Mirages of the Mind

Mushtaq Ahmed Yousufi

MIRAGES
OF THE MIND

Translated from the Urdu by Matt Reeck and Aftab Ahmad

A NEW DIRECTIONS BOOK

First published by Random House India in 2014
First published as New Directions Paperbook 1310 in 2015
Manufactured in the United States of America
New Directions Books are printed on acid-free paper
Design by Erik Rieselbach

Library of Congress Cataloging-in-Publication Data
Yusufi, Mushtaq Ahmad, 1923–
[Ab-i gum. English]
Mirages of the mind / Mushtaq Ahmed Yousufi ; translated by Matt Reeck and Aftab Ahmad.
pages cm
ISBN 978-0-8112-2413-0 (alk. paper)
I. Reeck, Matt, translator. II. Ahmad, Aftab (translator). III. Title.
PK2200.Y89A2513 2015
891.4'39371—dc23   2015006801

New Directions Books are published for James Laughlin
By New Directions Publishing Corporation
80 Eighth Ave, New York 10011

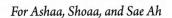

For Ashaa, Shoaa, and Sae Ah

Contents

Introduction

Mushtaq Ahmed Yousufi, a Biographical Sketch

Mushtaq Ahmed Yousufi was born in Tonk, sixty miles south of Jaipur, in what was then the British Indian state of Rajputana, and that is now Rajasthan. The year was 1922. His father was a local politician, and, in Yousufi's own words, 'a simple, God-fearing Muslim.' Yousufi was educated in Jaipur before receiving a law degree and an MA in Philosophy from the renowned Aligarh Muslim University. He married Idris Fatima in 1946, and the couple's four children live today in Pakistan, America, and England. After a brief stint in the Indian civil service, he left for Pakistan. He arrived in Karachi in January 1950, and, aside from an eleven-year stint in London, he has lived there ever since.

Yousufi has won national awards for his contribution to Pakistani arts and letters, and critics and readers alike have praised his work, so much so that one critic has called contemporary Urdu humour and satire writing, the 'age of Yousufi.' He has written four works, each of which has been extensively reprinted. Yet despite his national stature and the recognition that he ranks among the best humour and satire writers in the history of Urdu literature, not much is known about his life. That may be in part because he spent his professional life in banking: after his first job at Muslim Commercial Bank, he rose rapidly in the ranks, becoming President of United Bank in 1974 and the chairman of the Pakistan Banking Council in 1977. But the scarcity of biographical information may also be due to his personality and the fact that he shuns the limelight. In one of the few interviews he has granted, he readily admits to being a private person, and states that all he has to say is in his books.

Yousufi is known as a humour and satire writer, and the two together form one genre in Urdu literature. Humour and satire writing has been a vital part of Urdu literature since its prose traditions began to flower in the 1870s. It can be commonly found in newspapers and literary magazines, and it is often used to satirize society. Little is done to differentiate between the genre's two aspects, and the resulting confusion has been perhaps the single-most important reason why the genre has not gained as much critical attention as short stories and classical poetry, the ghazal tradition. Yousufi, the leading contemporary practitioner of this hybrid craft, has stated that more care should be taken to separate the two, as there is a real difference—namely, that of love, 'You cannot write humour until you love your target or subject of attack. Love is the foremost condition. In satire it's not necessary.' While there are moments of political and social satire in his writing, humour is the chief vehicle of Yousufi's craft, and, love, in one form or another, its chief object.

Reading Guide

Mirages of the Mind (in Urdu, *Aab-e-gum*) is a challenging book. It is challenging because of its length but more so due to its erudition. Yousufi acknowledges the difficulty of his work. On the occasion of his being awarded the Sir Syed Ahmed Khan Lifetime Achievement Award in New York in 2008, he recited an anecdote about how a schoolboy admonished him for the difficulty of his Urdu. On a visit to the Karachi Grammar School, the boy asked him, 'Uncle, do you find it very difficult to write in simple Urdu?' When Yousufi asked why, the boy said, 'Because so many of us have failed Urdu because of you!'

Yousufi's use of different rhetorical registers, his punning on Urdu poetry, and his encyclopedic descriptions of regional cultures mean that even the most astute Urdu reader will miss some of the subtle humour or will be unaware of certain cultural references. While we have tried to leave this experience intact as much as possible, English doesn't have as many rhetorical registers as Urdu does, and so it inevitably flattens some of the irony that comes when Yousufi writes in the decadent, florid, 'high' Urdu of old. In light of its challenges, we would like to give several examples of the book's main idiosyncrasies, namely, encyclopedic culture, poetry punning, narrative digressions, and cultural nostalgia.

ENCYCLOPEDIC CULTURE

The narratives of this book span the entire east-west axis of the northern Indian subcontinent, from the Khyber Pass to the floodplains of Bangladesh, and Yousufi documents regional culture each step of the way. He is fond of turning his attention toward subcultural traditions that are quickly becoming obsolete. This book is, as well as being 'The Adventures of Basharat Ali Farooqi, Bumbler and Bungler Extraordinaire,' an encyclopedia of Pakistani and North Indian regional cultures in the twentieth century.

When Basharat goes back to Kanpur, his hometown, in his attempt to find the things that he has missed since immigrating to Pakistan, he meets a number of old men who, like him, want to know about their hometown, but, unlike him, haven't had a chance to travel over the border. One such man is Ramesh Chander Advani. Basharat narrates his encounter, in which this man speaks longingly, and in great detail, about his native Baluchistan:

> So, sir, I talked to Advani. Or not so much that as listened to his monologue. It was like being taken prisoner. He wanted to confirm that Jacobabad was as beautiful as it had been when he had left it as a young man. I mean, was the full moon as full as it had been? Do the palla fish still jump around in the Sindh River's waves, shining

and glimmering in the sun? Is the weather still good? (Meaning, is it still 46 degrees in summer or has that declined as well?) Does the hot wind still blow from Khairpur with its sweet scent of dates? Was there still the yearly cattle fair in Sibi or not? What about the Sibi darbar? When I told him that at the fair there was now a poetry festival and poets came from great distances to participate, he went on for a long time lamenting the fair's deterioration.

This is only the first third of his monologue. Yousufi takes the time to fold such evocative, elegant sketches of regional, and increasingly historical, culture into the overarching narrative of Basharat's adventures. Often he colours these descriptions with slight exaggeration to make them lightly humorous.

POETRY PUNNING

The reader will see that sections of the text are indented, and that some are in italics. All of these passages are lines of poetry: the ones that remain in Roman type are direct quotes from canonical English poems, given in the English original; and those that are in italics are Urdu, or occasionally Persian, poetry, that we have translated. The majority of these lines have been altered by Yousufi for humorous effects. In 'A Schoolteacher's Dream,' Basharat goes to confront Maulana Karamat Hussain, a worker for the Society for the Prevention of Cruelty to Animals, who has been giving him tickets for using an injured horse. He finds the man's shack in one of the poorest sections of Karachi. The man is absent, but his children, in a seemingly endless string, come out of the shack to greet Basharat. To this, Yousufi quips, 'The entire universe is one big net of children.' This plays off a line of Ghalib's poetry:

Yousufi: alam tamam halqa-e-dam-e-ayal hai
Ghalib: alam tamam halqa-e-dam-e-khayal hai

The only difference is one syllable in the second to last word. Ghalib's couplet is full of metaphysical implications.

> *Don't be beguiled by being, O, Asad,*
> *The world is but a single loop in thought's net*

Yousufi changes Ghalib's line into something entirely worldly and more practically challenging—raising a bevy of kids on close to no income at all.

NARRATIVE DIGRESSIONS

Yousufi's style is situated between the oral and the written, as it toggles between the recitation of anecdotes, third-person accounts, and intellectual asides. Yousufi himself functions as the narrator and scribe whom Basharat occasionally addresses in the course of telling his stories. This oral-textual style appears immediately in the first chapter, 'The Mansion': 'Long Live Qibla! When I first met him in 1945, he was as old as I am now. But since I'm talking about my good friend Basharat Ali Farooqi's father-in-law, it would be good to let Basharat say a few things. I've heard the stories dozens of times. Now it's time for you.' Here, Yousufi writes in the first person. But he immediately passes the narrative task to a new storyteller. This back-and-forth between Yousufi and Basharat continues throughout the book, and it creates the story-within-a-story texture familiar from classic Eastern, or Oriental, tales.

Yousufi's narrative style favours the anecdote, the vignette, and the digressive. The book is episodic and picaresque. Its chapters are arranged not in strict chronological order but associatively, providing, in toto, the story of some fifty years of Basharat's life, and doing so in the way that events are recalled in conversation. Yousufi has chosen this form self-consciously, or, perhaps, it has chosen him:

Writing about Basharat's love for phaetons and horses has brought me far afield. My mentor and master Mirza Abdul Wadud Baig once shared with me a great piece of wisdom: 'When you slip on a banana peel, you should never ever try to stop yourself or put on the brakes because that will only cause greater injury. Just slip without a care in the world. Enjoy it. In the words of the great poet Zauq, "Go as far as it goes." When the banana peel becomes tired, it will stop on its own. Just relax.' So I use this principle not only when walking but also when writing and thinking. But why shouldn't I go ahead and tell you the whole truth? All my life, the banana peel and the banana peel alone has been my sole means of conveyance. If you happen to notice a youthful spring to my step, it's due to the banana peel. If my pen happens to slip, then I go along with it happily.

Not only does his own writing lead to digressions, but he also presents characters that prefer this method of telling:

Now listen to the rest of the story as told by Basharat in his circuitous way. (The fun of it is not 'long story short' but 'short story long.') In so far as my pen and my memory allow, I will try to recreate word for word his special idioms, his way of talking, and his lilt and stutter. Whenever he starts telling a story, his digressions and random asides start telling their own story. He doesn't even let you catch your breath.

Digressions are so thoroughly interwoven into the fabric of the book that it would be wrong to consider them secondary to a supposedly primary narrative. The book's reading pleasure is found in 'short story long' and not 'long story short.' Not only does Yousufi, the narrator-cum-scribe, intrude upon Basharat's stories to offer his own opinion, but two other characters also frequently provide commentary, though they themselves never appear within the stories themselves. Mirza Abdul Wadud Baig, mentioned in the quote just above, and Professor Qazi Abdul Quddus, MA, BT, offer comments in every chapter. Both pretend to be fonts of wisdom, and their comments demonstrate varying degrees of ridiculousness. In a way, they resemble Statler and Waldorf, the two hack critics from the Muppets, who provide inappropriate commentary from the balcony and yet find themselves intensely funny.

CULTURAL NOSTALGIA

Nostalgia is the feeling of loss over what has disappeared; it can range from innocent daydreams to a deep and persistent desire to return to the past to recover what has been left behind. These attempts are almost always futile: what has disappeared is not simply a person or a place, but that person and place in time, as they existed then. Outside of that time, they are not the same, and the difference between the two—the one known and the one returned to—is enough to frustrate any sense of recovery. Strong nostalgia can disable a person. But most people live with a weak sense of nostalgia, a tendency to think back to past times, people, and places, and to reminisce fondly.

Yousufi contextualizes this book as, in part, a critique of nostalgia. It goes without saying that the partition of the subcontinent created cultural nostalgia for many displaced people, and so this book can be read as another volume of Partition literature, a dominant subgenre of north Indian and Pakistani letters. While Yousufi's general critique is never directed explicitly toward those displaced by Partition, inevitably those characters at which he pokes fun for their symptoms of nostalgia are these very ones. Perhaps as a defense mechanism against the real losses that immigration entails, including those of the 'muhajirs,' or Urdu-speaking Indian Muslims, to the new state of Pakistan, he criticizes the tendency, especially prevalent among the elderly, to long for the 'good old' times and the places and experiences of youth. Examples of this outward critique are numerous. In his afterword, he likens nostalgia to a drug:

> Most of the characters in this book are lost. They live in the past and avoid people at all costs. They suffer from nostalgia for a different time and place, and they suffer from this individually and collectively. When someone falls in love with the past and stops anticipating the future, they get old fast. (Bear in mind that anyone can age before their time — even the young.) If they can't get drugs, then the depressed and defeated can find their last refuge in the intoxication of memories and fantasy: just as the determined and diligent use their iron will to shape their future, the dead-to-the-world use their imagination to lose themselves in visions of their past, and the heady rivers of memory descend into the mirages of the mind.

Nostalgia, he writes, is like a drug, or a mirage, something that promises much and delivers only a paltry version of that promise, if at all.

'Two Tales of the City' deals directly with Basharat's nostalgia for Kanpur, his hometown. After his wife's death, a sharp pang of nostalgia overwhelms him:

> According to an old saying, regardless of exactly how many defects old age has, it has one more burdensome than all the rest combined. And that's nostalgia. In old age, a person prefers to turn back from their unwanted, imminent end to recall the places they used to know. In old age, the past flashes all its dangerous charms. Old, lonely people live in sad houses where they have to have lights on even at noon; and when bedtime rolls around and they put out the lights, their minds are lit by the bright glow of memories. As this glow becomes brighter, so too their desolation becomes more pronounced.
>
> So something like this happened to him as well.

And yet when it comes to characters suffering from nostalgia, Basharat or otherwise, Yousufi treats them so gently, and their depictions are so endearing that we can't take the author's stated objection too literally. Certainly, those who suffer from nostalgia are easy, and rewarding, targets of humour, as who, other than the truly enlightened, hasn't looked back from time to time with a sense of longing for yesteryear? Furthermore, Yousufi himself suffers from a sort of nostalgia—his penchant for antique words—which he acknowledges without regret:

> 'Mirza often taunts me about this,' I replied. 'He says that I'm one of the very few who hasn't filed a claim for property abandoned back in India, and the reason for this is that before coming to Pakistan, I dug up all the local Rosetta Stones, stuffed them into my travel-all, and headed over here. He was just kidding, but, in fact, if I'm able to resurrect one word—yes, just one word—then I'll consider my life's work done.'

It seems as though Yousufi's position is bound in situational irony: either he intends for his admonishments to be taken at face value and thus he too is subject to them, or his scolding is like between friends and so without real bite. Despite his occasional protests to the contrary, we're left with reading the book in quite different terms from those of an express critique of nostalgia. It reads more like a sympathetic portrait of the same.

Master Fakhir Hussain, Basharat's grade-school teacher, helps elucidate the book's point of view. Basharat remains quite fond of his teacher, warts and all, so much so that he makes the seemingly outrageous statement that, were he a student today, he would prefer his old teacher's eccentricity and obvious gaps in knowledge to today's rational, knowledgeable teacher: 'Master Fakhir Hussain couldn't hide his ignorance from even no-good students like me. I've met important intellectuals, but if you give me the choice, I'd prefer to learn from Master Fakhir Hussain. Sir, he was a real man. He wasn't a book.

He taught you about life.' We don't take at face value, however, the statement that Basharat would prefer an ignorant teacher to a distinguished intellectual; rather we understand his rhetorical emphasis on how learning must take place outside as well as inside the classroom. The last two sentences quoted above sound like an adage, and so something with a pre-approved truthfulness—real life teaches you more than books. Since it is hard for us to imagine loveable ignorance in adults, especially those entrusted to guide children, we treat the entire passage as a type of rhetorical flourish.

But this isn't the last mention of Master Fakhir Hussain. Basharat then recounts how his teacher had to fill in for a colleague and teach English grammar to ninth-graders and how, despite his can-do attitude, he was woefully unprepared to deal with this subject:

Once he wrote 'TO GO' on the blackboard and then asked the boys, 'OK, then, someone tell me—what is this?' One boy raised his hand, 'A simple infinitive!' He nodded his head approvingly, 'Exactly right.' But then he saw that another boy still had his hand up. He asked, 'Is there anything wrong?' The boy answered, 'No, sir. It's a noun infinitive.' Master Fakhir Hussain answered, 'Oh, you mean from that perspective.' But then he saw that the smartest boy in class still had his hand raised. He said, 'You still haven't put down your hand. What is it? Please speak up.' He said, 'It's a gerundial infinitive, but not a reflexive verb. Nesfield's grammar says so.' And with this, it was clear to him that

He was voyaging across uncharted waters.

He said in a calm and understanding way, 'Oh, you mean from that perspective.' Then he saw that the fluent English-speaking boy who had gone to an English-medium school had his hand up. He said, 'Well? Well? Well?' The boy said, 'Sir, I am afraid this is an intransitive verb.' So he said, 'Oh, you mean from that perspective.'

But he didn't understand the idiomatic expression 'I am afraid,' and so he said to the boy in a tone full of love, 'But, my dear, what's there to be afraid of?'

He always said that people should always leave the door open to knowledge. But he himself had never opened any of the doors. Find me a teacher nowadays for whose ignorance you feel any love!

Despite the humour of this situation, we are still prone to read Basharat's avowal of love for his teacher as hyperbole.

But there is a way to understand Basharat's fondness for his former teacher as being quite real, and this way also helps us resolve the book's rather ambivalent comments about nostalgia. It involves local, or regional, culture, which we have already suggested is one of the book's implicit concerns. Master Fakhir Hussain, like all the characters of this book, is nothing if not an emblem of local culture—the good, the bad, and the ugly. This sort of character is what Yousufi means when he refers to 'common' people: 'In all, the characters, whether they be central, secondary, or merely to fill out the scenes, are all by definition "common," and when it comes to social status, ordinary; for this reason, they deserve extra attention and consideration.' The word 'common' implies a lot: it suggests the poor, the uneducated, and the non-mobile; or the opposite of the wealthy, the well-educated, and the mobile. We think the word 'local' describes better the book's characters. For one, Basharat himself, a business owner, is resolutely middle class, and he is mobile, as his trip to India shows.

The book criticizes intellectuals at several points, and yet, if we weigh this criticism of intellectuals against Yousufi's professed love for common people, we see no necessary conflict in these terms. To be an intellectual suggests nothing about income or mobility; it only designates a level of education. So, if we are to take these complaints against intellectuals seriously, the focus of these attacks must lie first in their pretensions toward exceeding local knowledge and culture. Basheer, the school servant, whom Basharat returns to see in Kanpur, puts it like this: 'Today's scholars are so arrogant that they think of themselves as wisdom incarnate. New things cramp their style, like new shoes. But even though they've swallowed the entire ocean with all the oysters in it, they still can't spit out even one pearl.'

In his afterword, Yousufi states that local people are the true source of what good he finds in life, and that, by contrast, those who, through education and privilege, have escaped narrow cultural confines, risk being less grounded and suffer more often from the ills of egotism: 'It's been my bad luck that the "great" or "successful" people I've happened to run across have been entirely second-rate, rancorous, and superficial.' In Master Fakhir Hussain, Basharat sees someone who, even if ignorant, is still honest; and someone who does not seek to repudiate the way that local culture has shaped him. And these local cranks are the characters—indeed, the 'characters'—that Yousufi loves most.

Nostalgia, then, is good, insofar as it reminds us of a cultural value—the local. Without putting his sentiments into exactly these words, Basharat may appreciate in his old 'master' how he represented a time when local ambitions, local personality quirks, and local cultural attitudes weren't deemed backward, retrograde, or thought of as being contrary to progress and the imperatives of a modern mindset. This book recalls a time when life was, for better or worse, more fully local, and it reminds us how the circumscription of culture held people in closer contact. Values were more locally defined, and people were seen in their many lights at once, and that surpasses what most of us in our fragmented, hyperkinetic, and global mindsets can offer today.

MIRAGES OF THE MIND

The Mansion

1.

He's Human but Don't Look into His Eyes

Long Live Qibla! When I first met him in 1945, he was as old as I am now. But since I'm talking about my good friend Basharat Ali Farooqi's father-in-law, it would be good to let Basharat say a few things. I've heard the stories dozens of times. Now it's time for you.

He had always been my relative somehow or the other. Before he became my father-in-law, he was my phuppa. Before that, I called him Dear Chacha Uncle. And before that, he must have been something else, but I hadn't yet learned to speak. My extended family lives in Muradabad and Kanpur, and how everyone is related to everyone else is as mixed up as a pot of sewaiyan. I've never met any man as foul-tempered and awe-inspiring as Qibla. When he died, I must have been half done too, I mean, around forty years old. But, sir, his eyes were so threatening that they terrorized me every day of his life, and they will continue to terrorize me till the day I die. His big eyes bulged from their sockets. They were always bloodshot—really bloodshot. As red as pigeon's blood. I thought the red veins around his pupils would burst in a fountain of blood to spray across my face. He was always as mad as hell, God knows why. He swore as a matter of habit. His writing was as foul as his speech. The pen would start smouldering in his hand. Of course there were some people he couldn't curse out. In those cases, he would look at them in a way that suggested real physical violence. Well, no one dared disagree with him. And if

3

someone happened to blubber 'yes' to something he said, he would flip his stance and start arguing from the opposite perspective.

Sir, sometimes it didn't even take talking to him—sometimes a simple 'hello' would send him into a tizzy! No matter how rational or straightforward you were, he would be sure to refute whatever you said. He considered it unbecoming to agree with anyone. He started each sentence with 'no.' One day I said, 'It's really cold today.' He said, 'No, tomorrow will be colder.'

He had been my uncle several times over, and he became my finger-pointing father-in-law, but even as he lay dying I couldn't muster the courage to look him in the eyes while speaking to him. At my wedding, he had sat next to the officiant. The officiant asked me, 'Do you accept her?' In Qibla's presence, I didn't have enough courage to say 'yes.' I nodded respectfully twice, but the officiant and Qibla didn't think that was enough. Qibla erupted, 'Boy, why don't you say something?' Being scolded made me more nervous. The officiant hadn't yet had a chance to ask me again when I blurted out, 'Yes, I accept!' My voice was so loud it surprised me, and the officiant hid behind my wedding garland. Everyone started laughing. But Qibla was furious. He interpreted such a loud 'yes' to be an insult to his family. He was like this till he died. All my life I suffered beneath one bellowing blast or another.

He had just one child, a girl. His wife had high hopes for her daughter's marriage. On the day before the wedding, when the female members of my family were just about to slather unguents over my body to make it glisten, Qibla sent a message: 'The bridegroom will not reveal his face in my presence. He will dismount from horseback two hundred feet in front of me and walk to the marriage hall.' He made 'marriage hall' sound like our Faiz's famous slaughterhouse. And the truth of it was that I was so terrified of Qibla that even the nuptial bed seemed a gallows. He also made sure that after wolfing down the pulao and zardah, the wedding guests would never complain that there hadn't been enough meat in the pulao and that the zardah hadn't been sweet enough. He said to me, 'Listen, keep your band away from my house. If you're thinking about having a bachelor party, it will be over my dead body. Go ogle whores at your own whorehouse.'

There was a time when Rajputs and Arabs thought a girl's birth inauspicious and a sign of God's displeasure. They couldn't stand the thought of the marriage procession coming to their house. Not wanting to have a son-in-law, they would bury their newborn daughter alive. Qibla was against this barbarian custom. He wanted to bury the son-in-law alive.

Looking at his face and comportment, you would think he was a police chief. Who would have thought that he owned a very ordinary-looking store in Bansmandi? He had a towering frame. When he walked, he would stand up straight and stick out his chest and glare at people. Sir, it's best not to ask. I never dared look at him directly. And when I found the courage to do so, all I saw was his beet-red, blood-shot eyes. His stinging glance spewed fire, O, Asad! His skin was light coloured like yours, Mushtaq Sahib. You say that it looks like the wheat that Adam ate that led to his being immediately kicked out of paradise with his wife. He was always spitting and fuming. He had no control over his temper, tongue, or fists. Because he was always shaking with anger, bricks, stones, sticks, bullets, and curses could never find their mark. He would twirl the ends of his moustache before and after insulting someone. When he got old, he started doing the same with his eyebrows. His athletic frame looked very good in a muslin kurta. His kurta's sleeves were meticulously pleated, and his dopalli hat was in even better shape. He used itr-e-khas cologne in the summer. The folds around the ankles of his kekri pyjamas were so many that all you saw were folds and no pyjamas. The washerman didn't hang these on the line to dry, but, like fine gloves, he put them on a bamboo drying rack. If you happened to go to his house at two in the morning, even then he would answer the door wearing his churidar pyjamas.

My God! I have a hard time believing that even his wet nurse would have seen him in anything but these pyjamas. Their tight fit looked so good on his shapely calves. Tied to the hand-woven silk drawstring of his pyjamas, his keys would jingle with his movements. He continued to keep keys for locks that had been broken long ago. In this bunch, there was even the key for a lock stolen five years ago. The neighbourhood talked about that for years because the thief had taken only the lock, the watchdog, and a copy of Qibla's family tree. He said that only a close relative could have committed such a dastardly crime. By the end, this key ring had become so heavy that his drawstring's knot would frequently come undone on its own and his pyjamas would fall down. When occasionally he bowed while shaking someone's hand, his other hand would hold his key ring. In May and June, when the temperature reached 43 degrees and the hot wind slapped his face, he would use his pyjamas as air conditioning. I mean, he would soak his pyjamas up to his knees, put a hand-towel on his head, and eat watermelon; he couldn't afford a sweet-scented grass screen and ice water. He didn't miss them, though. He never closed his store on account of the heat. He would say, 'This is a business. How else are you going to eat? Do you think your gut cares about hot or cold?' If an unfortunate customer happened to show up, he would thunder at him and drive him away. Yet the customer would have to come back. That was because nowhere else in Kanpur could you find such good lumber. He said, 'I never sell bad wood. Wood shouldn't be blemished. Blemishes are becoming only on lovers and teenagers.'

A Word's Flavours and 'Outside' Paan

He ordered tobacco, qiwam paste, watermelons, and embroidered kurtas from Lucknow; hookahs from Muradabad; and locks from Aligarh. He got halva sohan and idioms, like those of Deputy Nazir Ahmad, from Delhi. (After he lost his teeth, only the idioms passed through his mouth.) That said, his curses were always local; in fact, they were homemade. They rolled off his tongue quite easily. While they were original, they weren't very precise — they only gave a vague idea of what he meant. He ordered scarves and Salim Shahi shoes from Jaipur. Mushtaq Sahib, your Rajasthan is really great! What were all its rarities that you enumerated the other day? Khand, sand, bhand, and rand? It's very funny that Marwaris add retroflexes to the names of everything they love. I couldn't believe that you said a 'rand' means a beautiful woman. You really don't have a Marwari word for 'widow'? Or are all widows there like the houris of paradise? But it's also true that up till one hundred years ago the word 'randi' [prostitute] meant a woman. As men's intentions toward women worsened, this word's flavour changed as well. Sir, I also very much appreciate the three exquisite gifts of Rajasthan — Mira Bai, Mehdi Hasan, and Reshman.

So I was saying that whenever Qibla went out, he took his purse as well as a little box of paan. He never ate 'outside' paan. He said, 'Only widows, degenerates, and Bombayites eat that.' Sir, I learned my refinement and fastidiousness from him. His paan box was silver. It was engraved, heavy, and completely solid. It had dents; these were impressions left by human heads. When really pissed off, he would often throw this box at people. In the aftermath, no one would know whether the red meant blood or a paan stain. He got his purses from your hometown, Tonk. He said, 'Tonk's leatherworkers are so good that their leather purse straps open with just the slightest pressure, just like a sycophant smiles at almost anything.' He got gutka from

7

Bhopal. But he didn't chew that. He said, 'Sweet paan, thumri songs, gutka, and novels are for teenagers.' He didn't particularly like poetry. He couldn't stand free verse. Someone said that free verse is like a tennis game without a net, and that person is probably right. But it's also true that he had memorized all Urdu and Persian poetry that mentions wood, fire, smoke, bullying, fighting to the death, failure, and disgrace. When arguments started to get out of hand, he would quell these fires with couplets. In his last days, he was a recluse and a misanthrope; he left the house only to walk in his enemies' funeral processions. He liked cornflower blue, and his wife liked cream. He always wore a cream-coloured coarse silk shervani.

Wow! You Can't Praise Enough This New Earthen Jar!

Basharat's introduction ends here. Now please listen to my rendition. It will be punctuated by Basharat's narration and the words of others—accurate or not.

Qibla had a lumber store first in Bansmandi and then in Cooper Ganj. It provided the façade of a livelihood; it was really his means to torment humanity. He also sold a little bit of firewood, but he never called it 'wood.' He called it 'timber' or 'faggots.' If someone unfamiliar with his quirks called his store a 'wood lot,' he would race after them with a two-kilo weight. When he was younger, he had used a five-kilo weight. He used stone weights his whole life. He would say that foreign weights were heavy and inauspicious. To lift a stone weight, you had to gather it in your arms and then rest it against your chest. Leave alone doubting his intentions, no one had the courage to test his weights to see if they were really as heavy as he said they were. After getting back change, no one dared count it. At that time, I mean, in the twenties, lumber wasn't in great demand. Sal and pine were the most popular. People used rosewood only for doors and doorframes. Teak was used only for two purposes: the rich used it for their dining-room tables, and the British used it for coffins. There was no such thing as furniture back then. In fairly well-off homes, a charpoy was passed off as furniture. As far as I can remember, chairs were used only on two occasions. First, after the hakim, ved, homeopath, saint, fakir, and exorcist failed to cure the patient, the doctor would be called in. He sat on the chair and used his stethoscope to see how much closer to death these men had already brought the patient with their medications, amulets, and charms. In those days, wherever oranges, five grapes wrapped in cotton in a wicker basket, or a doctor wearing a pith helmet arrived (the patient's caretaker in front of him carrying his leather bag and shooing away the children), then the neighbours quickly ate and prepared themselves to offer condolences and walk in the funeral procession. In fact, doctors were called in only when the patient was in the worst way possible, just as two thousand years earlier people had tried Jesus. The second and last occasion was when the chair was used during circumcision. The boy in question would be dressed up like a bridegroom, given an earthen toy, and seated. Just seeing this execrable chair would cause even the most courageous boys to blubber. For this same ceremony poor people would buy a new earthen jar.* They would turn it upside down and cover it with a red cloth.

---

* The mention of an earthen jar automatically reminds me of a Nazir Akbarabadi couplet that goes like this:

> *Your young heart and fresh body*
> *Wow! A new earthen jar is wonderful*

Nazir Akbarabadi is truly wonderful. Look at any of his poems. Whenever he encounters nature's handiwork or evidence of God's glory, he falls to his knees and offers paeans to its beauty. So as soon as he saw a new earthen jar on the girl's head, he started composing verses while staring darts at her. Then 'a ripple went through

The Charpoy

The truth of the matter is that if you have a charpoy, you never have room for furniture or any reason for it. If England's weather weren't so awful, and if the English had discovered how to build charpoys, then not only would they have saved themselves from the nuisances of modern furniture but they also would never have had the inclination to leave their charpoys, go outside, and conquer the world. Thus the 'overworked' sun would have been saved from shining over their empire for a century. (Also, they would now have something appropriate to lie down on when they retreat to their bedrooms to protest the state of the world.) One day I said to Professor Qazi Abdul Quddus, MA, BT, 'You say the English invented everything. That they love comfort and are relentlessly practical. So why didn't they come up with the charpoy?' He said, 'They can't stand tightening its ropes.' In this writer's opinion, we must keep one fundamental difference in mind. That is, Europeans use furniture only for sitting; but we don't sit on anything we can't also lie down on. For instance, rugs, quilted mattresses, carpets, picnic blankets, white sheets, charpoys, a favourite alley, or a lover's lap. There was only one thing we used exclusively for sitting. That was the ruler's takht [throne]. But after the ruler was executed on it, the takht was called a takhta [bier], and this reversal was called a coup d'état.

---

her body.' He can't control his heart and his poems. Wherever they go, he follows happily. It gets so bad that whenever he sees a stand for a water pitcher or a jug with a spout, he loses all sense of proportion. Depraved thoughts take over his mind.

I saw a jug with a spout
And my heart drowned in lechery

The poor jug bears blame only for having a passing resemblance to Nazir's lover.

The Bad Fortunes of the Station, Lumber Market, and Red-Light District

The purpose of this tedious introduction was simply to say that wherever charpoys are in vogue, the furniture business suffers. In fact, the entire lumber industry was lethargic, and the number of stores exceeded the number of customers. If someone showed up in the lumber market, and by his gait and comportment, the shopkeepers suspected this man of being even remotely interested in wood, then they fell upon him. Most customers came from the countryside around Kanpur. They needed wood only twice in their lives—to build their homes and for their last rites.

Those readers familiar with the Delhi or Lahore railway stations as they existed prior to Pakistan's coming into being can easily imagine the following scene's mad scramble. It was 1945. The train from Delhi arrived in Lahore. As soon as any traveller stuck any body part outside the door or window, a porter would grab him and, lifting him onto the palm of his hand, would transport said passenger through the air to land him on the platform on top of a hookah or thin-necked jug. Those passengers who were pushed out of the cabin were subjected to the same harsh treatment that a new Urdu book gets from critics. People made off with whatsoever fell into their hands. Then the second phase began. The hotel touts sprang upon the travellers. They wore white suits, white shirts, white handkerchiefs, white canvas shoes, and white socks. Their teeth were white too. And yet you couldn't quote Muhammad Hussain Azad's line that 'a pile of jasmine flowers lies nearby laughing.' While just about everything about them was white and clean, their faces weren't. When one laughed, it looked like a frying pan was laughing. They rushed upon the travellers as rugby players pounce simultaneously upon the ball. Their purpose was not to secure anything for themselves but rather to prevent anyone else from securing anything. The Muslim touts were recognizable due to their fezzes. They immediately identified folks from Delhi and UP by their special water pitchers, their women in niqabs, their large number of children, and the rancid smell of meat-stuffed parathas. They shouted out, 'Assalam Alaikum, brother!' and hugged them tight. Only the Muslim touts could lasso these folks. The tout whose hand ended up on the strongest part of the traveller's outfit would grab ahold and pull him out of the pell-mell. And those touts who laid hands on the threadbare portions of the traveller's outfit would later use these pieces as hankies. The half-naked traveller, being subjected to further disrobement with each step, arrived outside only to fall prey to an endless string of wrestlers, who, having found the wrestling pit an insufficient arena, had taken up the profession of driving horse-drawn carts. At this point, if the traveller wore any cloth remnant at all, these men would tear it off to decorate the backside of their carts, as though it were Ramchandraji's sandal. If a driver got ahold of the drawstring of the traveller's churidar pyjamas, he would be towed along without any resistance. One driver would pull the traveller's kurta from behind, and another man would pull it from the front. In the final round, one muscular driver would yank on the traveller's right hand, and another brawny soul would grasp his left hand to begin their tug of war. Before the two opponents were able to rend him into two separate parts, a third nimble driver would hunch down between the traveller's spread-eagled legs, and then, quite suddenly, get up, and, with the traveller on his shoulders, throw him into his cart and disappear.

This was more or less the state of affairs in Cooper Ganj, as well, and Qibla's store rested in the very heart of this. Usually the lumberyards were just behind the stores proper. To entrap customers, Qibla and a couple of other overly aggressive shopkeepers built small wooden cabins on the road. Qibla's cabin was outfitted with a bolster pillow, a hookah, a spittoon, and a switchblade. In fact, the cabins were like blinds from which the shopkeepers hunted customers. They lured them in hoping they would not leave empty-handed and heavy-pursed. As soon as a likely customer walked by, the shopkeepers near and far would try to wave him over, crying out, 'Sir! Sir!' During their struggles to win them over, shopkeepers exerted so much energy that their turbans fell off. They quarrelled over customers so much that eventually they held a community meeting at which they decided that a shopkeeper could shout out only when a potential customer was directly in front of his store; if the customer left his kill zone, he was to say nothing. And yet discord only increased, and so the shopkeepers drew lines in chalk on the pavement to mark their property. This changed everything. The game changed to kabaddi. Some shopkeepers hired goons, thugs, and wastrels on a part-time basis. Their job was to forcibly round up customers. Business was at an all-time low. During the day, these men pressured customers into buying defective wares at the lumber market, and at night they did the same in the red-light district. Some prostitutes hired these men as pimps in order to get more business, and thus to save their dishonourable honour. Qibla didn't hire any such bully because he could bully people well enough with his own arms. Sawing to size was still a part of the lumber's price, but now he, like everyone else, added the expenses of physical coercion.

Bloodletting Tools: Leech, Cupping Horn, Police Baton

Qibla's anger never relented. Before going to bed, he made sure his mood was foul enough that he would wake up mad. Three furrows permanently creased his brow. The purest sort of rage is that which doesn't rely upon any provocation or that which flares up at the slightest thing. By the time his anger subsided, he couldn't remember why he had been angry in the first place. His wife didn't let him fast. It was probably 1935. One day he was praying to God—nay, imploring

God—to end his everlasting problems. But then he thought of a more recent problem, and he became incensed. He addressed God, 'You didn't take care of the old ones, so I'm sure you can't do much about the new one!' That night he folded up his prayer mat for the final time.

That reminds me of when ear-cleaners used to roam the neighbourhoods. You could get a lot done in those days without leaving the house, not just ear cleaning, but practically everything. You could buy vegetables, meat, household goods. You could get your hair cut or get an education; you could give birth too. You could get your stools fixed, your charpoys fixed; you could even get yourself fixed without stepping one foot outside! The wives of barbers would come to the homes of the well-off to give massages to the ladies of the house, as well as to cut their nails. Lady tailors came to the houses to sew these ladies' clothes so that outsiders would have no clue what size they wore. This was actually unnecessary because those specimens of women's clothing from that era that I've seen were no better fitting than clothes measured around a mailbox. But the point is that everything was done at home. Even dying. There was no need to go out in order to get run over by a truck. If you suffered from boils and welts because of 'bad' blood, or if perverted thoughts were afflicting your mind even during daylight hours, then you could have your blood let at home. In order to drain some perverted, pent-up blood, there was no need to put your head beneath a police baton, either at a political function or during a demonstration against the government. In those days, batons weren't used as bloodletting instruments. Kanjari women made daily rounds with their leeches and cupping horns.* If hakims looked into the minds of today's youth, not one young man would escape the cupping horn. As far as us, the older generation,

---

* Cupping horn: The site of the pain or puss was first cut. Then the big end of the cupping horn was affixed to the skin, and, putting the mouth on the small end of the horn, they would suck out all tainted (and untainted) blood.

Whoever we speak to, we give them advice …

If hakims were still around, they would be sure to apply leeches to our tongues.

One summer day Qibla was taking a nap in his cabin after having eaten a lunch of qorma and cantaloupe. Suddenly, at the cabin's door, an ear-cleaner shouted out quite loudly, 'Ear cleaning!' God knows if Qibla had been deep in sleep, or dreaming a beautiful dream of customers buying lumber for triple its real rate, but he awoke flummoxed. He stared ahead, befuddled. Then he grabbed a piece of wood lying nearby and began chasing the ear-cleaner. The gall of that man! He had yelled out so loudly from a metre away—no, a metre *close*! It wouldn't be right to say that Qibla ran after the ear-cleaner because his anger was so great that at times he overtook him. The ear-cleaner entered a maze of alleys and disappeared. Qibla continued running in the direction that his sixth sense told him to go; unfortunately, that was in the direction that a man in control of his first five senses and brandishing a stick above his head would never go—i.e. the police station. In this mad dash, Qibla eventually lost his stick, and the ear-cleaner lost his turban and ear-cleaning instruments, each of which was folded into one pleat or another of his headgear. This included a little can in which he kept earwax. When you weren't looking, he would take a pinch of this and show it to you, saying, 'Look how dirty your ears were!' He would point out big black flies and say the buzzing sound in your ears was due to them. But it was true that he would twist and turn his swabs so carefully through your ear canals that it felt as though he was digging out your guts and would soon present them to you for your inspection. Qibla took this turban and put it on a pole outside his cabin, as in olden times an impatient successor would cut off the head of the emperor (or if one of those wasn't available, then that of an enemy) and put it on a spear for everyone to bear witness. This struck such fear into the hearts of carpenters, charpoy

15

weavers, bloodletters, and Ramadan morning announcers that they all stopped walking by his shop. Added to that, the tone-deaf muezzin from the neighbouring mosque started using the back alley.

Bronze Pots, Teenage Girls, and Scraggly Beards

Qibla loved showing off his lumber. I say 'love' because even though he watched his customers as a lion watches its prey, he stroked his lumber with great affection. From memory alone, he could have traced out the grain of each teak board in stock. He was the only shopkeeper in the lumber market who made his customers memorize the family tree of each and every post and beam. (His own family tree was longer than that of any piece of wood. He hung a copy of it over a photo of his grandfather.) He would point out a good-looking four-by-four, 'It's a quarter inch over thirty-nine feet. It's from Gonda. It's too bad that Asghar Gondvi's wonderful poetry has made people forget about its wood. Now no one will believe you if you say that Gonda was famous first for lumber. Before Asghar Gondvi, you got beams so straight that if you put a big ring around the top and let it fall, it would slide straight down all forty feet and hit the ground with a resounding clatter.' Each piece in his store was an original and descended from noble heritage. They were like purebred Mughals or Rohilkhand Pathans: they ripped the clothes of everyone, and would hardly, if ever, submit to being sawed.

Sometimes Qibla would point to this or that piece of 'seasoned' wood, and his manner was so respectful that it seemed as though the board in question had just been brought for his own special approval from Noah's Ark in the foothills of Mount Ararat. He would stroke fondly a beam of Burmese teak, 'Now, how old do you think he is? He's just a kid. No more than eighty years old. There're trees in the Irrawaddy forests that have withstood typhoons for one hundred and fifty years. Sir, that's seasoned! This one's lived through hundreds of rainstorms, and it's floated down seven rivers. On top of that, a crocodile peed on it.' He pointed to a spot. 'You see, he pissed right here on this lotus-eyed burl. If you've a board that a crocodile has pissed on, no termite or fire can touch it. It'll be with you till Judgement Day.' So once Khwaja Abdul Majid, who had come to buy wood for a writing desk, asked, 'Dogs pee on electric poles, but crocodiles pee on trees?' He was going to say something else when Qibla angrily interrupted him, 'Not at all! During Muharram, crocodiles drink water from tin glasses tied to water stalls, and then they dry their dicks with dirt clods while walking down the street—just like your glorious father. Got it, sir?'

He was a twenty-four-hours-a-day volcano. One day Haji Muhammad Ishaq, the leatherworker, came to buy some rosewood. Qibla sang the high praises of all his wood, but he really loved rosewood. He would say, 'Shah Jahan used rosewood for his peacock throne. People today don't know how to appreciate it. But it's so lovely! The more you use it, the more you realize how great it is. I was born on the same rosewood charpoy that my grandfather was.' Qibla thought of his own glorious arrival in the world as an honour for not just his grandfather but also the charpoy.

Haji Muhammad Ishaq replied, 'This wood has too many burls.' After an interminable pause, Qibla smiled. He stared at Mr Haji's beard and said, 'The one thing I've noticed about rosewood, bronze pots, teenage girls, and scraggly beards is that the more you stroke them, the more they glow. The true mark of quality rosewood is that it renders saws, carpenter's planes, and drills useless, and hands stiff. It's the furthest thing from pine. With pine, just tap a nail in, and it splits in half. But there's one thing about pine. Freshly cut pine smells so good—just like the forest does. On those days I'm going to cut pine, I don't bother with cologne.'

Seeing Qibla's mood improve, Haji Muhammad Ishaq felt embold-ened. He said, 'This does look like quality wood, but it doesn't look seasoned.' This lit a fire under Qibla. 'Seasoned?' he exclaimed. 'What do you know about seasoning? If you're only concerned about season-ing, then go over to the mosque where they wash the corpses. That's seasoned wood. Do you want that? Should I bring that for you?'

Honour and Advance—Gone at Once

Qibla's principles in life completely contradicted those of Dale Carnegie, and yet in his business life he had come up with his own special methods. He wouldn't utter the price of anything until the customer had admitted to liking it. If a customer asked the price, he dodged the question, 'What're you asking? You like it. Take it. We're friends.' When the customer said he liked it, Qibla would stretch out his hand for an advance. Those were the days when everything was cheap. Two to four annas should have been enough. But he would scold, 'At least show me some silver. I mean, at least one rupee.' The poor, ashamed soul would bring out a rupee, which in those days was equal to fifteen kilos of wheat or one kilo of pure ghee. Qibla would hold it in his palm so that the customer could have the consolation of seeing it even though he couldn't grab it. Qibla wouldn't pocket the money lest the customer get wary and the deal fall through. Then he would declare unilaterally, 'Congratulations! The deal's done!' He would mention the price, and this would flabbergast the customer. If the customer started to haggle, Qibla would say, 'Are you a fool? You just gave me the advance, and now you want it back? The advance sealed the deal. The coin's still warm, and you want it back? You're telling me the coin's not yours? Just say it. Say it.' Qibla priced things so well that even the craftiest customer wouldn't be able to see him-self out of the conundrum of what was the worse deal—forfeiting the advance or buying the wood at the stated price.

Howsoever heated the argument would become, Qibla continued to hold out the coin. He never pocketed it. The disgraced customer rested content that at least his money was not yet stolen. There's a famous story about a fight that broke out between a crazy customer and him. In a swift wrestling move, Qibla threw the customer over his shoulder, planted him on the ground, and sat on his chest. Even then he held the customer's advance in the palm of his hand so that he could see he wasn't being cheated. Yet it was true that you couldn't get such pristine wood from even the trees of paradise, or so he said: 'I've never sold bad wood. A hundred years from now if any termites infest the wood, I'll give you your money back.' He lived by his principles. Which is to say, 'Quality Store, Quality Product, Wrong Price.' I've heard that Harrods, the world's most famous store, advertises itself as having everything from sewing needles to elephants. But I've also heard that the price for either is the same! If Harrods sold lumber, I swear they would follow Qibla's price points.

2.

We Left This to Come Here

When he left Kanpur and came to Karachi, he found himself in another world altogether. It felt strange. He was unemployed. And homeless. He brought with him a dozen or so photos of the family mansion. 'Look at this profile. And this photo's excellent,' he would say, showing the photos to everyone. 'We left this to come here.' When he went to apply for housing at the Allotment Offices, he showed the photos to the officials from where he stood on the other side of the fence, saying, 'We left this to come here.' Whether or not he had anything else in the pockets of his waistcoat or shervani, he was sure to have a photo of the mansion. Whenever he met someone new, he showed it to them. He called Karachi apartments different things—matchboxes, chicken coops, and pigeon lofts. But when he couldn't get even the most measly of apartments after three months of tireless searching, he realized what was going on. His friends explained to him, 'You can get an apartment in an hour. Just give the custodian some money, and he'll give you the keys.' But Qibla was used to receiving bribes, not giving them. For months, he schlepped like a mendicant to the various offices trying to get a house, but to no avail. He'd never been a guest in anyone's house. But now he had to suffer the torment of living with his daughter and son-in-law.

And … Now?

When a person experiences an excruciating pain or ordeal, it seems like each moment lasts for a year, or as though

> *Every year has 50,000 days.*

He could never have imagined himself being a burden to his daughter. In Kanpur, when he went to her house, he would give her a little money even for a glass of water. But now? He would eat his breakfast with head bowed, then leave to wander around all day before coming home right before the sunset prayer. At dinnertime, he would say he had eaten at an Iranian restaurant. Back home he had had his shoes made at Rahim Bakhsh Cobblers because their shoes always squeaked like new. But now his shoes were completely worn out. His feet developed calluses. And his shervanis became too big. His sick wife couldn't groan at night for fear of disturbing her in-laws. Dirt started to obscure the Lucknavi embroidery of his muslin kurtas. As his sleeves lost their fit, they fell past his hands. His dyed handlebar mustache remained firmly in place, but only the ends of it remained black. Sometimes it would be as many as four days between baths, and yet his jasmine cologne had run out four months previously.

When worried, his wife would ask innocently, 'And ... now?' instead of asking 'What are we going to do?' Coming from her, it sounded very dear. Her words were laden with all her fears, naivety, and helplessness, as well as her faith in her husband's clairvoyance and charity. Qibla would always answer her in a very confident and dignified manner, 'We'll see.' It consoled her.

The Situation Called for a Steady Hand and Immediate Action

Through each sadness, through each bout of suffering, life reveals something to us. Under the pipal tree in Bodh Gaya, the Buddha underwent a terrible trial. When his stomach had sunk through to his backbone, his eyes had descended deep into their lightless sockets, and while his breath clung tenuously to his skeleton's bony garland, then Gautama Buddha too discovered something. To the very same extent, depth, and reason that each person suffers, a secret is revealed to them. You have to seek nirvana to find nirvana; and when you suffer for the sake of something, eventually it shows you the way forward.

So after he had wandered from alley to alley and had got kicked out of countless offices, a revelation descended upon his sad heart. Tyrants and their like take advantage of the cowardly. The man who looks for the reins of the elephant will never ride it. The wine glass belongs to the man who has the courage to pick it up and the wine-bearer as well. In other words, the house belongs to the man who breaks its lock. When Qibla came from Kanpur, he brought his savings, his family tree, his switchblade, Akhtari Bai Faizabadi's three records, a bronze stand for his Muradabadi hookah and pitcher, and, lastly, the padlock from his shop. (He had specially ordered it from Aligarh; it weighed at least six pounds.) After the aforementioned revelation, he chose for himself a nice apartment on Burns Road. It had marble tiles and stained glass windows that let in the ocean breeze. With just one blow from his made-in-Aligarh padlock, he broke the front door's rusted lock and so claimed the apartment for himself, bypassing all the government nonsense. He redid the nameplate and stuck it back on. It had read CUSTODIAN OF ABANDONED PROPERTIES. In a fit of rage, Qibla yanked it out with the nails still attached. Before his name, he added, 'Muzaffar Kanpuri.' His longtime friends asked when he had become a poet, and he answered, 'I've never heard of a civil court case against a poet—foreclosures, either.'

He had been in the apartment for four months when one day, while he was darning the knees of his churidar pyjamas, he heard a rude knock at the door. I mean, the person was rapping on his nameplate. When Qibla nervously answered the door, the man standing there introduced himself as though he were foisting his title directly into Qibla's face: 'Officer, Department of the Custodian of Evacuee Properties.' Then he yelled, 'Old man, show me your Allotment Order!' Qibla took from his waistcoat's pocket a photo of the mansion and showed it to the man, 'We left this to come here.' The man didn't look at the photo but said somewhat harshly, 'Old man, didn't you hear me? Show me your Allotment Order!' Very slowly, Qibla removed from his left foot his Salim Shahi shoe—so slowly that he lost track of what exactly he was doing—but then he struck the man in the face and said, 'This is my Allotment Order! You want to see its carbon copy too?' Up till this disgraceful moment, the man had had only bribes thrown at him, never shoes! He never went there again.

The Mansion That Was Our Home

Finally Qibla managed to build a lumber store in Lee Market. He sold the jewellery from his wife's dowry and his Webley Scott shotgun for close to nothing. Then he bought some lumber on credit. Things were barely up and running when an income tax inspector showed up. He wanted to see the accounts, the shop's registration, the cash box, and the receipts. The next day, Qibla said to me, 'Mushtaq, did you hear? For months I wandered around wasting my time at government offices. No one even bothered to ask my name. Now look at their fun and games. Yesterday this fine fellow, a tax inspector, comes strutting in with his chest stuck out like some fan-tailed pigeon. I show the bastard this photo, "We left this to come here." He pretends he doesn't understand. He asks, "What's that?" I say, "Back home we call it a seraglio."'

Only Mirza knows if this is true, as he's the one who tells the story, but it goes like this. Qibla got a photo of the mansion enlarged and framed, and when he was hammering a nail into his apartment's paper-thin wall, the neighbour on the other side came over and asked whether he could place the nail a foot higher so that he could use the nail's other end to hang up his shervani. Whenever anyone slammed the front door, the seraglio would swing like a pendulum on the rusty nail. If the mailman came by, or a new washerwoman, he would show them as well, 'We left this to come here.'

I had seen his photos countless times. They were all blurry. But Qibla's strong storytelling skills made up for this. In fact, the past has a way of surrounding everything with a romantic halo. Even past pains feel pleasant. When everything's been taken from you, you either become a wandering Sufi or you take refuge in some fantasyland.

Without this sustaining illusion, you die

His family tree and the mansion were his refuge. It's possible that looking at the photos, a person with an unsympathetic eye would only see a ruin, but when Qibla explained the mansion's architectural niceties, suddenly the Taj Mahal itself seemed nothing more than a crude mud house made by kids. For example, there was a doorway on the second floor that had lost not only its door but its frame as well; Qibla called it

French windows. If there had been French windows anywhere in the house, it would have been those windows (in whose frames mirrors had been inlaid) through which the entire East India Company had come, spritzing the locals with dust from off their shoes. The gateless entry leading to the foyer was a Shahjahani arch. Above this was a decrepit ledge where a kite was relaxing after lunch. Qibla said that this was all that remained of a princely gallery where in his grandfather's time Iranian carpets had been laid for the performance of Azerbaijani qawwali. In those days, when the last hours of night set in and everyone's heavy eyes began to droop, rosewater was sprinkled from time to time on the VIPs from silver rosewater dispensers. The walls, as well as the floor, were covered in carpets. Qibla liked to intone, 'There are just as many flowers on the rugs as in the gardens outside.' On top of a gold-embroidered Italian velvet carpet rested crystal spittoons with intricate gold and silver designs, and after the men had chewed the silver-wrapped paan they spat into these spittoons' throats where they watched the spit fall like mercury in a thermometer.

It's So Crowded There's No Room for Thoughts

He had some interior close-ups too. Some were actual photos, and some were by way of his imagination. In one photo, there was a three-window arcade, and where some of its Byzantine-era bricks had fallen, local birds had built their nests. Qibla referred to it as Moorish arches. A lamp-niche in the wall had sunk at such an artistic angle that he imagined Portuguese influences. To its side, there was a wooden stand for a water pitcher whose design his grandfather had stolen from Shah Jahan's special bathroom. Whether that was true or not, the table was definitely Mughal, or so its broken-down state suggested. In all the photos, there was no trace of the servants' quarters, but in one neighbour's account these were crammed with elderly relatives fallen on hard times. The mansion's northern section had a roofless part: having thrown off the ceiling's yoke, a pillar had been standing there insolently from time immemorial. This was, according to Qibla, a rare example of Roman pillars. While it's a wonder the pillar hadn't fallen down before the roof fell in, one reason could have been that it was surrounded by so much junk that there was no place for it to fall. On one dilapidated wall, there leaned a rotten wooden ladder in such a fashion that it was difficult to say which was holding up which. Qibla said that before the second floor had caved in, a grand Victorian stair-case had led up to it. Qibla pointed toward the nonexistent roof where iron beams had supported an Albanian chandelier in his grandfather's time. It was in the golden light of this chandelier, he said, that they had listened to the music of jingling tambourines brought by the women who had arrived inside litters on top of two-humped Bactrian camels. If his running commentary had not accompanied the presentation of his photos, I would never have imagined that a ramshackle 'mansion' of fifteen hundred square feet could have had so many architectural features and borne witness to so many cultures, so many that they hardly left a person any room to think. The first time you saw the photos you would think that the photographer had shaken the camera. Then after a moment you would begin to wonder how on earth such a wreck had remained standing for so long. Mirza's opinion was that it didn't even have the strength to fall down.

I Remember When You Came Barefoot to My Roof

A couple steps removed from the mansion's main gate (where in the present photo there was a trash heap on top of which stood a black rooster crowing with his neck puffed out), you could see the remains of a raised sitting platform. Plants shot through cracks in its stony joints in their relentless search for light. One day he pointed at this structure and said, 'European goldfish used to swim here. It was once an octagonal pond of the purest water, encased in red sandstone. Arif used to make paper boats out of the *Pioneer* and float them here.' Telling the story, Qibla got so worked up that he hoisted himself up with his walking cane, then used his cane to start outlining the pond's octagon on the frayed rug. One side came out crooked, and he erased it with his foot. He pointed with his cane toward the preferred spot of one rowdy fish that liked to fight with the others. Then he pointed to where one nauseated fish hid in the corner. He didn't come out and say it (I was younger than him, after all), but I understood that this fish was craving sour things and dirt — that is, she was expecting.

When Qibla got really wistful, he had the habit of reciting to his only good friend Rais Ahmad Qidwai how he still remembered the times when a beautiful young gal used to brave the May and June afternoon heat to come onto his sultry roof. Mirza never could figure out this scenario because the mansion was three storeys tall and yet the houses on either side were only one storey. Even if the girl was barefoot and brazen, something was still amiss. Unless, of course, she was not only beautiful but also possessed the power to levitate.

Pilkhan

In one photo, there was a sad-looking mushroom-shaped pilkhan tree* in front of the mansion. His great-great-grandfather had brought its seed hidden within his embroidered cloak when he had arrived on

---

* Pilkhan: Readers who have never seen this type of tree can find one in Qurratulain Hyder's novel *Kar-e-Jahan Daraz Hai* [*I Have A Lot To Do Here*]. I've only seen this tree in photos. I can't find mention of it in any dictionary. I have no idea what its grammatical gender is either, but if the love with which Hyder speaks of it is any indication, my guess is it's feminine.

the back of a black stallion from Damascus in a time of great famine. The story goes that Qibla's great-great-grandfather used to recount the following story: 'I came in a state of dire want. I was an embarrassment to the human race, to my ancestors, and to my country. I came with my head exposed to the heavens, my feet exposed to the earth, my rump exposed to my horse's back, and my sword drawn and held in my bare hand. I vaulted over the stripped and crushed Khyber Mountains and arrived in India.' Although Qibla told the story with great pride, it actually showed that the old man had only had the horse's tail to cover his ass. His property, his seraglio, his servants, his wealth—he had left it all behind. Yet he managed to bring his most valuable assets, I mean, his family tree and the pilkhan's seed. Like the man riding him, the horse was a purebred fed up with his homeland; it fidgeted beneath the weight of tree and seed.

On Each Branch of This Tree Sits a Rare Genius

Life was an endless ordeal. Because they had lost their land, the family's coming generations took shelter beneath these trees, real and figurative. Qibla was very proud of his family's brains. He considered his each and every ancestor a rare species of his time; on each branch of his family tree, a genius sat, nodding off to sleep.

In one photo, Qibla was standing beneath the pilkhan tree in exactly that spot where his umbilical cord had been buried. He said that if any bastard doubted his ownership of the mansion, he could go dig up his umbilical cord for proof. He said that when a person doesn't know where his umbilical cord is buried (and his ancestors' bones too), he becomes like a plant that can't take root anywhere but in pots. Talking about these matters—umbilical cord, family tree, pilkhan—got him so worked up that he lost track of what was what.

Ancestors (Imported) and Nose (Grecian)

Things were different back then, including standards of class. No Indian Muslim considered himself noble if his ancestors hadn't been imported, that is, if they hadn't come through Transoxiana and the Khyber Pass. Ghalib even imported from Iran a fake Persian teacher (named Mullah Abdus Samad) so that he could brag about it. When Qibla's ancestors left their homeland due to unemployment and poverty, their eyes were brimming with tears and their hearts were heavy. They slapped the flanks of their horses and, according to one spellbinding storyteller, they pulled on each other's beards and wailed, 'God forbid! God forbid!' Needless to say, they charmed everyone they met in their new land.

First they were like a new lover, then a great lover, then an even better lover

Or, these fine folks became

First middle class, then upper middle class, then upper upper class.

Like the mansion's designs, Qibla's diseases were royal. As a kid he got an abscess on his right cheek during the mango season, and this left a scar. He said, 'The very year, no, the very week, I got this Aurangzebi abscess, Queen Victoria became a widow.' At sixty, he started to suffer from Shah Jahan's disease, which made it hard to pee. He said Ghalib was Mughal royalty, and although Ghalib killed his lover with the poison of love, he died by the same disease, the enlarged prostate, which Qibla also suffered from. Ghalib wrote that he drank wine drop by drop and peed that way too. If Qibla's asthma let up enough for him to catch his breath, he boasted that Faizi suffered from the same disease. He wrote in a quatrain, 'I've swallowed two worlds inside my chest / but I can't seem to suck down even half a breath!' Qibla said his father died of a royal disease. Indigestion. Or, in other words, TB of the guts. Aside from his family diseases, he claimed royal provenance for even his big nose. To him, it was Greek.

3.

The Dead Come Back to Perform a Miracle

Qibla had two sorrows. The first I'll get to later, since it's too heart-breaking to mention now. The second was not so much his as his wife's, as she was dying to have a son. That poor soul had promised countless acts of charity if only her prayers were met. She made Qibla drink cold concoctions with naqsh charms dissolved in them. She put amulets beneath his pillow. She secretly went to saints' shrines and draped sheets over their tombs as offerings. In our country, when people are this disappointed with life, only one hope remains:

The dead come back to perform a miracle.

There wasn't a shrine within fifty miles that she hadn't visited. She would stand near the grave's head and cry and cry. In fact, she must have cried more than the friends and family had when attending the funerals of these men so long ago. In those days, whether the dead were miracle workers or not is one thing, but at least you could be sure their corpses were in their tombs. It's not the same today. Now we don't know what's inside. The best scenario is that nothing is in there. Then the yearly commemoration, which is held with much pomp and circumstance, is celebrating nothing more than nothing-ness. That said, not a day goes by in Karachi without another news-paper ad along the following lines: 'Today offerings will be made at such-n-such holy shrine. At five, the holy water will be taken out to head the procession. Then the anointment of the holy shrine will be performed. Holy food will be distributed afterwards.' I've seen so much emphasis placed on the word 'holy' in reference to the shrines springing up for newly discovered saints that my mind is awash with all sorts of doubt. I'm neither gullible nor a Wahhabi, so I have to say that when it comes to the one shrine in Karachi whose construction I've followed, I'm ready to believe that everything about it is holy, except the body inside.

Actually, Qibla thought of himself as nothing less than a living saint. When he learned that his wife was secretly going to shrines, he got very upset. And in this condition, he never ate regular meals. He went to the sweetshop to order rabri, moti choor ke laddu, and kachori. But the next day his wife put on her cornflower blue scarf and whipped him up his favourite food in an effort to win him over: do piyaza, super-sweet zardah, and extremely spicy dahi bade. He offered portions of these delicacies to his Persian and Arab ancestors, although he made sure the dahi bade weren't too spicy. Then he placed restrictions on her going to shrines. When his wife started tearing up, Qibla relented a little. He said she could go on the one condition that the saint wasn't from the kamboh caste. 'Women must stay away from ghazal poets and kamboh men, whether they're alive or not. I know just what they're like,' he said. His enemies liked to say that Qibla himself was a poet during his youth and a kamboh on his mother's side. He liked to say, riffing on a proverb, 'A kamboh's death is a festival by itself.'

The Alley Cat's Collar

Gradually his wife grew accepting of her lot. Then they had a girl. Qibla grew fonder of her by the day. He grew so content that he took to saying that God was merciful and kind. 'If I had a son like me, his life would be rough. And if he wasn't like me, I'd disown him.'

However darling a grown daughter may be, she remains an enormous burden resting on the collective chest of her parents. Even though some people write in their daughter's matrimonial ad that she is good-looking, well-mannered, and knows how to run a household, for Qibla's daughter, this was actually true. But who would dare ask him for her hand? I don't have personal experience in jumping into Nimrod's fire, but I can say for sure that it's less dangerous jumping into that than into his family tree. I mean, as I have mentioned, Qibla was the uncle many times over to my friend Basharat. They were neighbours, and their shops were next to each other. Basharat's father didn't have any objections to his son marrying Qibla's daughter, but he didn't initiate the conversation since he figured that he could live easily enough without a daughter-in-law but would look awkward without a nose and legs. Basharat threatened to commit suicide by tying himself to the railroad tracks—the wide-gauge ones—when an express train was set to come through. (The ropes were to prevent his changing his mind at the last minute.) But his father said, not mincing words, 'Then you put the collar on the alley cat.'

Qibla was not only famous for being arrogant and insulting, he really was. He respected hardly anyone. He always found some reason to insult others. For example, if a man was only a month younger, he would call him 'kid,' and if a man was only a year older, he would call him 'gramps.'

K.I.S.S. or Four Blanks

Basharat had just taken his BA exams and was waiting for the results. He thought he had a 50–50 chance of passing. He said '50–50' with such gusto, pride, and certainty that it was as if he were challenging his examiners to find any fault in his merely passing competence. In the meantime, he had absolutely nothing to do. He played carom and coat pass. He spoke to the dead, asking them questions he didn't dare ask the living. He spent days filling in the blanks in Nazir Akbarabadi's *Collected Poems* that Munshi Nawal Kishore Press had put in for fear of violating the Indian Penal Code. While talking to others, he finished each sentence with a poetic petit four. He was also deep in the throes of writing short stories. In those days, Niyaz Fatehpuri's ornate phrases and Abul Kalam's swirling prose had taken possession of even the best writers' minds. In some cases, the style shone out like bright wedding jewellery; in other cases, it rose up like the many scars on a washerman's body; and in yet other cases, it was like the girlfriend tattoos with which English sailors decorated their bodies. Urdu prose was suffering from elephantiasis. Once it recovered a little, it was struck by Tagore and his ecstatic flying carpets rising toward the heavens. One of Basharat's stories had a climax something like the following: '*Anjum Ara's beauty, charms, and flirtatious gestures filled his body's every pore with their fragrance. Tripping forward, she was the epitome of modesty, cowering behind her satiny arms, stealing glances here and there. Salim took Anjum Ara's henna-dyed hands into his steely clutches, and with an awestruck aspect stared shamelessly at her diamond-chiselled wrists and crystal calves, and then on her rosy lips he planted a big _ _ _ _.*' In those days, the word 'kiss' was considered obscene, and so the four blanks. Basharat was punctilious about using what the era considered the correct number of blanks; prevailing standards of modesty, as well as ideas of the heroine, determined this. I remember how the Urdu Progressive Writers' magazine published an article in which Maulvi Abdul Haq had replaced that word, for propriety's sake, with its letters spaced one by one, and thus, how contrary to his intentions, had only increased the reader's attention and pleasure. But I don't mean to make fun of him or my dear friend; each era has its own style. Sometimes words are dressed up in angarkha gowns, sometimes in floor-length cloaks, sometimes in scholarly turbans, sometimes in dinner jackets, and sometimes in fool's caps. Sometimes words wear anklets, and sometimes they wear fetters. And sometimes they are like trained monkeys that dance on a showman's command.

Maulana Abul Kalam Azad wrote about his birth like this: 'I, alien to time itself, born into the wrong era, a stranger amidst my own people, raised by pious folk, ruined by desire, named Ahmad, called Kalam, came from the world of non-being into the world of being in 1888 (1305 Hijra), and thus was accused of living.'

People don't write like that anymore. People aren't born like that anymore. Not even a C-section takes that long and causes that much suffering.*

A Leap into the Volcano

Then one fine morning, Basharat took upon himself the task of writing to Qibla, and he sent the letter through registered mail even though his house was right next door. The letter ran to twenty-three pages and contained at least fifty couplets, of which half were Basharat's and the others were those of Andleeb Shadani, who was

---

* A passage just like this exists in *Nau Tarz e Murassa*, [*The New Ornate Style*]: 'When the moons of my life had accrued to those of fourteen years, the dazzling light of the happy day turned darker than the darkest night of winter, that is, the goblets of my parents' days were filled with all sensual pleasures only to spill over upon fate's hands.'

All he really wants to say is that his parents died when he was fourteen. But because of his turgid style, not only did his parents die but the meaning did too. Mirza Abdul Wadud Baig came up with a new term for this pompous style of Indo-Persian writing: ustu khuddus [bitter medicine]. Please see my footnote on this in the fifth part of 'The First Memorable Poetry Festival of Dhiraj Ganj.' Actually, the literal meaning of Mirza's term is the medicine for the common cold (and madness) that doctors refer to as 'the mind's broom.'

friends with Qibla. In those days, such letters were written with saffron, but this letter would have used up more than an entire field and so he used saffron only for the salutation and parting and otherwise used a wide-nibbed fountain pen and red ink. Then, for those parts he meant to draw special attention to, he used blue ink and wrote really small. Although he was being quite presumptuous in writing, his tone was worshipful and his points, flattering. He praised Qibla's good manners, affectionate nature, pleasant company, fair business practices, compassion, soft-spokenness, and handsomeness—in short, all those things that were entirely absent in the real man. Then he went on to chastize all of Qibla's enemies man by man. This called for special skill to accomplish in under twenty-three pages. Finally, Basharat drew up the courage to say that he wanted to get married, and yet he didn't have enough chutzpah to specify to whom. No doubt the point of the letter was difficult to decipher, and yet Qibla was pleased to hear himself praised and his enemies slandered: no one had ever told him he was handsome. He read the letter twice and then handed it to his secretary with these words, 'Read this and tell me who this prince wants to marry. He's described me quite well, though.'

For quite a while, Qibla luxuriated in the praises of his good character. The glacier was beginning to melt. He smiled at his secretary and said, 'Many untrained poets have trouble rhyming this sound or that, but he can't rhyme anything. From A to Z. It's so discombobulated it's like praying at Eid when no one knows what to do.'

When people heard of Basharat's temerity, they were shocked. They thought the volcano was about to erupt. If Qibla took mercy upon Basharat's family members and didn't murder them all, then surely he was going to break all their legs. But nothing like this happened. Qibla accepted Basharat as his son-in-law.

4.

Why Was Ravana Killed?

It's hard to choose just one anecdote of Qibla's salesmanship. Examples of its disastrous consequences are so many. If a customer so much as insinuated that he had a problem with Qibla's prices, then not only this man's honour but also his physical person would be at risk. Once Qibla was in a hurry. He immediately stated the price to be ten rupees. The customer, who was from the countryside, set his own price at nine rupees seventy-five paise. Qibla swore nastily at him and chased him out of the store, incensed that this yokel had dared bargain. There was a broken-down charpoy in the shop. The shop's carpenters had the habit of stealing its ropes to use to light their hookahs. When Qibla wanted to attack someone, he would take a leg of the charpoy and chase his enemy, meaning, the customer. He often stroked this piece fondly, saying, 'It's real tough. It's as solid as ever. Only cowards and the debased carry bludgeons. And only butchers, vegetable sellers, goons, and the police wield billy clubs.' After using his weapon, he would give it first aid, that is, wipe it down neatly with a hand-towel then refit it into his pathetic charpoy. He probably put it back so that in going to retrieve it he would have time to cool his heels a little. Also, it allowed the object of his displeasure to gather his wits and take advantage of the fact that he had legs. An ancient Chinese saying goes that of the three hundred and seventy means of fighting that wise men have laid down, the most effective remains fleeing! This is confirmed by Hindu mythology. Ravana had ten heads and twenty hands, yet he was killed. The only conceivable reason for this was that he could run only as fast as his two legs could carry him. Before attacking, Qibla would huff and puff for a while so that if the opponent wished to save himself, he could flee. He said, 'Not once have I not warned my enemy by swearing at him first.' What is that couplet? Oh, yes,

You can learn about chivalry from mosquitos
Before they suck your blood, they warn you.

I've never met another person who took such pride in being mosquito-like. Professor Qazi Abdul Quddus, MA, BT, was so impressed by Qibla's thinking that he made up outlines for two sophic, if not solipsistic, lectures, entitled 'The Place of Mosquitos in the Poetic Traditions of the East: The Objective Perspective in History' and 'A Comparison of Mosquitos and Falcons.' Thank God my readers are intelligent. There's no need to state which one won that one.

I Deserve to Be Punished, but for a Different Crime

Everyone was scared shitless of Qibla, except for the shopkeeper whose shop was just to the right. He was from Kannauj. He was arrogant, violent, dishonest, and rude. Twenty years younger than Qibla, he was still young and headstrong. In fact, he had recently retired from professional wrestling. People called him Mr Wrestler. One day a customer was just entering the zone in front of Qibla's shop when Mr Wrestler grabbed him and dragged him into his own, leaving on Qibla's lips the words, 'Sir! Sir!' But when Qibla entered his store to repossess the customer, Mr Wrestler uttered the one curse that Qibla himself was famous for. That was going too far. Qibla went back to his store, ripped out his special weapon—meaning, the leg of his charpoy—and raced back barefoot into Mr Wrestler's store. The customer tried to intervene, but he lost a tooth in this impulsiveness and so retired from his peacekeeping efforts. The impudent Mr Wrestler took to flight, sprinting out of the store. Qibla followed hot on his trail. But when Mr Wrestler was crossing some railroad tracks, his foot got caught and he fell facedown right there. Qibla caught up. He hit him so hard with the charpoy's leg that it broke in two. God knows if this blow was what injured him or if it was his falling, but Mr Wrestler lay unconscious for a while, and a pool of blood grew around him.

His leg was fractured in several places, and because gangrene developed, the leg was amputated. Qibla was brought to trial since Mr Wrestler had paid the authorities handsomely. The police charged Qibla with attempted murder and held the motive to be longstanding animosity. Then they added whatever else they could from the Indian Penal Code. After listening to the rap sheet, Qibla said, 'It's not his leg that's broken, but the law.' When the police came to take him away, his wife said, 'And what now?' He shrugged his shoulders, 'We'll see.'

In court, both the peacekeeping customer's tooth and the murder weapon—the bloodstained charpoy leg—were presented as formal exhibits. The case went to the Sessions Court. Qibla had already been in custody for several days, but now he was put in jail alongside hardened murderers, robbers, pickpockets, and recidivist criminals. That said, after a couple fistfights, they accepted him and began to call him 'uncle.'

One of Kanpur's best lawyers, Barrister Mustafa Raza Qazalbash, took up Qibla's defense. But the two of them couldn't agree on a single thing. Qibla swore that under oath he would say that the plaintiff had lied about his parentage—he didn't resemble his father but rather one of his father's dissolute friends. His lawyer wanted to argue that the man in question had got injured falling on the railway track and not because of Qibla's bludgeoning. When it came time for Qibla to enter the courtroom, he wanted to walk in casually like lawyers do in the movies; and when he took the witness stand, he wanted to bang on its iron bars and announce, 'I'm a soldier's son! I don't need my store to give me a sense of dignity. Anyway, it hasn't been profitable for a long time. As a soldier and a man, it was wrong for me to hit him on the legs. I really should have bashed in his skull. So if you have to punish me, don't do so for what I did to his legs. Punish me for hitting the wrong part. I deserve to be punished, but for a different crime.'

Prison Life and a Blood Test for Lice

His case was brought to court. The circumstantial evidence suggested he would be convicted and that the sentence would be fairly severe. Every day during the trial there was a lot of crying and carrying on at his house. His friends and loved ones were very worried that such a small matter had grown so out-of-proportion. The police would come to his cell and take him away in handcuffs. They would parade him around town before winding up at the courthouse. Mr Wrestler had paid them to do so. Qibla's naïve wife couldn't believe what she heard. She asked each and every person she spoke to, 'Now, is it true? Do they lead him around town in handcuffs?' Inside the courtroom and outside as well, Qibla's enemies gathered—that is, the entire town. His entire family was ashamed. But Qibla never hid his face, and he never covered his handcuffed hands with a hankie. When the police led him around town, he twirled his moustache, and this made the handcuffs jingle. When Ramadan rolled around, someone suggested he start praying and fasting—Maulana Hasrat Mohani from our own little Kanpur* had used to work at the mill even while fasting during Ramadan. Qibla didn't think much of this: 'You've got to be kidding! I'm not a poet. People will make fun of me, saying I couldn't take it.'

> His wife kept asking, 'What now?'
> He kept saying, 'We'll soon see.'

---

* This person said 'Kan *hi* pur.' Sometimes people from Kanpur say 'Kan *hi* pur' instead of 'Kanpur *hi*.'

He never regretted anything he said or did out of anger. He used to say that only then could you glimpse a man's true character. He thought it beneath himself to worry about whatever missteps he had made when angry—i.e. to worry about his true character. One evening his nephew came to the jail with food and lice medicine. The medicine said that it would blind the lice, which you could then easily find and kill. It also mentioned the traditional way of killing lice and nits, that is, put the louse on the nail of your left thumb and crush it with the nail of your right thumb. Then, if the blood released from the louse's stomach was black or crimson, immediately take some of their Jalinous Elixir to purify your blood. The instruction sheet also said that you should continue treating yourself until the lice's blood was pure red. Qibla instructed his nephew to lean toward the iron bars so that he could tell him something. He whispered, 'Son, you can't trust life. The world, and this jail too, is fleeting. Listen here. You must do this for me. In my wardrobe, I hid two thousand rupees for a rainy day. It's underneath the old newspapers. Give it to Allan.' (He was the town thug.) 'Try to reassure your aunt for me. Give Allan my blessings, and tell him to beat up the six witnesses so that even their families won't recognize them.' Then he gave his nephew a crumpled-up piece of newspaper on which was written the names of the plaintiff's six witnesses—a plan he had formed while in jail charged with having committed a similar crime.

One Sunday his nephew came for a visit. His nephew reported that it wouldn't be difficult to befriend the guards. If Qibla wanted something special to eat, like zardah or dahi bade, or if he needed some of Shauq's sexy masnavi poetry, or any cigarettes or mahva paan, then he would be able to get it at least once a week. His wife was asking after him. Eid was approaching, and her eyes were always swollen from crying. Just then Qibla trapped a bug on his coarse jail shorts. He said, 'I don't need anything. But when you come next time, ask Siraj the photographer to take a picture of the mansion, and bring that. I haven't seen it in months. Try to get him to take the photo so that he gets your aunt's balcony and its bamboo blinds.'

The guard stamped his boots and banged the butt of his 303 rifle on the ground. He said in a threatening voice, 'Time's up.' Qibla's nephew thought about Eid, and his eyes welled up with tears. He lowered his head. His upper lip quivered. Qibla pulled on his ear, and drawing it close to his mouth, he said, 'OK, if you can, slip a knife into some double roti or sewaiyan, but its blade has to be at least six inches long. Also, the Pentangular* is about to start. If you can find a way to get me the score every day, then, I swear to God, each day will be Eid, and each night, a Shab-e-barat! If I can get news of how Wazir Ali does, that will be really great.'

He was found guilty. He was sentenced to one and a half years of hard labour. While listening to the sentence, he looked up, as though he were asking the heavens, 'Are you watching? What's going on? How's that?' The police handcuffed him. Qibla didn't react at all. Right before he was led to jail, he sent a message to his wife: 'How happy my grandfather's soul must be! How lucky you are to see your bridegroom...' (He actually used that word.) '...going to jail wearing men's jewellery after having laid waste to that bastard. I'm not going home with a wooden leg. Pray two rakats to thank God.' He tasked his nephew with keeping up the mansion and looking after his wife. He told him to pass along the following message: 'These days will pass too. Don't be heavyhearted, and make sure to keep wearing your cornflower blue scarf every Friday.'

His wife wanted to know, 'What now?'
He answered, 'Let's wait and see.'

---

* Pentangular: A yearly cricket tournament in Bombay in which Hindu, Muslim, Parsi, English, and European teams participated.

His shop remained closed for two years. People thought that after being released he would quietly move on. But when he came back, he was exactly the same—he hadn't changed a bit. Being in jail hadn't broken him at all. A Japanese idiom goes that a monkey is still a monkey even if it falls from a tree. He came out of the jail screaming like Tarzan, 'Aauuaauuuu!' He went straight to his family's graveyard. Over his head, he sprinkled dirt that he had taken from the foot of his father's grave; then he prayed the fatiha; and then something came to mind that made him smile. The next day he opened up shop. He installed a pole outside his cabin and hung on it a wooden leg, which he had had made by a carpenter. Each morning and evening he would raise and lower this leg, just like the Union Jack was raised and lowered in those days in military camps. He sent threatening letters to those who hadn't paid their bills for two years. And after his name, he wrote the phrase 'ex-con' in parentheses. Before going to jail, he had used to take special pride in referring to himself as 'the shame of my forefathers.' (No one had had the courage to agree with him, but no one had had the courage to disagree, either. They were simply too scared of him.) Now he began writing after his name 'ex-con,' and he did so in the way that others write after their names the initials of their degrees and awards. Now jail and the law no longer scared him.

Qibla returned the same man. His intimidating bearing and booming voice hadn't changed in the least. If things had changed in the outside world in his absence, he didn't care a whit. His opinions had gone from being very self-assured to being the absolute final word. Previously he had expressed himself with conviction; now he spoke in judicial sentences. He wore his black velvet hat from Rampur at an even more rakish angle. I mean, he pulled it down so severely that he couldn't open his right eye. When his wife asked, 'And what now?' he never said, 'We'll see,' but rather, 'We'll soon see' or 'You'll soon see.'

In jail, his beard had grown so thick that it entwined with his bushy mustache so that while eating he had to use one hand to raise his facial hair and the other to stuff food into his mouth. Jail hadn't made any impression upon him. He said, 'There was a guy, a clerk, in our cell block, Fasahat Yar Khan. He was in for three years hard labour for embezzlement and fraud. He had gone by the penname of Shola [Flame], but inside he changed it to Hazin [Miserable]. He never shut up. He recited his newly-minted ghazals as he ground grain, which he did poorly, and so got beaten for it. Poetry isn't much use in milling grain. He thought he was at least on par with Ghalib, but the only similarity was that they both spent time in jail. He called himself a Rohilla. Maybe. He didn't look like one. He tried to avoid his fellow inmates. He told his son to tell anyone who asked about him that he had temporarily moved away. He never called jail by that name; instead, he said 'the slammer.' He didn't refer to himself as a prisoner but as 'jailbird.' Sir, it's good that he didn't refer to the guards as Potiphar! He probably would have called a mill something else if he had known a synonym for it. He never said 'vomit' or 'diarrhea,' maybe because he thought that if euphemisms can't stop them from happening, at least they won't smell as bad. He must have known because his father had died of cholera. Sir, I'm not a pickpocket. If you put a lion in jail, he's still a lion. Release a jackal into a river valley, and you're going to get jackal behavior. I'm not one of your limp dicks who once in jail shorts turns into a snivelling ninny.' Actually, it seemed that Qibla thought of his time in jail wearing raggedy clothes as the same as the trials of Joseph. Qibla's bad humour got worse. A crow's feathers stay black no matter how much the bird goes through, no matter how old it gets. Unsociable—curt—rough—genuine—fake—whatever he was, you got what you saw, and you saw what you got.

> They have clean bodies and dark hearts like herons
> Crows are better—what you see is what you get

Qibla said, 'Thank God I'm no hypocrite. I know what sins I've committed.'

His shop was closed for two years. When he got home from jail, his wife asked, 'And what now?' He said, 'My dear, you'll soon see.'

My Sweetheart's Lips

His business picked up so much so that not only others but Qibla too was surprised. He set up shop in his blind, that is, his cabin. He leaned against a bolster in the same haughty posture as before, except now he spread himself out even more, with his legs directed less toward the floor than the sky. Before his jail residency, he had called out to customers by gesticulating politely. Now he ordered them near with just the slightest wiggle of his index finger. His finger moved as though it was changing a wayward kite's direction. For his hookah, he got a pipe that was one foot longer. He smoked on it less; he used it more to produce gurgling sounds. He exhaled the foul-smelling smoke rings so that they pierced the noses of his customers and hung there like nose rings. He liked to say, 'Wajid Ali Shah, The World's Beloved, was unparalleled in giving beautiful names to things. He gave his hookah a lovely name—My Sweetheart's Lips! If you've ever seen a hookah up close, you can guess which sort of lips these were. When he was dethroned, he took only his hookah to Matiya Burj. He left all his beloved Fairy House girls in Lucknow. That was because girls don't gurgle when you grab them by the waist.'

I'll Hang You from This Pole

Qibla got the calligraphist from Munshi Daya Narayan Nigam's magazine *Zamanah* to write on his fence with coal tar a famous couplet from Urfi:

O, Urfi, don't worry about your rivals' plots
Dogs may bark, but beggars get their daily bread just the same.

(I sense racial profiling and discrimination in this couplet. If dogs wrote poetry, the second line would be something like this: *Beggars may cry, but dogs get their daily bread just the same.*)

Several days after Qibla's return, his lame enemy—Mr Wrestler—closed his shop for good. Qibla started threatening people over almost nothing. He said, 'I'll hang you from this pole, just like I did that fucker!' Everyone was so scared of him that Qibla didn't have to motion a customer over; all he had to do was look in his general direction, and the customer was his. If a customer happened to enter someone else's store by accident, that store's owner wouldn't show him anything. One day a man was walking down the street when Qibla wiggled his finger at him. The owner and assistant of the store in front of which the man was passing grabbed this man and pushed him into Qibla's shop. Inside, the man beat back his tears to say he was on his way to Mool Ganj to watch a kite-flying competition!

5.

This Is Not the Tree I Was Looking For

Then suddenly business dried up. He was a diehard Muslim League supporter, and this affected things. Then Pakistan came into being. The rallying cries he had been shouting came true, and he paid the price twice over. Customers turned away. The mice of the lumber market turned into lions. The friends and family with whom he had constantly bickered (and whom he hated) left one by one for Pakistan, and he realized suddenly that he couldn't live without hating them. When his daughter and son-in-law sold their shop and left for Karachi, he too cut the cord. He sold his shop to a broker for next to nothing. People suspected that Mr Wrestler had used the broker as an intermediary to buy the store. Qibla suspected as much. But he couldn't have cared less. In a flash, his ancestral connection to the place was severed, and he left his homeland and headed toward the new dreamland.

Qibla had always been proud as a peacock. But when he immigrated to Karachi, not only did he find the land strange but his own feet as well. Somehow or the other he managed to open a shop on Harchandrai Road in Lee Market. But things didn't work out. There's a phrase in Gujarati that goes, 'You can't put a new rim on an old jar.' He had left for greener pastures, but his old eyes couldn't spot a pilkhan tree. No, he couldn't even find a neem tree. What people called a neem tree was really a hoop tree. In Lucknow, Hakim Sahib-e-Alam prescribed its fruit for dysentery or piles.

This is not the tree I was looking for!

The fussy teak buyers of Karachi were nothing like the countrified customers of Kanpur. In fact, what troubled him most was how there wasn't one person in the vicinity—i.e. one person that fell beneath his terrifying shadow—that he could curse out without reason and without fear of retaliation. One day he said to me, 'Here, carpenters cut with their tongues. Four or five days ago, this saucy carpenter was in the store. His name was Iqbal Maseeh [Messiah]. I said, "Hey, stand to the side a bit." He said, "Jesus Christ was a Turkhan too." I said, "This is blasphemy! I'll hang you from this pole!" He said, in dialect, "That's what they said to Jesus too."'

Mir Taqi Mir in Karachi

From the very start, Qibla couldn't stand Karachi, and vice versa. All day long he would nitpick. His complaints ran like this:

'Man alive, are these mosquitos or man-eaters? Even DDT can't kill them. They only die when they land inside the hands of a clapping qawwal singer. If one happens to bite a poet, they go crazy, and then go sterile, and then die. The reprobate Nimrod died when a mosquito went up his nose. Karachi's mosquitos are all related to that murderous one. Listen to the way they speak. For the first time in my life I heard a man call another man by what I thought you said only to dogs. In fact, he was addressing his servant.

'Mir Taqi Mir didn't say anything while he sat in the cart that the camel was pulling toward Lucknow. He didn't talk to his fellow traveller because their way of talking would have polluted his own. If Mir had lived in Karachi, I swear to God, he would have bound his mouth shut for good. He would have ended up getting arrested in conjunction with some thievery just because of his suspicious appearance. I swear! People in Tonk call guavas "safri," and I've heard that too. But here people call them "jaam." Where I was from the name "Victoria" meant Queen Victoria. Here, if you can get a dozen people onto a horse-drawn cart, they call that a "Victoria." Once I was in Lahore for two days. There you call the red-light district the "diamond district." There's a new craze for calling singers "music men" and writers "pen men." Sir, in our day there were only good and bad men, and that didn't have anything to do with their jobs!

'I've seen every last inch of Lalukhet, Bihar Colony, Chakiwara, and Golimar. A million and a half people must live there. (Journalists are ashamed of this, and so they call these people "individuals" or "beings"!) You won't find a bookstore or a perfumery there. You won't even find fake flowers. In Kanpur, in the houses of good families like ours, you would always find jasmine vines here and there. But, sir, the only thing flowering here is depression! It's too much! In Karachi, the rich and the really rich buy wood as though they're buying fine brocade! If I sell two feet of wood in a day, the lines for sawdust don't end! I grew up eating food cooked on cow-dung fires. But food cooked over sawdust fires is fit only for the forty-day memorial services of the hell-bound dead!

'I'm sick of lumber. Money's important, but it's not everything. Money makes things possible. That's true. But if money is an end in itself, you'll never be satisfied. I've never sold bad wood—not lumber, not firewood. Here carpenters are so forward that they demand a commission. If you don't give it, you won't sell a thing. I mean, really! In Kanpur, I would have cut the guy's nose off with an axe, put it in his hand, and told him to go give it to his bride as a wedding gift! My God! Everything here is out of whack. I've heard that as soon as the red lights come on in the red-light district here at the intersection of Napier and Japan Roads, the prostitutes come out to sit behind the windows and advertise their pointy breasts. In films, too, actresses strut their slutty stuff. This is like the saying, "The cultureless don't know what to do with a partridge—tie it up outside or inside." The Islamic Republic doesn't even blink. But if you want to bring in a prostitute to dance for your wedding, well, then, you have to register her at the nearest police station! Only here do you have to have a ration card to get a prostitute. If you can't get a prostitute when you want one, then what's the use? What use is a government promissory note in the red-light district?'

Mirza Abdul Wadud Baig has a more elaborate interpretation of these matters. He says that a prostitute has to get an NOC [No Objection Certificate] from the police station so as to reassure them that she's going about her proper business and not about to go listen to a sermon or participate in politics.

One day Qibla said, 'A while ago I got to hear a famous prostitute from these parts sing. My God, her pronunciation was worse than her manners! I mean, really? Once upon a time the good families would send their kids to the brothels in Chowk to learn culture and refinement.'

Mirza thinks differently about this. He says, 'The real reason they sent their sons to brothels was to save them from the bad company of their own grandparents and the bad environment of their home.'

The Running Tree

In no form or fashion did he like Karachi. He often got annoyed, 'My God, is this a city, or is it hell?' About this, Mirza has slightly altered the words of a wise man to say, 'After Qibla leaves this world of sorrows, if, God forbid, he ends up in the place against which he compares Karachi, he'll take a good look around and then say, "I thought Karachi was a little hell, but it turns out hell is a big Karachi."'

Once a good friend asked him, 'If you think society's one bad thing after another, why don't you stop whining and get up and do something?'

He answered, 'Look, I used to work for the PWD [Public Welfare Department], but I can't install air conditioners in hell.'

The fact of the matter was that the mirror into which he had used to look for reassurance now reflected back not his authority, customs, and charm, but rather a new land entirely; the passage of time had turned it into a 'distorting mirror' that only mocked him.

His business quickly went from bad to worse. Then it ground to a halt. One day I felt very sad when I saw a new piece of calligraphy hanging from his wall:

> Don't ask about me; I'm the desert's dried wood.
> The caravan lit me on fire, then left.

I tried to cheer him up, 'How can anyone call you "dried wood"? I'm jealous of your youthful vitality.' Contrary to all expectation, he smiled. Since his dentures had already broken, he covered his mouth with his handkerchief when he laughed. He said, 'Yes, well, you're a young man, but I'm like this ...'

My organs have become 'flaccid.'
Now where's my old 'perversity'?

He removed the hankie from his mouth and said, 'Son, I'm that tree that the passenger on the moving train thinks is running.'

My Own Mind Attacks Me

Qibla tried his best never to let his ire die. He used to say, 'I don't ever want to live in a place where I can't be mad at people.' And when he found himself in one such place, his ire turned inward. Now he started hating himself.

My own mind attacks me.
I'm the fire. I'm the fuel.

He had used to say, 'Beware, if you stop being angry, you start being sad. And that's for cowards.' Adrift in such cowardice, he began to daydream uncontrollably about his childhood home and the village of his ancestors. The careworn take refuge in their memories. It is as if the photo album of life opens. Blurry, faded pictures start crowding each other out in your mind's eye. Each picture takes you back to another age. Each snapshot has its own story: the strong odour of horses sweating while they walk down the road, which is glistening with mica; farmers returning home in the evening with lambs draped over their shoulders like scarves; scarves dyed with night-flowering jasmine that hang from the tops of bamboo screens; the paths that part the rich, green fields of arhar lentils; in the dry years, desperate eyes glancing now and then toward the empty monsoon skies; the unlucky sounds of jackals calling out on desolate winter nights; the jingling of cowbells as the cows return at dusk to their pens; the drags on the dying chillum coals getting longer and longer as the pipe is passed through the village assembly hall on pitch-black nights; the fresh scent of young bodies and jasmine bracelets; the coiling smoke rising from incense sticks lit above a new grave in the golden light of the setting sun; nostrils flaring to inhale the scent of chickpeas being roasted in the hot sand; and the stench of government-issue kerosene lanterns. This was what his village had smelled like. And this was the fragrance that overwhelmed him like musk straight from a deer.

The Eaves' Tap-Tap-Tap

In a seventy-year-old child's mind, things start to get mixed up.

Smells, tactile sensations, and sounds turned into images: the sound of each raindrop hitting like a drum on the village house's tin roof; the sharp sound of the rain striking dry leaves; the way the little pools of water collecting on the floor toss up a crown of pearls when the heavy raindrops hit their surface; the roof tiles sizzling when the first rain strikes; the sensation of the shower's deluge on the baby's irritated skin, as though someone were bathing the baby in mint; the first rain to fall on a young son's grave, his mother racing bareheaded to and from the courtyard, looking up at the sky; the first flash of lightning from the clouds that will unleash their water on the waiting, thirsty ground; the sound of bangles chinking and girls' laughter as the monsoon songs are played on the drums; the rush of water finding the seams in the dry pond's cracked bottom; the delicate pattering of raindrops fanning out in the arc of light cast by the lanterns that hang on the verandah's support posts; the sound of the heavy rain on the mango trees clanging like cymbals; and the young girls playing on swings. Then the silence of a restless night, and the tap-tap-tap sound of water dripping from the eaves.*

---

* These eaves were those for thatched or tiled roofs.

By the time that Qibla got to this last sound, he was drowned in tears. While I could have introduced him to the rainstorms of Lahore and Nathia Gali that would have made him forget the showers of his past, how was I going to recreate those special eaves? Likewise, I could get him good mangos from Multan—dashari, langara, samar bahisht, or anwar ratol. But in the Punjab, you won't find any young girls swinging playfully from mango trees.

Whenever he got like this, I sat silently listening to the patter-patter of the rain of bygone years.

Qibla's Radio Was Hard of Hearing

There is no real harm in swimming against a river's current. I mean, none for the river. But Qibla didn't just want to swim against the current; he wanted to scale Niagara Falls.

One day he said to me, 'Mushtaq, your Karachi is yet another city that doesn't recognize good men for who they are. Buying is just buying; there's no art to it. The young don't know how to behave. And people don't know how to address their elders. When I was living with Basharat in Bihar Colony, I bought a battery-operated radio. I ran it off a car battery. There was no electricity in Bihar Colony. It was a constant worry. Basharat took it with him to work to charge it on his power saw. If he charged it for eight hours, I could listen to half an hour of the BBC. Then it would start to sound like a power saw. In the backyard, I had installed an antenna on top of a pristine twenty-five-foot wooden pole. But I still couldn't get any reception. The neighbourhood boys would get their kites entangled on it and then try to wrench them free. Their strings broke, and the antenna did too. Well, you really couldn't call it an "antenna." It was more like an aerial kite cemetery. The kites would flutter all day long like the flags on a newly dead saint's roadside shrine. It was a real pain in the ass to climb up and fix it. Think of it like this—I listened to the BBC from a hanging noose. When I began planning to move to the apartment on Burns Road, I thought I should sell it. Basharat was sick of it too. He said all he heard was the fluttering of kites. Someone from the neighbourhood agreed to pay 250 rupees. Early the next morning, he brought over the cash, and I gave him the radio. When I got home at eleven thirty, what do you think I saw but this man and his two bull-necked sons having a good old time prying up the antenna with the help of a pickaxe and shovel. I yelled, "What do you think you're doing?" He said, "We're taking the antenna. It's ours." I said, "I sold the radio for 250. Not the antenna." He said, "Without the antenna, the radio doesn't work. They go together."

'If it had been Kanpur, I'd have ripped the asshole's tongue out and cut off his bastard sons' necks in one fell swoop. I'd never met such a scheming and dishonest man. The wretch had already uprooted the pole and laid it on the ground. For a moment I felt like going inside to get my twelve-gauge rifle and then laying him flat like the antenna. But then I remembered that my gun license had expired. And what good was going to come out of arguing anyway? His poor wife would become a widow. But he wouldn't stop telling me about all his rights, and so I said, "Fine, take it, I don't care. You think it's that important to me? Look, we left this to come here."'

The three of them hauled off the antenna while Qibla stood holding out the photo of his mansion.

6.

A Disabled Wife and an Old Chillum Pipe

But there was one aspect of his life that he never spoke about, not even obliquely. I alluded to what this was much earlier. His wedding was an event of great celebration. His wife was very pretty, well-mannered, and cultured. Several years after their wedding, she suffered from an illness that rendered her hands useless. Then even her close relatives started to avoid her. She gradually stopped socializing—not only daily interactions with friends and family, and weddings and funerals, but everything else too. Of course the servants couldn't do all the housework. So Qibla dedicated his life to helping her, and he did so in such a selfless and loving way that it beggared description. Her hair was always braided. Her scarf was always pleated, and on Friday, it was always cornflower blue. With the passage of time, her hair grew grey. But Qibla's love for her didn't weaken in the least. You couldn't imagine that this embodiment of sacrifice and love was the same person who, when out of the house, raged and fumed like a sword cutting through air. If you live with someone your whole life, there will be thousands of moments when your patience and good nature are tested. But not even once did he raise his voice while talking to his poor wife.

Some people trace his vengeful nature back to the incident that crippled his wife. Right afterwards, his wife started praying so fervently that the world slipped away and heaven seemed nearby. No one ever saw Qibla pray. But the way he took care of her for forty years—waking in the middle of the night without complaint—perhaps figured as his prayers, fasts, and charitable deeds. God is merciful. These acts don't go unnoticed.

There was a time when his wife couldn't stand to bear her hardships anymore. She said, 'You should marry some widow.' He said, 'Oh, sure, why not? There's a little bit of land somewhere that's been waiting for me. My palanquin bearers will take me there. My dear, the earth never lacks for bridegrooms. One day I'll fall asleep covering myself with dirt for a blanket.'

He noticed tears in his wife's eyes, and so he changed the subject.

He relied upon lumber, hookahs, and tobacco for all his figures of speech, and so he asked, 'My dear, why do you restrict me to widows?

I agree with what Shaikh Sadi said, "Don't marry a widow even if she's a houri." You probably haven't heard this bit of Eastern wisdom, "The first smoker's an idiot, the second knows tobacco, and the third gets the chillum." Meaning, the first person to smoke is an idiot because he just gets the hookah ready; the second person gets to enjoy the tobacco; and the third person has to make due with sucking on the pipe for whatever he can get.'

I Burn (Like a Fire) Wherever I Go

Although his shop in Karachi was doing OK, Qibla wasn't. After all, who can escape time's ravages? He couldn't. You can't stop things from happening. But you can lessen their impact by disciplining your senses. If your personality has flaws, they will hurt yourself as well as others. Yet when you try to correct these flaws, they become even more painful. After coming to Karachi, he would often say, 'I was in jail for a year and a half, but that didn't change me as much as a week here did. Doing business here is like swimming in a pond full of water chestnuts. Once the rogues of Kanpur got here, they turned into lions and started hunting in the open. And the elite are like jackals hiding in some hole with their tails stuck between their legs. People are going into hiding on their own free will.'

One of Qibla's friends laid his honor on the line and said, 'You can't go back to the olden days. Things have changed. You too have to change.' Qibla smiled. He said, 'Even if a cantaloupe finds its way into being round, it's still not a watermelon.'

The truth of the matter was that Qibla couldn't recognize how the times had changed; he lacked the necessary parts of a personality to do so—tolerance, patience, gentleness, and flexibility. The fact was that these qualities weren't considered attributes in feudal society. Strictness, wilfulness, haughtiness, harshness, and a bad temper were all thought to be the strengths—and true qualities—of a feudal character. But this wasn't true just for feudal landlords; even scholars took pride in being this way.

> *I'm neither a fragrance nor a flower*
> *I burn like a fire wherever I go*

Things began to deteriorate quickly for Qibla. His friend Mian Inam Ilahi, who had a lot of influence over him despite being younger, advised him to get rid of the shop and buy a bus because that was a good way of earning income while sitting at home. He said he would take care of getting a route permit. Then he said, 'You can earn a tidy sum.' Qibla took this amiss. He said, 'You can earn good money playing the tabla and sarangi. There's a time-honoured tradition in my family that even if you're destined to fall into ruin and disgrace, it's better to do so in the family line of work. I don't give a damn about tidy sums!'

> *Now whatever heaven has in store for me, I'm not going to take it*
> *Even if it's this world and the hereafter, I'm not going to take it*
> *It doesn't give it the way I want it*
> *The way it gives it to me, I'm not going to take it*

Last Curse

His business wasn't just in a slump, it was dead. His mood was similar. He moped all day. He went to the shop not because business required him to, but for psychological reasons. He dreaded the thought of closing up and sitting around at home. Then one day it happened that his new Pathan servant Zarrin Gul Khan was several hours late. He tried not to be upset, but his old habit got the better of him.

Several months earlier he had hired a sixty-year-old accountant on half wages. This man had worn a long ochre robe. He had sat barefoot and cross-legged on the floor while he did his work. It was against his belief to sit in a chair or on any raised thing. He was devoted to a saint in the Warsi order. He was dutiful, honest, regular in his prayers and fasting, hypersensitive, and completely useless. Once Qibla had got upset and cursed him, 'Filth merchant!' Qibla didn't care about his white beard either. This man had replied very calmly, 'Exactly, sir. What else can this old man peddle if that's all you sell? Goodbye.' And he left. The next day he didn't come back, and Qibla stopped using that term for good. But that wasn't the only insult he knew.

So when he got mad at Zarrin Gul Khan, an insult slipped from his lips that had once been his favourite. The curse's terrible echo reached all the way to the Adam Khel Mountains where it resounded in the valleys. That's where Zarrin Gul Khan's widowed mother lived. His mother had lost her husband when the boy had been six. At twelve, he had promised that after he grew up he would move to Karachi for work and once he had enough money he would buy her brand-new sheets and send them to her.

No one had ever insulted him like that. He was young and head-strong. Qibla had insulted his honour and Pakhtun pride. Zarrin Gul Khan snatched Qibla's hat from his head and threw it to the floor. He brandished his knife and stood at the ready. He said, 'You old fool. Get lost. Or else I'll rip out your guts and eat your liver raw. Then I'll hang your filthy corpse from this pole!'

A customer disarmed the man. Qibla bent down, picked up his velvet hat, and, without wiping off the dirt, put it on his head.

Look How You Break Down

Fifteen minutes later he shut down the store and went home. There he told his wife, 'I'm not going back anymore.' A little while later, he heard the call to prayer coming from the neighbourhood mosque. After only the second iteration of 'Allah hu Akbar,' Qibla washed his hands and feet and, for the first time in forty years, stood ready to pray. His wife's jaw dropped in amazement. And he too froze because he realized that he could remember only two chapters of the Quran! He couldn't even recall the invocation of prayers! So, he finished up quickly.

He couldn't have imagined that a person could break from the inside. And to break in this fashion! When you break down, you make peace with your friends and family, with strangers, and even with your worst enemy—that is, you make peace with yourself. Then enlightenment becomes possible. The book of true wisdom opens.

If you have eyes, the world's a house of mirrors
You see faces everywhere you turn

There are those cautious types who ensconce themselves within the protective walls of inaction in order to escape the trials and tribulations of life. Like heavy, expensive curtains, they too eventually fray. Then there are those overly serious people who crack like walls: tiny cracks appear that could easily be painted over or covered with decorations, but these cracks reveal that the walls are collapsing slowly from the inside. Some people crack like porcelain. They're easily fixed with glue, but all you see are the cracks. On the other hand, there are shameless sycophants made of unbreakable stuff. They are like chewing gum: regardless of how much you chew them, they don't break. They bend but never break. If you contemptuously spit them out, they stick to your shoes and won't let go. You'll stop to question why you spat in the first place: at least when they were in your mouth, you were able to chew on them! These people are not really human, but they do understand human psychology. These are the successful ones, the lucky ones. They observe, test, and measure people, and when they find them useless, they turn their backs on them. The vagaries of time place a crown of spume on their heads as they sit for a moment on a wave's flying throne.

There are also people who are like windshields. When they are whole, they are as clean and transparent as a mystic's heart: through them, you can see the whole world. And when they suddenly break, they do so completely. They don't ding, chink, or split. Rather, they shatter into a thousand pieces so that there remains no evidence of the mystic, the world, or the glass. Nor is there any fear any longer; the only thing that remains is mystical ecstasy.

There are egos that break like the fortune of tyrants, or like Solomon's staff, against which he was leaning when the bird of his soul flew from the cage of his body. His lifeless body stood for many years, and no one suspected that he had died. He was dead and soulless, but because his authority had grown so overwhelming, the affairs of state continued as per usual. Termites were eating away at his staff, and one day it snapped in two. Solomon's empty body fell to the earth. That was when his nation and his people learned that he had already died.

So that evening Qibla's ego broke like a termite-infested staff, one that he had long been using as a crutch for his anger, that had allowed him to live a carefree life, and that had been the source of his vanity, as well as his vim and vigour.

I Burnt, but I Never Turned into Coals or Ashes

That night Qibla couldn't sleep. The muezzin was announcing the morning prayers when a watchman from the lumber market came to his house. He was panting and trembling, 'Sir, your shop and lumberyard are on fire. The fire engines got there at three. Everything's burnt to coals. Sir, fires don't start on their own!' By the time he got to the shop, everything was, in the government's terminology, 'under control.' That was due to the firemen's prompt action as well as the fact that there was nothing left to burn. The forked tongues of the leaping flames were now black. But the pine boards were still burn-

58

ing and sputtering, and they were showering the environs near and far with their heady scent.

Everything was ashes. Only his small side-office was safe. A long time ago in Kanpur, Lala Ramesh Chandra had said to him, 'Things are dangerous these days. You should get insurance.' In response, Qibla had turned up the pleated sleeve of his muslin kurta to show the throbbing muscles of his arm. 'This is my insurance policy!' he had said. He had flexed them, then asked Lala Ramesh Chandra to touch them. Lala had said with surprise, 'It's iron. Iron.' Qibla had replied, 'No, that's steel.'

There was a big crowd in front of his shop. People gave way for him the way people let a funeral pass. His face was expressionless. He had nothing to say. He unlocked his office. He picked up his accounting books, stuffed them under his arm, and raced to the western end of the lumberyard where the pine was still burning. First he committed the accounting books to the fire, then his keys. Then, without looking right or left, he slowly walked back to his office. He removed the photo of his mansion and wiped it down with his hankie. Then he put it under his arm and, with the pine still burning, went home.

His wife asked, 'What now?' He bowed his head.

I often imagine that if the angels took him to the heaven of cream-coloured light and cornflower blue clouds, he would stop at the gates for a second. Rizwan would motion him to quickly enter, and he would puff out his chest and step closer. Producing the photo of his mansion, he would say, 'We left this to come here.'

A Schoolteacher's Dream

1.

A Feudal Fantasy

Everyone dreams a dream of a fantasy life that they've copied from others, but whatever sadness a person experiences is strictly their own. No one can experience it with them. It is exclusive and personal. Who can understand the bone-melting fire they walk through? Even the fires of hell are not so hot! My toothache? No one has ever had one so bad, and no one ever will. But, on the other hand, the dream of a fantasy life is always copied from others. The dream that occupied Basharat's mind resembled the extremely colourful patchwork quilts that our dear grandmothers stitched together from thousands of scraps of cloth. And in this dream many things from those bygone days were jumbled up: feudal shows of pomp and circumstance; the dissolute nobility's haughtiness and elegance; the middle class's showiness; the small-town person's airs; and the slickness, simplicity, and stinginess of a person with a good job. Basharat himself said that in his childhood his greatest desire had been to toss aside his writing slate, to rip up his primers, and to become a wandering juggler. He wanted to go from town to town beating his drum, getting his monkey, bear, and young assistant to dance, and encouraging the kids in the audience to clap. But when he grew up a little and was able to distinguish a bad idea from worse, he exchanged that dream with wanting to become a schoolteacher. And after he became a schoolteacher in the village of Dhiraj Ganj, he dreamt of wearing corduroy

pants, a silken Two Horse Brand boski shirt, two-ounce gold cuf-
flinks in his double cuffs, a new sola hat without its khaki protective
covering, and patent leather pumps; and he dreamt of going to school
to teach the boys his own ghazals. Then the dream took on a more
mature form: a white silk achkan coat with bidri engraved buttons
rising up to his Adam's apple; in his pocket a little paan box with
ganga-jamuni engraving on it; a white brocade Rampuri hat on his
head worn at a rakish though somewhat modest angle (though not
so modest that he would seem entirely respectable); a white chikan-
embroidered kurta with small flowery designs soaked in itr-e-henna
or itr-e-khas, depending upon the weather; churidar pyjamas with
a white silk drawstring woven by a beautiful young woman; white
sheep's hide Salim Shahi shoes; an Italian blanket for show and to
protect his pyjamas from the tail and the projectile piss and poop of
the white horse yoked to the phaeton; and, on the running board at
the rear of the phaeton, a groom wearing a large belt around his waist
stitched with zardozi embroidery, as well as woolen livery chaps from
knees to ankles, who would be yelling 'Get away, kids!' while whipping kids as they tried to catch a ride. Youth had passed him by, but
his childishness was still intact.

The depth of concentration, complete involvement, and self-
forgetfulness with which a child plays a game outstrips by a factor
of ten that which adults demonstrate in the course of their business
and other doings. It goes without saying that even the world's most
famous philosopher isn't more engrossed in his task than a child
playing a game. When the child's toy breaks, he suddenly looks into
the light, and in his tears a rainbow begins to glimmer. Then he falls
asleep sobbing. If magically this toy is brought to the man after he has
grown old, he will be speechless as to how this toy's getting broken
could have caused him to cry so much. This is the same for those toys
that people play with their entire lives. Yes, it's true that as we age, our
toys change. Some break on their own. Some are broken by others.

Some toys change into gods for you. And some goddesses (toys) fall from grace and you realize they are just rag dolls. Then there are the unfortunate moments that spare none of the toys. And in those moments, you too break.

I made, I worshipped, I was conquered

Now Basharat himself can laugh at these childish desires. But things were different then. To a child, there can never be anything more real in all of creation than his toys. Whether dreaming at midnight or daydreaming in the middle of the day, that dream is for that moment the only truth there is. This broken toy. This tear-stained kite for which the child was spanked so many times. This firefly flashing on and off. This taut balloon that in a second will turn into a flaccid blob of rubber. This scarlet fly that tickles my palm. This train made from matchboxes that flies faster than the speed of sound. This soap bubble quivering with the child's breath. This fairies' chariot that is drawn along by butterflies. This second. This moment. This is the one and only reality.

And this world is nothing but illusions, spells, and shadows

I Took Some Colours from the Rainbow and Stole Some Light from the Stars

This Story Takes Place Before The Toy Broke

He had just become a schoolteacher and the height of his desire was a black phaeton. In fact, his going to the trouble of wearing a white uniform, a white achkan coat, white shoes, white kurta pyjamas, a white drawstring, and so on was only so that he could match the white horse. Otherwise, only a duck could find such a duck-like get-up attractive. He actually hated churidar pyjamas. But since he wanted to have a white drawstring woven by a beautiful young woman, he was forced to cover his legs with this 'sitar cover' (the tight-fitting pyjamas). Each brick of his castle in the sky was formed from the clay of the feudal system and kneaded with bourgeois dreams. And each brick was not only of different size and colour from the others, but each was embossed with his image. Some bricks were even round! He had fantasized about everything so clearly that he had already determined to what degree the white horse could raise its tail in his presence so as to preserve the rules of decorum; behind which window-blinds along his route which wrists would jingle which colour of bangles; which girl would have written his name (along with BA) on her palm; and which kohl-rimmed eyes would watch anxiously from behind which blinds and which fingers would separate the bamboo's slats to look for the revolutionary prince who will declare

You, my dear, wave the flag, and I will play the drums.

I must add, what could be a safer division of labour? The sweetheart carries the flag into the thick of the battle risking her life, and the poet sits in a marble tower far away playing a period instrument and singing an antedated song (meaning his own). In prose, this situation has been described as persuading others to slip the noose over their own necks; in a Punjabi saying, the same thing is said, but with a little too much clumsy honesty. Look, something quite presumptuous happened from the very first verse (moment). In any event, I meant only that Basharat dreamed at all times of being a schoolteacher, and he never thought of anything else: for only a teacher could a phaeton and a silk drawstring mean so much. Landlords and the feudal elite couldn't care less. Even after twenty years, he could still feel the fiery slashes on his back where he had been whipped as he ran with the neighbourhood boys hooting and hollering behind a nobleman's phaeton and its white horse.

At the Crossroads of a Dilemma

He left poetry behind to become a schoolteacher. Then he quit that and became a shop owner. And then he closed up shop and moved to Karachi where he opened another lumber store on Harchandrai Road. It was a new world with a new lifestyle. He had thrust his foot into a new, busy world. But the dream of a white horse and a phaeton never left him. You can break a daydream or a fantasy in only two ways. One, it becomes a reality. Two, at the crossroads of your dilemma, you are granted a reprieve from your obsession and are allowed to go on your way.

Heart-breaker, dream-maker, thank you for the dream!

Then you finally round a bend beyond which no one has ever returned. That is, the family life. And yet this too didn't cure Basharat. He had sold his lovely house for close to nothing and, according to him, had arrived in Karachi robbed and beaten. Then in the next two years, God rewarded him so grandly that Kanpur began to seem quite paltry. All his dreams had come true. I mean, his house was crammed full of all sorts of useless material goods. There was only one thing missing: God had given him everything but a horse! While he couldn't have bought a new car, he could have bought a second-hand one. Back in those days, you could get a car for less than what you have to pay to get four tires today. But, to him, a car didn't have the same aristocratic splendour and feudal elegance as a phaeton or buggy. Horses are beyond compare.

Chivalry Died with the Horses

Mirza Abdul Wadud Baig says that trying to talk sense into an overwrought person is like trying to sow seeds in a windstorm. So instead of trying to dissuade Basharat from pursuing his worthless obsession, he encouraged him. One day, in the way that you would extinguish a fire by spraying it with gas, Mirza mentioned that chivalry, sacrifice, valour, and fearlessness became foreign concepts once horses fell out of favour. Out of all the animals, dogs and horses are man's first and best friends; they have left behind the natural world for us. Dogs are still around because of their dogged nature, but humans haven't been faithful to horses. With the departure of horses, the feudal chapter of human history has ended. It was a chapter in which enemies warned before attacking and fought looking their adversaries right in the eyes. Death was a spear's length away, and both parties held spears. No doubt death still tasted strange, but at least the killer and the victim could recognize each other. Firebombs and atom bombs didn't rain down on anonymous, sleeping cities. A horse shows cowardice only when its rider does. Galloping horses make hearts race and the ground tremble beneath their hooves. The dust stirred up in their wake, the sparks flying off their hooves, the sun glinting off the spear-points, and the men's breaths transformed into storms of panting announced the attacking horsemen from miles away. Even today the sound of horses galloping together lights in our blood the savage fire of thousands of years ago.

But, Mirza, just a minute: rein in your rhetoric a little. What sort of horse are you talking about? A horse that pulls carts?

Gulji's Horses

But I do accept that without horses, we could hardly imagine an age of adventures, conquest, bravery, and chivalry. *The horse's saddle is our imperial throne . . .* The Gaekwads were very proud of their ancient royal motto. It's said that the Hun horsemen who raped and pillaged their way across Europe never got off their horses. They slept in the saddle, relaxed there, ate there, drank there, and conducted trade there; they even performed their calls of nature there. In England, there was a painter named Stub who only painted purebred horses. (In Europe, people still care a little bit about lineage when it comes to horses, dogs, and royalty.) The apparent reason why Stub preferred horses to naked models is that women don't have tails. Add to that, horses never demand that their likenesses trump reality. For eleven years, we've lived next door to Pakistan's renowned artist Gulji. I've been able to observe his painting habits quite closely. He always paints at night, and that, after midnight. For a long time I thought that perhaps he did so because he saw better at night. But then, when I had to start writing at night because of an ulcer, I stopped being so curious.

Who knows who's living it up and where?

His love for horses is limitless. He earns hundreds of thousands of rupees from his paintings. Someone once teased him (it wasn't me) that for the price of one horse painting, you could easily buy three live horses! After that, I noticed that he had at least three horses in each painting. I also noticed that he doesn't give one hundredth of the love, detail (down to the last hair), and inspiration to the rest of the horse and its rider that he does to the horse's tail. Not just the horse's entire personality but that of the rider as well is sucked into the tail. It's like each and every hair has been stroked by the affectionate hand of the horse's owner: each hair is unique, becoming, and priceless. If you ask the truth, he would rather paint only the tail. He paints the rest of the horse against his will and only so that he can hang the tail on it. If it should ever come to pass that he has to paint a very beautiful and minutely detailed portrait of some VIP lady, he would be sure to paint her ponytail so well that if a horse saw it, he (the male horse) would start pawing the ground.

He also specializes in painting cute camels, though what he has done with them is absurd. That is, he has exported these oils in the dozens to Arab countries. Some of these paintings are so expensive that only banks, Arab sheikhs, foreign diplomats, and Pakistani smugglers can afford them. The rare camels that the United Bank bought from him proved so large that the bank had to construct an entirely new wall in the middle of the hallway to hang them up. After the sheikhs saw them, they were so happy that a handful demanded where they could get the real (meaning identical) camels. The bank was thus faced with a dilemma:

Where can I get one just like you?

In its greed for petrodollars, the bank was forced to find some camels to export (along with their fodder) that kind of resembled these painted camels. When I came onboard at United, one day I timidly asked Gulji, 'Sir, if you could please paint camels that resemble the camels of this earth, it would make the bank's job of meeting the sheikhs' demands much easier. My job's on the line. And, also, please avoid painting on their backs beautiful women without veils.' Gulji is a very crafty, hypersensitive, and witty artist. My suggestion pissed him off. He took a moment to compose himself and then spoke in English, 'Baba, I'm a simple and craftless Agha Khani worker. And I'm obedient. But this will be possible if and only when I mix a debauched camel's milk with my paints, and if and only when I paint with a brush made from the tail of a virgin mare. This will be worth double. Think about it.' Then he added in Urdu, 'Sir, you're poking fun at us fakirs! Picasso said that painting is a blind man's profession. An artist doesn't paint what he sees, but he paints what he thinks he sees.' I didn't mind his sarcasm because

Fiery, fumbled words don't affect wise men.

Also, I read somewhere that the bright, beautiful colours of Rajput paintings from three or four hundred years ago (colours that were brighter than turmeric) were made by feeding mango leaves to a cow continuously over the course of several days and then collecting its urine. This colour was used for ripe, juicy mangos, for cholis, and for the uppity turbans of the kings.

In any event, Gulji's camels couldn't match his horses. And how could they? How can you compare a horse's long, thick, royal-fly-whisk of a tail to a camel's little stub? It's not really a tail but a tale of a tail. Mirza says that a camel's tail isn't big enough even to cover its privates. But every animal's tail serves some purpose. For instance, a monkey's. That's good for hanging around in trees and for using like a ladder to pluck off half-ripe fruit and female monkeys. A dog's tail, wagging helplessly in front of its master, was a brown-noser's tongue in a previous life. (A dog doesn't use its tongue for that purpose.) An ostrich's tail is made to adorn the heads of Western women. For many animals, the only reason they have a tail is so that the poor creatures have something to stick between their legs as they run away. A peacock's tail isn't for dancing in front of people but for impressing female peacocks in the wild and for sweeping saints' shrines. If not for that, why would they carry around such an overblown corsage on such a frail frame? Close your eyes and tell me—if a peacock were shaved, wouldn't it look just like a cowering owl?

The Best Tail

But forget charming the opposite sex with a tail. A camel's tail can't express anything—profound or silly. It doesn't even really hang right. If you ask the truth, only peacocks, birds of paradise and casino bunnies have tails worth mentioning, and when it comes to the last one, the reason I like them is that they aren't their own and they tickle awake the sleeping, soon-to-be-losing rabbits in men's souls. A bird of paradise is the size of a red partridge, but, I swear to God, the males have tails a full fifteen feet long! If male birds of paradise are sitting high in some trees with their tails hanging down hoping to attract females, then the females judge their husbandly qualities by the same methods that in a previous age people used to measure Muslim theologians' knowledge. That is, only by those things that hang: the length of their beards, the loose ends of their turbans, and their retinues. The female puts her beak into the tiny beak of the male with the longest tail. But the most efficacious tail goes to the scorpion. If a snake's poison is in its fangs, a scorpion's is in its tail. A wasp has its poison in its stinger, and a rabid dog's is in its tongue. Humans are the only animals with poison in their hearts. Writing this makes me think about whom I would sting if I were a scorpion. Thinking about all the people I don't like, I have to say that one lifetime wouldn't be enough to take care of things. Then again, it would never work because the very first name on my shit list is my own. As far as snakes' tails go, I don't like them, but they do fascinate me. And that's because they have the same virtue that my forehead does: no one can tell where it starts. Setting aside the snake's hood, I would say that a snake is nothing more than a big tail. But the very best tail must be that one which has already fallen off. It was only after that incident that humankind was dubbed the most noble of all creation and the viceroy of God on earth.

My Means of Conveyance: A Banana Peel

Writing about Basharat's love for phaetons and horses has brought me far afield. My mentor and master Mirza Abdul Wadud Baig once shared with me a great piece of wisdom: 'When you slip on a banana peel, you should never ever try to stop yourself or put on the brakes because that will only cause greater injury. Just slip without a care in the world. Enjoy it. In the words of the great poet Zauq, "Go as far as it goes." When the banana peel becomes tired, it will stop on its own. Just relax.' So I use this principle not only when walking but also when writing and thinking. But why shouldn't I go ahead and tell you the whole truth? All my life, the banana peel and the banana peel alone has been my sole means of conveyance. If you happen to notice a youthful spring to my step, it's due to the banana peel. If my pen happens to slip, then I go along with it happily. I don't try to control my pen at all. And when it reveals my malice, then I'm like the boy who has had all his secrets suddenly taken out of his stuffed pockets and laid upon a desk. But, that said, the old folks feel even worse than the boy because this reminds them of their forgotten youths and of the current contents of their desk drawers. The day that children begin to keep in their pockets money instead of worthless things is the last day they will ever be able to sleep without worry.

From Race Course to Horse-Drawn Cart

As his business started to do better, his desire to have a phaeton only grew. Basharat spent months looking for a horse. It seemed as though a horse meant everything to him, and, like Richard III, he was ready to give up everything for one:

A horse! A horse! My kingdom for a horse!

His neighbour Chaudhuri Karam Ilahi told him that he should go to the police stud farm near Sargodha because the police breed thoroughbreds and other top-notch horses there. If the father is a purebred, then its son is bound to be as well. The saying goes that a son is like his father, and a horse is like its father as well, and if not in features, then at least in feelings. Basharat said, 'I don't believe that. The fact is that any horse born from the police's breeding and midwifery can never be purebred. It will only be a police horse.'

Hearing this talk of horses, Professor Qazi Abdul Quddus, MA, BT, recited that famous couplet (and, as usual, his choice was quite out of place), in which a narcissus flower cries for thousands of years in the fear of the complications attendant upon the birth of a sage. Mirza says that Professor Qazi Abdul Quddus always looks foolish when he interrupts others to impart some nugget of wisdom. And if he doesn't say anything, he looks even more foolish, thanks to his normal facial expression, which is as though,

If I speak, it's meaningless; if I don't speak, the same.

As for his normal expression, it is the flush of blood that comes over his face when he sees someone's zipper stuck halfway down.

Finally Basharat took a liking to a horse owned by a businessman who had a steel rerolling mill. He went to see the horse three or four times, and each time he returned liking it even more. He was taken so much by its white coat that it was all he talked about: he loved talking about it. When I asked if it didn't just have a little white on its forehead and hooves, he scoffed, 'Even a water buffalo can have that. A horse isn't revered just for having a little white here and there. All eight leg-joints should be strong. All four ankles and all four knees should be strong. This isn't some hired horse. It's from a family of racehorses.' The businessman also showed him the brochure of the Karachi Race Club that was printed by Associated Press and that noted that this horse not only had run in such-n-such race but had won as well. The brochure had a picture and notes about the horse's character, as well as a family tree, which went like this—White Rose, son of Wild Oats, son of Old Devil. From the moment he set eyes upon this magnificent horse, Basharat stopped feeling any pride about his own ancestry. According to him, the horse's grandfather had won three races in Bombay. He was running in his fourth when he had a heart attack and died. His grandmother was a real slut. She had relations with all of the most famous English stallions of that era. Thanks to these stallions having held onto the hem of her chastity, she gave birth to six colts. Each took after his father. A degenerate nobleman had owned White Rose before the businessman. This man was building for his Anglo-Indian wife Alice a mansion called Wonderland on Bath Island. He bought rebar from the rerolling mill, and yet after several months had passed he still hadn't paid his bill. He went bankrupt from racing and gambling debts, and so the construction of Wonderland stopped. Alice hastily left him, hooked up with a landlord from Multan, and then took off with him to Europe. The day that the businessman heard that one of the man's creditors had gone to Wonderland's construction site and had taken away sacks of cement and rebar, he sent his manager with a mercenary troupe of five guards armed with clubs with the instructions to take whatever at all they could get their hands on. That meant the horse. And a Siamese cat, which they stuffed into a gunnysack and brought as well. To drive home the point of the horse's tragedy, Basharat expressed his sympathy for me: 'This horse was hardly born to be yoked to a cart. The businessman didn't treat him right. But that's fate for you. Sir, three or four years ago, who would have guessed that you would be stuck in a bank? You could have been Deputy Commissioner or District Magistrate, and now look at your tiny bank teller's stool!'

A Kingly Ride

He had fallen in love with the horse at first sight. And love is blind, even when it comes to horses. It never occurred to him that the couplets of the Urdu masters that he had a penchant for reciting at inappropriate times didn't have anything to do with those horses that pull carts. There's no harm in admitting that a horse is a kingly ride. The image of kingly pomp and splendour is incomplete—nay, half of itself—without a horse. If you put a king on a horse, then at last he looks as tall as a regular man. But if you look at it closely, a horse is only the second of kingly conveyances. That's because a king's favourite ride is always actually his people. Once they've gotten a chance to ride them, then there are no wells, no ditches, no fences, and no obstacles in their way. Blinded by power, they don't see the writing on the walls. They'll be able to read only after it's rewritten in Braille. What kings think of as their court is really their Bastille, and this prevents them from understanding that if you just let the headstrong horse neigh a little, then all will be well. But you can't rely upon this means of conveyance because this piebald horse doesn't walk at a consistent gait:

Often it got testy and difficult to ride.

Kill the Poor on the First Day

But those rulers who are clever and who understand human nature and statecraft kill the poor on the very first day and thus teach a lesson to the elite.

Kill the poor on the first day

But the elite (and the dignitaries of state) don't need a warning, or to be pricked with an elephant goad. They are always ready to become the show elephant for whoever gives them a gold canopy, silver bells, and a brocade elephant covering strung with a lanyard of medals. First, they are obsequious and willing to do anything. The next day, their lips are sealed. And the next day, they are relegated to the outhouse.

Their life is four days long. Two days are spent yearning for power. And two days are spent as Yes-men.

Our Camel Saddle

One day I happened to vent a little contempt toward horses, and Basharat got hot under the collar. I had satirized the historical example that when the Mongols rode out in the thousands upon their horses, the stench was so putrid that you could smell it from twenty miles away. He replied, 'Excuse me, but you grew up in Rajasthan where you only saw camels, starched white Rajputi turbans, thick beards, and guns ten-feet long; and below this, the Jat servants walking with their clubs resting on their shoulders and freshly made, oil-soaked leather shoes hanging from those. You saw horses for the first time when you came to Pakistan. Mian Ahsan Ilahi is my witness. He was there when you told the story of the feudal baron who was a cavalry officer in the king's camel platoon. When he retired and returned home—what was that place called?—oh, yes, Udaipur Torawati— he had a dozen or so reed stools set up for visitors and, for himself, his old government saddle from his camel Jung Bahadur. And on this saddle, he sat fidgeting from dawn till dusk wearing his platoon's vermillion turban and his medals on his chest. One day, as he sat fidgeting while recounting the exploits of Jung Bahadur, and as his medals tinkled away, he had a heart attack. From the saddle itself, the bird of his soul flew from the cage of the elements. At the moment of death, he was smiling with the name of Jung Bahadur on his lips.

'Mushtaq Sahib, I'm sorry, but you were the one who told me this story. My lord, why don't you get off your high horse and stop making fun of others? Anyway, what do you know about horses? You don't even know what a blacklegged thoroughbred is. Or how to cross-breed a donkey. Or what a curry comb looks like. Or where on the head the horse's ears are. Or where to prick an ox with an awl. Or from which language the word "pine nut" comes.'

The last two statements finished our conversation. Seeing how personal it had become, I decided not to say anything. His banter wasn't pleasing to me in the least; I didn't know the answer to a single one of his questions. He's not a difficult person by nature; he's soft-spoken and sweet. But when he gets derailed like this, he drags me along in the mud for quite a ways. He said, 'If you haven't ridden a horse, you'll never be happy, high-minded, or lion-hearted.' He must have been right because he himself had never ridden a horse.

Keep Far Away from Funerals

The horse filled a spiritual vacuum that had existed in him for quite a while. He was very surprised to think how (and why) he had made it up till then:

> I wonder by my troth what thou and I did till we loved.
>
> (Donne)

This love for the horse had grown so much that he agreed to buy from the businessman a horse-drawn cart as well, and that for 450 rupees, even though he didn't like it at all. It was really big and bulky. But what could he do? There wasn't a single phaeton in all of Karachi. The businessman wanted to sell the horse and cart together. Well, not just those, but he also forced him to buy two sacks of grain, five lots of hay, the horse's framed photo, digestive salts, a long tube to administer medicine orally, a curry comb, and a nosebag. This lot cost twenty-nine and a half rupees, and the businessman called this swindle a 'package deal.' He had to overspend for the horse too. If he had asked the price straight from the horse's mouth, it never would have been what he paid—900 rupees. And throughout this, Basharat also had to put up with the businessman's pet interjections—'you know' and 'fucking.' After he had made the down payment and had taken the reins in hand, and thinking then that nothing in the world could prevent his dream from coming true, Basharat asked why he was selling such a good horse—was there some hidden flaw? The businessman answered, 'Two months ago I was on Lawrence Road going to the market. I must have been in front of the City Workshop when a fucking funeral appeared in front of me, you know? It was a fucking police officer's. The horse shied all of a sudden. But the people in the fucking procession freaked out even more. For no reason at all, they took off, you know? The body was dropped right there in the middle of the fucking road. And I stood watching it like some dumb fuck. From that day, the horse hasn't been worth the grain it takes to fucking feed him. I've fallen out of love, you know? So there's nothing really wrong with him. Just keep him away from fucking funerals. See ya!'

'Why didn't you tell me before?'
'Why didn't you ask before? See ya—'

2.

I Wandered the World like a Will-o'-the-Wisp

He hired a driver named Rahim Bakhsh. He agreed to the salary that Rahim Bakhsh proposed: forty-five rupees, food, and clothes. He had bought the horse after seeing its colour, teeth, and thick tail; he was so satisfied by those parts that he didn't think it was necessary to inspect anything else. He hired his driver in much the same way. That is, based only on his way of talking. He was a master of the tall tale. His face looked like a horse's. When he laughed, he looked like a horse neighing. From living among horses for thirty years, he had taken on all of their habits, defects, and bad odours. If a horse had only two legs, it would walk exactly like him. He would amuse kids by wiggling his left ear. When he scored a goal in soccer by kicking the ball backwards off his heel, kids would erupt in applause. He stole the chickpeas intended for the horse. Basharat said, 'The ingrate also steals hay and eats it. How could one horse eat so much? That's why his hair is still black. Don't you see? The bastard has had three wives!' Whatever the conversation was, Rahim Bakhsh expressed himself using a groom's vocabulary, and at night he slept with a whip. Whenever a horse (male or female) should come within two miles, he would immediately start flaring his nostrils to get its scent. If he should happen to cross paths with a good-looking mare on the street, he would stop, wink at the driver, and ask how old she was. Then he would peel back his horse's leather blinders and say, 'Take it in, buddy. She's something to remember!' Then he would start singing a tune of his own devising in a voice like Pankaj Malik's to the beat of the horse's hooves, 'I wandered the world like a will-o'-the-wisp,' and then head off down the road. Mirza says that he was a horse in his last life and that he will be a horse in his next life; and that only great prophets, sages, and saints have the good luck to be the same thing in former and upcoming lives. The rest of us have no such luck.

I Went Along Hugging the Wall

Call it what you will—the horse and cart's unveiling, its confirmation ceremony, or its breaking in—but Basharat's father took care of it. After he turned seventy, he was almost always sick. After he moved to Karachi, despite his best efforts, he couldn't get a house or any other property through the Allotment, and his attempts at going into business failed. At heart, he was a very simple man. He would have considered himself an absolute villain had he changed his time-honoured principles and out-of-date views to match his new circumstances. So instead of being disappointed or embarrassed by his failures, he felt a kind of pride and satisfaction. He was the sort of person who took failure to be the absolute proof of his goodness and integrity. He was a hypersensitive, introverted, and self-respecting man. He had never asked for handouts, not even from a palm reader; but then that changed. He had never offered false praise; this too fell by the wayside. But nothing worked. In the words of Mirza Abdul Wadud Baig, 'When high-minded, principled people suffer a lot beneath the Wheel of Fortune, they become demoralized and so try to implement clumsily the tricks of the successful, and yet this only worsens the situation.' Then suddenly he suffered a stroke. His left side became paralysed. He developed diabetes, allergies, Parkinson's, and God knows what other maladies. Some said that his battered ego had taken refuge in disease and that he himself didn't want to get well because then no one would feel any sympathy for him. Now he wasn't as sad about his failures as he was about his turning his back on his time-honoured principles. When people came by to console him and suggest ways of improving his situation, his eyes filled with tears.

You're living the life of Riley, and yours truly is left with nothing

The biggest fall from grace, indignity, and dishonour that anyone can experience is when you have become worthless in your own eyes. So he too passed through this hell.

I shouldn't have, but I went there one hundred times
I was so weak I hugged the wall at times
Without any bread, I was close to starving at times
Not seeing any way out, I was going mad at times
*   I had a weak soul, but I was still patient*

79

I went to flatter at the door of every fool
I lost my self-respect begging from fools
Getting nothing in return, I too become a fool
When she rejected me, I became the king of fools
Now in the city, I'm the infamous patient

Basharat says that when his father recited 'I was so weak I hugged the wall at times,' he would act as though he was leaning against the wall with his right hand and stumbling forward like the line said. But his lifeless left hand told its own story. He didn't need to expend any extra effort in painting a picture of helplessness. Throughout his life, listening to Dagh's ghazals would send him into ecstasy. He had never heard a prostitute sing either Fani's or Mir's ghazals. In fact, back in those days to request a hot dancer or musician to perform one of Fani's or Mir's ghazals was like asking to have some lemon juice mixed into your liquor! Forgive my impertinence, but after drinking such a 'man-conquering concoction,' a man would be able to play only the tabla! His father had always detested Fani and Mir. But in old age what consolation he could find came from their verses alone. He had always been a strong, brave man. Basharat said he could never have imagined seeing him cry. But then he did. With his own eyes. A lot.

In Karachi, he wasted half his time thinking about his long-lost friends. The other half was wasted by his new good-for-nothing friends.

Aladdin the Eighth

Basharat's father's diseases were numerous and infectious. The worst of them was old age. One of his sons-in-law returned from England having just received his FRCS in surgery. At his in-laws' house, no one's appendix was safe. If someone was suffering from eye pain, he took out their appendix. The surprising thing was that their eye pain went away. Throughout his life Basharat's father had suffered from GI tract pain, but he put his hand on his stomach and swore to God that he had never let any doctor touch his appendix. He had been bedridden for quite a while, but his disability was still incomplete. I mean, he could walk, if he had something to lean on.

So he performed the inauguration of the horse like this: he had a red ribbon tied to his bedroom door (from which he had not emerged for several months) and then cut it with his shaky hand. Then, after distributing laddoos to the children who had clapped during the ribbon-cutting ceremony, he prayed two rakats in thanks. Then he hung a marigold garland over the horse's neck. The horse had a big whorl on his forehead. He dipped his finger in saffron and wrote 'Allah' on it, muttered some prayers and blew on it. Then he smeared vermillion paste on the horse's four hooves and the cart's two wheels and intoned the blessing that they should race forward at full speed for as long as they lived. He had Rahim Bakhsh open his mouth, and he stuffed in one laddoo. For himself, he slipped a silver-wrapped paan between his jaws. He wrapped himself in his old Kashmiri shawl and sat in the cart's backseat. Then he had his 20-year-old harmonium put in the front seat, and he set off for Master Baqar Ali's shop to have it repaired.

Basharat's father gave the horse a new name—Balban. He told the driver, 'I don't like your name Rahim Bakhsh at all. From now on, I'll call you Aladdin.' Since his memory had started to go wonky, he called all servants by this name. This was Aladdin the Eighth. His predecessor, Aladdin the Seventh, had a big family. He had been fired for stealing hookah tobacco and bread. He had tied warm bread to his midriff and was walking out when his clumsy gait gave him away. Basharat's father called the current Aladdin, meaning Rahim Bakhsh, just Aladdin. But if there was something special to be done, like massaging his feet or refilling his hookah at some unusual hour, or just out of love and affection, he would call him Aladdin Mian. Only when he cursed him out would he call him by his real name.

Half-Mast Whip

The next day the kids were taken to school in the cart. Then Basharat was taken to his shop. For three days, this continued. Then on the fourth day, the driver was very upset when he came back from dropping the kids at school. He tied the horse to the gate and went directly to find Basharat. He was holding the whip like in bygone eras standard bearers carried flags into battle. In fact he had his hand raised to the very last possible centimetre like the Statue of Liberty does in New York (thus keeping the torch of freedom high). Later, Basharat learned that if Rahim Bakhsh had to relate some misfortune or break bad news, he would come carrying his whip like that. Seeing the whip raised horizontally would unsettle Basharat like Hamlet seeing his father's ghost:

Here it cometh, my lord!

When Rahim Bakhsh got to Basharat, he lowered the flag to half-mast and asked for fifteen rupees. He said, 'I'd just got to the corner of the alley by the school when I was suddenly stopped and given a ticket. The horse's left leg was limping. As soon as I left the school, the Cruelty Cops* swooped in. With a lot of cringing and begging, I got off with a fifteen-rupee ticket. Otherwise, boss, you too would have been in for it. Right in front of me the Cruelty Cops whipped a donkey-cart owner all the way to the police station. And that donkey wasn't even remotely as lame as our horse.' Rahim Bakhsh mentioned

---

* Cruelty Cops: The driver called (and cursed) the Society for the Prevention of Cruelty to Animals (SPCA) by this nickname.

the donkey's trivial lameness with such contempt, and he exaggerated their horse's serious disability with such pride that it incensed Basharat, and so, with a quivering hand, he thrust the fifteen rupees at him just to shut him up.

A Lion's Intentions and a Goat's Intelligence Fall into Question

He immediately called in a veterinarian and showed him the horse. When the vet rubbed its left shin, the horse flinched. He diagnosed it as being an old injury. So then the whole thing started to become clear. Probably—no, *most definitely*—this was the reason why the horse had been disqualified from racing. Horses like this are always put down on the spot so as to prevent them from being yoked to a cart and condemned to a wretched life of disgrace. But, at the same time, the vet gave him the hope that the horse's condition would improve if the horse was massaged with heron oil. The price of this oil was five rupees a day, which meant 150 rupees a month. That would be 900 rupees in half a year. The horse cost 900, and now the massaging would cost the same! It was like stitching a burlap quilt with patches of brocade! Just recently he had hired a man to massage his father's feet for eighty rupees a month. This meant that he was going to have half his earnings confiscated by income tax, and a third eaten up by masseurs! He had never imagined that so much of his hard-earned money would be legally embezzled by such riffraff! At four in the afternoon, he yoked the horse to the cart and set off to confront the businessman. Before leaving, he made sure to put on heavily tinted sunglasses so that he wouldn't hesitate to speak harsh words and in order to give a mysterious expression of bloodthirstiness. He had gone about halfway when someone grabbed the cart's yoke and stopped them cold. The man said, 'Your horse is limping badly. You're going to get a ticket.' Basharat was shocked. The Cruelty Cops were cracking down. Every corner had one on the prowl. And they were giving tickets for each and every little thing. When the inspector didn't relent, Basharat started to split legal hairs: 'I just got a ticket this morning. You can't get ticketed for the same offense within seven hours.' The inspector added this to his charge sheet and said that things had turned much more serious. When Basharat didn't see any way out of it, he said, 'OK, baba, you're right. Take ten rupees and let's call it over with. It's a brand-new horse. I bought it three days ago.' But this sent the inspector into a tizzy. He said, 'Look, mister, you seem nice enough, despite your sunglasses. You should know you might be able to buy a lame horse but you can't buy off a person.' So Basharat got a ticket.

When Basharat arrived at the steel rerolling mill, the businessman was getting ready to go home. That day, he was feeding pulao to somewhere in the vicinity of 200 beggars as a way to honour a saint. He believed that doing this would sanctify his month's earnings. And this sort of laundering was nothing new. For as many as twenty years, one certain bank had been serving dinner to just as many beggars as new accounts had been opened in all its branches on that day. (It wasn't clear whether this was done out of happiness for the new accounts or to atone for the uptick in the usury business.) Once, I happened to travel to Multan. That day a very senior executive from the bank's hierarchy was there for an inspection. That evening I witnessed a truly righteous scene that made me happier than anything: the senior executive sat on his haunches alongside fifteen or twenty beggars as they all ate pulao, and he was going from man to man asking in detail about his (bad) health and that of his people. But Mirza Abdul Wadud Baig has a bad habit of popping my balloons. He ruined my good mood: 'When a lion and a goat drink from the same well, realize that the lion's intentions and the goat's intelligence fall into question. That Mahmood and Ayaz are sitting together eating is also part of the audit and inspection. The executive wants to find out whether the beggars are truly beggars or whether they're not the manager's friends and relatives come for handouts.'

But back to the matter at hand. I was talking about the businessman from the steel mill and how he 'laundered' his income by performing monthly religious functions. Back then the invention of a new magic wand* was still far in the future, and our intelligent and creative Minister of the (Empty) Treasury and other economic gurus were still busy studying for their final high-school exams. Back then the transubstantiation of black into white was a conjuring performed only by spiritual masters, swindlers, occultists, and kitchen cleaners.

Mahatma Buddha Was Bihari!

The businessman denied vociferously that he had known anything about the horse's injury. He turned the tables on Basharat: 'You came to see the fucking horse a half dozen times. The horse even began to fucking recognize you. You counted its teeth ten times, you know? You even brought cookies once! You said the horse was nine hands' long. You thought the horse was a fucking giant. Now you come four days later wearing your horse blinders to accuse me of atrocities, you know? Even the dead lying in their fucking graves have their accounts settled in three days. You didn't notice any defects then. You yoked him to the cart and took him to your humble fucking abode, and still you didn't notice anything wrong!' (Basharat had called his house

---

* In 1985, with just one twirl of the pen, the government turned seventeen billion rupees from black to white, in the hopes that people would stop their illegal practices. But black money is like the mythological snake with a thousand heads: if you cut one off, a hundred grow in its place.

his 'humble abode' so many times that the businessman thought that was its name.)

Basharat wanted to say something, but the businessman went on, 'Look, baba, there isn't any part of the horse that you didn't stroke ten fucking times, you know? You say you're a businessman, and yet if you start lying through your teeth, what do you think I'm supposed to do? Tell me! Don't keep going on like a fucking imbecile, you know?'

Basharat got upset, 'Was it too much to ask for you to tell me that the horse had desecrated a funeral procession? And you call yourself a Muslim and a Pakistani!'

Pointing at his chest, he answered, 'Do I look like a fucking Buddhist to you? I'm from Junagadh in Kathiawar, you know? I have a domicile certificate from Sindh. Mahatma Buddha was Bihari!' (Then pointing at the paan in his mouth.) 'I swear by the food in my mouth, I cannot lie. Now, swear on your children's good health, when you asked why I was selling the horse, I told you immediately. If you had asked before the deal was done, I would have told you then. You sell lumber, you know? Do you point out each fucking burl and impurity and ask the customer to look them over? Should I have done business with you or told you the horse's fucking biography? My father always told me that if a customer looks like a fraud make sure to get a good fucking look at him. Then, when doing business with him, make sure to talk less and watch more. Then you started singing 'Untie it, untie it now!' It was like coins were jingling in your fucking mouth. In Gujarati there's a saying that goes that money is a lioness's milk. It's hard to get, and it's hard to digest. But you're trying to fucking milk a lion! I do business in the millions. To this very day I've never reneged on my word. OK, if you swear on the Quran that you were drunk at the time of the purchase, I'll refund you every fucking penny.'

Basharat started to plead, 'Sir, take 100 or 150 rupees for yourself, but please take back the horse and refund me. I have a family. I will be grateful to you forever.'

The businessman lost his mind, 'Oh my God, baba! You're being as stubborn as a fucking mule! Don't use such difficult Urdu! Why did you come here like some film's villain wearing your fucking sunglasses and trying to intimidate me? Sir, you're an educated man. You're not some scum of a pimp, some malbari, who goes around threatening decent people. You read the signboard, baba! This is a rerolling mill—a steel rerolling mill. It's not a fucking horse shop, you know? Tomorrow you'll come trying to get me to take back the cart. If I start fucking selling horses and carts, what will my family do? Sit around at home singing qawwali? Sir, my house is a family house, not some fucking saint's shrine where prostitutes come to let down their long hair and make a ruckus singing dhama dham mast qalandar!'

Basharat parked the cart outside the rerolling mill. He sat down on a raised platform, dangling his legs, and waited for the cover of darkness before returning home so that he wouldn't get his third ticket in nine hours. His ears were still burning with anger, and his throat was like a cactus. Balban was standing with his head down and tied to a gulmohar tree. Basharat went to a paan shop and bought a bottle of lemonade. After only one swig, he realized that this Codd-neck bottle had been waiting for him in the sun for several months. And then he suddenly remembered that in all the running around of that afternoon, Balban hadn't been fed or given anything to drink. Basharat poured the lemonade into the sand, and he took off his sunglasses.

'Nevertheless, They Caught Us'

Somehow the cart managed to lumber on. Rahim Bakhsh got caught several more times, but things were resolved with the exchange of a little money. About two weeks later, he approached again with his whip raised in the air. He said, 'Boss, nevertheless, they caught us. Though I didn't have any money on me today, he asked for more. He wanted twenty-five rupees. So the officer took over the cart, and I came straight here. But the kids are in the cart, the horse is with it too. You always think that Rahim Bakhsh is making things up, so please come with me to get them back. Although the inconvenience…' At the time, Basharat was squatting and inspecting the knotty grain of a board. He sprang up in anger. Since there was no one else to take his anger out on, he grabbed the whip from the bringer of bad news and snapped it hard upon the ground, 'You ninny! If you ever again say "although," "nevertheless," or "so" in my presence, I'll flay you with this whip!'

While Basharat was rebuking him, Rahim Bakhsh suddenly wiggled his left ear. Basharat couldn't believe it. To extinguish his anger, he swore once, drank a glass of water, and then, with the whip still in his hand, set out with Rahim Bakhsh with the full intention of dropping the filthy liar at his house once and for all. When they reached the site of the incident, one of the Cruelty Cops really was standing there with the horse's reins in hand. Basharat's kids were scared. They were standing in the sun with their bags and thermoses strung from their necks. Seeing this caused his boiling blood to cool to the freezing point. He felt like a ball of wool had caught in his throat. He had to lean on the whip to stand straight. He took the Cruelty Cop aside and appealed for his compassion. He emphasized in his special shopkeeper way that he was now their permanent client; he wasn't some gypsy or here-today-gone-tomorrow type. So the man gave him a twenty-rupee discount, and things were settled.

So 'cruelty week' began, though it lasted for twenty-one days. Before it ended badly, the three of them—the horse, the vet, and Rahim Bakhsh—were tied up, made to stand around, and forced to eat to stave off boredom, respectively. (It's necessary to put an asterisk after Rahim Bakhsh's name because he ate no less than a horse.) While the horse had indigestion every third or fourth day, Rahim Bakhsh's stomach was not only made of steel but also always seemed as empty as a steel drum. In our culture, we have only one way of spoiling new pets, new brides, and little children: each person thinks it's their duty to overfeed them. This happened with the horse too. So, as a result, the horse kept getting sent to Richmond Crawford Animal Hospital. Basharat says that one evening he saw Rahim Bakhsh stuff his mouth full of the horse's purgative powder and swallow it down—no problem.

At the end of the 'week,' the kids started to go by cart to school again. Basharat's shop was not far away, so he walked. Three weeks passed without incident. That is, the horse's injury grew worse, but the tickets stopped coming. The fourth week had just started when one day Rahim Bakhsh came with the whip raised in the air, sighing and lamenting, and limping heavily on his left side. (He was now limping in imitation of the horse.) He said, 'Boss, they caught us again. They caught us without even warning us! So I paid them twenty rupees, though I tried to talk them down.' Basharat threw him the twenty rupees quite reluctantly. Now the tickets came so fast and furious that Basharat had no time to lick his wounds. He gave Rahim Bakhsh strict instructions to proceed very cautiously, to change up his routes, and to keep to the alleys. To these means of concealment, Rahim Bakhsh added one more. That is, he covered himself from head to foot in a red sheet before driving. Only his cigarette could be seen from underneath the sheet's hood. This made only one big difference. Now instead of having to make out the horse, the inspector only had to see the red sheet from a distance before he began to draw up the ticket.

3.

Basharat's Father's Miracle Cures

Now the money spent on bribes and massaging had exceeded the amount spent on the horse and Basharat's patience. The string of ticketing continued unabated. He became so helpless that he had

Rahim Bakhsh tell the inspector to go to his store where he would employ him as an accountant, and that he would pay him more than his current wages. The word came back to say hello to Basharat but that there were three inspectors.

He wanted to sell the horse and cart, but no one offered so much as one hundred rupees. So he ended up mentioning his problem to his father. His father listened to everything and then said, 'Don't worry yourself over this. I will pray. Before yoking the horse to the cart, make it drink a glass of blessed milk. If it's God's will, the horse's leg will heal, and so the tickets will stop. Just try it once.'

Then his father asked right then and there for Rahim Bakhsh to bring his harmonium to his bed. Rahim Bakhsh operated the bellows, and Basharat's father began singing a hymn in a quavering, unsteady voice: *Annihilation and salvation are in your hands, O, Your Splendour, Glorious One, O, Your Splendour, Glorious One.*

Basharat's father couldn't manage to press the keys he wanted to. And then, with his finger on a key, he didn't have enough strength to lift it. After singing one line, he lay down and said that the harmonium's keys were jammed. Master Baqar Ali hadn't fixed a thing.

The next day Basharat's father's charpoy was moved into the living room. That was the only room in which the horse could be brought indoors in the early morning to have 'Allah' written on its forehead and then holy breath exhaled over it as well. Early the next day, Basharat's father prayed two nafils, dipped his index finger in rosewater, wrote 'Allah' on the horse's forehead, and then coated its hooves in the smoke of frankincense. A little while later, when the horse was being outfitted, Basharat came running; he said that the horse was not drinking the blessed milk. His father was surprised. Then he closed his eyes and fell deep into thought. After a moment, he opened his eyes a little, 'No problem. Make the driver drink it. The horse has a toothache.' After this, the routine became that Rahim Bakhsh would drink the milk. He did this with the aversion that people used to show while taking their huge doses of Unani medicine, which is to say, pinching the nose, making a funny face, and intoning, 'God forbid! God forbid!' God knows where Rahim Bakhsh got such a big metal glass for the milk: it reached from his lips to his bellybutton.

And the effects of these miracle cures manifested on the very first day. That day it was a bearded man who gave them the ticket! Rahim Bakhsh lowered the whip to half-mast and said, 'Boss, nevertheless, they caught us.' Then he sketched in the scene: 'A bearded man has just been transferred in from the Jamshed Road area. He's a very compassionate, pious man, so he took only three and a half rupees, and that as a donation for medicine for a widow's child in his neighbourhood. If you want, go see for yourself. He'll be pleased to meet you. He's always muttering prayers under his breath. A light emanates from the prayer-mark on his forehead that's so bright that you could thread a needle by it in the dead of night.' Then Rahim Bakhsh took something from his arm-pouch and said that the man had given him this amulet for the horse.

Just think—from twenty-five to three and a half rupees! What a difference! Basharat's father attributed the reduction to his miracle-cure prayers. He said, 'Now wait and see. If it's God's will, in forty days or so, the Cruelty Cops won't be able to see the horse's leg.' Now Basharat's father took up permanent residence in the living room along with all his paraphernalia: medicine, bedpan, hookah, bowl for washing hands before prayer, harmonium, Agha Hashr's plays, the collector's edition of Maulana Azad's *Al-Hilal* newspaper, enema necessaries, and a picture of the actress Kajjan. The living room was hereby transformed into a space that only the horse, Basharat's father, and the cleaning lady who came to take away their feces could stand for more than five minutes. Basharat's friends stopped coming, but he put up with his father for the horse's sake.

How Many Mouths Can a Horse Feed?

From the day the bearded preacher had been employed, Rahim Bakhsh would appear every fourth or fifth day to say, 'The donation, please.' But two and a half or three rupees were enough (five at the very most) to avert disaster. Under cross-examination, Basharat learned from Rahim Bakhsh that, in all of Karachi, horse-drawn carts were in operation in only their neighbourhood, and that the condition of the cart-drivers was actually worse than that of the horses. The sum they set aside each month for the Cruelty Cops was hardly enough to satisfy them. By way of contrast, the donkey-cart drivers—those of naked feet and hungry stomachs—were always ready to fight back. The injured donkey, the hard-working donkey-cart driver, and the wretched Cruelty Cop: it was difficult to decide who was worse off and who was suffering more. It was like one bone-dry leech trying to suck blood from another bone-dry leech. So, consequently, the Cruelty Cops showed up first thing in the morning to wait on the street corner for the cart of their only reliable patron, and once they got their money they would leave. One single horse was feeding the families of all the men. But it was a little different with Karamat Hussain, the bearded preacher. His evident wretchedness made him so pitiful that giving him bribes seemed a virtuous act; his accepting bribes was, thus, him giving you the opportunity to be virtuous. He asked for the bribe in the same way that someone asks for a charitable donation. It seemed as though his entire livelihood descended from heaven via that horse's lame leg. But Basharat felt no sympathy and no fear for such a sorry bribe-taker.

Worrying about the Moral Conduct of Dogs

His friends told him he should have the horse put down at the Richmond Crawford Animal Hospital. But he couldn't. His father became sentimental at its very mention. He said, 'Today it's your lame horse. Tomorrow it will be your crippled father. The ladies and pets of respectable households show themselves in public for the first time *after* they die.' He had had three wives die on him, so he must have known when it comes to horses. Rahim Bakhsh was also very much opposed to killing the horse. As soon as it was brought up, he mentioned his thirty years of experience: if we've heard tell that history is really the biographies of rich people, then for Rahim Bakhsh, his autobiography was in fact a biography of horses. Hardly had one horse left his life when another entered it. He told the story of his three ex-bosses, each of whom had got a vet to put down a horse. The first boss died within three days. The second suffered a stroke that left his face contorted so that the right side of his mouth touched his earlobe. One day he happened to look at himself in a mirror by mistake, and he almost died gagging on the spot. The third's wife ran off with a jockey. If you are the discerning sort, you will recognize that the one who died immediately met the most respectable fate.

It was then that a groom came with the news that in Larkana there was a reddish-brown mare being sold for absolutely nothing, meaning, three hundred rupees. Mr Vadera, the owner, had grown sick of her. From his sugarcane harvest's profits, he had bought a big American car that he measured with a length of sugarcane. 'If he likes your face, it's possible he'll just give her to you for free,' the man said. At first, I was the one who argued against this, and then it was Basharat's father. In those days, I had just grown really interested in dogs. I brought them up in every conversation. Suddenly, I had so much respect for their species that I began referring to female dogs not as bitches but as 'she' dogs. I warned Basharat, 'For God's sake, don't buy a mare. In Amil Colony, Mr Dastgir got a she-dog. A well-wisher of his had told him that angels, old people, and robbers avoid houses with dogs. But this fine soul hadn't told him that only dogs will come by. Now all the adult dogs of the city are laying siege to his mansion.

The chaste one herself has taken sides with the enemies. I've never seen such a generous body-giver. Her motto is the very one the Boy Scouts use—*be prepared*. Meaning, she's ready to cooperate bodily with each and every assailant. Opening the front gate is now out of the question. The women of the house have stopped going out. The men have set up a stool that they use to jump the gate as well as the mass of dogs outside. Mr Dastgir feeds the dogs on a regular schedule of twice daily so that they don't take to preying upon the calves of passers-by. Once he had their food poisoned. The dogs' corpses lay in heaps in the alley. He paid for their burial out of his own pocket. That night, one man's dog, having fallen into bad company, had slipped out of his house and come by to look on. He too died. The vacuum that arose from the demise of these good dogs was filled in the same manner that vacuums are filled in literature and politics: the youths of the new generation sprang forward so quickly that the void wasn't big enough for everyone to fit in. I know only too well that the only vacuum that arises after the death of those who think they are indispensable, absolutely unique, and unparalleled is that of the six feet of earth removed and then immediately covered over with their corpse inside. But that's another story. Mr Dastgir is very worried. His she-dog is purebred. He is fearful that some low-class dog will ruin her pedigree. So I told him that he should get a female mutt to divert the dogs' attention. Then at least he could stop worrying about that. Then he could sleep at night. He's the only person in history to take upon himself the duty of worrying about the moral conduct of dogs.'

Miserable Company

I told him this story to teach him about life. Basharat's father was opposed to getting a mare for another reason. He was very upset because Basharat didn't believe in his miracle cures. He was prone to cursing out people. He didn't openly curse out his son, but he said that if he needed to have a purebred mare to keep his line going, then, please, go ahead, but he himself wouldn't set foot in such a house, not even for a minute. He also threatened that he would go wherever Balban the horse went. The fact of the matter was that his father and the horse had become so close, that if the family had not forbidden it, the old man would have kept the horse tied to his charpoy's leg while he slept at night. When the horse approached, he would lower his head so that Basharat's father could stroke him while seated. He would put his nose to the horse's muzzle and, for hours, bitch and moan about the household's members, including his daughters-in-law. For the kids, the horse was a live plaything. Basharat's father said that since they got the horse, his hands shook less and he had stopped having nightmares. He had started calling the horse his son. Everyone gets sick of a chronic patient. One day, he lay moaning on the charpoy for four or five hours. No one paid him any mind. In the evening, when his heart symptoms (and his depression) increased, he said to the cook, 'Please bring Balban, my son.' The sad horse was the man's only companion in his old age and failing health.

Something Good to Eat

He couldn't yoke the horse to the cart. He couldn't sell him. He couldn't get him put down. But he also couldn't afford to feed him without getting anything out of him. What was there to do? When a black mood descended upon him, he would think that the era's bad name was due to the villainy and corruption of big businessmen, capitalists, the Vadera caste, feudal landlords, and high-ranking officials. But the piece-of-shit Cruelty Cops weren't any better. He had never been one to think conservatively or in such a contemptuous way. But now a cynical feeling of annoyance entered into his thoughts—that of one man wronged by another. He thought, 'The people are poor and oppressed, but whom do they spare? The night watchman is also poor. When does he spare a fruit-seller? And last night, the poor fruit-seller slipped two rotten apples into the kilo the customer ordered. He always underweighs the fruit by a little; but it's only just a little because he can't get away with underweighing it any more. Schoolteachers deserve a lot of mercy and respect. For years, Master Najmuddin has gone around dressed in rags bemoaning the state of society. I gave him 430 rupees; only then did he boost my niece's final high-school exam scores. And who could be more pitiable than Rahim Bakhsh, the cart-driver? Oppression ruins the tyrant and the oppressed alike. When the wheel of oppression comes full circle, the oppressed enacts what was done to him. Boa constrictors swallow their prey whole. Sharks chomp their prey into bloody pieces. Lions, as doctors advise us to do too, chew their food thoroughly before swallowing. Cats, lizards, spiders, and mosquitos, all according to their needs and abilities, suck blood. My God! No one spares anyone!' Then he remembered how he lied on his income tax, and he smiled, 'My God! No one spares anyone! We are each other's fodder. We rip and claw at each other with great zeal. Only then do we have something good to eat.'

4.

Below Sea Level and the Poverty Line

Basharat grew sick of the continual tickets. He thought, 'What a joke! This is the only crime left in all of Pakistan! Enough is enough!' Now he wasn't going to rest until things were set right. By this time, he had already met Maulana Karamat Hussain, and he was no longer terrified of him: he was a midget an inch short of five feet, and his neck was about as thick as Basharat's wrist. On his round face and small forehead, pockmarks shined like dings on a copper pot. Having discovered where he lived, he was going to tell him off. He had prepared everything he was going to say, as well as his hand gestures and vocal inflections. He was going to grab his beard and say, 'So you go around showing off your half-finished trademark on your forehead. Why don't you go to a smith's and have it branded on so you don't have to bother hitting your forehead on the ground five times a day?' He remembered the witty words apropos beards that some black-hearted man had coined: 'The eaves of the sacred ...' All his sarcasm was tied to praying and having a beard, as though those things were the real sin! He would go on, 'You think you're special? I've squashed a million lice like you. You religious perverts eat your halva and pulao and stroke each other's beards and think you're sitting on the right hand of God the Almighty! And you call yourself Muslim! If I decide to show you what I'm made of, I'll have you cough up each and every cent that you've swallowed!' His rehearsals were so specific that he had already decided to ask God for forgiveness right before uttering the 'right hand of God' line.

He got to Liyari, but then he had a hard time finding Maulana Karamat Hussain's shack. The directions that he had got were accurate. Look for electricity pole #23, go behind it, to the other side of the mud pit. (They had been waiting for three years for electricity.) Then, on the right, look for a pregnant brown water buffalo. It would be around there. In areas like this, there are no roads or streets, no alleys or footpaths. There are no house-numbers or -names. Each house has its own personal, identifying character. While he was looking for the electricity pole, he suddenly saw the name Karamat Hussain written in red ink on a piece of burlap serving as a shack's door. The effects of rain had turned the good calligraphy into something like the khatt-e-ghubar style [big letters filled with flourishes]. This, the worst of the Karachi slums, was several metres below sea level and the poverty line. The sea was held back by a dike of human bodies. Alkaline water rose from the ground so that wood and steel rotted in just a couple of months. The reek of the dead sea permeated the wind, and this was worse than the stench of rotten fish. There was knee-deep mud in every direction. Basharat didn't see dry land anywhere. To make a pathway through this, people had placed stones and bricks. A -year-old girl was approaching with a bucket of water on her head that was heavier than she was; by moving her neck and waist, she was balancing her feet on the loose stones and the bucket on her head. Sweat streamed down her face. Everyone told her to walk carefully. Every so often, there was a traffic island of five or six bricks, where people waited to let others pass. And inside the shacks, it proved to be more of the same. Kids, the elderly, and the sick clung to stilt-legged cots. The Holy Quran, folded up bedrolls, pots and pans, paperwork from abandoned property, and high-school diplomas were kept in bamboo scaffolding underneath a tarp on top of which were kept chickens. In one corner, Maulana Karamat Hussain had set up a brazier on top of a little mound of earth. A goat was tethered to the leg of one cot. In front of some of the shacks, water buffalos waded in the mud, and their backs were coated with mud-plaster. It was heaven for them. No one picked up their dung because there were no walls or dry land on which to dry the dung into cakes. The dung disappeared into the muck along with human excrement. Inside these shacks, Basharat saw the tin milk canisters recognizable from the white-tiled dairy shops of Saddar. A lame dog stood outside a shack. When he suddenly shook himself, the flies that had been sitting on his wounds and the half-dried mud flicked off and onto Basharat's shirt and face. For those readers who never saw Bihar Colony, Chakiwada, and Liyari back in those days, it might be difficult to imagine how people not only live in such filthy places but also give birth there as well. I haven't seen such foul places even in East Pakistan. There, while people might not be any different, at least nature is better. The sun, the water, and the wind clean and purify each and every thing: the scorching sun, the sandstorms, the monsoons that fall like children's tears, the floods of the foaming sea, the cyclones. What's a quicker and more thorough—a more merciless and sure-fire—disinfectant than them? I will never forget two images from Barisal. It's like they were engraved in my mind with an acid pen.

My Golden Bengal!

In 1967, I had the chance to travel through East Pakistan by car and ferry. Out of the seven hundred miles across which my journey took me, there wasn't one eighth-of-a-mile stretch where I didn't see a half dozen people walking along. On average, only one out of twenty wore sandals. And I never saw anyone whose clothes covered their entire body, except for corpses! I saw three funeral processions where the shroud was made by tying together two lungis of different colours. In another procession, an old man was holding a broken umbrella above the corpse. This was the father of the young boy who had died. He was crying, and the rain was streaming off his beard. We were passing through Barisal. The humidity was unbelievable. We were dying from thirst. Drinking water or lemonade was out of the question because cholera was sweeping through the area. It was one funeral procession after another. A close friend of mine said that if I was in the mood to commit suicide, then I could go buy anything to eat and that would be it. A Bengali friend said to me about coconuts the same thing that Ghalib said about mangos:

> By God's command
> Sealed glasses filled with honey have been sent ...

This friend told me that germs can't get into coconuts; that instead of drinking water, I should drink coconut water; and that it's good for ulcers, too. I bought two coconuts for six paise each. My driver asked the coconut-seller for water. He drank it, and then he put his coconut in the trunk. Then I broke my coconut. The coconut had very tender, soft flesh. The water of green coconuts is very pleasant, good for digestion, and sweet. After drinking its water, I flung the shell onto a trash heap. I bought a pack of Three Castle cigarettes from a paan shop. When I opened the pack, I saw that they were extremely old and withered. Bugs had eaten little holes in the cigarettes, and so I had problems drawing on them from time to time. In our culture, you get 'treated' to cigarettes like these only in those houses where the man of the house doesn't smoke: during Eid, he tests the throats and morality of his guests by forcing upon them the cigarettes he bought the previous Eid. It made me think about which sneaky little bugger it was that ate tobacco to sustain itself. We can treat cancer by making a soup or paste of them!

Just then an old woman walked toward the trash heap. By pelting them with clumps of dirt, she chased off the cats that were digging deep into the trash, as well as a dog gnawing on a placenta. She wore nothing other than a loose, tattered sari. (Without a choli.) She climbed the trash heap step by deliberate step. Just as she kicked aside the placenta, a kite swooped down and grabbed it by its end, although, even before the bird managed to regain any altitude, the placenta fell from its grasp. The old woman very gently picked up the coconut because no one else wanted it. She was probably the grandmother of the little girl and the two stark naked boys with her. She was eating the coconut's flesh so greedily that the little boy took her hand and put it into his mouth. She gave the two boys some of the flesh. The little girl was so young that the old woman first chewed the flesh in her toothless mouth, then pressed her mouth against the girl's mouth, and then spat the flesh into her mouth. When she had bent over to pick up the coconut from the trash heap, her naked breasts, which looked like withered eggplants roasted over hot coals, quivered like empty intestines. Her breasts looked like mushrooms borne from that very ground. Neither did anyone looking at her breasts, nor the old woman herself, mind her nakedness, but that day I felt completely naked.

The second scene took place in the market just a little ways ahead. In front of the bank, a man was selling fish from a platform raised four feet off the ground. His undershirt had countless holes in it. His undershirt and lungi were covered in fish blood and guts. When his hands got dirty, he wiped them on his lungi so that the old gunk absorbed the new gunk. From time to time, when he splashed water over the fish, a swarm of flies flew up, and only then could you see how small the fish were, and which type. The filthy water and cast-off fish parts flowed down a drain and collected in a canister. When he sold a big fish, he used a cleaver to hack at it, and the blood and guts flowed into this canister. When the canister filled up, he set it to the side and started using another. Standing on their hind legs, cats would dart their mouths forward to catch the discarded meat parts as the refuse slid toward the canister. Those watching were terrified that the cleaver might suddenly clip one of the cat's heads and then— POP! When a young woman came to buy fish, the fish-seller would make a fist and shout curses longingly at the cats. In one hour, he sold two full canisters for one anna each. A man told me that the poor would cook their rice in it to give it a fishy aroma. Three households shared one canister. Among the poor, only those that were relatively better off could afford this luxury!

The Mughal Dynasty's Decline (Descending from on High)

Though there was hardly any difference between inside and outside, Basharat called out Maulana's name from where he stood outside the shack. Only a straw mat, a burlap curtain, and some bamboo slats separated the muck outside from that inside and so provided an imaginary sense of privacy as well as a property line.

This is my grave and that is yours

When no one answered, Basharat clapped in the Hyderabadi style, and then from inside six children came out, one after another, from biggest to smallest, just like a stack of pots. The age difference between them didn't even seem to be nine months! The eldest boy said, 'He's gone to sunset prayer. Please make yourself comfortable.' Basharat couldn't see how that was possible. He was standing on wobbly bricks. His mind was about to explode from the stench. If there were a hell on earth,

It was here! It was here! It was here!

On the walk there, he had rehearsed what he was going to say: 'Maulana, what kind of crap is this?' He had planned to say 'Maulana' in a thoroughly sarcastic and bitter way, the same you use when you are going to launch a horrible insult at someone. But when he saw the shack and the muck, he thought that if this man were taken to jail, it would be for him a life of luxury. All the taunts and insults that Basharat had prepared were focused on his beard and prayer rugs so that if the words didn't injure him at least they would make him feel ashamed. But all that fell to the wayside. His hands froze. What was the use of cursing him out? His life itself was an insult. When the kids started carrying on around him, Basharat's thoughts turned to them. He asked them their names. Timur, Babur, Humayun, Jahangir, Shah

Jahan, Aurangzeb. My God! In this wretched, wet shack, the entire Mughal dynasty had descended from on high in chronological order!

While the line of Mughal kings had ended, the line of children didn't. So even the lesser princes were called into service. For instance, one darling boy was named Mirza Koka, Akbar's foster brother, and whom Akbar had ordered thrown from the castle's ramparts. (If he had been a real brother, Akbar would have used even worse means to take care of him—that is, he would have sent him on a pilgrimage to Mecca so that robbers could kill him, or he would have blinded him. If he had appealed for mercy, Akbar, out of kingly kindness and brotherly love, would have cut off his head in one stroke, so as to make his situation more bearable.) The little kids and suckling babes who remained inside had names that invoked the majesty of crown and throne, although Basharat couldn't remember which of them had been killed before climbing onto a throne, and which, after. The truth was that the death of Aurangzeb had spelled the end of the dynasty and the beginning of a period of anarchy. In twelve years, eight kings had come to power in such a way that they hadn't properly sat down on their throne before they were deposed. Crowns and heads were being tossed in the air like a juggler's balls. While Aurangzeb had hated music, as soon as his eyes closed for the final time, the claimants to the throne started playing musical chairs. The one little alteration they made was that instead of music, poets would recite passionate encomiums, and whenever they suddenly stopped short, a new prince would spring onto the throne. Nadir Shah was so taken by this Mughal game that he took the peacock throne with him when he went back to Persia. And yet the game continued unabated. Talking about taking the throne with him, I intentionally didn't use the idiom 'when there's no bamboo, no flutes can play' because kings and royals don't need bamboo flutes to carry on.

So, about the rest of the descendants of Timur the Great who were still inside the shack: their names too must have been in correct order (or the order of their deposition) because it seemed like Maulana had a very good grasp of history. It seemed as though the pregnancies had overridden family planning in order to satisfy the requirements of Mughal history. Basharat asked, 'None of you is named Akbar?' The eldest boy replied, 'No, that's the penname of our grandfather.'

He talked to the kids for a while. He asked, 'How many brothers and sisters do you have?' One of the boys answered, 'How many uncles do you have?' He asked, 'Are any of you educated?' The eldest boy raised his hand, 'Yes, I am.' Then he learned that this boy, who looked to be thirteen or so, had long ago graduated from a mosque having studied the *Baghdadi Primer*. Then for three years, he had served as an unpaid intern at a fan factory. Last year, his right thumb had got caught in a machine. It was sliced off. Now he was studying Arabic with a mullah. Humayun, like his namesake, was still living a life of disgrace and wandering. By the time Jahangir was born, pyjamas had been sacrificed to anarchy. However, Shah Jahan's private parts were covered quite well with the bandages that had been applied to his boils and sores. All that Aurangzeb wore was his father's fez. Basharat couldn't see his eyes, and the boy couldn't see Basharat at all. He was only seven but extremely talkative. He said, 'In all my life, I've never seen such rain!' His limbs were as thin as matchsticks, but looking at his balloon-like belly, Basharat grew scared that it might explode at any minute. A little while later, the young Noor Jahan came out. Her big, beautiful, intelligent eyes were lined with kohl, and she wore an amulet around her wrist to ward off the evil eye. Her entire face was smeared with dirt, kohl, and snot, except for those parts that had just been cleaned with tears. Basharat patted her on her head. Her light-coloured hair smelled like the harsh smoke of wet wood. A cute, little boy came forward to say that his name was Shah Alam, and then he disappeared. Suddenly he returned to say that he had forgotten:

Shah Alam was his big brother's name. All these Mughal royals were splashing so happily through the muck and mire that it seemed as though their lineage was not that of royalty but of swans.

Kids were gushing forth from every nook and cranny. Such a big family, and only one salary! Basharat couldn't believe it.

The entire universe is one big net of children

A Wall Has Just Collapsed

A little while later, Maulana appeared. He carefully stepped from brick to wobbly brick through the muck. The uncertain path forced everyone to walk like a woman juggler walking on a tightrope at the circus. And what a sight she is! She balances herself with an open umbrella. And if she sways just a little, the spectators hold their breaths. God knows if Maulana saw Basharat and so got startled, or whether his wooden sandal just slipped, but he stumbled to the right, where, in his hand, he was carrying a glass of blessed water. His lungi and beard were slimed with muck, and it looked like his hand was wearing a muck sock. His son poured water from a dirty little pot for him to wash his hands and face. (Without soap.) He daubed clean his rosary, hands, and face with his cotton scarf; then he shook Basharat's hand and stood with head bowed. Basharat was already defeated. His rehearsed, sarcastic remarks about his beard, praying, and his forehead's permanent prayer scar drowned in the muck, and his witticism about 'the eaves of the sacred' sank as well into the fermenting funk. He wanted more than anything to flee. But whoever tries to flee through such muck ends up sinking into it as quickly as they tread.

Basharat couldn't figure out where to begin. Faced with this dilemma, he happened to scratch his lip with his right hand, the very hand with which, just a little while earlier, he had reluctantly shook hands; smelling his hand, he felt like throwing up. After this, he made sure not to touch his clothes and person. Maulana guessed why Basharat was there. He took the initiative and admitted that he was taking money from his cart-driver Rahim Bakhsh in order to pay for medicine for a neighbour's girl. He also said that before he had been hired, it was customary for Rahim Bakhsh to keep half of the ticket-money, but now everything that Basharat spent reached him. Rahim Bakhsh got nothing. That was because one day he had given the driver an amulet for his wife, and God had cured her. God alone is the cure, God alone. He gives life, and He takes life. So Rahim Bakhsh had become his devotee. He was a very miserable person.

Maulana also told him that whenever Basharat ordered Rahim Bakhsh to use detours to avoid getting tickets and so having to pay bribes, he would forewarn the Cruelty Cops. He was always willingly and happily caught. In fact, it went so far that when one of their officers caught pneumonia and had to stay home for three weeks, Rahim Bakhsh ended up coming to the office to ask why we hadn't given him a ticket in so long. Was everything OK?

Basharat did ask him a couple of questions about his driver, but now he had no desire to confront Maulana. So he continued, and Basharat listened in shame, 'My dad broke his hip two years ago. Take a look at him. He can't even sit up. I've cut the charpoy. Since he's always lying down, he's developed fistulas. One's so deep that I can stick my entire finger into it. It's so wide that I can see a vein inside that's as thick as twine. It's always emitting puss. While cleaning it, I've thrown up several times. I've put Dalda [vegetable oil] cans filled with water underneath the charpoy's legs so that red ants won't climb into his wounds again. My neighbour is often at my throat. He says my father snores all day and screams all night, and that because of the reek coming from his wounds, they aren't able to eat. And he's right. Only a reed mat separates our homes. By God's good grace, four months ago we had another boy. He is God's gift. God gives pearls without asking; people don't give anything even to those forced to beg. God increases the number of the Prophet's people. After my wife gave birth, she had white leg disease. She still can't walk. It's God's will. I put her in a rickshaw and took her to Jinnah Hospital. They said, 'You have to admit her to the hospital right away. But there's no beds here.' I took her back after a month. This time they said, 'You bring her now? She's been sick for so long. We can't admit someone like her.' So I've learned to live with it. God's will is my will. I clean their bedpans before morning and sunset prayers. After praying, I cook some food so the kids will have something in their stomachs. Once, when Noor Jahan was warming some goat's milk for her mom, her clothes caught on fire. Thanks be to God—a million thanks—that I'm still healthy.'

Basharat reached a new plane of existence. He neither smelled the stink nor felt like throwing up. He was numb.

What could we understand?
But we listened to the story of the world anyway.
When we understood
We didn't want to hear any more.

Maulana said, 'A midwife is treating her. She's prescribed a paste of black nightshade, Turkish gum mastic, sparrow brains, and opium. She's a very compassionate woman. After morning and sunset prayers, I bring a glass of blessed water from the mosque. Even the rich and famous don't have the good fortune to be blessed by the breaths of two hundred men who have just prayed. But maybe God doesn't want to heal them. God's will is above all else.'

In that half hour, Basharat heard mention of God's will more than he had heard in the previous ten years. Listening to Maulana made it seem like everything that happened in that godforsaken place was God's will.

And at the end of the tunnel, all he saw was darkness. Only Dante could portray such a hopeless, helpless, dark, dismal place.

Dirty Hands

Then all of a sudden, as though he had just remembered something, Maulana excused himself and went inside. Outside, Basharat was soon lost in thought, 'In this open-air shack without rooms and without curtains, without walls and without doors, where sounds, groans, and thoughts are bared to all, and where probably even dreams aren't private, here, in one corner, an old man is dying, and there, in another corner, a baby is being born, and in between the girls are growing up. My brother! When you're already accepting bribes, what's the problem with asking for a little bigger bribe so that you can take your wife to the hospital? Even liquor isn't forbidden, if it's a matter of life and death. Who'll cook? Who'll sweep the floor? How will the kids eat?' Maulana said that the day after delivering the child, his wife was up, cooking for the kids, and washing clothes. Basharat started to think about how history was full of encomiums written to the Tartar warrior women who, according to Arab Shah, had fought shoulder to shoulder and spear to sword with Timur's army. If a woman began to go into labour, she first let the rest of the cavalry pass. Then she dismounted from her horse and gave birth. Then she made a swaddling cloth, tied it around her neck, and with the baby inside, mounted the horse, and, riding bareback, caught up with the forces. But who is going to write the elegies of these women who die without complaint in their shacks? Basharat felt like he was suffocating. Up till then, Maulana hadn't even taken 150 rupees. He shouldn't have come. He began to think about the effects of the blessed water. Now the poor woman was suffering from one disease, but after drinking the blessed water — breathed on by two hundred men — she would have a hundred more.

Maulana set up purdah conditions in the house—meaning, Noor Jahan covered her sick mother from head to foot in a greasy blanket and made her lie down—and then Basharat was asked inside. Both men sat at the foot of the charpoy, dangling their feet off its edge. On the charpoy's foot there rested an embossed tray with a blue, enamelware kettle and two cups. Maulana filled a cup with a little tea, which he used to clean the cup by rubbing his finger vigorously this way and that. Then he filled the cup to the rim and offered it to Basharat. Basharat might not have felt such revulsion had that finger not have been smeared with muck just a short while before. As Maulana bent over to hand him the tea, his beard smelled like a sewer.

Then he started talking again, but Basharat no longer had enough courage to raise his head to meet his gaze: 'The Society for the Prevention of Cruelty to Animals gives me sixty rupees as a salary. I've a son. He's seven. He's the smartest, most muscular, and best looking of my kids. Four months ago, he had a terrible fever for three days. On the fourth day, his left leg went limp. I took him to the doctor's. He said it was polio. He wrote a prescription for a course of shots. Thank God that polio took only one leg. In the neighbourhood, in a shack just four down that way, it took both legs of one young girl. It's an epidemic. Whatever happens is God's will. The girl doesn't have a father. Where will she get the money to go to the doctor? I gave her three of the shots meant for my son. I can't tell you how her widowed mother has thanked me. I pray five times a day for that girl. Every Friday, I massage my son's leg, and her legs as well, with a mixture of wild pigeon blood, and clove and almond oil. And then there are the doctor's treatments. Whatever money I've taken from your driver has been for this.'

Basharat felt as though his mind had gone blank. Sickness, sickness, sickness! Did people here do anything other than producing numberless children and sicknesses? In the past half hour, Basharat hadn't said any more than a dozen sentences. Maulana had held the floor. One question kept coming back to Basharat: Were all the shacks like this? Did everyone live such a miserable life?

Maulana went on, 'Please consider it a loan. Your driver said, "My boss told me to tell that bearded mullah that he'll give him a thrashing that he'll never forget." You see all this. The raincloud is our blanket and this filth is our bed. What could be worse? I prayed to God that I would earn money legally and speak the truth—that I wouldn't have to stoop to anything to provide food. I'm a sinner. My prayers didn't come true. God knows everything. This morning, I ate one piece of bread for breakfast. If even one morsel has passed through my lips since then, call me a liar. He gives more than is enough food to whomever He wishes. He says, "You are so helpless, so pitiful, that if a fly picked a piece of food from your hand, you wouldn't be able to get it back."'

Maulana lifted his kurta to show his caved-in stomach. It rose and fell like bellows. Basharat lowered his gaze.

Maulana continued: 'For quite a while, I've been trying to join the disciples of Hazrat Zaheen Shah Taji. A neighbour that wants to marry that widow, and thinks that I'm an obstacle in the way, wrote an anonymous letter to His Holiness saying that I take bribes. Now His Holiness tells me that Hazrat Baba Fareeduddin Ganj-e-Shakar (God's blessings be onto him) says that an honest income is Islam's sixth pillar. He has told me that he won't take me on as a disciple until I have paid back all of the bribe-money. God have mercy on me! Please pray for me!'

Maulana stood with his hands locked in supplication. His off-white kurta was stained with tears that formed a pattern like a black, chain necklace. Basharat put his hands on top of Maulana's.

5.

Two Lonely Souls

A week later Maulana Karamat Hussain was working at Basharat's shop as a secretary, and as he carried around a measuring tape and sized up different planks of Himalayan cedar and pine, he looked quite happy. His salary was three times greater than before. After three or four days, Basharat had to say something, 'Maulana, being honest is a good thing, but please don't stare at the wood's burls as though you're inspecting a wound on a horse's neck.' There had been no need to fire Rahim Bakhsh, the driver; as soon as Maulana came to work the first day, he vanished on his own.

Still, no one came forth to buy the horse. As a favour to Maulana, the Cruelty Cops stopped coming after the horse. Basharat insinuated to his father that the tickets had stopped because of his prayers, and so he should relocate from the living room back to his bedroom. But his father had grown so accustomed to performing the morning rituals with the horse that he wasn't ready to stop. As soon as the horse saw the old man, he would, in driver-talk, start to 'buchiyana'—that is, he would perk up so much that his ears touched at their tips. First thing in the morning, the horse would be led into the living room with insistence and ritual punctuality; as soon as the cry 'the horse is coming' went up in the house, then anyone who cared about their religion, their person, or anything else for that matter, would step out of the way and watch the spectacle from a safe distance. This reminded me of the bride and bridegroom ritual. When the groom is called into the women's quarters, the cry is raised over and over, 'The boy is coming! The boy is coming!' When the girls and women in purdah hear this, they raise their veils and stare with their faces as wide as washing tubs. The suspicion that some old men get married only to hear 'The boy is coming!' doesn't seem that far-fetched, because, otherwise, when it comes to marriage and the duties of conjugal life,

What sinner finds pleasure there?

Basharat's father wrote 'Allah' on the horse's forehead. He had already switched to blowing holy breaths on the horse's hooves and massaging them. He had started complaining about the members of the household by name while he combed the horse's mane, and from that day forward it was no longer a relationship between man and animal. Basharat's father would recount his new problems and then fall quiet, and the horse would brush his face against the half-paralysed man's body, and then lower his head as though he were saying, 'Baba, now you seem worse off than me!' Basharat's father would say, 'I feel like I'm getting feeling back in my left leg.'

Long story short, Basharat's father stopped treating the horse like a horse. And, for the horse's part, he had grown so close to the old man that he no longer seemed human. Basharat's father no longer called him a horse. Instead, he called him Balban or 'my son.' Whenever they met, it was worth watching and listening, it was

As though a crazy fakir showed up at another crazy fakir's house.

One day, Basharat's father said that the horse was suffering from chronic osteoarthritis. (He used an Arabic phrase for this diagnosis.) Then he elucidated this comment by saying that his joints were jammed. So, in order to unjam the joints, he had a brazier brought into the living room where, under his supervision, he had gheekawar halva made from three kilos of cream and pure ghee, which he ate for forty days, thus reactivating his appetite. He had also begun to say that the horse was possessed by djinns. In order to cure him, every

Thursday he would burn chilli incense and distribute the best qalaqand sweets to the deserving. That is, he ate half of it himself and
sent the other half over to his friend Chaudhuri Karam Ilahi's house.
He went on eating qalaqand and saying that some djinns were never
satisfied. The ex-driver Rahim Bakhsh also had taken to saying that it
wasn't a horse but a djinn, and that corrupt men couldn't see djinns.
According to him, one morning he hadn't been able to take Balban
into the living room in the morning, and so after sunset prayers, the
horse snapped his tether, went in by himself to get blessed by the holy
breath, and then came back. When he brought his food, he couldn't
believe what he saw. His hooves had turned into camphor, and they
radiated such dazzling rays that you couldn't look at them straight on.
The smoke of frankincense was streaming out of his nostrils. Abdullah, the snack vendor, swore on Rahim Bakhsh's good name that as
this was happening, he saw the horse in Clifton in front of Abdullah
Shah Ghazi's tomb. On his back was a bearded holy man wearing
green robes and radiating light.

Basharat's father thought the miracle of the horse was related
to him. He kept asking what the green-robed old man looked like,
and he got annoyed each time the answer came back that he didn't
look like him. Then he started calling for his son Balban after sunset
prayers as well. They would put their heads close to each other and
talk until the day's last prayers, and

If people could hear what they were saying, they'd think them crazy.

After the miracle, Rahim Bakhsh had started to call the horse Balban Sahib and Shahji. Basharat's father took to saying that the horse
was auspicious. He even attributed the birth of Basharat's son to the
horse's presence! Several barren women from the neighbourhood
came to get blessed by Shahji.

Shit Happens

I forgot to mention that after Rahim Bakhsh left, Basharat hired a new driver. His name was Mirza Wahid-uz-Zaman Baig. But, according to the conditions of his employ, Basharat's father called him Aladdin as well. He talked meekly, and looked meek too. He made sure he looked like this so that for no rhyme or reason you would want to do something for him: Mongol features, dark skin, muscular body, tiny ears, and a broad forehead. He was in such good shape that you couldn't tell how old he was. Inside his vest's pocket, he didn't keep a pistol but rather a sharp lion's claw made from a worn-out horse-shoe. Behind Bandar Road near the tram depot, there was a drama company, and in their production of 'Rustam and Sohrab' he had played Rustam's horse Rakhsh for a month and a half. When, on stage, he would neigh with all his might, the mares yoked to carts outside would strain on their reins, wanting to get inside. One audience member had thrown that horseshoe on stage in a show of appreciation for his acting. Even though he was short, he had a very deep voice. In everyday conversation, if he should happen to remember the theatre, he would substitute the Persian words for 'horse' and 'singer,' and he would call himself 'rusiyah' [sinner]. He knew the stentorian style from Agha Hashr's fiery plays, and he practiced lines with the horse. And the truth is that perhaps this was the best audience for these lines. In Agha Hashr's dialogues, even in the nuptial chamber, men wear helmets and chainmail and carry naked swords, while on the battlefield their every step strikes the war-drum. The main characters all have ankle-bells strapped to their swords for them to jangle about. And if right in the middle of the battle, there comes a romantic interlude (whether due to human nature or the public's demands), even then the heroes talk to their beloveds in the same ornate and swordy language that they have used to drive back their dire enemies. Even in those critical moments, when it's so hard to control oneself, the heroes still speak in rhyme. The lives and honour of Agha Hashr's heroes are reduced to parroting words, and despite the small size of these parrots, they still fire enormous cannons. Back then, cart-drivers, factory-workers, and street-vendors all used lines from these plays to talk to each other.

Mirza Wahid-uz-Zaman Baig (whom I have a hard time dignifying with the title of 'driver') started every sentence with the phrase 'Forgive my mistakes!' During his job interview, he stated that he also drove cars very well. This irritated Basharat, and so he asked contemptuously, 'Then why do you want to drive a cart?' Mirza had put his hands together as though praying and said, 'When God, the Cherisher, decides to give you a car, then I'll drive that as well.'

Basharat hired him under the belief that he was a meek person who would be easy to control. Mirza Abdul Wadud Baig gave him the tip to never employ anyone on the basis of his intelligence. The more dull-witted a servant, the more obedient and helpful he will be. He was very helpful for a couple days, and then that stopped. Sometimes he came back from school an hour late. Sometimes he disappeared altogether for several hours in the middle of the day. Once Basharat had to send an important invoice to the Pakistan Tobacco Company. He returned after four hours. The kids were still standing hungry and thirsty in front of the school's gate. Basharat scolded him. He pointed toward his special box (he called it his tool box) that he always kept with him in the cart. He said, 'Forgive my mistakes! Shit happens! On the road next to the Municipal Corporation Building, the horse tripped. He broke one girth. His horseshoe started jingling like ankle-bells. I was fixing them up. Forgive my mistakes. If so much as one nail has fallen out of a horseshoe, I can tell from a mile's distance which horse's it is.' Basharat asked with surprise, '*You* were fixing the horseshoe?' He answered, 'Of course. Who else? There's a saying that anything related to farming, water, humble requests, and horse's girths should be done by yourself even if there are hundreds of men with you. You have to attend to horses by yourself.'

Each time something went wrong, he came up with new stories and new excuses. The problem with chronic liars is that even when they're telling the truth, you assume it's a lie. It often came to pass that what he had said was true. Yet it was very difficult to believe him. One day he came back very late. Basharat rushed toward him, scolding him. Mirza defended himself, 'Sir, please hear me out! I was going by the Race Club's stables when suddenly the horse pulled up. When I whipped him, he raised onto his hind legs. The passers-by on the road stopped to watch. But then a vet happened to come out from inside. He recognized the horse, "Hey, hey, why're you whipping this prince? He's seen good days. Prey can't blame the hunter for his bad luck. What's happened is that he's smelled Dur-e-Shahwar. She was running in the race when he sprained his ankle. Two Sundays ago she came in first again. Photos of her were published in the newspaper. God has made her owner a millionaire." Then he called out to the horse's former groom. The three of us unyoked him from the cart and took him inside. He knew the way. He took us straight to his stall. Nearby a jet black, ungainly horse was bucking. Beyond that, but in the other direction, Dur-e-Shahwar was standing. Recognizing Balban, she got restless. Earlier he had been so restless, but now he was entirely still and powerless. He didn't even try to shoo away the flies on his neck's wound. Sir, his wound's gotten much worse. The groom fondly caressed him. Then he said, "Son, we should have put you down. Then you wouldn't have had to go through this. But your owner couldn't do it." Then he gave him some of the race club's fodder. Sir, that grain was better than some people eat. But, I swear, he didn't touch it. He just stood with his head bowed. The groom said the horse had a fever. Then he took off all his equipment, hugged him, and started crying.

'Sir, I couldn't take it. We were both crying when the race club's physician came in. He kicked the three of us out. He said, "Hey, why the hell did you drag this rotting carcass here? You want to kill the other horses too?"'

The Size of a Nose Ring

When he returned late on another occasion, before Basharat could start scolding him, he started up, 'Sir, forgive my mistakes! Shit happens. We were going by the Municipal Corporation Building when we saw a black mare. She took off and Balban started running after her. They didn't stop till we had reached Clifton. The mare finished first, then Balban. Then me, this sinner. The horse's owner came in fourth. Sir, our horse was running so smoothly it was like cream going down your throat!'

Then he put his whip between his legs and started running, demonstrating how the horse, himself, and the mare's owner all galloped one after the other in pursuit of the desired object. Mirza Wahid-uz-Zaman Baig started up again, 'Sir, that man looked at me with, what do you call it, nargisi kofta-like eyes! Then he growled at me even though it wasn't my horse's fault. His mare kept turning the whole time to see if our horse was following or not. I asked him, if he cared so much, why hadn't he controlled his unbridled sankhni?* An owner's honour rests in his horse's hands. As she ran along, she was flirting with my horse. She tested him like you would test a prophet. In the end, he's a man. He's not a cold-blooded statue. Sir, I told that what's-its-name—yes, that cuckold—I said, "Get out of here! Get out! I've seen a lot of mares like yours. There's a vixen just like her in

---

* Sankhni: A type of woman mentioned in the scriptures. The dictionary that I have here, *Scholarly Urdu Dictionary*, says that she's tall, slim, irascible, and that her tresses and bodily desires are very sizeable.

the Karachi Theatre Company. Her whore of a mother still has her wear the sort of nose ring that only virgins wear. The more skanky she gets, the bigger the ring gets." Sir, hearing this, he stopped being mad. Instead, he asked for the address of the theatre company and the name of the girl. At first, he was spewing one insult after another, and now his throat was getting dry from calling me "master" so many times! He said, "Master, calm down, and eat this paan." But, I swear, our horse lowered his eyes, stuck his mouth into his nosebag, and started chewing his cud. Sir, it's something to think about. His mare was quite tall, just like a big, strapping man. But your horse isn't any taller than you.'

Basharat flew into a rage, 'Are you a fucking measuring stick? Why is it that "shit happens" every time you're near the Municipal Corporation Building?'

He folded his hands in supplication and said, 'Forgive my mistakes. This time shit didn't happen with your horse but …'

Basharat Haircutting Salon

At last the riddle of the Municipal Corporation Building was solved. At the time, Basharat wanted to change the front of his shop and to expand toward the street, so in order to get approval for his plans he had to go to the Municipal Corporation. And yet his driver was nowhere to be seen. Finally, he grew tired of waiting. At three o'clock, he hired a rickshaw and set off for the Municipal Corporation Building. And what did he see, but right there on the sidewalk, Mirza Wahid-uz-Zaman Baig had spread out a threadbare rug and was shaving a man! He stood out of his line of sight and watched. After shaving him, he cleaned off the soap and stubble from his wrist with the razor, and then he sharpened the razor with a strop laid on his wrist. Then he put his knees on the ground, and from this height, he shaved the man's armpits. Basharat couldn't believe his eyes. But when Mirza took a clump of alum and Tibetan talcum powder from his 'toolbox,' Basharat started trusting his eyes again. Looking closely at the scene, he saw a sign written on a piece of cardboard near the edge of the rug; in bold and beautiful calligraphy was written the following:

Basharat Haircutting Salon
Main Office
Harchandrai Road

He didn't think it right to insult him right there in the busy market. Full of anger, he took a rickshaw back to his shop. That night, Mirza brought the kids home from school at seven in the evening. Basharat couldn't control himself; he grabbed the whip from his hand, and brandishing it threateningly, he said, 'Tell me the truth, or else I'll rip the flesh right off of you! Bastard, you're a barber! Why didn't you tell me? Everything has been a lie. Everything you've said has been a lie. Today I'll see what kind of liar you are. Tell me the truth—where were you?' The driver clapped his hands together pitifully and, while shaking, said, 'Forgive my mistakes! Boss, you're absolutely right. I swear to the One Beyond Compare, from this day forward I'll tell the truth.'

So from that day forward, whatever disgrace he experienced was due to his telling the truth. Mirza Abdul Wadud Baig says that it's relatively better to tell lies and so suffer disgrace and insult than to tell the truth and suffer the same fate. At least then you understand why you're being punished.

Under Basharat's cross-examination, the first truth that Mirza revealed was that after finishing up work at the Municipal Corporation Building, he had had to perform a circumcision on Burns Road at four thirty. But the circumcision party was quite late in arriving. And then the boy didn't want to have anything to do with it. He was an only child and so everyone's darling. He was eight years old and a little raging bull. His grandfather, Haji Maqsood Ilahi Punjabi, Merchant of Delhi, tried his best to coax him into it, 'Son, Muslims don't get scared. There's nothing to it.' But the boy was obstinate. He said, 'You first! You have a long beard too!'

Basharat's Face Went Red with Anger

Basharat extracted another truth from him under the threat of the whip: his real name was Buddhan. His son, who had graduated from high school, was staunchly opposed both to his name and to his profession. Over and over, he had threatened to commit suicide. He had explained, 'Son, our ancestors used to have names like this. What's in a name?' His son had been furious, 'Dad, Sheikh Pir [Shakespeare] said just that, but his dad's name was nothing close to Buddhan. What did he know? If you can't change anything else, at least change your name.' So a couple days after that conversation when Mirza had got a job at Eastern Federal Insurance Company, he had introduced himself as Mirza Wahid-uz-Zaman Baig. And the name had stuck. Actually, it was the name of an executive that he had used to shave twenty years ago. That man had died childless. His nephews had taken his property (which he had accumulated through accepting bribes), and he had taken over his name.

Now that the poor guy had begun to tell the truth, he couldn't stop himself. Mirza Abdul Wadud Baig says that in this day and age to live a life telling the truth 100% of the time is like building a house but forgetting to mix pebbles into the cement. Mirza, the driver, said, 'Forgive my mistakes! Now I want to tell the truth in one fell swoop. My family has its self-respect. Thank God I'm not a groom by caste. For a hundred years, my family's been barbers. God be praised—there are about a dozen in my family. Boss, you know very well that my salary is only half of what we spend on the horse. Seventy rupees disappears like that. That's why I'm forced into having this private practice. For years, my wife and kids sacrificed meals so that my eldest boy could get through high school. I've been cutting Mr Alimuddin's hair for twenty years. Now there's nothing left on his head. I just trim his eyebrows. Boss, all the connoisseurs of my art have passed on. Today's barbers shave people like they're shearing sheep. My vision's become weak, but even now I can pare off the excess from a big toe in one motion with my nail-parer. So I begged Mr Alimuddin, and so he hired my son as a clerk at Muslim Commercial Bank. Now my boy says he's ashamed of me being a barber. He wants me to change jobs. Boss, my father and his father were barbers, not nawabs! I earn my money through sweat and hard work. But, sir, I've noticed that people consider those jobs that require hard work to be beneath them. My son says, 'All the boys from my class have become accountants. They go around jingling the keys to the moneybox. I'm being held back only because of my father's name. If you don't stop being a barber, I'm going to cut my throat with your razor.' Sometimes, late at night, in order to scare his mother he made sounds like a goat being slaughtered. And so the good woman made me promise to find another job. So I had to start being a cart-driver. I haven't told him I'm still a barber on the side. I never take home my strop, tools, barber's bag, and stuff because I don't want him to feel disgraced by me. Please believe me, that's the reason I've used the name Basharat Haircutting Salon. Your name is very auspicious. Forgive my mistakes!'

The Lampless Aladdin

He joined his hands in supplication, sat down, and then started to massage his knees very fervently. The moment Basharat's countenance softened, Mirza Wahid-uz-Zaman Baig told another truth: 'It pains me to see cuts on your face every morning. Domestic razors take off more skin than they do hair. You always have stubble. Forgive my mistakes! Your sideburns are off too. They look like a clock's striking nine twenty.' He requested that he be allowed to shave him before currying the horse. He could also cut the kids' hair. Also, his speciality dishes were Bihari biryani, Bombay biryani, chicken qorma, and shahi tukre. And his deg halim and dhubri firni* were so good that you wouldn't be able to stop licking your fingers. He could cook pulao and zardah for a big party of up to 150 in under three hours. Basharat was a gourmand. And like the English saying goes, the way to a man's heart goes through his stomach.

He began to like the barber

He also offered that after currying the horse, he would massage Basharat's father's feet. At night, he would massage Basharat. There is a vein on your neck where your spine starts, and if you have it pressed just right with a delicate, warm touch, then all your pain goes away. You can't see it. His teacher, the late Laddan Mian, had used to say that a masseur sees through the tips of his fingers. His fingers are his pain binoculars; as soon as they touch someone, they know where the pain is. Then Mirza Wahid-uz-Zaman Baig enticed Basharat with the idea of giving him an almond oil head massage. And after that, he would press his thumbs gently into Basharat's temples, and then using both his hands like birds' wings, he would drub his skull up and down so that Basharat felt as though sleep fairies were descending slowly and gently from the clouds in layer upon layer of fluffy balls of carded cotton—so slowly, so gently, so slowly, so gently.

Basharat was exhausted after a long day. As he heard this, his eyes closed on their own.

---

* Dhubri: This firni is made in a shallow earthenware pot. The scent of the earthenware is infused into the firni, and this is considered a good thing!

Then the crafty bastard threw the knockout punch: 'God be praised! Your little one is almost three months' old. The younger he is when circumcised, the quicker his scabs will heal.'

Basharat's face bloomed like a rose, 'My gosh, Khalifaji. Why didn't you say so earlier? Why were you so secretive? It turns out you're a real Rustam!'

At this, he got out the horseshoe to show Basharat, the one that he had been given as a token of appreciation for the role of Rustam's horse.

Mirza Wahid-uz-Zaman Baig became Khalifa. Or, Aladdin the Ninth. From then on, he worked less and bragged much more. Mirza Abdul Wadud Baig called him the Lampless Aladdin. Basharat's father agreed to call him Khalifa (instead of Aladdin) on the condition that if they got a new driver or any other servant in the future, they would call him Khalifa as well.

6.

The Snake Charmer in Front of the Horse

Gradually, Maulana, Khalifa, the horse, and Basharat's father, in this order of importance, became accepted as members of the family, and this merger became so complete that the horse's lame leg too was then considered an inseparable part of the family. Thanks to the horse, Basharat's father again had a say in household matters. I've used this phrase idiomatically because otherwise his say counted for shit. There comes a time in people's lives when all they do is meddle, and this they consider to be their good work. Some people spend their entire lives counting others' mistakes and correcting their follies, I mean, they waste their lives meddling in others' business. They never have any time to think about themselves.

When the Day of Resurrection came, Shaikh had empty hands
He called himself a merchant, but he had only empty hands

Everyone in the house took turns petting the horse. His diet was probably the same as before, but from all the love he was getting, now his mane and coat shone with such a brilliant lustre that glances and flies slipped right off. The kids fed him their own sweets on the sly and, like him, tried to wiggle their ears. Now, while playing soccer, some kids started kicking goals backwards with their heels. During poetry contests, when one boy ran out of ammunition or when he messed up while reciting a poem, the opposing team (as well as the audience) would neigh as one big group. Basharat's father would grab his harmonium and start singing to the horse whenever he got good news or whenever a dark cloud passed in front of the sun. He said that whenever he played well, the horse would instinctively start wagging his tail like a fly-whisk. I have never doubted the veracity of his claims—not before, not now. The only surprising thing was that Basharat's father had never noticed which part of the body the horse had used to show his appreciation for his art!

Balban was everything to Basharat's father: a plaything, a substitute for a son, a companion in solitude, and a pillow to cry on. Before the horse had arrived, Basharat's father would groan like a creaky door about his rusted joints, whether he was in actual pain or not. If someone happened to pick up something heavy in front of him, he would groan as though he himself were dying under its weight. If someone asked him how he was doing, he would raise his right hand toward the heavens and shake it, as though he were shaking a juggler's drum back and forth; then he would cough for three or four minutes in a range of pitches. It seemed like he had begun to enjoy his bad health. Some virtuosos of the sickbed consider it insulting to the high status of their disease to admit that they feel better. Basharat's father had great willpower. Whenever he started to feel better, he would forcibly make himself feel worse again. You've never seen him, but you must know old people who talk about their pet ailments just like cricket batsmen, having got out with ninety-nine runs, talk about their incomplete centuries, or how village women talk about their labours and deliveries—that is, each time with new commentaries and new regrets. Before Balban came, Basharat's father always had a prickly temper. People had stopped asking after his health. They left him to himself. No one had the courage to interfere in the joys of ailing.

But now his mood not only moderated but also expanded. He told each and every person about the newest symptoms of his sicknesses. He told them the details of his pleuritis, his osteoarthritis, and his chronic constipation. He would stroke his stomach and talk about his flatulence and the grumbling of his bowels, and he would accompany this with the corresponding sound effects. He would list the names of the neighbours who had died in his dreams and then advise them to sacrifice a goat immediately. Sometimes he told about how his phlegm would remain so viscous for three days that only after shaking his head quite vigorously a dozen times would he be able to spit it out into the spittoon. Back in those days, the most ignorant people in Bihar Colony—including the street-sweeper women and Professor Abdul Quddus—knew what viscosity* meant (and knew

---

* Viscosity: This word was implanted so deeply in Professor Qazi Abdul Quddus's conscious and subconscious minds (MA, BT) that he made it the subject of his thesis: 'The Viscous in Milton, Josh, Abul Kalam Azad, Allama Mashriqi, Agha Hashr Kashmiri, Abdul Aziz Khalid, and Mushtaq Ahmed Yousufi.' The professor included my name with these famous people not because he wanted to honour me. He bound me to these notables in a three-legged race in order to chastise them and to drive me away. I heard that the professors rejected his thesis's outline because they didn't think he could kill so many birds with just one stone! No one

its examples too). Mirza used to say that Basharat's father's diseases had germs that spoke Arabic; English medicine couldn't do anything for them.

The Intoxication Grows When One Drunk Meets Another Drunk

One of his oldest and most loyal of friends, Fida Hussain Khan Taib (the Penitent), came every Friday to ask after his health. Once upon a time, he had been a very social and jovial sort. He had used to drink on the sly, but only when it was free. Drinking on the sly is a sin that has one benefit: you get as drunk on one shot as you would otherwise on a hundred bottles. He had one odd and nasty habit. Whenever he got really drunk, he left off all other conversation and would only talk about Islam. Because of this, he had been beaten up three or four times by drunks. But Shaikh Hamiduddin, with whom he drank, didn't mind this choice of topic. Mr Shaikh put a lot of effort in his drinking parties. He served the best whisky from Czechoslovakian crystal, along with spicy liver and kebabs, and Riyaz Khairabadi's poetry. And there was a towel. Because as soon as Taib got drunk, he would think about his first wife and start sobbing away. He would use the towel to wipe away his tears. If he hadn't drunk for a while, he would rush back to the bottle, thinking,

It's been a long time since I've enjoyed a good cry.

---

took the time to explain to them that Professor Qazi Abdul Quddus doesn't need arrows, guns, or stones.

Why would a hunter hunt on a horse
When the prey presents itself on its own—their heads bowed low ...

When he got extremely drunk, he would wander around his house or through the neighbourhood on moonlit nights thinking about his dead wife, moaning and crying so much that his present wife joined forces with neighbours to get a water carrier to douse him with water. One January, he was doused with such cold water that it led to him coming down with a fever, and then pneumonia after that. From then on, his wife made sure to put a fez on his head before dousing him with water.

Fida Hussain Khan Taib

Fida Hussain Khan Taib must have been around sixty, but he had never stopped ogling women. According to one source, he looked at other people's daughters and wives in just the way that his wife was dying to be looked at herself. What happened after the birth of their third child was that, as happens in our culture, the child acted as a roadblock for conjugal love. His wandering eye was not content with just one wife. For a long time, he had sought out nirvana in the happy bed of prostitutes. Until he could afford to take the wrong road, he left the narrow confines of married life to ambush what he might find outside of it. His long-suffering wife put up with it, as she thought

My husband needs bigger pastures in which to roam.

People couldn't understand why he had chosen the penname of Taib. What defect of character *didn't* he have? In the end, what had he renounced? But then people just figured that he had probably renounced all good.

Once upon a time, Taib had worked and written poetry at Cooperative Bank. He tried to compose poetry with the accounting books as well and so was fired on the charge that he had embezzled money. He still wrote poetry, but only one day each year. After he turned fifty, he had written his epitaph (in a quatrain) on the first day of the new year, and yet for a dozen years not one had been put to use. His poetry was elegant and simple; his words were well-chosen and full of poetic imagery and foreboding. During the year, should one of his friends or acquaintances die, he would scrunch in their name and hand over the quatrain, saying,

Thy need is yet greater than mine.*

His poems were neither natural nor baroque. They featured only dead people. Basharat's father praised his poetry in a bizarre way that can be imitated but never fully described. It was something like an imbalanced mixture of forced appreciation, social grace, intentional sarcasm, and spontaneous laughter. His laughter was such that if someone should hear it from a distance, they wouldn't be able to tell if he was laughing or crying. That is, he was laughing bitterly.

Due to the substitution of other people's names into his quatrains, some lines had broken the metre, but he considered this permissible under the demands of poetry and death. Some of his friends who were on the brink of dying put it off simply out of fear of his quatrains. Basharat's father began to dislike Mr Taib's visits. One day he said, 'Why is this bad-luck charm hanging around here? I think he's hoping for the worst for me. He wants to stick this year's quatrain to my head—no, to my gravestone.' Then he wrote a special will that stipulated that, even though he would never let it come to pass, if we consider the impossible possible, then if he should die before Fida Hussain Khan Taib (which he would never let happen), then affix the quatrain to the foot of my grave. From those headstones with epi-

---

* During the Battle of Zutphen (1586), Sir Philip Sidney uttered these immortal words, as he lay wounded and just about to die, and as he handed his flask to a dying soldier.

graphs containing the quatrain, the name of the deceased, and Taib's penname, it was never that clear who actually was buried there. Or, in the words of Professor Qazi Abdul Quddus, it was hard to decide whether the grave was that of the dead person or that of the poet. Many wondered, as they looked at the epigraphs, why one poet had been buried so many times. But after reading the words, they saw that it was entirely appropriate. A poet once said that after poets die, many live on in their words. The poet dies; the words don't. This has been to the detriment of Urdu poetry.

A Party of Ear-Scratching Music

Not a single day passed when Basharat's father didn't threaten dying. Like General Sher Ali, he had bought a plot in the cemetery where he had had built a mausoleum that had been unoccupied for a long time because he had avoided moving in. Often he would make himself depressed then recite the couplet,

> *Any time now I'll leave the world behind*
> *The world will watch in amazement as I go.*

In this, there is a play of words regarding one's imminent demise. By playing with the gender, he wants to show simultaneously the delicacy of language, the agony of the last, dying breath, and the fun of figurative speech. According to Mirza Abdul Wadud Baig, you can tell from this that Basharat's father eventually died due to his taste for spiciness. It was as though he had dug his own grave with his tongue. God have mercy on him. He used idioms and everyday language religiously.

When the horse began to participate in his ear-scratching music parties, Basharat's father got his old silk brocade achkan coat undone and, out of that, he had the tailor make a sheet to cover his harmonium. Khalifa would push in and out the harmonium's bellows, and Basharat's father would press on its keys with trembling fingers. Sometimes when the spirit really moved him, he would involuntarily begin to sing as well. At times, it was difficult to figure out whether his voice or his fingers were quavering more. As soon as he started singing the song's second line, his neighbour, the retired excise inspector, Chaudhuri Karam Ilahi, would waddle over. He had lost his vision to glaucoma a long time ago. He had special-ordered a bright red terracotta pot from Gujarat and on it had painted Sindhi hala tile designs. He said that at least others could see them. Whenever he accompanied Basharat's father's singing on the pot, he rolled up his sleeves and wrapped a jasmine garland around his big wrists; and he cast a deep spell. He would often say that ever since he had gone blind, God had given him countless secret powers in classical music and in matters olfactory. After they had finished singing the gammat, the sweet fragrance of their ragas would waft over everything and everyone, and Basharat's father would say, 'Wow, Choi Sahib, you play so well!' And Mr Chaudhuri would close his lightless eyes in ecstasy and say, 'You too were playing really great!' And what in fact could you call this other than great art? Two disabled, old men were swaying away as they played simultaneously their own songs on their own instruments. I mean, the one played in raag darbari, and the other, in a syncopated rhythm, played mahiya. As they accompanied each other, it was hard to tell who wasn't following whom.

Look How the Rainy Season Is Celebrated, Friends!

While Basharat's father asked Chaudhuri Karam Ilahi to help him change the position of his paralysed leg, he would often say that in his youth he had played the harmonium so well that the masters of the craft acknowledged his superiority. His love of music reminded him of those days when the Bombay Theatrical Company had come to town and he had watched the same play every day for a month, and for the rest of the year he had gone around mouthing lines from it. Beginning in 1925, he had watched every show from the orchestra pit, which was considered in those days the height of all connoisseurship and status. He had learned to play the harmonium from one theatre company's retired harmonium player who was called the peti master. He said that to keep his finger-joints and the veins and muscles of his fingers nimble he had the habit of wrapping cracked-wheat halva around his fingers for months on end. He was light-skinned and delicate. Despite being ill for so long, even now his cheeks were rosy in the winter. His velvety eyes looked even more beautiful when he closed them. He wore a white achkan coat. His churidar pyjamas clung to his thick calves. During his youth, he was a very handsome, well-dressed man. Now any mention of his youth caused him to writhe in pain.

You shot an arrow at my heart! Oh, oh!

How full of longing it was when each day bloomed like a new lotus! 'When the shadows were green, and the sunlight rosy . . .' Just thinking about them made his breathing speed up. The days, months, and years of the past started to swirl around him like autumn leaves. Oh my! Ustad Faiyaz Khan's wild, whirlwind-like alap gaining momentum; Gauhar Jan's crystalline voice; Mukhtar Begum's rich voice! Basharat's father measured his youth in these memories. Then these dream fragments began to melt away. The river of memories flowed on, but it descended into the mirages of the mind. A heavy rain started to fall. A fragrance rose from the earth, and a hot, intoxicating odour wafted off the body. Thin kurtas, soaked through and through, couldn't hide anything. The clouds erupted; the rain carried with it everything in its path.

The clouds rise from the breast, the rain falls from the eyes
It's not the rain of Phagun, which lasts a moment then dies
It's Bhadon's rain—a downpour that never dies

(Insha Allah Khan Insha)

While it rained cats and dogs—*jham jham jham*—Basharat's father
would play the harmonium with both hands—sometimes he played
the snake charmer's songs and sometimes the light-hearted and soul-
searching dirges of Ustad Jhande Khan; people said that the black
cobras would come out of their holes and start to dance, and the
moon would appear in the window. Somewhere else, on roofs that
were still sizzling from the rain, the scarves of the girls looking out
at the rainbow took on the rainbow's colours. Somewhere else, despite their best efforts, the pinch-marks and stains from cheap chunri
scarves wouldn't leave girls' pretty arms. When the melody sped up,
the surroundings echoed—*jhun jhun jhun*—as though someone had
ecstatically picked up both heaven and earth and smashed them together like a pair of cymbals, and now their reverberations coursed
through everyone's bodies and couldn't be stopped.

7.

A Newspaper Hat

Three or four months passed without incident. The kids' school
closed for summer vacation. One day Basharat had the horse yoked
to the cart, and, for the tenth time, went to the Municipal Corporation Building to get approval for his plans. As he left, he said to Maulana that he wouldn't return until he got approval. Enough is enough.
How can the bastards deny him again? This wasn't just empty boasting. He had already plied them with all sorts of examples, ratiocina-

tions, and arguments. Now he was going with five 'greens'* because the sword of wealth cuts through all riddles and burls. He had to go from alley to alley because there were few roads left in Karachi where a horse-drawn cart was still allowed. Horse-drawn carts were considered worse than rickshaws, and so they were in operation only in those extremely poor sections of the city that, while they were in the city, weren't considered to be part of it. Who would have thought it? He left Kanpur dreaming that one day, by the grace of God, he would sit with an Italian blanket on his lap as his phaeton went through the streets and people would ask who that fine gentleman was. But the world had changed so much that by the time his dream came true, not only did he have to operate the cart on the sly but, while seated in the cart, he also sat slouched over. If he had had his way, he would have covered himself from head to foot in his Italian blanket so that no one could recognize him. Whenever he went out at day, he would sit with *The Dawn* newspaper spread out covering his face and torso so that only his legs peeked out as though they were appendages to the paper itself. One day, Mirza Abdul Wadud Baig said that he should make a hat out of the paper so that no one could see his face—a hat just like the horrible ones that criminals wear before they're hung. He went so far as to say that only newspaper-hats should be worn by criminals walking to the gallows so that the editors too might learn something about life.

A Horse's Long Jump

The Municipal Corporation Building was still some five hundred metres away when they saw a funeral procession coming around the

* A green: A 100-rupee note was called a 'green' because of its colour. When this note became red, only then did people start calling it a 'note.' No one calls it a 'red.'

alley's corner. When Basharat had hired Khalifa, he had given him strict instructions to avoid funeral processions. But Khalifa's mind was on something else, and the funeral procession was advancing menacingly upon the horse. Basharat threw the newspaper down and yelled at the top of his lungs, 'Funeral! Funeral! Khalifa, funeral!' And so Khalifa started whipping the horse. The horse reared and started neighing. Khalifa lost his wits. Basharat took the reins in hand and tried to turn the horse around. But he turned stubborn and started kicking with his hind legs. Basharat didn't know that this was the very spot where Khalifa would tie up the horse before leaving to set up his haircutting business. Basharat yelled, 'Hit him hard!' In front of them, the danger (meaning, the funeral procession) was inching forward. He was terrified. Guessing from Basharat's disturbed state, the funeral procession was now within the same 'range' that, several months earlier, according to the steel businessman,

The story finished with one long jump of the horse.

Now Basharat was more scared than the horse because he was trying to kick the horse in the side. The horse's neighing was drowned beneath Basharat's yelling. Khalifa was whipping the horse like a madman. When the whip struck a heavy blow, the horse reared. Khalifa was beside himself with anger, and when he twice cursed it, 'May your owner die!' Basharat was speechless. But at that moment he was busy trying to bring the horse under control. He scolded Khalifa, 'Khalifa, why are you whipping him like a wussy?'

Upon hearing this, Khalifa got down and then, like a fast bowler in cricket, took a running start at him. With his teeth bared and his eyes closed, he lashed down with the whip with all his might. The whip's tip caught Basharat on the mouth and on his eyes. He felt as though someone had drawn a line on his face with acid. Later he said, 'It would be an understatement to say that everything went dark. It felt as though I was blinded.' In just one sentence, his curses jumped from 'idiot' to 'asshole' to 'motherfucker.' How he then got to Khalifa—whether it was by vaulting over the horse or by ducking beneath his legs—no one knows; but when he got there, he grabbed the whip from Khalifa and whipped the horse so hard that it wondered what was going on.

The burning in the one eye was so bad that he had to close the other as well. And so, with his eyes shut, he kept whipping at the horse. After a little while, though, he felt as though there was nothing at the other end of his whipping. He put his hand over his wounded eye and opened his left one; what he saw was unexpected. The open casket was lying diagonally in the middle of the street. The cart was racing off wildly. The casket-bearers were nowhere to be seen. Khalifa was gone, as well. But one elderly man in mourning, who was suspended from a golden shower tree, was cursing out the horse's family tree, from top to bottom.

After a couple minutes, everyone came out of hiding and began to accost Basharat. Each person fired his own missiles; no one wanted to hear him out. He heard many voices and many vituperations.

And this asshole calls himself a Muslim!

Let's shoot the horse!

No, let's shoot the owner!

Let's take him to the police station!

(Grabbing Basharat by the tie) *He's sullied our funeral. Let's cover his face with soot, tie him up, and send him out on the horse!*

Basharat decided right then and there to put down Balban.

When he got home, he thrashed the horse so much that neighbours came to watch.

That night, neither he nor Balban could sleep. Basharat didn't know that Khalifa had threaded the whip with wire.

8.

Balban Gets the Death Penalty

The next morning Basharat fired Khalifa. He put his toolbox beneath his arm, and, as he was leaving, he folded his hands together in supplication and said, 'I swear on your children! The horse didn't do anything. He was just standing there. You were beating him for no rhyme or reason. You beat him so much that even a dead horse would have stood up and run away. See ya!' He left, then returned, 'Forgive my mistakes! What time should I come on Friday to shave you?'

A friend advised him not to let a vet put him down. He said, 'It's a bad way to go. It's not pretty. When I put my Alsatian down at a hospital, I saw it dying. I couldn't eat for two days afterwards. He had been by my side through a lot. He was looking at me pleadingly. I sat with my hand on his forehead. This is a very inauspicious, a very miserable, horse. Despite his disability and pain, he served you and your children well.'

This friend arranged over the phone for Balban to be shot to death.

Maulana Karamat Hussain was put in charge of leading Balban to his death. He didn't like this at all. He argued that a pet or a working animal isn't an animal; it's like a son or daughter. Basharat answered, 'Do you know how long a horse lives? Who's going to feed this lame ass for nine years? I didn't sign up for stuffing its mouth just so it can live.' Maulana forgot his subservient position; he got angry. He took these earthly matters and made them heavenly: 'Since when are people in control of who gets food and who doesn't? There is only one sustainer—He gives food even to the insects under rocks. Anyone who thinks that he's in charge of providing food to anyone else thinks of himself as God. Each animate being has its own food already provided for. God's promise is the truth. He always provides, always.'

'Of course! Of course! Even for bribe-takers!' Basharat blurted out. The words were like arrows. Not just Maulana but Basharat too stood there numb, taking in what he had just said. If, for years, you hold in your heart a horrible, vengeful utterance, it will eventually come out; putting a gag in your mouth won't stop it. And as long as it remains inside you, you remain upset:

What was on the tip of my tongue finally came out today.

Maulana came early the next morning to pick up Balban. He was going to be killed in the foothills of North Nazimabad at eleven.

When Basharat sat down for breakfast, he couldn't swallow. He hadn't seen Balban that morning. He thought, 'Of course they'll shoot him in the forehead. The swirl above his left eye proved really inauspicious. It took his life.' The previous night he had instructed Maulana to have the corpse buried right before him so that it wouldn't be left for wild kites and crows to feed on. He shivered. He left for the shop without eating his kebab paratha. As he was leaving, he saw the horse's gear and the bloody rag that had covered his neck's wound. He felt like something was happening to him; he started to walk faster.

Basharat's father was not informed about what was going on. He was only told that Balban was going to the Punjab to graze for a couple months. His father said, 'I've heard of cows and water buffalos being sent to pasture, but this is the first time I've heard of a horse being sent from Karachi to the Punjab to graze! Every summer, only businessmen and millionaires get to escape Karachi for Mt Murree.' This was not the time to tell him. His blood pressure had been very high for a while. There was once a time when he had been very proud of his strong and muscular body. Even now he took great pride in saying that his blood pressure was equal to that of two men combined. I can confirm that he had blood pressure equal to that of two men because I have seen that even an ordinary pain made him yell as loudly as two men. So Basharat stuck to the prudent path. And it was good he did. Mirza often says that you shouldn't lie to people younger than you because you don't want to inspire them to lie as well. But it's different with old folks: they don't rely upon any external inspiration for their lying.

Holding the reins, Maulana took Balban to see Basharat's father. More than half of his possessions had already been removed to his bedroom. The harmonium was being wrapped in Rahim Bakhsh's red sheet. The only thing left on the wall was the photo of Balban that had been published in the newspaper after he had won that one race. Basharat's father had felt uneasy since the previous night. After the night's last prayers, he had smoked on his hookah twice. (This was against habit.) How was he going to while away his time now? When Balban was brought to him, the horse hung his head and let him run his fingers through his mane for a long time. Basharat's father didn't bless his hooves with his holy breath. When he started to write 'Allah' on the horse's forehead, his fingers found the long line of a scar where the horse had been whipped. This stopped him cold. He ran his finger along the entire length of this line and so took on this pain for himself. In a sad voice, he said, 'Who hit you, son?' When Maulana made ready to take him away, Basharat's father rested his hand on the horse's head, 'Well, Balban, son, I don't know if I'll be here when you get back. I give you over to God.'

Separation anxiety overwhelmed Basharat's father. Who would he tell all his worries to now? For whose health would he now pray? He had never imagined that God would begrudge him such a small crutch; after all, it was just an animal. Someone who has never undergone the agony of loneliness can't imagine the importance of having someone else. Charles Lamb, the unparalleled essayist, once underwent a period of terrible loneliness. On Monday, May 12, 1800, he wrote to Coleridge that, 'Last Friday, Haity [his old nurse] died after eight days. Her corpse is lying in front of me right now. Mary [his crazy sister] couldn't stand the sight of it, and she suffered a terrible fit. She's been taken away. Now I'm alone at home, and I have no one to be with but Haity's corpse. Tomorrow I'll bury her, and then I'll really be alone. Then, except for this cat, there won't be anyone to remind me that I saw this house in better, happy days, and that once there were other living, breathing beings like me.'

Maulana was absent the whole day. The next day when he came, he looked upset. Basharat wanted to ask questions, but he didn't dare. No one had the courage to ask where Balban had been shot. People say that animals know when they are about to die. So did he try to run away when he was being led into the desolate foothills? Sometimes miracles happen at the very last moment. He had been a very hard-working, tough, and courageous animal. It was hard to believe that he would have gone quietly.

> Do not go gentle into that good night,
> Rage, rage against the dying of the light.

9.

Ah! Ah! It's Raining Again!

About two weeks later, Basharat ran into Tahir Ali Mussa Bhai in front of Spencer Eye Hospital. Mussa Bhai was a Bohri, and his lumber store was so close to Basharat's that if he threw a stone it would land on his golden turban. I give this example because on many occasions Basharat had wanted to throw a stone at him. He was very arrogant. He was always after Basharat's customers, and he spread rumours about him. In fact, he wanted to ruin Basharat's business and buy his store. His scraggly beard was curled inward like a parrot's beak.

He said, 'Basharat, sir! Last month I heard you were going to have your horse killed. I said, "No way! This is definitely murder!" That horse was Duldul during Asharah [Muharram]. There's a guy, Turab Ali, who works my power-saw. He said that the procession went right by his shack. It was your horse! Exactly the same. 100%. Turab Ali fed it milk and jalebis out of his own two hands. That day your driver spared no one. He raked in fifty rupees. He said that his boss wanted to turn Duldul into a taxi. He walked in front singing "The King of Men" and "The Lion of God" and so on. That was fifteen more rupees. He even brought the horse over to me to say "hi." The man's got a big family.'

The next day Maulana didn't come to work. It rained for two days straight. Four days before that, when Radio Karachi had seen the first drops of rain, they started raining down the songs of the monsoon. If the songs hadn't told them it was the rainy season, then, in Karachi, they wouldn't have known. But if you call the rainy season by the words 'June' and 'July,' monsoon songs won't have the same romantic air. Basharat smiled. That morning, while leaving the house, he had told his wife, 'Begum, you should fry some things up today. I've missed eating the monsoon foods in Karachi—crispy samosas, crunchy papad, and kachoris. I've gotten flabby eating Karachi papayas.' That evening, as he was about to close the shop, a man came with the news that Maulana's father had died the night before. He had been buried that afternoon. *We belong to God, and to God we shall return.* It was good. God had heard his cries. His years of agony were over. He was finally home. In fact, he had been raised up from the muck and buried in solid ground. He went straight to Maulana's to offer his condolences. The rain had stopped, and the moon had come out. It seemed as though the moon was running quickly through the sky while the clouds were locked in place. The bricks, stones, and Dalda cans that made the paths through the muck were drowned in places. A group of butt-naked children were taking turns putting their mouths on top of the small opening of a water pot to sing film songs;

as they did so, the pot bobbed up and down in the watery muck. In front of a collapsed shack, a man with an awful voice was singing the call to prayer so that the rain would stop. He stretched out so many syllables that it seemed like he was using the call to prayer as an excuse to sing the beginning of a classical raga. He had jammed his fingers up to the first knuckle into his ears so that he would escape having to experience the torment of hearing his own voice. The previous week the same man had stood in front of his shack and had sung the call to prayer in order to *bring* the rain. But, that day, small groups of children were going door-to-door singing, 'Please, God, make it rain. Please, God, let it rain. All the ponds, wells, and jars are dry! God! Rain! Rain! Rain!' And for this, they were being roundly scolded.

It was a strange state of helplessness. In one direction, the roofs made of matting, burlap sacks, reed mats, and scrap-paper were sinking under the weight of the water. In another direction, the men of the houses were patching one tattered mat with parts of another tattered mat. One man was pouring tar onto a burlap sack to make a tarp to cover his sick mother's charpoy. Another man's shack had completely collapsed. He couldn't figure out where to begin repairing it. And so he started hitting a child. Here and there people were making drains whose function seemed to be to separate their muck from their neighbours.' One man had thrust his arm (up to his armpit) into a sack of wet flour to see if any of it was still dry or whether it had all become dough. Outside one hut, monsoon flies were sitting on top of a heap of goat's guts, and, like lazy aide-de-camps, they weren't budging even when a scabby dog tried to shoo them away. These were the guts of a milk-giving (but old and dying) goat, that, just a little while before, had been slaughtered by three neighbours a metre in front of her two-month-old kid so that she wouldn't die before she could be killed halal style. Her blood had spread through the network of drains into the far distance. The three men were congratulating themselves for having prevented their brother's rightful earnings from going to waste at the last minute. How cleverly they had stolen the goat from death's jaws! In several shacks, they would eat meat for the first time in months. Basharat was most taken aback when he passed in front of one shack in which girls were singing wedding songs. He couldn't see anymore the colourful paper flags that had been hung outside, but the burlap was still stained with the streaks of their colours in psychedelic patterns. One girl was accompanying the singers on a large, flat bowl used for kneading flour.

> *Mom, send my brother because the rain has come!*
> *Mom, send my brother because the rain has come!*
> *The rain has come!*

After every refrain, the girls laughed uncontrollably. Laughing while singing, and singing while laughing, the girls would lose themselves and become mixed up in the crazy hopes of youth. Actually, the giggling of these inexperienced girls was the cutest thing about the song.

In front of one shack, a man and wife were wringing out a quilt. The wife's wet veil was hanging from her; it looked like an elephant's trunk. Because of the rain, the twenty thousand people in the area hadn't been able to light a cooking fire for two days. In the low-lying areas, shacks stood in water that went up to people's knees. In front of the first row of shacks, a well-intentioned, God-fearing, bearded elderly man was trying to distribute the qorma and tandoori bread that he had brought in a rickshaw. He had also brought three quilts to distribute to the needy. But, leaving the house, he had had no idea that bringing three quilts to an area of twenty thousand people was like trying to put out a fire by squirting water from a syringe. But it was also true that no shack had even a dry island of two metres on which someone could lie down, pull the quilt on top, and go to sleep. The old man was surrounded by a crowd of two hundred butt-naked children to whom he was trying to explain the benefits of forming a line.

But these illiterate, thick-skulled kids were better with numbers than the old man because their internal mathematician knew very well that if you divide thirty pieces of bread by two hundred hungry people, and three quilts by twenty thousand needy people, then the quotient will be nothing more than the old man's body stripped to the bone. And things were becoming something like this. Basharat pressed on, and he noticed that there wasn't a single shack from which he didn't hear the crying of children. For the first time, he understood that the cries of children emanate from the guts. In half the shacks, children were being beaten because they were crying; in the other half, they were crying because they were being beaten.

He thought to himself, 'You set off to comfort one man, but what is this ocean of sadness?' Thoughts rushed through his mind, 'Maulana's father must have been buried in a wet shroud. What kind of place is this where kids can't play inside or outside? Where little girls grow up on two metres' worth of land? After a girl gets married and moves to her in-laws,' what memories will she have of her childhood and her parents' house?' But then he thought, 'She won't go anywhere. There's nowhere to go. She'll put on her red clothes and walk to some other shack somewhere around here. While singing "Why Did You Marry Me So Far Away, O, My Millionaire Father!" her friends will take her to her new two-metre plot. Then on a rainy day just like today, she'll be taken from there and laid in two metres of earth, and earth's burden will be folded back onto earth's breast. But look here—why are you getting so depressed? Why is your outlook on life so teary-eyed? Trees don't shrink back from the muck. Do flowers cringe at the smell of shit?'

He shivered, and then he twisted the corner of his lips up into a smile. Those who can't cry, smile like this.

When he had first seen this filthy neighbourhood, he had wanted to throw up. But now he was scared. In the wet, moonlit night, it looked like a ghost town, and not a part of Karachi at all. In all directions, he could only see the shacks' bamboo walls and their roofs' dripping mats. It wasn't a neighbourhood but the skeleton of one: it looked like what the survivors of an atomic bomb would erect. Every puddle reflected the moon, and the ghostly beams of light were dancing their freak show in the muck and mire. The sound of crickets came from everywhere, and yet they couldn't be seen at all. Fearing monsoon flies and moths, people had put out their kerosene lanterns. Right above Basharat's head, a curlew cried as it cut across the face of the moon. The wind from the beating wings seemed to ruffle his hair. No, this was all a terrifying dream. Then just as he rounded a bend, he walked into the smoke of burning incense, and his eyes were dazzled. 'My God, is this real, or am I dreaming?' he thought.

Outside Maulana Karamat Hussain's shack, a kerosene lantern was burning. A handful of people were standing there offering their condolences. And outside the hut, there was his white horse standing on a brick plinth!

Maulana's polio-stricken son was feeding him a piece of nan that a neighbour had sent to the mourners.

The Car, the Man from Kabul, and the Lampless Aladdin

1.

Obsessed with Horses

Allama Iqbal has expressed his sympathy for those poets, artists, and fiction-writers who are obsessed with women. But my wise friend, the venerable Basharat Farooqi, is counted among those unfortunate souls whose spotless youths were like poetry that is both free of errors and pleasure! Basharat's tragedy was much worse than that of the poets, artists, and fiction-writers. That's because the poor guy was always obsessed with something, just never women. In that period that has been inaptly called his 'crazy youth,' he was obsessed with, in order, mullahs, mentors, Master Fakhir Hussain, examiners, Maulvi Muzaffar, Dagh Dehlvi, Saigal, and his revered father-in-law. By and by, he lost interest in these people, and so he became obsessed with horses—the story of which I've just presented in 'A Schoolteacher's

The Man from Kabul: In almost every big city before the partition of the subcontinent, you could find Afghanis who gave loans on interest. They usually set interest at more than 100% and their ways of collecting were even more despotic. The people who took loans from them were usually the poor and or working class: once you took the loan, you would be paying off its interest until your dying day; that is, until your dying day, the principal of the loan and the Man from Kabul would be standing over you. In Bengal and other regions as well, these Afghanis were known as the men from Kabul. Tagore wrote a very beautiful story by this title that has nothing to do with my problematic story.

Dream.' That godforsaken thing ruined his sleep, his peace of mind, and his household budget. He had become so sick of daily tickets and bribes that he often said that if he were given the choice of being a horse, a horse's owner, or a cart-driver, he would say without the least hesitation that he wanted to be the SPCA inspector who gave tickets to all three.

Like those who demonstrate hindsight after committing a serious blunder, in those days he spoke a lot about choices. But where was the choice? Mahatma Buddha said unequivocally that if he had been given a choice, then he would have refused to be born. But I can say with confidence that if a horse were given the choice, he would like to be reborn a horse and not as Mahatma Buddha because a horse would never stoop to doing what Gautama Buddha did to Yashodhara. I mean, he would never leave his sleeping wife for some desolate wilderness, he would never run off with some jockey. A horse is never ashamed of being a horse. The poor soul will never complain about heaven's unfairness. He will never complain about his chivalrous rider, or about the infidelity of promiscuous mares. It's only people who are always ashamed of and complain about their humanity; it's only them who are wallowing in the thought that

'Being' drowned me—if I didn't exist, then so what?

After having bought a horse and cart, and then after having gotten rid of both, Basharat experienced two apparently contradictory changes. First, he started hating horses and everything associated with them, no matter how remote the connection. One single, crippled horse had caused him so much grief—all elephants combined must not have wrecked so much havoc on King Porus! Second, he could no longer live without a ride. Once someone has gotten used to transportation, he starts to feel contempt for putting his legs to their natural use, and he becomes too weak to do so as well. His lumber business had expanded a lot, which sometimes he attributed to his own hard work and sometimes to the intervention of his father's shoes, whereas his father pointed to the blessings received from the auspicious horse. In any case, what is worth noting is that the inspiration for his advancement never rose above the knees: it was either his father's shoes or the horse's hooves. But no one, not even himself, gave credit to his intelligence and foresight. As his business grew, he had to go around town more. So he needed a ride that much more. Back in those days, business didn't work through bribes; you had to suffer a lot more disgrace and humiliation to get a deal done. The problem with honest public servants in our society is that they don't consider their jobs safe until they've endlessly harassed everyone with their needless strictness, nitpicking, stubbornness, and peevishness. A businessman works easily with corrupt public servants, but he feels scared of honest ones. So what ended up happening was that he had to go five times to the various companies before they would put in an order, and he had to go ten times to collect payments. When the companies cried poverty, he tacked on the expenses of the round-trips and the extra work. For their part, the companies declared the new prices highway robbery and offered instead 10 percent less. So it ended up being even-steven. The only difference was that both parties started thinking of the other as greedy, crafty, and bent on theft. This happens to be the fundamental principle of an alert and successful businessman.

Now he couldn't survive without some mode of transport. But he couldn't figure out which kind would be best. Taxis weren't yet popular. Back then, they were used only on very special occasions, like taking someone who has just had a heart attack to the hospital, kidnapping, robbery, or giving a lift to a police officer. And in the case of the heart-attack patient, it was used only to confirm that the person was not yet dead! That was because even back then Jinnah

Hospital and Civil Hospital admitted only those patients who, after having already undergone treatment in one of the hospital's doctors' private clinics, found their conditions deteriorate so much that, upon this doctor's recommendation, they gained admittance just to ease their way into the sweet hereafter. I have no objections to dying in a hospital. Actually, there's no inappropriate place to die. It's just that a private clinic or hospital is best because then there will be no blood-letting among the deceased's survivors, seeing as how all the person's property, possessions, and savings will fall into the doctor's hands! Alas! In the time of Shah Jahan, there were no private hospitals. If he had been admitted into a private hospital, then he would have been spared his long imprisonment at Agra Fort, and so saved himself from living out such a miserable life. And then his four sons wouldn't have played Hide-and-Seek all over India as they sought the throne (and sought to behead one another) because the root of the conflict—the throne and its treasury—would have been peacefully transferred to its legitimate heirs, meaning, the doctors.

A Wind Blew from the West

In his collection rounds, Basharat took a cycle rickshaw several times. But it unsettled him. The rickshaw cyclist would have to carry a load double his own weight, and Basharat suffered under an even greater weight—his conscience was killing him. In my opinion, men should be allowed to carry other men in only two circumstances. One, when one of them is already dead. Two, when one is an Urdu critic, for whom carrying dead people is not only a part of the job, but also his livelihood, and the reason for his fame. Twice during bus-strikes, he had to ride a bicycle. He realized that, in Karachi, due to the wind that blows in your face for all twelve months of the year, bicyclists and politicians can't advance even ten steps. Sometimes he felt as though the entire city was stuck in a whirlwind's eye. Call it the malice of the western wind blowing off the ocean, or call it the bad luck of Karachi's people, but if you set out in politics or on a bike, whichever direction you go, you'll find a headwind. Both are like trying to fly a kite in a storm.

Suicide Is Beyond the Reach of the Poor

Once or twice it occurred to Basharat that it would be much better to buy a motorcycle than to suffer the harum-scarum push-em-pull-em of buses. The motorcycle rickshaw was out of the question; committing suicide this way was not yet in vogue. Back in those days, an ordinary person had to go through a lot in order to commit suicide. Houses were so tightly packed that in one room you would have ten people crammed together so closely that each one could hear the next one's stomach growling. In such a situation, where could you find enough privacy to string up a noose to hang yourself in peace and quiet? Moreover, each room had only one beam, from which a ceiling fan was hung, and the residents of each hot room would have refused to let anything else be hung from it. As for pistols and guns, you had to get a license, and only the rich, Vaderas, and government officials could get those. So, a man wanting to commit suicide would have to lay himself down on the railroad tracks for an entire day since trains were often twenty hours late. Then, despairing of not dying, the poor soul would get up, dust off his clothes, and walk off.

To Basharat, the biggest problem with motorcycles was that wherever they were on the street, they seemed to be in the wrong place. After conducting research and collecting data about traffic accidents, I've come to the same conclusion: on our streets, pedestrians and motorcyclists find their normal habitat underneath trucks and minibuses! The second problem is that I've not yet met any man who

149

has ridden a motorcycle in Karachi for five years who hasn't suffered broken bones in an accident. But wait, something just occurred to me. There was one man I met who rode a motorcycle in Karachi for seven years without getting into an accident, but he rode in the circus's Well of Death. The third problem that Basharat saw was that the Karachi Municipal Corporation always keeps in mind two things when it comes to manhole covers. One, they should always remain open because if robbers and their like should see them with their lids down, they would become unduly curious as to what is inside. Two, they should be wide enough so that motorcyclists should fall in without any discomfort. Very easily. Very quickly. And with a passenger seated behind him, as well.

Donkeyography

It's likely that the question has arisen in your mind that, with all this talk about modes of conveyance, why didn't I suggest donkeys and donkey-carts? The first reason is the one that you have already thought of. The second is that after reading Chesterton's excellent poem about donkeys, I stopped laughing at them and considering them ridiculous. I've lived in London for eleven years, and so now I know that the West doesn't consider donkeys and owls as terms of insult. Especially owls, which are considered symbols of wisdom. In the first place, in the West, you won't find someone who truly deserves to be called an owl, and, if someone gets called an owl, they will be happier than a clam. In London Zoo, there must be at least fifteen cages for owls. Each big, Western country has a representative there. Each cage is as large as those we have for lions. And each owl is as big as each of our asses. In comparison to them, our owls look like real dunces. England's largest eyeglass maker, Donald Aitcheson, uses an owl for his company's logo; it's reproduced on their billboards, their letterhead, and their receipts. And, in America, the owl is the logo of a big brokerage firm. This isn't just hearsay, it actually happened to me, that after I started wearing Donald Aitcheson glasses, and after I took the advice of the abovementioned stockbroker and did advance trading on his company's stocks and bonds, I was left looking like both companies' mascots.

The mascot of the Democratic Party has always been the donkey. It's on the party flag. The entire American people were like this donkey in their single-minded opposition to Iran. I mean, they were numb, dumb, and frozen in place. In the West, the donkey does not inspire any satire. In fact, the French philosopher and essayist Montaigne was so impressed with the noble qualities of this animal that he wrote, 'Nowhere on earth can you find an animal more certain, decided, disdainful, contemplative, grave, and serious than a donkey.' We Asians think ill of donkeys because they have some human qualities. That is, they carry loads heavier than their power of endurance and strength will allow; and they are obedient, obliging, and grateful to their master to the same degree that they are beaten.

Don't Be Found Without a Job

By presenting the pros and cons of different types of transportation, I only meant to show that, after much weighing and reweighing, Basharat reached the conclusion that he had to buy a car; that it was more than a business necessity, it was in fact a logical imperative; and that if he didn't get one, not only would his business go belly up, but it would also offend reason, and Aristotle himself in heaven (or wherever he is) would cry out in pain. But the truth of the matter was just the opposite. What he wanted wasn't really a car but a status symbol. When someone takes recourse to philosophy and logic in order to convince others, understand that they themselves are equivocating and that they are searching for a good reason to justify an emotional and rash decision they have already made. Henry VIII severed his country from the Roman Papacy and laid the groundwork for a new religion only because he wanted to divorce one woman and marry another. Mirza says that there's no better reason to create a new religion in our day and age than that.

2.

The Cost of a Widow's Smile

Basharat had been going around looking for a secondhand car for a while when he heard that the big, six-cylinder car of an executive at a British company was on sale. Two months previously, this man had suddenly died, and now his young widow wanted to get rid of it for whatever price. As soon as Basharat saw the widow, he fell for the car. (He hadn't yet seen the car even from a distance.) He had been selling pine packing crates and wood to the company for three years. The Parsi accountant said that he could have the car for 3483 rupees, 10 annas, and 11 paisas. It's possible that readers will find this figure strange, but Basharat didn't. That was because this was the very amount that for quite some time the company had refused to pay Basharat on the excuse that he had supplied inferior quality wood and that, due to this, during the floods in Chiniot and Sialkot, all their goods had been turned into mush. Basharat's argument was that he had sold them wood at twelve annas for each pine crate—he hadn't sold them submarines or Noah's Ark—and so the embarrassed executives were blaming him for what was really an act of God.

The beautiful woman—whose widowhood didn't make Basharat feel sad at all, and whom Basharat couldn't call a 'widow' without feeling sick to his stomach—added one condition to the sale, and that was that in three months when she was to travel back to London on the MS Batory, Basharat should supply free packing crates, along with bananas and a carpenter. Not only did Basharat agree, but he also suggested that he himself could come every day to her house to oversee the packing with his own two hands (and other body parts). Basharat told the chief accountant that the car was so old that they should sell it to him for 2500 rupees. The man accepted on the condition that Basharat lower the amount owed for his bad wood to the same figure. Basharat complained to the woman, 'It's a lot of money. Please tell him to lower it a little.' And, to win over her sympathy, he added, 'I'm a poor man. I have had seven or eight children, one right after the other. And I have thirteen siblings younger than me.'

The woman reacted with surprise, sympathy, and wonderment. She said, 'Oh, dear, dear! I see what you mean. Your parents too were poor but passionate.' Hearing this enraged him. He wanted to shout back, 'Why do you have to drag my father into this?' But he couldn't find an idiomatic way of expressing this in English, and the words that he almost blurted out made him start giggling. Right then, he decided that he would never again exaggerate the numbers of his children and siblings, except when applying for a ration card. The woman explained, 'It's really not that much. My husband's teak coffin cost more.' Caught up in the zeal of salesmanship, Basharat replied, 'Madam, in the future I'll sell you one for half that price!' The woman smiled, and that sealed the deal. I mean, Basharat got the car for 3483 rupees, 10 annas, and 11 paisas.

The incident made such an impression upon him that he decided he would sell things in the future at the lowest possible price. Then, if he had to recover goods in lieu of cash from a deceased debtor's beautiful widow, his losses would be less, and his self-regard would escape intact.

I Didn't Come Here by Myself, I Was Dragged Here!

Basharat was quite proud of having got the car for cheap, but the reality was that he had sold his crates at a loss. But if such optimism, or if a misconception, makes you happy, where's the harm in that? Mirza says in his philosophical way, 'We've seen fifty-two-foot wells that think that if they turn themselves upside down, I mean, if they were stood on their head, then they would be fifty-two-foot minarets.' Anyway, Basharat bought the beige-coloured car. He's a very modest man. So he didn't brag to his friends that he too now had a car. Instead, he asked each one, 'Do you know what the colour beige is?' Each man shook his head. So he said, 'Sir, the British have invented a strange colour. In Urdu, there's no word for it.* I'll show you what it looks like.'

As soon as he bought the car, he became very social. He started going over to people's homes that he didn't even visit on Eid and Bakrid. None of those friends and family members who came over to see the curiosity left without being plied with sweets. A month of congratulations passed. Then one day when he was en route to a friend's to show off the car, it jerked violently in the middle of the road. Then it suffered a bout of whooping cough. Its pulse was so faint that sometimes there was a little whisper and sometimes abso-

---

* It's sad that we're quickly losing track of the old and beautiful names of colours. Tomorrow who will be able to recognize them? Vermillion, nut brown, aloeswood, jujube, cotton, azure, camel, emerald, red onion, scarlet, grass, dark purple, chicory, nacre, pearl, lotus, light green, pale yellow, falsa-berry purple, jamun-fruit mauve, tobacco, golden, watermelon, earthen, ochre, mung dal, mulberry, orange, grape, raisin, dove, deep purple, pistachio, peach, peacock, ebony, ambergris, henna, violet, saffron, pale purple, as well as mystical and vulgar. If we've buried our word-hoards in the earth, then that's one thing. But we've also buried the rainbows that sprang from the womb of our land.

lutely nothing. He thought it was faking it. Then suddenly it recovered. For a second, the headlights went on. The horn wanted to say something, but it was too weak to speak. Then, after sputtering and gasping for a moment, it died right where it was. Steam rose from one end of the radiator, and water started dripping from the other. He had it yoked to a donkey-cart and hauled home. He had a mechanic come, and he showed it to him. As soon as he raised the hood, the mechanic hit himself on the forehead three times with his right hand. Basharat asked, 'Is everything OK?' He said, 'It's too late. It's all shot. It's answered the call of duty for the last time. You should have called me six months ago.' Basharat answered, 'Six months ago? I bought it just a month ago.' The mechanic said, 'Then you should have called when you were buying it. When you're buying a pitcher, you rap on it a couple times to see if it's good. It's a car, after all. If you don't want to spend a lot, I can jimmy-rig something for the time being. Our elders have said that when you get cataracts or arthritis, then pot and massages don't work anymore. Then you get a cane, crutches, or a young wife.' Basharat didn't like at all the man's informality, but, in the end, beggars can't be choosers.

After this, the car was always breaking down. Nothing worked right. Only the rearview mirror worked. The car was often slower than donkey-carts because it was tied to the cart and dragged slowly home.

I didn't come here on my own, I was dragged here.

Before leaving the house, he would make sure to have money for a donkey-cart and the necessary ropes and supplies. This funeral procession that wended its way through the alleys (and which he called 'being towed') was repeated so often that eventually everybody's drawstrings and all the tightening ropes of the house's charpoys were confiscated. And those who slept in the charpoys found themselves swinging around in a loose net all night long. Things got so bad that one night the chain of the goat belonging to Benaras Khan, the night-watchman, was stolen. Mirza protested: 'The chain couldn't hold back a scrawny goat that has given birth three times, so how is it going to control your wayward car?'

3.

Jack of All Trades: The Lampless Aladdin

The problem of who was going to drive the car was solved when Mirza Wahid-uz-Zaman Baig, alias Khalifa, hired himself for this job. But he demanded twice as much money because now he wouldn't get to buy fodder for the horse at the market. When he saw the car, he was very happy; it was a good three hands longer than the horse. More-over, he wouldn't have to bother with curry-combing it every morn-ing and night. He was a barber by birth, but he considered himself a jack—no, a master—of all trades. There wasn't any job that he hadn't already done and already messed up at. He used to say that when he was on the Burma Front defeating the Japanese, then whatever time he had off from driving the Japanese into the ground—and that was very little—he did some driving for the army. Not one passenger ever complained about his driving. And there were no fatalities— not even in the worst accidents. That was because he drove around the dead British soldiers. From his boastful stories, it was clear that

The Lampless Aladdin: Basharat's old and permanently sick father couldn't re-member names. So he called all his servants 'Aladdin.' This is Aladdin, the Ninth, whose extended introduction I've given already in 'A Schoolteacher's Dream.' He thought of himself as a jack of all trades. But he ruined everything he put his hands on. He often said, 'I have magic in my hands. If I touch gold, it becomes brass.' Mirza sarcastically called him the Lampless Aladdin.

he had put his life on the line to transport the regiment's corpses to their shallow graves and to perform his duties as barber for those not yet dead. And that for his bravery, he had received a bronze medal that a Sikh man, baring his kirpan dagger, stole from him during the commotion of 1947.

There's no real need to puncture the balloons of such egotism, but I can vouch for the fact that it was only when he learned that Basharat was going to buy a car that he got Gul Badshah Khan, the truck driver, to teach him how to drive a car. But that was like serving an apprenticeship under a blacksmith before becoming a goldsmith. At the time, an Anglo-Indian sergeant conducted the driving test; Khalifa had been cutting his entire family's hair for the last six years. This is Khalifa's narration of the events: 'The sergeant conducted the test in the big open field near the Jinnah Court. But you couldn't call it a test, it was just a formality. The sergeant said, "OK, caliph, make a figure eight, in English, with the car. Do it in front of me. I'll stand here with this red flag. Don't cross beyond this line. And do it in reverse." Hearing this, I got really nervous. I'd never learned to drive in reverse. Once I had asked Gul Badshah Khan to teach me to drive in reverse. But he answered, "My teacher never taught me. And I've never had the need for it. My teacher Chinar Gul Khan told me that lions, airplanes, bullets, trucks, and Pathans can't do backwards."

'I cursed out the sergeant under my breath, "You ape, if I could make a figure 8, then I'd hardly have to shave bears like you. I'd be the personal masseur of Ghulam Muhammad, the Governor General." I've done so many things in my life for money. I've even been the gardener at GG House. I haven't grown mustard in the palm of my hand, but in Karanchi, what's it called, oh, yes, I've grown tulips. But no one among the rich looks for long at the flowers planted in their yards. Only the gardener. He plants the flowers, and he alone enjoys them. Hidayatullah, the waiter, told me that every limb of the

GG Sahib was paralysed. Even his tongue. But he still manages to slander everyone who comes by. But he's a real man. He never wastes time cursing out inferiors. As he grows weaker, his curses grow worse. Now only his butler, after putting his ear next to his mouth, listens to him. He translates his Punjabi curses into Delhi Urdu and then relays them to Qurratullah Shabab. Then Shabab translates them quickly into English and tells them to GG Sahib's American secretary, Miss Ruth Moral. Then this firecracker strides sexily up to the assembled foreigners, ministers, and diplomats and tells them that the GG Sahib is very happy to meet them. Many times I've wanted to set him straight with a good massage. In a couple minutes I could wring him out so good that he would start springing around like a deer. But I never say anything because if he should happen to die, and he's about to, they'll send me to jail and my oil bottle off to get inspected.

'So, dear sir, the sergeant drew a figure eight in the dirt with his boot. My God! I was scared for nothing. I figured out that a figure eight in English is only what grooms call breaking a horse. To break a wild horse, and to drain all the lust out of him, they spin him around very quickly in a couple circles. This was what the driving test's purpose was! So I let it rip. Instead of a figure eight, I slammed it into reverse and started doing a tangled-drawstring sort of thing. Then I heard the sergeant yelling from behind, "Stop! Stop! You idiot!" To save himself, he had jumped onto the car's bumper while still holding his red flag. He had barely escaped getting knotted up in the drawstring, I mean, getting run over. I said, "Sir, should I come again?" But he didn't think it right for me to come for another test. I got my license the next day.

'Thanks to you, I'm a master of all trades. What haven't I done? I've even performed operations. But one went south, so I gave that up. What happened was my friend Allan fell head over heels in love with his cousin. But she wouldn't agree to marry him—no matter what he tried. Who knows why Allan got it into his mind that the reason she wouldn't marry him was the mole on his left thigh. So I cut it off. But it got infected. Now he has a limp. From that day on, I stopped doing surgeries. In the end, I married that girl. I've a mole on my right thigh.'

To Hell with It, and Marconi's Grave

The car was suffering from many diseases—both those internal and external, both those secret and obvious. Once one part was fixed, another gave out. The car burned as much Mobil oil as it did gas, and Basharat's blood burned twice as hot. One day the clutch burned out, and the next, the dynamo went kaput. He switched out the gearbox, but then it felt like someone was banging on the car with a spade from underneath the seats. Khalifa offered this diagnosis: 'Sir, now, the universal's acting up.' Then the brakes started to fail. The mechanic said, 'This model's very old. They don't make parts for it anymore. If you want me to, I'll fix the brakes. But then you'll either have to have the brakes pressed down all the time or never touch them again. Tell me what you'd like to do.' Two weeks later, Khalifa informed him that the shock observers weren't working. He called shock absorbers by that name. And the truth was that they no longer absorbed any shock. They were like worn-out old-timers who sit in some half-dark corner or lie in some half-dark niche and can only observe. They watch helplessly as their progeny screws up; this is the phase of life of true wisdom and understanding. When a man sees absurd acts being committed, and yet this doesn't distress him or make him mad (and he doesn't say to hell with it all), there can only be two reasons for this. I'll tell you the second reason first: he has become so wise that he's now tolerant and forgiving. And the first reason is that the stupidity is his own.

Once, when they were coming back from Zarif Jabalpuri's house, right as they passed by the British cemetery, and as he was laying on the horn, suddenly it started to quaver strangely. It sounded like ankle-bells jingling. Then everything went dark; the headlights had gone out. Khalifa said, 'Dear sir, the battery just died.' This shocked Basharat because every day as soon as he got to the lumber store he took the battery out of the car and hooked it up to his power-saw so that it would get charged for eight hours. Then, at night, as soon as he got home, he would take the battery out and hook it up to his radio.* Then, at midnight or one in the morning, when the radio shows stopped, he would unhook the battery and put it back in the car so that Khalifa wouldn't gripe about it in the morning. So the battery worked three shifts of eight hours and was hooked up to three separate things. No wonder it gave out. It was completely confused. I saw for myself that instead of broadcasting radio shows the machine occasionally growled like a power-saw, and yet he thought these were great ragas and swayed and dipped to their melodies. In the same way, the car's engine started broadcasting inclement weather updates. It was a strange state of affairs. In the dead of the night when the family members heard strange sounds start up, they didn't know if they were coming from the radio, the car, or whether a qawwal singer had fallen into the power-saw. But the inability of his family members to figure things out was excusable because the origin of the sounds was Basharat's throat! (He was snoring!) He said that his throat was permanently sore because of Karachi radio. The other problem was that a number of neighbours hung around until the end of the programming to listen to the shows. Now Basharat really hated this dratted thing. It was probably in such a black mood that English poet Philip Larkin said that a public toilet should be constructed on top of Marconi's grave.†

---

* In those days, you had to run a radio with a car battery and not the batteries you put in a flashlight; you had to charge it every day. Where he lived in Bihar Colony, there was still no electricity.
† Marconi: the inventor of the radio.

Four Wheels with a Crazy and Parochial Temperament

A little while later, when it got really hot, the four wheels turned crazy and parochial. I mean, each wheel wanted to go in a different direction, and they stopped obeying the steering wheel. Not only that, but on many occasions, the steering wheel would actually start to revolve based upon the wheels' whims. Basharat asked Khalifa, 'What's going on?' Khalifa replied, 'Sir, it's called wobbling.' Basharat sighed deeply: once you know the name of the illness, you rest easier. A little while later, he smiled as he thought that for a car it was called wobbling, for a swan it's called waddling, for a cobra it's called wriggling, and for a woman it's called wiggling.

Was the shore moving or the boat?
Wow—I just had a great idea ...

This time he too went along to the auto-body shop. The mechanic said that the muffler was just about to fall off because it was so rusty. Mirza says, 'There's so much humidity in the air in Karachi and so much love in the people's hearts that if you stand with your eyes half closed and palms extended for just five minutes, you'll get a handful of water and a handful of coins. Then, if you stand there for just one more minute, the money will disappear. Here, hair, mufflers, and libido disappear before their time. Lahore is better because at least there mufflers don't fall off.' The mechanic advised, 'When it's time to get a new horn next month, then change your muffler as well. Right now it's working great as a horn!' Then Basharat got upset and asked whether there wasn't any part that was working. The mechanic fell silent for a moment and then replied that the odometer was working at double speed! Actually, instead of referring to the car's performance it was best to say it's non-performance because it was operating entirely in accordance with Murphy's Law, which says that what can go wrong will go wrong. In this condition, a government can run, but not a car.

Camel Anthem

Despite the constant repairing, the brakes still weren't right. But he didn't feel their lack because he never got to use them: the car always gave out a mile before he reached his destination. Basharat started to learn how to drive; he used electricity poles for brakes. Over this, he got into some fights with some dogs. But now some of these dogs were using his shiny hubcaps as poles. As they peed on the hubcaps, they kept turning around to look at their reflections. Basharat noticed that the car had become even more oversensitive and touchy. Now it pulled up short if someone crossing the street happened to curse at it, provided the curse was in English. The car had passed from elegance, to nimble-footedness, to intoxication, to slowness, to being permanently stationary; now it was passing through the stage of total insubordination. Its gait now resembled that of Rudyard Kipling's laggard camels that, in their marching song, moan,

> Can't! Don't! Shan't! Won't!

Without a doubt, this true-to-life song should become the national anthem of those Third World countries that absolutely refuse to progress.

Dialogue with 'A Stupid Cow'

For three months or so, Basharat invested all his time, hard work, earnings, prayers, and curses in this worthless car. His wounds from the wicked horse (Balban) had still not fully healed. Ustad Qamar Jalalvi says,

> I still wasn't on firm ground after my last slip-up when this new slip-up tripped me up.

The car had a mind of its own. When you pressed on its gas pedal, it stubbornly refused to move; when you pressed on the brake, it playfully drove on. I mean, it wouldn't budge at intersections and when the traffic cops motioned it forward, but it inched forward when any passer-by walked in front of its bumper. The traffic was held hostage by its stops and starts, which gives you something opposite of Faiz's line:

When we walked, we were a huge mountain; when we stopped,
we died.

Basharat gave up and took the car back to the white lady and pleaded with her to take back the car and return him the money, less 500 rupees. She refused. He pleaded fake poverty, and she cited her widowhood. Since justice was now out of the question, each tried to prove themselves the more pitiable and more helpless than the other. Both were in dire straits. Both were aggrieved. Both, afflicted. But each remained cold-hearted to the other. Basharat tried to induce a weepy sound in his voice, and he kept wiping at his nose with his handkerchief. In response to this, the woman actually cried. Basharat opened and closed his eyes rapidly in order to induce tearing, but this only made him feel like laughing. Now he imagined a couple extremely painful but completely fake scenes in order to try to get himself to weep. (For example, scenes of his house and shop falling into foreclosure and being auctioned off; and scenes of his untimely death in a traffic accident, and how his wife, as soon as she heard the news, would immediately start wearing a coarse white scarf and dash all her bangles onto the floor—her crying making her eyes puffy.) But neither did his heart melt, nor his eyes well up with tears. For the first time in his life, he grew extremely upset that he was Sunni. But suddenly he remembered his tax notice, and he started whimpering. He pleaded, 'I'm telling you the truth. If this car stays in my possession, I'm either going to go crazy or I'm going to die young!'

This turned the tide. Tears welled up again in the white lady's eyes, and she spoke, 'What will happen to your children? You don't even know whether you have seven or eight. Actually, my husband's heart attack was because of this damn car. He died in it. He collapsed right on top of its steering wheel.'

Hearing this, Basharat inadvertently blurted out that he ought to have put up with the horse. Upon this, the chaste woman enquired with great interest and impatience, 'You mean a real horse? My first husband died when he fell off a horse. He was playing polo. The horse had a heart attack and fell on top of him. He used to call me very affectionately a "stupid cow."' Now tears were really flowing from her Anglo-Saxon blue-grey eyes.

Basharat was a tenderhearted man. Seeing a young woman in such a sad state, he really wanted to wipe away her tears with his silk handkerchief and end her widowhood right then and there. It would be an understatement to say that he had a soft spot in his heart for beautiful women because each and every spot of his desolate heart was reserved for them.

In waiting for his lover, he never sleeps

… Friends Have Turned into Preachers

Failing at something is never as bad as having to listen to all the unwanted advice from people who don't know the ABCs of it. A wise man once said that the best thing about success is that then no one dares give you any advice. It's not my place to propound on things, big or small, and I can't tell you if I've been successful or not; but I can offer this little tidbit that if we were held together with screws and nuts, then all our friends, family, and well-wishers would drop their work and rush toward us with screwdrivers and wrenches. One would try to untwist our round nuts with a square-headed wrench. Another would try to hammer a screw into our oil valve. A third would try to tighten all our screws day in and day out. Then they would all get together and remove all our screws and nuts. And that just to see if, by the force of their will, they could get us to move around and eat and drink, or not. Both sides would pass their days in this worthless conundrum. Something like this happened to Basharat. Each time the car broke down, he was flooded with advice that didn't address the car's flaws but rather his own, and none of it was what you might call brilliant. On the other hand, passers-by that had no cars offered thanks to God that they were among the lucky ones to escape having them.

Out of all these advisors, only Haji Abdur Rahman Ali Muhammad of Bantua had anything worthwhile to say: 'If you ever have to go to a saint's shrine, an income tax office, or a doctor's private clinic, then park the car a mile away. A week before going, stop cleaning your teeth after you chew paan. Leave the spittle lines on the corners of your mouth. Don't change clothes for four days, and don't shave. If you're a factory owner, then put a look on your face like those of cart-vendors. Otherwise the bastards will flay you, sprinkle salt and chilli pepper over your naked flesh, and send you to Hawa Bandar. You'll run around for the rest of your life screaming, "Brother! I tell you, if you ever go to see an income tax officer, to the police, to your young wife, or to see a guru, never go empty-handed and double marching like a soldier. Always take some fruit or money or something. Otherwise the bastards will flay you and stuff your effigy with leftover copies of the newspaper *Dawn*. After seeing a green, if someone's eyes don't shine with 200 candlepower, he must be colourblind or a saint. Or the head of the State Bank who signs the notes himself."'

4.

Dialogue Condemning the Neem Tree

Sometimes while talking freely about the car's infirmities, Khalifa would start recounting his own misdeeds as though he were speaking about the miracles of saints. Only someone familiar with the inner workings of the human mind could tell if he was telling the truth, or if he was running an imaginary horse through the fields of longing. One day he told Fakir Muhammad, the cook, 'Today in front of the Saeed House, our horse went totally mad. Its every part started chanting, "I am the truth, I am the truth." At first the engine overheated. Then the radiator, whose leak I'd stopped up with a soap cake, exploded. Then one of the rear tires started leaking. To pump up the tire, I got out a pump that was the same age as the car. And do you know what happened? I found out that the pump itself was leaking! The fan belt got overheated and snapped too. Since she had to drive around British folks, she too got a little crazy. Hakim Fahim-ud-din from Agra used to say that if the woman is crazy, the man should be hot-tempered. Man, "hot-tempered" reminds me of something. Abdur Rahim, the dandy—you know him, he used to be the gatekeeper at the Naz Cinema—got syphilis. The bastard got his just deserts. He said that his blood ran hot from watching English films, eating gazak snacks, and listening to Noor Jahan's songs. Back in those days, I don't know if it was the same for you or not, but if someone picked up herpes or syphilis* from some contact sport or another, he had to wear a high-water lungi and carry around a neem twig. When I was a boy, I saw many of the upper echelon carrying around these green flags in their

---

* Herpes and syphilis, or the gifts of foreigners. Some people say that along with the gifts of potatoes, tobacco, trains, horseracing, European flowers, Shakespeare, gin and tonics, tea, cricket, and countless others, the British brought with them these STD 'gifts.' Only God knows if this is true or not.

neighbourhoods. Everyone thought that a neem twig would ward off contagious diseases. But I think they used this excuse just to show off their achievement. To clean their minds and bodies, they had to drink such a bitter concoction that as soon as they swallowed it their eyes rolled back in their heads. Back then there was punishment hidden in the cure. Maulvi Yaqub Ali Naqshbandi used to say that that was the reason they called Unani treatment real wizardry.

'Man, that fucking neem tree was such a pain in the ass. If you were poor and you happened to get this rich man's disease—or even if you just had ordinary blisters or warts—then the country doctors would treat you only with neem. All medicine was neem-based. They told you to bathe with neem soap. They prescribed a paste made from neem fruit and bark. They applied neem ointment. They burnt dried neem twigs and leaves and blew the smoke over you. If your young blood was running too hot, they made you drink something made of neem shoots and flowers. They would make you lick a sticky paste made of neem sap. They would force you to ingest a powder made from neem fruit seeds. They would make you brush your teeth with a neem twig before each meal so that all food tasted like neem. Under the excuse of draining the bad blood from your body, they would re- peatedly have leeches drink off several kilos of your blood—so much so that you ended up looking like a withered, old mango, and, forget acts of debauchery, if you so much as performed two prostrations in prayer, your knees would start making creaking sounds. Water boiled with neem leaves would be poured over open sores to kill the germs. And if, thanks to the doctor, the patient should die before the germs, then neem leaves would be boiled in a pot and the water used to wash the corpse, which would then be placed beneath a neem tree. They would throw three buckets of water over the fresh grave and stick in a neem twig at the grave's head. They would go to the home of the deceased man, take out his widow's gold nose ring, and replace it with a neem twig from the very tree from whose branches she had swung during the rainy season. Then they would make her wear a white scarf, they would put a betel-nut cutter in one hand and a long whip-like twig from a neem tree in the other so that she would be able to fight away the crows, and then they would have her go sit in a neem tree's shade.

'When I immigrated to Pakistan, I came across the Wagah Border with nothing but the clothes on my back and a razor—nothing more, I swear. What I have now is due to God's good graces and to Pakistan. The day after crossing the border, I went with my friend Muhammad Hussain to Shalimar Gardens. He told me there were no neem trees in Pakistan. I swear to God—I fell in love with Pakistan right then! Right there, next to the Mughal fountain, I prostrated in thanks before God.'

Khalifa's Record of Sin

Khalifa's problem was that once he got started, he couldn't find a way to stop. He had grown old, but, in listening to his boasting, you would think that old age had turned his fantasies and carnal desires into absolute fact. And there was nothing unusual about this. There's an old saying that in old age a person's carnal powers relocate to the tongue. Whether or not his exaggerated stories had some basis in fact, his manner of storytelling was true and sincere. The simpleminded folks who listened to his tales were so hypnotized that they didn't think about whether his stories were true or not. They just wanted him to go on. So here is more of Khalifa's story, unedited. I've just given it the new title listed above.

'So Gulabiya Natni was a real wheel.* Even if you would just glance

---

* Natni: the lowest class of prostitute, also called a 'takhiyai' because her customers couldn't pay more than a taka [old coin worth 1/32 of a rupee]—as though the real reason for their ridicule and disgrace wasn't their profession but their low wages!

　Wheel: a type of small firework that moves very spastically in circles across the ground.

her way, she would hand you a neem twig. Man, I can't lie to you. On Doomsday, I'll have to show my face to my father, in addition to God. Why should I hide anything from you? I'm no saint. I'm a man of the flesh. Like Maulvi Hashmatullah says, people are puppets of mistakes and women. My friend, the fact is that I had to carry a neem twig too. I wasn't yet a grown man. I was seventeen when the tragedy struck. But, believe me, Tamizan was a first-class, respectable woman. She wasn't some whore. She was married. She lived in the neighbourhood. Actually, I became a man in her house. She must have been fifteen, if not twenty, years older than me. But still her body was like a taut drumhead. If the wind just grazed across her, she started to rumble. I used to go to her roof to fly kites. She was used to me being around. Sometimes she would give me gazak snacks, and sometimes she gave me halva that she herself had made. Her husband, who was probably twenty years older—well, at least fifteen—had gone to Faridabad to get an amulet to speed along the birth of a child.' (At this, he started giggling despite himself.) 'I'd already cut four kites when I reeled it in, put it under my arm, and went downstairs. The damsel was taking a bath behind the see-through screen of a charpoy stood on its side. The wonderful scene is still fresh in my eyes. When she saw me, she stood up, naked. Man, what should I say? Alarm bells went off inside me. In a second, I turned her inside out like a pair of socks. The thing about gazak is that it makes your blood run fast and hot.

'When news got out, my father, may God have mercy on his soul, was beside himself with anger. He menaced me with his shoe. He said, "You're no son of mine! Get out of here, or else I'll cut your throat." But there wasn't a sword in the house; there wasn't even a dull kitchen knife with which he could have carried out his threat. And, anyway, I was a foot taller than him! But I was in such awe of him that I was trembling badly in my colourful lungi. My mom was standing in between us, protecting me. She grabbed his hand. I remember everything about it. In the commotion, she'd broken her bangles, and her wrists were bloody. She worked so hard, day and night. For as far back as I can remember, her face had always been wrinkled. Tears were running over her wrinkles. Even today I feel like her tears are staining my cheek. She said, "I swear to God, they're slandering my baby angel." I tried to explain to my father, "I got it from eating khichri made from buckwheat and from mangos picked raw. Please listen to me. I got this wretched disease from riding bareback on a black mare. Eating some chia seeds* will get rid of it." But he would never have believed me. He said, "Chia seeds, my ass! You think this is funny? You've ruined the honour of barbers. You've disgraced your ancestors." No one believed me but my mom. My younger brothers started fighting with me every day because my mom had stopped serving them—and my father—buckwheat khichri and mangos picked raw. Sometimes I think that if God loves his creatures as much as my illiterate mom loved me, then everything will be all right. On the Day of Judgement, all my sins will be forgiven and mullahs won't get hot from eating khichri and mangos. I hope to God this proves true!

'Well, whatever. The thing was that I had no idea that my uncle was already well acquainted with Tamizan. I swear on my youth! If I'd had the slightest doubt, I'd have kept my feelings to myself, and let him have his jollies. Man, in my youth, my pulse was so strong it beat like a hammer. I was handsome too. And strong. If I grabbed a girl's wrist, she wouldn't want me to let go. Anyway, those were the days. I was saying that the cure was worse than the disease. To cool me down, I had to drink heaping bowls of thandai sherbet, coriander juice, and goat's thorn potions three times a day. And twice a day I had to eat bland bread with salt-less, chilli-less kothmir chutney. In those days, everyone called me Brother Kothmir. My father was terribly upset by

* In the summer, people mix chia seeds with faloodah.

the whole ordeal. He was sceptical to begin with. Now whenever he heard about a child being born without a father anywhere in town, he looked at me with fire in his eyes. Whenever he saw a girl walking quickly through the neighbourhood, he assumed I was stalking her. His health got worse fast. His enemies spread the rumour that Tamizan had turned his beard grey overnight. He agreed. In order to humiliate me, he made me wear a beet-red lungi that was brighter than a railway guard's flag, and, instead of a neem twig, he made me carry around a full branch, which was bigger than me. On Shankarat, I cut eight kites with it. In childhood, you can really feel like a king. In those days, if someone had given me King Solomon's throne, a hoopoe, and the Queen of Sheba, I wouldn't have been as happy as I was from cutting a single kite. Man, I wish I could have some roasted makhana [fox nuts]. It's been ages. I don't remember what they taste like. My mom made them so good. Man, I made my mom so upset.'

Thinking of his mother made tears well up in his eyes.

Massacre of His Ancestors

Regardless of his present duties, Khalifa was still thinking about horses:

> *The smell of the black horse still wafts from his pillow.**

One day he said to Maulana Karamat Hussain, 'Maulana, all I know is that if you don't discipline kids and conveyances, you'll never, ever

---

* This line really isn't about horses but about the beloved. I took the liberty of changing 'fragrant tresses' to 'black horse.' This proves my ignorance about ghazals, beloveds, and poetic metre. I've read a thousand couplets like this, that, if no one tells me whom they are about, my mind will automatically go to horses and not women.

get them under control. That was the reason why Nadir Shah jumped from his elephant's howdah and, in a rage, started to massacre others. He massacred all my ancestors like he was cutting carrots and radishes in the field. He even speared the suckling babes and threw them to the side. He didn't leave even one man standing.' Maulana looked at him over the edge of his glasses, which were set on the end of his nose. Then he said, 'Khalifa, there hasn't been a single conflict in the last five hundred years in which you haven't killed off your ancestors one by one. If your seed was massacred, if your ancestors were all killed one by one, how is it that you're alive today?' He said, 'Through the blessings of pious souls like you!'

Out of all his ancestors, he took the most pride in his paternal grandfather about whom he knew only one thing: that when he was eighty-five, he could still thread a needle. Khalifa was so impressed, no, overawed, with this fact that he didn't worry himself about what his grandfather did with the needle after threading it.

5.

The Car's New Look

One day near the T-intersection at Robson Road, the car broke down near *Afkar* magazine's office. He yoked it to a donkey-cart and had it taken to Lawrence Road. This time the mechanic had pity upon him. He said, 'You're a good man. When are you going to stop ruining yourself? Trying to do things on the cheap kills a businessman, and a bad ride like this kills the passenger. I've heard of a car running over someone, but this piece of shit is killing the person sitting inside it! Listen to me. Cut off its body, and put a truck's frame onto its chassis. Use it to take lumber here and there. My brother-in-law just opened an auto-body shop. He'll do it for half price. I'll rebore your engine for 200 rupees. I charge 675 to others. Once the car gets its new look, you won't recognize it.'

And he was right. Afterwards, no one could figure out just what it was. A transport for taking accused prisoners to court? A dog-catcher's wagon? The bloody truck ferrying fresh carcasses from the slaughterhouse? It didn't resemble anything he had ever seen, not even remotely. The mechanic assured him that if he stared at it from dawn to dusk, then after three months he would get used to it. This got Mirza to say, 'Well, aren't you brilliant—this is hardly his wife!' He had the words on the back of his former car (and present truck) painted over, 'Keep going, old truck, God may see you home yet.' He also didn't like the next line, 'Pappu Yar, don't bother me.' Chaudhuri Karam Deen, the painter, said, 'Sir, if you don't like these names, then please pick some you like, and I'll paint them in.' He also had the following notorious couplet wiped out:

An adversary wishes a million harms, but what happens?
God's will alone is what happens.

After these emendations and excisions, whatever was left might have been God's will, but Basharat sure didn't approve of it.

The car's body was ungainly. But after the engine was rebored, all his worries vanished. Now it had the sort of unnecessary and ill-timed agility, as well as the showy healthiness, which those about to retire display when they decide to stay on for a little longer, or that some old people show after they get remarried: they jog while going to the bathroom; they bound up stairs two at a time. From the very first day, he put this truck-like car, or car-like truck, into lumber-delivery service, which lasted from nine in the morning to six in the evening. He multiplied that day's haul, meaning 45 rupees (which is like 450 rupees today), by thirty days; then he multiplied the day's haul by 365 days, and so he got 16,425 rupees. He told himself, 'And when the car itself cost only 3,483 rupees, are you insane? This isn't a day's haul, it's a life's haul!' So he started cursing himself for his foolishness—why hadn't he switched it to a truck earlier? But there is a time for each and every foolishness. Suddenly the line 'God's will alone is what happens' came to mind, and he couldn't help but smile.

It's Mine Too

Somehow the vehicle kept running for about a month, but the exhilaration he felt whenever he thought about the astronomical figure died out. He had to send it back to the auto-body shop ten times. The mechanic had guaranteed it would work for a month. That said, Basharat had had to pay for the donkey-carts with his own money. The driver of the donkey-cart came every morning to enquire when and where he would be needed that day. Then one day Basharat had had loaded two customers' lumber worth 7,000 rupees, and, at ten in the morning, he sent off Khalifa to make the deliveries. It must have been around two when he came back trembling and shaking. He kept using his hand-towel to wipe his face, and he kept sniffling loudly. He said, 'Boss, I've been robbed. I'm ruined. May God please take me now!' Basharat guessed that his chronically ill wife had died. He consoled him, 'No one can interfere with God's will. Bear with it the best you can … God's will alone …' But Basharat's apprehension subsided when Khalifa recited, '"When I cry, the world laughs. / When I say nothing, the world stabs me." Boss, my heart is crying tears of blood!' That was because if a person is able to use poetry and use idioms while lamenting occasions of great distress and suffering, then he doesn't want your sympathy—he wants you to appreciate his eloquence. When Khalifa stuffed his hand-towel into his mouth and began to cry, yelling reproaches at himself, Basharat suddenly realized that whatever bad had happened hadn't happened to that bastard; it had happened to him! He said, 'OK, what is it? What's my problem now?'

During his fake sobbing, he managed to say, 'It's mine too!' just like in the commercial for Habib Bank where men of every age and province hug the bank in their own way, and then a little, cute kid lisps, 'It's mine too!' Then he told the whole story. The truck was overloaded. Even first gear wouldn't work. He managed to get the truck out of the road on the strength of kids' pushing and his praying. But then some spring busted. In order to lighten the load, he took out half the wood and stacked it very neatly next to the steps leading into a mosque. And then he set out to deliver the rest of the wood to Nazimabad No. 4. But no one was at the construction site. So without dropping off the wood, he went back to the mosque. Once there, he saw that the wood he had left was gone! He said, 'Boss, I've been robbed in broad daylight! I'm ruined!'

They Are Old-Timers; Don't Talk Back to Them

Now Basharat began to regret his foolishness: why had he loaded into a ramshackle car goods worth twice the car's amount? Too bad thieves hadn't made off with the car. Then he would have been free of it. But he thought that it must have been due to Khalifa's old habit. He had probably parked the car somewhere with all the goods still in it, then gone off to shave someone, perform some circumcision, or gone to some wedding to collect congratulations money from a customer just because he had shown up. He had done things like this a thousand times. Suddenly he remembered the Persian saying, 'Mountains will get up and move before you teach an old dog new tricks.' And he remembered that it had been Master Fakhir Hussain who had used this phrase on him. He had been acting up in class, and so Master Fakhir Hussain had called him 'buznah' and then had crucified

175

him with this Persian saying. When calling him 'buznah' had no effect at all, Master Sahib asked what the word meant. He went through the class one by one, asking each boy. No one knew. So he made everyone stand on the benches and said, 'You worthless rascals! You'll be the death of me! "Buznah"—"b"—"u"—"z"—"n"—"ah"—the crying out in sadness "ah"—not the "halva" and "bastard" one—a "buznah" is a monkey—got it?' He thought to himself, 'My, such were the times, and such were the teachers! They explained the meaning of even the most absurd words. Even when they were mad, they abided by the prerogatives of education. They didn't just curse you out, they also told you the curse words' spellings and meanings. Where can you find such cranks today?'

Then Basharat said, 'Yes, I remember something else. Once for Urdu dictation he made us write something like, "Scholars are well respected in our culture." But I made a spelling mistake, and Master Fakhir Hussain bent over laughing for quite a while. Then he grabbed me by the ear and ordered me to write what I had written on the blackboard, "Go show everyone how you've written the plural of scholar." (My spelling mistake had turned the meaning of "scholar" [fuzala] to "shit" [fuzlah].) After I wrote it, he set the end of his five-foot-long pointer on the "ah" at the end of the word. Then he said, "Son, today I won't make you stand on the bench. That's because you, a boy, have summarized the quintessence of scholarship." Sir, it was none other than Master Fakhir Hussain who taught me how to get to the gist of something and how to call "reality" "quintessence."'

6.

It Turned Out to Be My Fault

He went straight to the Bolton Road Police Station to file a report. But a duty officer there told Basharat to go to the station where he lived and file an FIR [First Information Report] there. When he got there, they said, 'Sir, of course you can file an FIR in the neighbourhood where you live, on the condition that you've committed a crime. Go to the station in the neighbourhood where the incident took place, and file your report there.' He went there, and they said, 'The incident happened on the boundary between two precincts. Of course, the mosque is in our precinct, but its steps are in the adjoining precinct.' He went there, and he couldn't find anyone, except a man with a bloody forehead. His right hand had suffered a compound fracture, and his left eye had swollen shut. He said, 'I came to file a 324 report. I've been waiting for two hours. It's absurd. The Civil Hospital says that until the station files an FIR report and gives me a copy, they can't treat me. The wounded man was proudly holding the confiscated weapon—a walking stick with a ferrule that had split open his head. With him was his uncle, who was the secretary to a civil-court lawyer. He was assuring his nephew, 'When he picked up the walking stick and struck you over the head, the criminal took the law into his own hands. He not only broke your head, he broke the law too. If he isn't arrested, then I'm a bastard. He's committed a serious crime, after all. And I've sent many men to jail for absolutely no reason!' He gave Basharat the legal advice that he should go to the police station that had jurisdiction over where the accused lived, that is, where the thief lived; that that was how civil cases went. Basharat got fed up with him. He started asking this man pointed questions, and so he learned that the SHO was attending his daughter's engagement ceremony. Most of the station was there. They would be back in an hour and a half or so. The station's sub-inspector had been playing the role of a crossing guard since the afternoon; he was grouping schoolgirls on either side of the street because the prime minister was taking a tour of town. The head constable was out on business.

About two hours later, the SHO got out of a lawyer's car. The lawyer's client, who looked like a criminal, was carrying the lawyer's briefcase, which was covered in a khaki protective covering. The lawyer was carrying little boxes of sweets from the engagement ceremony, which he distributed to the station's staff. He gave one to Basharat as well. As soon as the SHO arrived, the entire staff came out of the woodwork and scurried around in front of him. They made it seem like they had been busy the whole time. The SHO listened to the outline of Basharat's story and then said, 'Please wait outside. The real "complaintiff" is the driver. We'll have to look into him.' Who knew what sort of grilling they were subjecting Khalifa to, but it took a full hour. When Khalifa came out, he wasn't just long in the face, his entire body looked as though it had been stretched out! The SHO called Basharat in, and his tone had changed completely. He didn't even invite him to sit down. Questions rained down. For a little while, Basharat got the feeling that the SHO thought he was the criminal. But that changed when he started to ask the sort of probing questions that only an income tax officer should ask. For instance, *When you sold the stolen lumber, did you record this in the account book, or did you plan to stuff all the money into your pockets? The salary you give your driver is what you record, or do you record more? You send him out every day without a delivery order form. How is it that you drive the truck without a learner's permit? When you were loading the wood to go to Nazimabad, did you, according to law nineteen hundred something something, stake out the area behind the truck with little red flags? Ah, yes, the mention of Nazimabad reminds me — my house in the PECHS Colony has been built up to the plinth level. How many square feet of wood do you think I need? Make an estimate. It's a 600-metre open corner-plot, facing west. And the radio you have — do you have a license for that? Is it true that on your incorporation papers, you've listed your seventy-five-year-old father, as well as your suckling babe, as partners? In delivering the wood from Lee Market to Nazimabad, what was the necessity of making a detour through Ranchore Line? Is it true that you pray five times and play the harmonium?* (Basharat explained that he prayed, and that his father played the harmonium. Hearing this, the SHO started fiddling with his handcuffs; this went on for quite a while. Then, for the first time, he smiled and turned to his secretary, 'So, did you hear that? It seems justifying the sin is more pleasurable than the sin itself!') *The report states that the wood was left right in front of the mosque's door. Did you mean to make it difficult on mosque-goers? Your driver cuts your entire clan's hair. He makes qorma for you. He circumcised your junior partner, I mean, your suckling prince. You forced him to drive a horse-drawn cart. This man curry-combed your horse and massaged your father. This is an outright violation of labour laws. Is it true that a while ago one of your carpenters got a splinter in his eye, and then after he got his eye bandaged at Spencer Eye Hospital, you sent him home, without any compensation? And why is it you charged twice the amount that this wood is worth? This is quite the situation … This is crazy. I can get wood for half of what you're selling it at. That's the going rate.*

In Violation of Penal Codes and Criminal Law

But Basharat's answers did little to satisfy the SHO, and so he said, 'I'll go look at the crime scene. Tomorrow's Sunday. I won't come to the office. Do you have a ride?' Basharat said 'yes.' And he took him outside.

'But what's this?' the SHO asked, in surprise.

'This is what delivered the wood.'

'But what is it?'

The SHO touched the neatly stacked lumber. He circled the vehicle and eyeballed its length. Then he suddenly got quite mad. Forget the scene of the crime—he grabbed Basharat and took him back inside the station, where he and his snivelling assistant started playing good-cop-bad-cop. *Who gave him permission to turn a passenger car into a truck? Also, you were going down a one-way alley the wrong way! Your insurance lapsed a long time ago. You haven't paid your wheel tax for a year. Just now your driver confessed to the crime of stopping the vehicle by shifting gears because it does not have brakes. Due to this, a couple days ago, in front of the Garden East slums, he ran over a hen. Khalifa had no money to pay them off. They impounded the car for the night and held him hostage, even though he kept yelling that the error hadn't been the car's, the hen had flown right under it. The next day, Khalifa cut the hair of the hen's owner, the man's kids, as well as his relatives and everyone in the vicinity—two dozen people, all told. That was to win his release. Then this man's neighbour came with his five-year-old, stark-naked boy (who was wearing a nice lace cap) and asked him, 'Please, could you circumcise him?' And, after all this heavy labour, when he arrived back at your place at two or so in the afternoon, what kind of welcome did he get but to be accused by you of going around town and barbering when he should be working. And you threatened not to pay him for the lost day. I guess that's an investigation for another day. But, tell me, why does your car spit out as much exhaust as an entire factory? Why does it pull up in the middle of the road? Hey, are you listening?* (He addresses his secretary.) *How many months is it for blocking a public road? Only that? No heavy labour?* (Turning back to Basharat.) *And so, sir, if it's true that it's a truck, then why do you load the whole family into it for evening drives?* (Turning back to his secretary.) *Hey, read him the part of the penal code about overloading.*

So it turned out that there wasn't a single provision within the Pakistani penal code and under criminal law for which he hadn't been caught red-handed. His each and every action was in violation of something or the other. He felt as though his entire life was in violation of the law. Basharat was flabbergasted: what intuition the SHO must have to already know about his law-breaking activities! But then he realized what was going on; he looked at Khalifa with murder in his eyes. As soon as their eyes met, Khalifa pressed his hands together in supplication.

The SHO shot a glance over to a constable, who came forward and handcuffed Khalifa. The head constable put his hand on Basharat's shoulder and led him into another room. He said, 'First there will be a warrant put out for your arrest. Since the vehicle in question is itself illegal, hence the goods within it are subject to confiscation. The secretary will prepare a transfer of property document. The "complaintiff" has himself committed various crimes, and so ...'

Basharat's head started to spin. If you asked him then, he wouldn't have been able to tell you the difference between up and down.

The Lowdown on the Lockup

Spending just four hours in a jail's holding cell will teach a man more about life (and about being human) than forty years at a university. Inside, Basharat grew wise fast, and he was scared. The most surprising thing was the sort of language they used in the station. While he could figure out what 'complaintiff' meant, the secretary was calling one man (who had forced a girl, still a minor, to marry him) a 'marriage-by-forcinicator.' He figured out by listening to the staff talk amongst themselves that they considered there to be two types of people: one, those who have been in jail; and, two, those who haven't been in jail yet but should be. The majority of the country's people were the not-yet-punished, and this was the fundamental reason for all mischief and violence. Whatever they talked about, they liked to use the suffixes 'yaftah' and 'shudah': the guy screaming out from time to time in the 'health spa' (the interrogation room) was either an ex-con [sabiq saza-*yaftah*] or out on bail [muchalke-*shudah*]. The assistant sub-inspector was dealing with two women arrested for public indecency: the one was a married woman [shadi-*shudah*], and the other was done for [*shudah*], meaning, someone of no standing. The head constable had won some awards [inam-*yaftah*]; he read aloud the last will and testament of a deceased man [vafat-*yaftah*]. One report detailed one thug's bad manners [ghair-qabu-*yaftah* chal-chalan]. With regard to one burned-out residential building, there was mention of destroyed things [barbad-*shudah*] and a ruined [tabah-*shudah*] reputation. In the course of one interrogation, the ASI was asking one 'complaintiff,' 'When did you learn of the abovementioned man's demise [vafat-*shudagi*]?' Every action was Persianized. For example, the execution of a summons by notarization; the reason for the deceased's expiration; the damage to all rifles (and their cartridges) of the existing police station due to their atrophication, iron oxidation, and prolongation of time; and the staff's collective stupefaction!

In the station, there were only two types of weapons: sharp-edged ones, and non-sharp-edged ones. About the weapon that had caused welts on the plaintiff's witness's butt and swelling on his head, it was reported in the station's logbook that the doctor had determined that the aforementioned witness had been bludgeoned by a non-sharp-edged weapon in the middle of the marketplace. Meaning, by a shoe! In the 'health spa,' one man was having the truth beaten out of him at ten at night. Basharat learned that those people who, after being beaten with a shoe, confessed to crimes they didn't commit were called 'royal witnesses.' The man was screaming a lot; this showed that he was still stubbornly holding onto his notion of truth. In Punjabi, you call this extracurricular activity of shoes 'chhitrol.' When business at the station slowed a little, three constables again brought in the eyewitness in a rape case, sat him down, and made him recite everything, which he did with the sort of pride that little kids show when reciting nursery rhymes to their parents' friends. Each time, he added new details; he coloured the scene in with new colours of criminal longing ... *It wasn't like that ... I just wanted it to be like that ...*

The three constables were listening attentively, as though he were reciting poetry. From time to time they offered him envious praise, and from time to time they cursed him out admiringly. The next morning, when they were taking the plaintiff's testimony, everyone, including the criminals in the holding cells, was listening with bated breath.

At the station, every incident only 'allegedly' happened. For example, *The accused came out of his alleged place of residence and attacked the plaintiff's witnesses. With his front teeth, he separated two inches off the end of the nose of Miss Naziran's alleged lover, Sher Dil Khan, and allegedly swallowed Exhibit A, meaning, the present nose's missing part. The disaffected witness, Miss Naziran, of unknown parentage, at first refused to sign the BSST in the presence of the ASI. But later, 'without any outside compulsion,' she signed the BSST with her left hand's thumbprint.*

At nine o'clock, an evening newspaper's crime reporter came. His paper's circulation was at a standstill. He said to the ASI, 'Ustad, you haven't given me anything for two weeks. Is this a police station or a paupers' cemetery? In your precinct, all the criminals have either renounced the life of crime or they've been recruited into the police ranks. If this keeps up, then we'll both be out of a job.' The ASI replied, 'My dear sir, sit down, sit down. Today we snared a live one. You don't get a scoop like this but once in a lifetime. He's in the side-room retelling his eyewitness account for the tenth time. Go listen to it. And, hey, in the last four days, you haven't published a single letter to the editor arguing against my transfer. If I'm not here, then who's going to get you the goods? Hey, Basheera! You hear me? Two cups of Sulemani tea. And hurry. Fill it to the rim. And thick with cream, so thick that a pencil should be able to stand up in it. And, Firozuddin, tell that revolutionary in the health spa to pipe down, will you? It's only evening, and the bastard's already moaning about something. I mean, the love has only just begun, and he's crying? He's already hoarse from screaming. Sir, there's nothing more disgraceful than a man crying. The bastard thinks he's Hasan Nasir or something. I gave him four ice-cold beers at five o'clock. He was so happy. After the third one, he started to explain to me—yes, sir, to *me*—the line "go on putting beneath the guillotine your revolutionary heads." He drank the fourth, and then I didn't let him go to the toilet. And so he stood up and lit a revolution in his pants three times. Sir, we're just following orders. He's just about to get transferred to Lahore Fort. They'll be able to get everything out of him. This bastard's tragedy is that he doesn't have anything to admit. So he'll get it even more.'

The Event Participants

Hearing about this, the reporter grinned ear to ear. He was so happy he ordered a cigarette and two sweet paans. Then he got out a peppermint and his notebook. It had been so long since he'd had a meaty story. He decided he would tell his short-story-writer friend, Sultan Khavar, about it; he asked every day for him to find a 'real-life drama.' Even before hearing the details of the rape case, his mind began to sizzle with headlines. He resolved to put his best foot forward in the headline itself ... *A 70-year-old Man Darkens the Face of a 7-year-old Girl* ... He'd written that headline last year; he'd subtracted ten years from the girl's age and added it to the man's age to make the crime appear that much more serious so as to increase the readers' interest.

Mirza Abdul Wadud Baig says that it's too bad that all the Urdu synonyms for such a bland word as 'rape' contain some hint of carnal pleasure; pick any headline at random, any phrase, and there will be some hint of sexual pleasure ... *The Accused Ripped the Hem of Chastity off the Beautiful Young Girl* ... *Under the Cover of Night's Darkness, a 70-year-old Man is Caught Red-handed in a Shameful Act* ... *A 65-year-old Man Played with the Young Virgin All Night Long* ... (As though the real objection was to the man's age, for which he could not be held responsible. In fact, this headline was a mix of ethics and the elements of surprise, curiosity, and jealousy, with ethics being only a quarter of the content.) *The Four Accused Made the Young Damsel the Target of Their Lust ... The Beastly Criminal Robbed the Woman of Her Chastity at Gunpoint; He Wouldn't Let Up till the Cops Showed Up ...*

I've quoted these headlines word for word from various newspapers. Some of the phrases in use—which I can't quote here for obvious reasons—make it seem as though the person writing them had a voyeuristic urge to participate in the incident himself. The result is that while the readers' legal sympathies go out to the poor young girls, their desires are more in line with those of the accused.

I'll always be where my heart is ...

We don't need any more pieces of coal to be brought out of this mine because we've already sullied our hands enough. In short, what I would like to say is that if you scratch even a little bit, you won't find a single word associated with sexual crimes that doesn't have within it a hint of carnal pleasure. Every word sighs, and every phrase smacks its lips. In English literature, you will find the best example of this in the work of the Russian-born Nabokov. His every word is like a balloon that he blows up with his slobbering spit almost up to the point where it explodes from pleasure, before he releases it to his readers.

Why Dogs Bite

For a while, Basharat couldn't believe his eyes. It was Karachi, after all, not some backwater princely state. It seemed like one big joke. But at nine that night, suddenly things seemed serious, indeed. ASI told him, 'You'll have to stay in the holding cell tonight, tomorrow, and tomorrow night. Tomorrow's Sunday. You won't be able to be bailed out until Monday.' He asked, 'Bailed out for what?' The ASI said,

'That's for the courts to decide.' He wasn't even allowed to phone home. He smelled urine coming from the cells at the other end of the station. Khalifa was over there, and from time to time he raised his handcuffed hands toward the heavens and whimpered in such a way that it made it seem like he was laughing. Basharat's anger was useless now. The station secretary finished up his night prayers, folded up his straw prayer mat, and came over to him. He was as withered out as a grasshopper, but, behind his glasses, there was still a sparkle in his eyes. He spoke to Basharat very kindly. He poured lemonade into a glass and gave it to him. Then the two exchanged paan from their own little boxes.

The secretary spoke in a very soft, sincere voice, 'Our boss is a good man. He's nice to nice people, and he's Halaku to scoundrels. I guarantee you that he'll get back your stolen goods in three days. My boss can get anyone to spill their guts. The neighbourhood's repeat criminals shiver in their boots hearing his name. The radiogram, jewellery, and saris that you saw in the other room was repossessed just this morning. What I mean is that, sir, please deliver the lumber in your vehicle to my boss's building site. He'll return to you your stolen lumber within three days. And, so, you won't lose any money in the bargain. I haven't mentioned anything to him yet. It's possible he won't like it. I just want to feel you out. It was very difficult for my boss to arrange his princess's engagement. She's thirty. She's a very good girl, very good at housekeeping. But she has a little bit of a lazy eye. The boy's side are demanding a car, furniture, a radiogram, and a house facing west.* They want doors and window-frames of the best quality wood. If you pick the wrong family, then this is what you're

* Facing west: Because, in Karachi, there is a cool breeze that comes off the ocean, meaning, from the west, that's why people prefer houses facing west. But they cost a lot.

left with. Usually, my boss isn't like this. These days he's quite upset and irritable. Everyone sees the rabid dog that goes around biting everyone. But no one sees that he hardly wished rabies upon himself. You must have noticed how he said a couple things that showed his nice, agreeable side. Up to three years ago, he was a poet. In the evenings, there were so many poets hanging around here that on several occasions we had to set up chairs in the holding cells as well. One evening, I mean, one night, there was a great poetry party going on. My boss was reciting a new ghazal in tarannum style. The entire staff couldn't get enough of it. At the beginning of the last couplet, our watchman Zardar Khan fired his 303 rifle; everyone thought that he was offering praises after a tribal fashion. But when he started to shout and holler, then everyone saw how during the party's climax, a suspect arrested in a robbery case, and who had been rapping against the holding cell's bars to show his appreciation, well, he'd escaped. All the poets took off after him. But, in fact, they weren't worried about catching him. They themselves were worried about getting away. God knows if he got away because the constables were lazy, or whether the accused wouldn't give himself up. But my boss didn't give up. He went out and caught a recidivist with the same name and brought him in. Then he changed his father's name on the paperwork. But since then he hasn't written any poetry. For three years, he hasn't got a promotion, and he hasn't written a thing. He's friends with the poet Adam Sahib. Last year he had to steal from the mouths of his own babes and give 150,000 rupees to his superior officers so that he wouldn't have to show his face in court. That's when he got the job here. After all, my boss isn't so loved by God that after performing his prayers, he can lift up the corner of his prayer rug to find 150,000 rupees left there by some invisible hand. After all, you have to pull on udders to get milk. If water buffalos aren't available, then sometimes you're forced to milk mice.'

Basharat was angrier about this disgraceful analogy than the loss of capital. If he'd said a goat, that would have been better. (Although a goat is low caste.) In any event, he was beginning to figure things out. He said, 'I want to rescind my report.' The ASI replied, 'Theft in broad daylight is such a heavy crime that there's no backtracking now, I mean, you've already involved the police. Who are you to change your mind? If you insist on withdrawing your complaint, I'll have you arrested on the spot for filing a false report. You'll be disgraced. If you get a good lawyer, you'll still get three months. The SHO will decide on Monday which charges to file against you.'

Basharat felt as though not just his life's every action was worthy of police activity, but that it was actually worthy of *humiliating* police activity, and that it had only been due to police negligence that up till then he had been able to get through life with his honour intact.

He got mad. He threatened, 'This is wrongful confinement. It's illegal. I'll file a habeas corpus petition in the high court.' The ASI replied, '*You* present a petition? We're going to present *you*! We're sure to get permission to hold you for ten days. Just see what happens.'

Autobiographers Go to Jail

After issuing this threat, the ASI left. Then, after several minutes, his boss, the SHO, with his billy club beneath his arm, left for home while clearing his throat. Just then the lawyer appeared from God knows where. Even at eleven at night, he was still wearing his black coat and white pants, as well as the special starched white collar that lawyers wear. He said, 'My friend, although your case has nothing to do with me, out of human sympathy I'm telling you that you can be charged with any number of crimes. God forbid your driver confesses to the violation of Article 164. Then you'll be in real trouble. You look like a family man. You're not a political figure angling to go to jail to make his memoirs more interesting. Things before Partition were different. Then, after delivering a fiery speech, a leader would be jailed, and, sir, the whole country waited for his release, anticipating that after two or three years, he would get out and then publish his memoirs, autobiography, or personal narrative. Too bad the British let Maulana Abul Kalam Azad out before his sentence was up because that meant his narrative was left incomplete. Anyway, that was a different era. It's not like today when they arrest you before you give the speech, and then when you get released, there's no one there to drape a marigold garland around your neck. "On the graves of the poor, there's no flowers or lamps." By God, I'm not suggesting that you take me as your lawyer, but I can't stop you if you want to. I'm just looking out for you. I'm only saying that I've been practicing law for twenty-five years and one month, and I've never seen a legal matter that can't be resolved with a little money. Money makes the world go round. Anyway, it's up to you. I'll leave you with some food for thought as you pass the night here. It's eleven thirty. What were you able to get done in the last eight hours? What will you get done in the next eight? Tomorrow's Sunday. You'll be crouched here just like this demanding your constitutional rights and protection under the law. If the courts are able to do anything, at the very most they'll get you released on Monday. But, sir, we want to see you sprung from this mousetrap before then. You *are* under arrest. OK, well, it's late. Good night! The secretary knows my number.'

After the lawyer left, the head constable gathered a reed mat, a little aluminum pot, and a date-palm fan, and pointed in the direction of Khalifa's cell. He said, 'Your hips and legs must be tired from squatting all day. Spread this out over there, and lie down. I have to lock the door. The mosquitos are really bad. Cover yourself with this blanket. If you get hot, then fan yourself. If you have to pee, then, of course, you can do so over there. I can't touch the lock after twelve.' Then he started to turn off the lights.

But Your Urine Tells Me Something Different!

As the lights were being turned off, Khalifa started crying out, 'Boss! Boss!' On the walls of the lockup, lines of bugs ran this way and that. And bloodthirsty mosquitos started to form a halo around his head. Just then the secretary appeared with the food he'd ordered from the Malbari Hotel and placed it before Basharat: qeema with its delicious smell of green chillies and hara dhaniya, and nan taken straight from the tandoor. The smell of the bread defied description: it must have been the same appetite-whetting smell that, thousands of years ago, humans had experienced when they put wheat to fire for the first time. Basharat wanted to say something to refuse the food, but he couldn't; he was so hungry that his mouth was drowned in saliva. He motioned weakly for the secretary to take it away. Then he turned around and sat down. The secretary spoke, 'I swear to God! I won't eat either, then. You'll be responsible. I had a roll dipped in tea at three. That's it. The doctor says I have TB of the guts. But Hakim Shifaul Malik in Pir Ilahi Bakhsh Colony says that my sickness is caused by eating too much. But, really! I said, "Doctor, look at my body!" He said, "But your urine tells me something different."'

Suddenly the secretary changed topics. He touched Basharat's knee, 'I'm the dust at your feet. But I know a thing or two about the world. You're a respectable man. But you don't understand the delicateness of the situation, you haven't read the pee right. I was once your father-in-law's neighbour. I was his humble devotee. Please look, offer up your goods to redeem your honour. Give him your wood. Get it over with. It's only a couple thousand rupees. Have you seen where you are? Think about how, if you give up this lot at 3,500, you're going to get the same amount back. So what's the big deal? My boss doesn't just steal prey from the lion's mouth, he takes the lion's teeth too. He knows about whatever's going on in the neighbourhood. It's like he intuits it. Sometimes he arrests people just because of how they look, and, I'm sorry to say it, but that's what happened to you. Last year about this time he arrested a man for swearing in public and for being a nuisance. It was hardly anything special. But his piss was telling him something else. Everyone was shocked. But two hours later my boss raided his house, and he found 300 bottles of whisky, two bolts of Two Horse Brand boski cloth, stolen jewellery, dozens of radiograms, and so many other stolen goods. Everything in the house had been stolen. Every single thing except his father, who immediately disinherited him. But my boss has a really big heart. Last year my daughter got married just about this time. He paid for everything. He slipped into the dowry a radiogram that he'd confiscated. I guarantee you that in no more than three days your missing lumber and the truck's registration papers will be delivered to your store. Please believe me. In this case, because of his daughter's wedding, bribes are like a wedding gift. Do you understand?'

My Bread Is Cut from Wood, and Hunger Is My Relish

Now everything was clear. He was only a little mad. When you finally understand the reason for your disgrace, you become resigned and start to think about things. You don't need to shout and scream anymore. He started to like the secretary.

'Mr Secretary, everybody here ... ?'

'Yes, sir, everyone.'

'Even the lawyer?'

'Yes, him, too.'

'Mr Secretary, then you ...'

'Sir, I have seven kids. My biggest boy is in middle school. My wife has TB too. She spits up blood a couple times each day. The doctor says I should take her to a sanitarium in Murree or Quetta. My salary,

* 'My Bread ...': A line from Baba Fareed.

191

after figuring in my raise this year, is twenty-eight rupees, five annas.'*

Basharat agreed to give the SHO the wood in the truck. So around midnight, they unlocked Khalifa's handcuffs, and he collapsed prostrate on the ground right there between the pisshole and the drainpipe and thanked God. He wasn't even done giving thanks to God when he motioned to the head constable for a bidi. Then he smoked. And Basharat was allowed to come out as well. The secretary congratulated him, and he brought a paan out from the little brass box he had. He said, 'My wife specially prepared this paan for me yesterday morning.' The head constable led Basharat to the side, and, by way of congratulations, he said, 'This is a special time. Please give the secretary twenty-five rupees. He's a poor, honest man, with a huge family. And, sir, why don't you treat us to some sweets? Occasions of great happiness happen so seldom. And, please, call home. They must be worried about why you haven't come home yet. They will be wondering whether you were in an accident. They must be desperately searching for you. They must be going round to all the hospital morgues and turning over sheets to see if it's you. Then when they can't find you, they must be going home disappointed.' Basharat took out a hundred rupees from his pocket for some sweets and gave it to him. Just a little while later, the lawyer came out of the SHO's room with four boxes of sweets (like he'd had before) stacked in a minaret; he was balancing them between his stomach and chin. He congratulated Basharat very warmly and praised his understanding and good thinking. He divided three boxes among the staff, and, as he presented the fourth to Basharat, he said, 'Please give this to your wife and kids from us.' After giving him the box, he took off his starched collar and black coat and hung them over his arm.

* In those days, a constable made seventeen rupees, and an ASI made seventy, which was equivalent to what a servant at a bank made.

Now Who's the Beggar?

When is the day of retribution, O, God?
Why do you delay justice?

A Parrot's Predictions

When he arrived home at two thirty in the morning, he had already decided that he would sell the 'automatic cart' at whatever price. He believed that houses, horses, wives, means of conveyance, and precious stones brought either good or bad luck. He remembered how in 1953 he had got wounded in a motorcycle rickshaw accident and how afterwards he had gone to Bandar Road near the Municipal Corporation Building to an astrologer sitting alongside the road and how this man had got his trained parrot to pick out an envelope that revealed Basharat's fortune to be that of one wife and three pilgrimages to Mecca. He said to himself, 'I wish it was the opposite!' (After all, only one pilgrimage is necessary in life. He was not greedy about the afterlife.) The astrologer made his horoscope and looked at the lines on his palms through a magnifying glass. He said, 'Two-, three-, and four-wheeled vehicles will be dangerous for you.' But he didn't need to draw up a horoscope and use a magnifying glass to see this; all he had to do was look at the bandages on his hands and neck. Anyway, he had come to the conclusion that until a vehicle with one or five wheels was invented, he must make do with his legs. It seemed as though the real purpose of his buying this vehicle was to expedite the delivery of lumber to thieves (and the SHO), and, thanks be to God, that was accomplished without any delay or interference.

7.

The Bengal Tiger Left, and the Lion Came

In the morning, when Basharat informed Khalifa that his services were no longer needed, he made a big fuss. At first he asked how he would be able to live without the vehicle. Then he asked where he should go. Then he gave a speech not only on the far-reaching consequences of the unbreakable relationship between a master and servant but also on loyalty in general. The speech's gist was that he felt for Basharat's loss, that he realized he had caused it, and that he was ready to make up for it in the following fashion: Basharat should keep whatever wages were due for shaving him for that year and so consider his loss that much less. Basharat yelled at him, 'Khalifa, you mean to tell me I was going to pay you 3,500 rupees a year to shave me?' Khalifa very cheerfully again admitted his mistake, and he suggested the very foolish idea that they turn the vehicle into a mobile barbershop, which Basharat also rejected out of hand. Khalifa was getting so desperate that he proposed to serve as his driver for absolutely free, till the end of time, that is, until either the car gave out or he did, whichever came first. So, in other words, the persecution to which he had subjected Basharat would now be provided free of charge. Long story short, Khalifa kept suggesting one idiotic thing after another and so continued to rub salt into Basharat's wounds.

When Basharat wouldn't relent, Khalifa gave up. But he did pick up his razor. I mean, he made his last wish known that despite their break-up he should be allowed to come shave him. Basharat agreed upon one condition, and that was that if in the future he should have a means of conveyance, and that of any sort, then the bastard would *not* be allowed to drive it.

After a few days, Khalifa came with news. He said, 'Sir, I got the idea that I should go by to look at the SHO's construction site. And I couldn't believe it. What did I see but that the stolen lumber was sitting right next to the bribe-lumber! Side by side! One lion snatched from another lion's mouth our goods and then gulped them down! What difference does it make if a Bengal tiger or a Barbary lion stole it? If you don't believe me, go see for yourself.'

Khalifa started to laugh. He had a bad habit of laughing uncontrollably and inappropriately about things he said. He would come up for air and then drown again in laughter. He laughed like other people sang. When he would breathe, he winked. One of his front teeth was missing, and when he tried to stop laughing, he really did look like a clown.

Truck for Sale

The vehicle stood unused for a month. No one offered to buy it, not even as a joke. In order to avoid any contemptuous overtones, I began referring to it as a 'vehicle.' Basharat had become over-sensitive. If someone called it a car, he thought they were poking fun at him; and if someone called it a truck, he thought they were insulting him. So he started calling it a 'vehicle.' He had lost all hope of selling it when suddenly he got offers on three consecutive days. The owner of the nearby cement company offered him thirteen rupees for the tarp that they had sometimes used to cover the vehicle. A donkey-cart driver offered twelve rupees for its four wheels. Basharat blew his top at the country idiot, 'They go together. You think it runs without wheels?' The man replied, 'My lord, it won't run with wheels either.' The third offer was the best, as far as money was concerned. It came from a man who looked like a smuggler. He offered two hundred for the vehicle's plates and tags.

After these insulting offers, Basharat put the tarp over it and resolved never again to buy a car. (When his economic situation and mood improved a little, he modified this to say that he would never buy a car from a dead white man's widow, howsoever pretty she may be.) Mirza recommended that Basharat give it as a gift to one of his enemies. Basharat said, 'You take it.' After several days, he removed the tarp and had a calligrapher write on a piece of cardboard, 'FOR SALE,' which he put on the vehicle. After a couple days, the cardboard sign, as well as the car, were covered in the sawdust flying off the shop's power-saw. Maulana Karamat Hussain, who was now called the firm's 'manager,' wrote with his finger on the grimy windshield, 'WELCOME' and 'TRUCK FOR SALE.' You could see this from afar. Every day in the afternoon after washing for prayers, he would use a wet finger to outline these words. After praying at the mosque, he would hurry back to blow holy breath over the vehicle. He said, 'With powerful incantations like this, within forty days, whatever gets the holy breath blown onto it will sell, or the blower will go blind.' Several times a day he would pass two or three fingers in front of him to check to see if he hadn't gone blind yet. On the way back from the mosque, he would hold his breath so that the holy breath should not leak onto something unintentionally.

8.

Haji Aurangzeb Khan, Lumber Merchant and Broker

Thin Gravy And Cracked Wheat Halva

The forty days of Maulana Karamat Hussain's special prayer had not yet passed when Basharat became involved in another mix-up, and that was that Haji Aurangzeb Khan, Lumber Merchant and Broker, showed up from Peshawar demanding his money. The year before, Khan Sahib had sold to Basharat through a Punjabi lumber broker a load of 'high-quality' wood. But it turned out to be bad wood. In fact, it was that very lumber about whose stealing, recovery, and loss I just wrote. Basharat claimed that when it hadn't sold after one year he'd sold it for 7,000 rupees. Khan Sahib replied, 'Half was stolen. Half went to the police. How can you call that selling? There's a real bad word in Pashto for this.'

According to Basharat's reckoning, the goods were worth no more than 7,000 rupees. And, for the sake of principle, Haji Aurangzeb Khan wasn't ready to accept one cent less, meaning, Basharat had to fork out the remaining 2573 rupees, 9 annas, and 3 paisas (which was equivalent to 15,000 rupees today). Khan Sahib said, 'You were much too hasty. Quick work is Satan's work. Sir, we're talking about wood here, not a young daughter you're trying to marry off.'

They had been exchanging letters about the money for quite a while. Who knows why, but one day after Khan Sahib had sent from the Peshawar Post Office a registered letter, he went straight home, packed his bags, and left for Karachi. He got there three days before the mail, and, in fact, he was there to snatch the letter from the mailman's hand, rip it up, and give the envelope to Basharat. He stayed at Basharat's, as well. In those days, it was customary for brokers or wholesale merchants to stay at the homes of those with whom they were doing business. In any event, Basharat and Khan Sahib got along well. Basharat liked Khan Sahib's affectionate and entertaining manner, and Khan Sahib enjoyed listening to Basharat's endless tales.

They squabbled during the day. Then in the evening, when they went back to Basharat's house, everyone treated Khan Sahib so well that it seemed as though the day's disagreements had meant nothing. Basharat's family left no stone unturned in extending their hospitality. And yet Khan Sahib complained that his eyesight was growing weak from eating Karachi's thin gravy. He began to walk with a limp. He said, 'The gravy's descended into my knees!' After dinner, he always demanded cracked-wheat halva. He said, 'If I don't eat halva, my ancestors come to me in my dreams to scold me.' He missed his hometown cuisine, and, as he remembered all the thighs he had eaten, he sighed a lot. His stomach was a graveyard for all the high-quality rams. In the afternoon, Basharat ordered for him thigh meat and chapli kebabs from the Frontier Hotel. Mirza repeatedly said that it would have been better to pay him the 2573 rupees, 9 annas, and 3 paisas and be done with it; that that would be cheaper. But Basharat said that it wasn't a question of money but of principle. And Khan Sahib too considered it a matter of principle and ego.

The devotion and focus that saints show when praying was nothing compared to that which Khan Sahib demonstrated while eating. He often said that if anyone interrupted him while praying, sleeping, eating, and insulting someone, then he would shoot him. When going to meet a stranger, an enemy, or an untrustworthy friend, he would tuck his .38-calibre revolver into his cartridge belt. People said that he had his revolver hidden somewhere beneath his pilgrim's robes when he circumambulated the Ka'aba. God knows if that's true. He brought with him a ten-kilo sack of cracked wheat as a gift when he came to Karachi. He ended up asking for Basharat's wife to make it into halva. Every day Basharat would peek into the sack, and every day he would be shocked to see how much was still left. Khan Sahib said that the next time he would bring a big sack of fresh jaggery from Mardan Sugar Mills because refined sugar made his blood run thin. One day Basharat started to get this foreboding feeling, and so trying to figure out his intentions, he asked him, 'Khan Sahib, what can you make out of jaggery?' Easing another handful of halva down his throat, he said, 'Ask your wife. At the moment, I'm not able to focus. The thing is that business losses, fighting, jaggery, and Ramadan make me lose my mind. I get into fights only during Ramadan. It's because you're not supposed to swear while fasting.'

Human Legs vs. Charpoy Legs

Khan Sahib's hospitality and cooking were famous. Basharat had the chance to go to Peshawar and stay at his house. For every meal, he was served goat or ram thighs, though for breakfast and for tea it was chicken legs. Basharat never saw hide nor hair of any cut of meat beyond thighs and legs. Nor did he ever see vegetables or fish because, after all, eggplants and fish don't have legs. It's hard to say what Khan Sahib would have said in Pashto had he seen the Folies Bergère or Lido Chorus Girls' Legs Show in Paris. But it's safe to say that he wasn't interested in any legs that he couldn't roast, eat, and serve.

Although Khan Sahib loved leg-meat, he absolutely detested Karachi's bong nihari stew, as well as the head-and-leg dish that was eaten there. He said, 'I can't bear to think of eating soup made from filthy, dung-caked cattle hooves. In our Frontier, if an old man should happen to marry a young girl, then the doctor and neighbours serve him this fiery concoction. He gets a GI-track disease and dies. I heard that in England they make glue out of hooves, not gravy. You guys are really something. Goat legs, sheep legs, ram legs, cow legs, cattle legs, water buffalo legs … I guess you leave charpoys alone because their legs are too clean.'

A Statue from the Previous Century

Khan Sahib was a commanding personality, and he had a remarkable frame. There was even something weighty to his babble and prattle. He was about six and a half feet tall, which came out to seven and a half when you added in his cap and turban. But he looked eight feet tall, and he thought of himself that way too. He was in such good health and he was so fit that you couldn't tell how old he was. You can guess how big he was from the fact that he had to wedge himself into an armchair, and how, when he got up, the chair went with him! He had a golden moustache and light brown eyes. There was a crescent-shaped scar on his left cheek without which his face would have seemed incomplete. One of his index fingers was missing down to its second joint. When he had to warn someone, or when he had to call on the heavens to be his witness in the midst of some dispute (which happened several times a day), then he would raise his tiny 'warning' finger and address them. Yet this finger was bigger than any of my fingers. He was both far- and near-sighted, but he avoided glasses as far as it was possible. He used them only when writing his name on checks and while looking at the faces of the objects of his displeasure after he had just cursed them out; in both cases, before he took them off, he quickly checked the surroundings. This geographical surveying was enough to last him the day. There was a hint of mischievousness in his eyes. When he burst out laughing, his face opened up like a pomegranate. After the effects of laughter had left his face, his stomach still jiggled from the laughter's interior aftershocks. On top of his pure yellow cap, his turban's starched crest stood permanently erect like his wounded 'warning finger.' He wore a dark brown Turkish coat, and his gold-laced Peshawari sandals were each large enough to fit both my feet front to back! And he wore an enormous, billowy white shalwar. Khan Sahib was an awe-inspiring, graceful man cut from the cloth of the previous century. For encomiums, caricatures, and statues, you need to be at least one-and-a-half times life-sized. Khan Sahib was his own statue.

The chain of the golden watch that he kept in the pocket of his waistcoat must have been two feet long, as that was the distance between the waistcoat's two pockets. In the time it took to string his shalwar's drawstring, you could go to Hyderabad and back. His nerves were so strong that he never got nervous. Normal pains, normal worries didn't affect him. Once the washerman found in his shalwar's waistband a small pencil! He ate a lot. He never spoke while eating, nor did he drink water, because he figured that they wasted precious time and space. He considered lentils a Hindu invention and an open encroachment on the rights of cattle. Fried meat didn't mean only that it was cooked in a frying pan; rather, it also meant that he would eat the entire frying pan's worth of meat. It's lucky that in those days people weren't in the habit of cooking their meat in buckets, because then he would have eaten buckets of meat. He considered spitting out partridge and quail bones, as well as spitting out grape seeds, orange seeds, and watermelon seeds, to be a feminine affectation. His big body (we should really call it his frightening form) frustrated him. He liked to go on walks, but with the one condition that after every forty steps or so he could take a break and eat something so that he had the strength to continue (meaning, for forty more steps). I agree that Khan Sahib was not so nimble that he would be able to rush forward to attack the enemy, but should he have simply fallen on top of the enemy, his foe would have had no recourse. That is, without even being able to wriggle his hands or legs, his foe would have expired on the spot. Whenever he came to Karachi to collect his debts, he never wore his cartridge belt. He said work got done the same without it. The cartridge belt had left a diagonal line across his chest and stomach that divided his upper torso into two identical isosceles triangles. He used to say that men can't sleep without mountain-winds and the sound of gunshots.

The story of his injured index finger goes back to his childhood. Boys were having a contest to open Codd-neck lemonade bottles. Khan Sahib had pressed his index finger down on top of the marble inside the bottle's neck and with his other hand he had hit down on his finger with all his might. The impact immediately broke the bottle and his finger. The bottle's neck latched onto his finger like a wedding ring. They had to use a hammer to break the bottle. His finger went septic. They had to cut it off two weeks later. He considered anaesthesia for wimps. So he had the operation without any. Before the operation, he instructed the surgeons to bind his head by tying a strip of cloth between his teeth.

If he considered what he was going to say as being very scholarly, then, in order to make it seem weighty and dignified, he would first massage his chin as though he had a big beard like Tagore had. He would raise his injured index finger toward the heavens, put on his glasses, and only then would he begin to talk. When he was in the midst of some complicated explanation, if some witty remark suddenly came to mind, then, before he laid into his listeners, he would first wink. And before that, he would take off his glasses so that everyone would be able to see it clearly.

It's very difficult to describe how he laughed. It seemed as though he wanted to laugh openly, and yet for some reason, he was trying to restrain himself. As a result, certain sounds kept escaping from his mouth that sounded like how a car sounds while you try to restart it after its battery has died. Before laughing, he would usually unbutton his waistcoat because, he explained, he had no one in that foreign land to stitch the buttons back on each and every day.

He had married only once. He believed in marrying only once and never to think about any other woman. His poor wife had requested on several occasions that he might like to take on another, so that she too might experience her good fortune.

From the Limping Cockroach to Shaikh Sadi

If you want, you can call Khan Sahib illiterate. But he was the furthest thing from uncouth and ignorant. He had a pleasant temperament, and he had a lot of commonsense, as well as a keen eye. He was a true gentleman; he had seen everything and had come out the other side.

He didn't read life through the lens of literature, and he didn't see life through the frame of art. Whatever life puts in front of you, and whatever it teaches you, that is what stays in your heart:

> O, Nazir, formal education only gives a man four eyes.
> The knowledge that gives you one hundred thousand eyes lies in
> the heart.

If Urfi called himself 'his own teacher,' he knew exactly what he was talking about. Khan Sahib was among the learned men, the graduates, of the School of Life.

For years, he had signed checks with his thumbprint. But when his bank balance exceeded 100,000 rupees, he had learned how to sign his name in Urdu. He said, 'There's nothing to be ashamed about signing for withdrawals with your thumbprint at usurious banks. But when it's hard-earned money, then you should think carefully about it.' His signature was truly bizarre. It looked like a cockroach had taken a bath in an inkwell and then had walked across a piece of paper. While signing something, he contorted his hand so strangely and, especially whenever he had to make a round shape, his wide-open mouth was locked in a circle that grew and shrank in concert with the letters, that when he was done, not only was his hand experiencing cramps but so were the eyes of anyone who had been watching him! In those days, his account was at the Chauk Yadgar branch of Muslim Commercial Bank, and at this branch the account-holders who signed their names in Urdu had to suffer the indignity of signing a guarantee that if their signatures were forged in the future and so some fraud committed, then the bank would not be responsible for their losses. Moreover, if the bank experienced losses, whether direct or indirect, then the account-holder would have to pay for them. When this was explained to Khan Sahib in Pashto, he almost lost it. He turned back to the accountant and said, 'There's a real bad word in Pashto for people like this who accept such absurd stipulations. I'm very upset.' He went in a huff to protest to the bank's English manager, Mr A. McClain (who had once been my boss). He said, 'My signature is so messy that no educated man could possibly fake it. If I sign my name with such difficulty, then who's going to forge it? You must have two dozen men working here. They all look like thieves, swindlers, and frauds. If any one of them can forge my signature, then I'll give him a 1000-rupee prize. Then I'll shoot him.' Mr McClain said, 'I can't change bank policy. It's the same at Grand Lease Bank. We copied the form from theirs. Not just copied, really, but slavishly followed. The thing is that the printers, due to their carelessness, transferred the name Grand Lease Bank onto our forms! Khan, if you learn how to sign your name in English instead of the vernacular, then you'll see yourself out of this mess at once.' In order to colour his command with a shade of entreaty, he offered Khan Sahib tea and pastries. So Khan Sahib was busy for two months in learning how to sign his name in English. Then when it was all ready to go, he went straight into Mr McClain's office and signed. It went like this: first, with his hand raised in the air, he practiced his signature four or five times, then suddenly he put his pen to the paper, and, bing bang boom, it was done. Mr McClain immediately wrote on a slip of paper to the bank's accountant: 'His indemnity is cancelled. I have verified that he has signed the card in English in my own presence.'

What had happened was that for two months instead of writing his Urdu signature right to left he had practiced writing it left to right and he had become very skilled at this. (This eliminated the dots and circles, which give away Urdu.) In front of Mr McClain, this left-to-right signature was what he did, and he kept to this 'English' signature afterwards for cheques and business papers. But if he was having a letter written to a friend or relative, or if he had to sign an affidavit, then afterwards he wrote his Urdu signature. Meaning, right to left.

Khan Sahib became so proficient that if someone asked him to sign in Japanese, he would have grabbed this cockroach by its whiskers and stood it on its head to fashion it anew.

If Khan Sahib wanted to end a conversation quickly, or if he wanted to throw someone to the proverbial mat, he would say, 'Shaikh Sadi said …' For him, Shaikh Sadi was the cat's meow. For extra emphasis, he quoted Shaikh Sadi all the time, even if it was really his own thoughts that he was conveying.

If anyone contradicted him, however petty the point, Khan Sahib was ready to fight to the death. To forgive and to compromise were unmanly. He often said, 'There's a real bad word in Pashto for a man who compromises before tasting blood.' Once Basharat had the chance to stay in his father's house in Bannu. He saw that whenever Khan Sahib won a heated argument or became excited because something good happened, he would go outside, mount his horse, ride around an enemy's house, and come back. Then he would ask his servant to pour him a bucket of cold water over his head because God doesn't like the arrogant.

9.

Khan Sahib Shed Crocodile Tears about His Plight

Two or three times a day Khan Sahib was sure to threaten Basharat that he wouldn't accept a penny less than what he was owed, even if that meant that he had to stay at Basharat's house for a full year. He also mentioned from time to time that the tribal rules of hospitality were different than others. He said, 'If you ask your guest when they're leaving, and if, in response, the guest doesn't kill you, then his nobility, sense of honour, and parentage fall into question.'

From morning till night, the two stags rammed against each other.

In addition to invocations for fair dealing, references to the customs of trading, appeals for mercy, warnings that the other should steer clear of unnecessarily tormenting the other, and warnings against cheating, there wasn't a single petty weapon that they didn't ruthlessly use. For instance, Khan Sahib cited his illiteracy. In response, Basharat cited himself as a cautionary tale, 'I'm a poet. I have a BA. I studied Persian. And now I'm selling wood!' Khan Sahib would note how his business wasn't doing well, and Basharat would say, 'Well, sir, there's no business here to begin with! Each day I cut into my savings.' Basharat had already rehearsed his narration about his fake indigence, his overgrown family, and his disaster with the white widow; but, when needed, Khan Sahib too could shed crocodile tears about his plight. One day his acting reached such a pinnacle that a very real tear, which was the shape and size of Sri Lanka, hung from his right eye. Another time, Khan Sahib threw the trump card of his fake victimization: his uncle had taken over land that was rightfully his and had kept it for himself for half a century. Basharat thrust back. He put his hand on his stomach and swore to God that he had been suffering from an ulcer for the same amount of time; he couldn't digest anything; even medicine and wind passed right through. Khan Sahib said, 'Oh, ho, ho! So you're fifty? You've been suffering that long?' In these quibbles, Basharat generally had the upper hand. But one day, when Khan Sahib said in a half-tearful voice* that his father had died, then Basharat got very angry at his own father for still being alive.

In arguments, whoever may win, only the truth is martyred.

Khan Sahib refused to leave without all of his money. He was driving Basharat mad. He said, 'Please stop talking about who was right and who was wrong. Look, we're going to be doing business in the

---

* 'Half-tearful' because his other eye was smiling.

future. Please ask for your money then. God forbid this is our last transaction.' Khan Sahib replied, 'Khan Sang Marjan Khan advised me to treat every meeting with a friend as the last, and every deal as the last. "The pimp won't show his face again!" Shaikh Sadi said even the craziest dog doesn't think that the man he's bitten will come back to be bitten again.'

Once Basharat let some bitterness slip in, and he started taunting him by calling him 'Khan Sahib.' Khan Sahib said, 'Look here, if you're going to start cursing me out, don't use "Khan Sahib." Call me "Haji Sahib," so we can both feel a little ashamed.'

Basharat hugged him and kissed his forehead.

Billionaires and Karachi's Five Gifts

Khan Sahib's frequent visits to Karachi to recover his arrears made him fluent in seven languages. I mean, he could curse in Urdu, Persian, Gujarati, and four local languages. As far as possible, he cursed out the objects of his displeasure in their mother tongue. But if he happened to run short of swearwords, or felt like they weren't having any impact, or if the person was really shameless, then he hammered the last nails into his coffin with some choice Pashto phrases, which cursed out several generations of his ancestors. There's no doubt that the *Koka Shastra*–curse words that are in vogue here make English curses (and those of all other languages) seem like feather pillows for a pillow fight, or the gurgling of babies burping up breast milk. For English and American readers, R. K. Narayan's novels are especially interesting because of their Indian curses, which he translates literally into English and spreads like mines throughout his dialogue. When I was in Dubai in 1975, I realized that our curses are filled with refinement, force, geographical pertinence, and sexiness. The Galadari brothers were counted among the billionaires of the UAE and the

Middle East—but, in fact, I should have said that they were among the richest billionaires because everyone there is a billionaire. So that's why I suggest that we call them not 'billionaires' but 'Arabaires.' Abdul Wahab Galadari and Abdul Lateef Galadari—who are Arab, and who speak Arabic—lived in Karachi for a while for schooling and to live it up. I was beyond surprised when I saw that when they got mad, or if they got into a fight with an Arab (and there wasn't a single Arab they didn't get into a fight with), they would slip in Urdu curse words throughout their Arabic, and these, in the context of Arabic's sacredness, felt even fouler. They were the first Arabs who could both speak Arabic and pronounce retroflexes. Abdul Lateef Galadari said that Karachi has at least five things that you couldn't find anywhere else in the world: studded jewellery, qawwali, biryani, curses, and aloewood perfume. In 1983, when his businesses went belly up, his jewellery, qawwali, biryani, and aloewood perfume fell into the possession of his enemies. Now he survives on the fifth gift alone. His wealth of curses suffers no decline. He gives one and gets seven in return.

Kebab Parathas and His (Extensive) Circle of Enemies

Khan Sahib was an affectionate, social, and loving man. Whatever fights he might get into, he never bore a grudge. He really liked to get under the skin of his friends, but only as a joke. For breakfast, he ate three parathas dripping with butter and two shami kebabs, and he also drank two glasses of lassi. He made it through the day half-asleep, looking out at the world and its denizens with half-open eyes. Yes, perhaps he looked out at the world from a remove, just as he yawned and burped to put people in their place. After such a stupefying breakfast, you can meditate, make abstract paintings, write stream-of-consciousness novels, and form government five-year plans. But you can't do any brainwork. And you can't argue properly. Khan Sahib couldn't remember what he'd said the previous day, and so, each time, he started up again as though he had never discussed the matter before. In Tasir's charming line, if you replace the word 'love' with the word 'argue,' then you get Khan Sahib's style of argumentation:

Every time I saw her, I argued with her anew.

He couldn't remain angry or mad at anyone for long. He hated poetry, and yet he often recited the couplet below, although he contorted the phrasing so much that it became prose:

For humans to bear malice for others is not good.
The man who bears malice for another is not good.

He added to this that to bear malice toward a Muslim was beyond reproach. It would be better to kill the man. He proudly said, 'I'm a free-range tribal man. While fighting with Karachi businessmen to get back my money, I've learned Urdu.' So his vocabulary became entirely worthless during peacetime. Like Rana Sanga's body, his feisty Urdu also had seventy-two wounds. From parsing his Urdu, you could figure out exactly where the men were from who had not paid him back.

Whose stamps are those on the affidavit?

Listening to the way he talked—listening to his Gujarati, his Hyderabadi Urdu, and his Delhi factory-dialect Urdu—you could fix the exact diameter of his every disputation.

Folk Accent

Khan Sahib's Urdu—his lingua franca and language for quarrelling—had been marked by all his debtors, and yet he spoke it in his pure, musical Pashto accent, which was pleasing to the ear. In comparison, Basharat felt like his own accent was bland and tasteless. Pashto Urdu has a winning brevity to it, and a fierce and fresh fragrance, that cannot put up with abstruse, double-dealing talk. Its thundering, daring accent can't support devious whispering. Similarly, Punjabi Urdu is full of grandeur, energy, and mellowness. It has the composure of the rivers, which cut zigzags across the plains, and the widening echo of a generous heart. In Balochi Urdu, in addition to a deep sigh, a leaping mountain echo, and an attractive anger, there is also an alertness that gives the mountains and the deserts over to its mendicants. Sindhi Urdu has a quavering, lively, lyrical accent. It's like a gush of feeling, an affectionate wave, kissing itself as it rolls forward. In regional Urdu, you get a folk scent, a sweetness, a flavour, and a zest that is entirely absent in our chaste and worn-out city Urdu. The new language that has formed through the amalgamation of these folk dialects is very powerful, fresh, sweet, and expansive.

The rivers of the four corners meet here

A City's Elegy and His Brethren, the Humble People of Bannu

Between their quarrels, Khan Sahib would take a walk. He had a dozen or so humble, needy folks from Kohat and Bannu always waiting outside, with pistols in their waistcoats, and they followed him wherever he went. They were not only Khan Sahib's devotees and companions, but they were also his commandos who, upon the signal of his half-finger, were ready to strap gunpowder to their waists and jump into Nimrod's fire without a second thought. For lounging about and passing the time, Khan Sahib had set up for them four charpoys and a Kabuli samovar. All day long tea boiled in the samovar, and so Basharat had to build a temporary outhouse from corrugated tin for the men to piss in. He put used blotting paper out there. When the men started to complain about Karachi's leaky ink, he gave them old issues of a newspaper infamous for voicing its approval of each and every government. It was to be used as toilet paper, and so finally it was being put to good use. All day they would gossip, joke around, and compete against one another in weightlifting competitions. The young guys talked about work, sports, inflation, movies, food and drink, and marksmanship, while the middle-aged men recharged their batteries with sticky sweet tea and obscene jokes. Fuelled with this heat, these men stilled for a moment the chilling onset of old age; they were possessed by a lust that fuelled such outrageous conversation that even young men would blush to hear them. The greyer the man's beard, and the more he bent at the waist, the more his jokes packed a punch and the more lecherous were his jokes. About this, Mirza once said,

The more bent the bow, the further its arrow will go …

When Khan Sahib told a particularly meaty story, he would put a cube of sugar between his teeth and drink tea through this with a 'si-si-si' sucking sound. He would sway and say, 'Yaraji! They drink tea like this in Samarkand and Fergana!'

Khan Sahib spent all of his free time observing Karachi and its people, and, subsequently, in giving them hell and encouraging others to do the same. He said, 'In Karachi, you have to make a personal effort just to breathe. In the tribal regions, the air is so light and pure. It goes in without any effort, just like a bullet. This morning, Radio Karachi said that the humidity was 90 percent. The 90 percent water that Karachi milkmen use to dilute their milk comes all from the city's air. While you all find occasions to shout slogans, recite poetry, and make incantatory offerings, we simply fire bullets into the air— POW POW POW. I've been in Karachi for a long time, and I've still to see anyone carrying a gun. For us, we pack even during weddings, because you never know if there will be gunplay over disagreements about the bride price. Sometimes brides' fathers and relatives turn out to be extremely wicked, stingy cuckolds. To be on the safe side, I took a small machinegun to my own wedding. In 1937, my uncle had used it to kill three white men in an ambush in a mountain cave in the Katori Khel region near Khaisora. One was a captain. He looked like a bulldog. That piece of shit had martyred countless disciples of the Fakir of Ipi. My uncle cut off his nose and ears and fed them to the birds. He took out of the pocket of one of the ordinary soldiers a photo of his infirm, old mother and one of his darling, little, 1-year-old girl. The girl was holding a doll. Seeing this, my uncle cried a lot. He replaced the gold watch that he had taken from the man's wrist. He moved the corpse into the shade. Then, when he was walking away, he had a thought, and so he went back and covered the corpse with his shoulder-wrap.'

Khan Sahib continued, 'So I was saying how I went to my wedding packing my uncle's submachine gun. Except for the kids, the officiant, and the barber, no one was unarmed. Right when we were about to exchange vows, someone on the girl's side raised objections. They said that they wanted 100,000 rupees. My uncle started to argue. He said he wanted it according to sharia law, which meant that the bride price should be equivalent in value to the weight of two-and-three-quarters-rupees' worth of silver, which was thirteen rupees and five and a half annas. A wise old man of the tribe said that the girl's side should come down a little, and the boy's side should go up a little, and when they split the difference, then both sides should be happy. Another wise old man said, "Sir, be reasonable. There's no reachable average between thirteen rupees, five and a half annas, and 100,000 rupees! In this case, the average is reached with swords."

'When the commotion grew, I took off the wedding garland and said, "I raise the bride price to five hundred thousand. Anything less will dishonour my family." Hearing this shocked my uncle. He whispered in my ear, "Are you high? We could get Calcutta's Gauhar Jan and one hundred and one dancing prostitutes for that." I said, "Uncle, please don't interfere. You sight your enemies down a gun's barrel, and you look at Queen Victoria on milled-edge rupee coins. You haven't seen the world. Nor do you understand a man's honour. If I'm going to have to go bankrupt, it's best to do so big. Only lowbred men and cuckolds try to do it cheap."

'I've been in Karachi a while, but I still haven't seen any streetfights.* What? Do people here not have relatives? Do you assume everyone's an orphan? Two days ago I went to meet a friend in Landhi. The bus conductor didn't give me change. When I was getting off, I swore at him, but he pretended not to hear. I said to myself, "Hey, buddy, I just swore at you. If it was advice, OK, I can see why you wouldn't care, but a curse is different."'

After this joke, he started laughing: noises sprung from his mouth that sounded like a car with a weak battery trying to start, and his body wobbled like jelly for minutes.

But this is not to say that Khan Sahib entirely hated Karachi. He said, 'If the people weren't here, and if the sea receded by 250 miles or so, the city wouldn't be half bad for driving trucks or riding horses.' He really liked some parts of the city. They were those poor sections with half-made houses that reminded him of the area around Kohat where, in his own words, once upon a time when he was younger he had reigned over the entire area.

O, earth, I like you because you smell like someone I love!

My Friends Are Still Alive, so Ignominy Lives On

Basharat and Khan Sahib's bickering and squabbling took place only during working hours, meaning, from nine to five, and, without

---

* This is old news. How sad it is that Karachi is now suffering the comeuppance for its previous vainglory.

resolving winners and losers, it was set aside for the next day so that they could engage again with a fresh start.

> *A truce is just another instrument of war*
> *The gun is emptied just to be filled again*

I've heard that neighbourhood women used to fight like this. After yelling at each other all day, implicating their own husbands in far-reaching, lecherous crimes, the women found that their throats had become hoarse. Then as the men were set to come home, they cleared the battlefield but placed at their property lines (meaning, the common wall between the two houses) an overturned pot to signify that the curse-war was temporarily suspended due to darkness. A cursefire was in effect. The next day the hostilities would begin again. The thing is that if you can't see your enemy, your curses will lack inspiration. At all hours, the store was filled with squabbling and wrestling, and outside the burly supporters sat around the samovar. Of course customers were scared away. According to my first teacher, Maulvi Muhammad Ismail Meruthi, whose school reader taught me my first lessons in self-defense and the art of running away,

> *When two brigands are fighting,*
> *Think first about how to save yourself.*

If a customer did come in, Khan Sahib would lament his losses in such a way that the customer either became scared or his eyes welled up with tears, and in both cases, he ran away.

The arguing proved salubrious for Khan Sahib. His tongue grew sharper, and his appetite picked up. He was in no way ready to accept less money because the price he was asking was exactly what he had paid. For his part, Basharat kept saying, 'First, the wood had a bad grain, and it was full of burls. Even the sharpest saw went dull from it. Second, it wasn't seasoned. Many planks were warped. There wasn't a single plank that was good. Third, there was a lot of "spoilage."* Fourth, it was infested with bugs.'

Khan Sahib quipped, 'Fifth, the wood was stolen. That's my fault too. Sixth, I gave you wood. I didn't give you a girl. In that case, it would've been fine for you to nitpick her dowry. Whenever you eat too much paan, you start arguing like a woman.'

Basharat didn't hear the last word right, and he got offended, 'You really are a man from Kabul!'

'What do you mean?'

Basharat explained to him the meaning of 'a man from Kabul.' He got enraged. He said, 'My tribe has never been in the usury business. It's no better than eating pork to us! But you thrust both your hands in, and don't even care to hide it. Even your homemade gravy is haram. It's half water, half chillies, and half usury! If you call me that again, watch out!'

Then, in his rage, he slammed his fist down on the table with such force that the cups, spoons, pens, and a dish of roasted peas jumped a foot in the air. The alarm clock on the table started ringing. And then, without saying anything, he took his loaded revolver from his Turkish jacket's pocket and set it on the table. After a minute, he swivelled the barrel to point toward himself.

Basharat grew scared. He didn't understand how to take back the poisoned arrow that had not only already left his bow but that had also already punctured the breast of his dear guest. Khan Sahib immediately ordered one of his commandos inside and told him to buy a ticket for him on the next train to Peshawar. He skipped lunch. Basharat begged for forgiveness. Khan Sahib kept getting angry, and so he kept walking out of the shop, although in such a manner that with every step,

---

* Spoilage: Wear and tear, or the loss of goods during loading and unloading.

He turned back to see if anyone was pleading with him to stay.

At four o'clock, Basharat fell to his feet. Khan Sahib agreed to return to his house if and only if Basharat fed him paan with his own hands.

Then Khan Sahib's attitude underwent a change for the better.

Basharat was very ashamed of what he had said. Like the English idiom goes, he was dying of shame. But Khan Sahib wasn't any less ashamed at his overreaction. He tried to make up for it and to console Basharat in a variety of ways. For example, if he saw that Basharat was sad or exhausted, or if suddenly in the midst of their arguing he should flee like a sissy from the battlefield leaving Khan Sahib like Don Quixote brandishing his sword in the air, then, with a unique and kind coquetry, he would say, 'Sir, the man from Kabul pays his respects and humbly asks you for a paan. Please feed me paan.' He had never even tasted paan before. Basharat was so ashamed he wanted to bury himself. So, from time to time, either out of embarrassment or in a mock-serious way, he would fold his hands together in supplication and get up. And sometimes he would touch Khan Sahib's knees. And sometimes Khan Sahib would kiss Basharat's hands and then put them over his own eyes.

10.

Mr Palangzeb (Bed-warmer) Khan

In the evening, he had a bed brought out into the courtyard and fitted with a mosquito net. For the last little while, he had given up sitting in chairs. He had accused Basharat of leaving nails exposed on the seats of the chairs reserved for his guests so that their shalwars would get caught. At an appropriate distance from his bed, he had four charpoys installed complete with mosquito nets for visitors to sit on. He said, 'If you put wings on one of our Frontier scorpions, you'll get Karachi mosquitos.' All conversing took place from within mosquito nets. But if someone should happen to get excited while talking, they would flick up the net like a bridegroom takes off his wedding garland after the ceremony. From the far-flung parts of the city, his Pathan friends, brothers in arms, and disciples came in droves to see him. He received them as though he was at home. Until late at night, blue enamelware trays were passed around, as well as a hookah. These tea connoisseurs mixed jaggery from Mardan and powdered poppy seeds into their boiling hot tea from Chura. Absolutely everyone brought something or another for Khan Sahib: walnuts; pine nuts; black gulab jamun dessert treats from Peshawar; honeycombs; Talagang and Dera Ismail Khan's white tobacco; and young, purebred roosters* from Qaraqul, which Khan Sahib ate with great gusto. The roosters went around the house all day strutting and shitting. The green poo on the red cement looked especially atrocious (if you replace 'atrocious' with 'obnoxious' the sentence will still be funny). When a rooster crowed at the wrong time or too loudly, that was the first that Khan Sahib slaughtered. In the morning when the full congregation of roosters crowed together, it sent a shock wave through the neighbourhood. One day a young man from Mohmand gave him

* Purebred rooster: A dark brown rooster with a tinge of red. They are very aggressive and attack-minded. Its meat was considered to be very invigorating. Maulana Abdul Halim Sharar wrote, 'There's no more courageous animal on earth than the purebred rooster. In fact, lions don't have the sort of courage that roosters do. He may die while fighting, but he doesn't shy away at all.' According to his research, it came to India from Arabia, while, also according to him, and I quote, 'the craze for quail fighting had come to Lucknow from the Punjab.' It seems as though Maulana had used the wrong source about quail fighting. I've never seen Punjabis engaged in the blood sport of quail fighting. Instead, they kill them with their own two hands and then eat them.

a hen by mistake. That day, all the roosters fought ferociously against one another. This was the first time that they had fought for a sensible, identifiable reason; otherwise, they fought till the death with one another for no known reason, cause, or purpose. No one tried to stop this, however; that was because if they weren't fighting amongst themselves, they started biting the family members. The roosters fought so much over the single hen that by morning they were too tuckered out to crow. Instead, they sat silently in the henhouse and listened to the mullah warble the call to prayer.

On Sundays, Khan Sahib reclined on his bed, and, with his eyes half open, resolved the tribal disputes and land claims of Bannu and Kohat. Now instead of Aurangzeb Khan (the King), he seemed more like Palangzeb Khan (the Bed-warmer). But at night he slept on the ground. He said, 'It's good for my arrogance and back. During our Frontier winters, the connoisseurs of sleep prefer soft hay. All night long, you smell the sweet scent of the wild expanses and the mountains. Whichever man takes in the sweet scent of the wild and likes it will be someone who can never be subjugated or made a slave.'

On Sundays, he ate lunch and then prayed. If lunch was bland, or if it had too many chillies, then his good mood was ruined, and he didn't pray. He said, 'How can I lie in front of the One Who Knows Men's Hearts? How can I say "God be praised" twelve times?' Usually there was arguing and backbiting going on in the room; nonetheless, he would go alone to the corner, unfold his prayer mat, and stand ready in prayer. But he kept listening. If, while praying, he heard something that put down him or his argument, he would immediately—right in the middle of bowing—leave off the prayer and start cursing out the offending soul in Pashto. Then he would put his hands on his belly, and with his ears still tuned in the other direction, continue praying.

After praying, he would take off his kurta and preside over his court. Most of his undershirts had big holes in them. He said, 'What can I do? Undershirts my size are smuggled in from Russia. Sometimes I can get them in Landi Kotal. Then I'm very happy. Some of the undershirts are so pretty that I really want to wear them on top of my kurta.' When he breathed deeply or when he laughed, penny-sized holes grew to the size of Ping-Pong balls, and his flesh popped out like blisters. Whatever the heat, even if he took off his kurta, he never took off his headgear. He said, 'As long as I'm wearing my cap, I don't feel naked and shameless. But this is why the British tip their caps immediately upon seeing a woman!'

One night, due to overloading, one charpoy collapsed to the ground with a dozen Pathans on it. For a good five minutes, the men couldn't get themselves untangled from the mosquito net and the charpoy's ropes. Inside the net, they kept jumping, hopping, and wriggling over one another like fish on the dock. One of the charpoy's legs broke, as did the wrist of a Pathan from Kohat. Once this man figured out that his wrist was broken, he thanked God because his wristwatch had escaped. The next day, Aurangzeb Khan had a white sheet spread out in his room, and he rolled up his bedding into a bolster pillow. This white sheet was the one that Basharat used during his regular Sunday poetry gatherings. Khan Sahib went to two such gatherings. If there was the slightest difficulty in the couplet, he turned to the man sitting next to him and asked what the poet was trying to say. When this man explained to him, then he would shout loudly, 'What the fuck?!'

The Ripped White Sheet and the Genitive Hater

After the second poetry gathering, Khan Sahib asked with great surprise, 'This is what a poetry reading is like?' The answer came: 'What else?' He said, 'I swear to God! So many lies have been told on this sheet that it's not fit for praying! The corpses of these lying poets

219

should be washed in hookah water so that the angels won't come to their graves for three days.' There were tiny holes on the white sheet wherever the poets had extinguished their cigarettes, and these holes grew to be quite large during the gatherings when the poets stuck a finger in while worrying over a line or while praising other poets. The white sheet was ripped in several places. When Khan Sahib mentioned praying on it, Mirza issued a very odd decree. He said, 'Only Zuleikha can pray sitting on Joseph's ripped hem.' Khan Sahib replied, 'There's a real bad word in Pashto for Zuleikha's husband.' For Khan Sahib, such a large gathering of poets was nothing less than a wonder. He said, 'In the tribal areas, there's only two possible explanations for such a large crowd to gather in front of a man's house. One, there's a tribal counsel to discuss a man's bad deeds. Or the man's father has died.'

When he liked a particular couplet, though this happened only once in a blue moon, he said, 'Yaoooww!' Then he would close his eyes and start to sway back and forth. But when the poet would begin to recite the same couplet again, Khan Sahib would signal abruptly for him to stop because he was interrupting his pleasure.

One day a young poet objected to another that he had composed a ghazal using his 'zameen' [prosody]. The other poet said, 'It's Sauda's—not your dad's!' He also shot back that the first had messed up the genitive. They kept on arguing for quite a while. At first, Khan Sahib couldn't understand what they were fighting over: if it was over agricultural land ['zameen'], then why were they using words to fight? When I explained to him the meaning of 'refrain,' 'rhyme,' and 'genitive,' Khan Sahib was speechless. Then he said, 'What the fuck? I'm so illiterate. I thought a 'genitive hater' was someone who took bribes or ate pork. Then I thought, "No, that's not it. One of them cursed out the other's father. That's why they're fighting." I've seen fighting over fake land for the first time today. Can they leave this land to their children as their inheritance? Can they say, "Son, we're moving on. Now it's time for you to watch over our land. Sow the seeds of rhymes, and make a jelly of genitives, and eat them to your heart's content!" There's a real bad word for this in Pashto.'

O Ghalib, It's Fine If I Don't Live Out My Natural Life

Often I saw him singing and whistling to himself out of happiness. His lively, undulating voice kept returning to a note in his lowest register—a bass note like on a tambura that was very pleasant to listen to. In his younger days, he had a particular liking for the tang takor raga. I mean, his expertise in music was enough that he knew he sang out of tune. He said, 'For us, the elite consider it a defect to sing well. I mean to sing badly.' Flawless singing was excusable only in the cases of professional singers, prostitutes, mirasi performers, and beautiful dancing boys. He knew a lot of songs. But his favourite was one Pashto song, and, singing it, he had ruined many a cloudy day and moonlit night. Its first line went something like, 'Look, my dear, for your love, I killed my rival with my steely sword.' After developing this with the repetition of the phrase, 'God, I sacrifice myself to you!' (during which time he put his hands to his ears), he sang with such ardour and passion that it became clear that the pleasure he got from loving wasn't anywhere close to the pleasure he got from killing. He sang this line with such brutal zeal and blind infatuation that his shalwar billowed with air.

He said, 'Without hatred and revenge life becomes purposeless, useless, and absurd. It's as though,

Life is absurd enough as it is; don't make it any more so.

You have to have at least a couple enemies. If you don't have enemies, then how can you seek revenge? Without enemies, what's the point of getting up early in the morning to work out, drinking buckets of milk, and sleeping with a pistol underneath your pillow? All our weapons would be useless. And, instead of dying a respectable death, all the respectable people will die with asthma, vomiting, and diarrhea! Only those animals that sharia laws forbid us to eat like crows, turtles, vultures, and donkeys will live out their natural lives! Until one of your ancestors has been mercilessly slaughtered you don't know the pleasure of revenge. The only people no one kills are beggars, mullahs, eunuchs, mirasi performers, childless men, and poets. There isn't anything more shameful than having an enemy who doesn't consider you worth killing. Blood will be shed. I swear by my faith! There's a really bad word in Pashto for men like that.

Pashto stones are not worn down in water!'

Horses, Slingshots, And Humility

'My grandfather was a very hot-tempered man. He murdered six men. And he performed the hajj six times. Then he renounced killing. He used to say, "I've grown old. I can't keep going on pilgrimage." He willingly went to meet his maker when he was ninety-five. He was unwilling to go until his last enemy had died. He used to say, "I won't let any of my enemies walk in my funeral procession. And I won't be able to bear seeing my wife become a widow." He was a very burly, truly intimidating man. Even when he walked, it seemed like he was on horseback. He was wise to the ways of the world. Mentioning horses reminds me how he used to say, "Walking is the best way to get around. You should use a horse only in two instances. One, to rush upon your enemy in the battlefield. Two, if that doesn't work, then to flee the battlefield in double time." I'm kidding. He never said that. He was like a Cossack horseman—he could leave the saddle, slide underneath the galloping horse, and then mount the saddle from the other side! I have his sword and fancy dagger. They were made from the same steel that was used to make Nadir Shah's sword. I'm the first man in my family for a hundred years who hasn't killed someone. At least till now. God be praised! Well, my uncle didn't kill anyone either, but that was because he was killed as a young man.'

There was no end to Khan Sahib's love of horses. He especially liked black horses. He always kept a half dozen horses in his stables in Bannu. They were all black. One purebred bay had been given to him as a gift. But he only liked the black on its tail and legs. He often said, 'In our tribe, it's forbidden to marry a bad marksman, a man whose ancestors were the killed and not the killers, and a man whose horse consistently bucks him off. I've always had horses. Even back in those days when I had nothing and went around on a brakeless bike, even then, outside my house there was a black stallion standing there neighing.' Someone asked him, 'How does that make sense, Khan Sahib?' And he said, 'For one, in our village, going everywhere on horseback was considered arrogant. Second, the horse was old. It was the last token I had of my father. My grandfather raised me. He hated any sign of arrogance. He used to say, "Always walk with your head bowed. This is the mark of a true Pakhtun." I'd just become a teenager. My blood was running hot. One day I was walking with my chest puffed out and my head raised so high and mighty that all I could see was the sky. He crossed my path. He stopped me. He grabbed the slingshot that my younger brother was carrying. Then he rammed its two ends into the back of my head so forcefully that my head bowed so low that all I could see were my heels. I promised to never strut around so proudly ever again. I took the slingshot and began to give it to my brother. But he stopped me. "Keep it," he said. "It will become useful. In old age, you can use it to prop up your chin."'

A Gypsy Song

When Khan Sahib, along with his hangers-on, would visit the poor areas where the Pathans lived, he would leap for joy when he saw a big stone lying on the road. He would stop. He would challenge the youths in his travelling party to lift it up. If no one could, then he would roll up his shirtsleeves, go forward, and, saying 'Yah, Ali!,' lift it above his head. The passers-by, as well as the neighbour kids, would stop to watch. When he had to pass through Karachi's nice, clean neighbourhoods, like PECHS, Bath Island, and KDA1, then he would get disappointed and say, 'What kind of shithole is this that there isn't a single big rock for a real man to lift up? In my village growing up there were so many boulders just lying around. We used to crawl on top of them and curse out our enemies. Or we would lean against them and relax. In the winter, the old folks would sit on these boulders with their slate-coloured blankets wrapped around them so that all you could see were their two eyes. Using the excuse of wanting to warm up in the sun, they kept an eye on the village's kids. And when, having come from the community well, the teenage girls — whose fair arms were as hard to get a hold of as fish in shallow water — would pass by with water pots on their heads, then the village's raring boys sat on these boulders watching them, and just from hearing the splish-splash of water in the pots, they could tell whose pot was filled to the brim, whose was half-empty, and which girls were smiling behind their veils. They could tell by a girl's gait whether she was wearing a skintight kurta beneath her heavy robes or whether she had brushed her teeth white with walnut paste. These girls walked with eyes in the back of their heads; they could tell who was watching them and what they were thinking. Where the four villages met near Malik Jahangir Khan's watchtower, there was a triangular boulder that lay half swallowed by the earth and half protruding like a demon's giant paw. It still has the marks that I left fifty years ago when using them for target practice on Eid. One bullet ricocheted off the boulder and into Nasir Gul's thigh. He was a good-looking young boy. Rumours spread about him. His dad yelled at him, "You son-of-a-bitch! I'll shoot such big holes in both your legs that a quilt-full of cotton won't be enough to staunch the gushing blood!" If anyone fired a round amidst the village's silence, the mountains near and far would double and then treble the sound into a great echo that made us tremble and quake in fear, and the women prayed that God would bring back their husbands safe and sound.'

Khan Sahib expressed his love and hatred through 'weightlifting.' I mean, if he lost an argument, he would lift up his adversary and throw him to the ground. And if he met a friend whom he hadn't seen in a long time, or if an unenviable physical specimen such as myself happened to greet him, then, as he embraced us, he would shake us as violently as you would a tree heavy with fruit. From his excess of love, he would lift us into the air, and then, with our foreheads at lip level, he would kiss us and then release us so that we would drop to the ground like Newton's apple.

Likewise, one of his favourite tunes (which he was always humming) indicated that he liked his beloved because he could lift her with both hands and put her on his head like he could a water pot:

My dear, come, become the water pot in my arms
I'll put you in my heart, then put you on my head.

While singing, he would trace out with his mutilated finger a diagonal line across his chest, as though,

I thought that you too were stuck on top my head.

It wasn't just her weight that he liked. He also considered her physical resemblance to a water pot (while not an absolute necessity) to be a big plus.

225

11.

Greetings!

Truth Be Told

As far as telling the truth is concerned, Khan Sahib was as helpless as we are when sneezing. There was nothing that could stop him from speaking his mind (and from burping). If anyone got dejected or angry because of something he said, he rested content that he had spoken the truth. He loved the truth as much as we love hiccups and poets love their just written ghazals. In French, a good writer is called an 'auteur,' and a good lover is called an 'amateur.' And, just like these examples, in Sindhi, someone who always tells the truth is called a 'sachar.' He belonged to this tribe. Once he asked a man right when meeting him, 'What are you trying to accomplish by having such a big mustache?' The man was offended. Khan Sahib said, 'Sorry. I'm an ignorant man. I asked because I really didn't know.' One time he asked Khalil Ahmad Khan Rind (the Boozer), 'Sorry, please, but were you born sick or have you ruined your health on purpose? Did your father too use the alias Khan?' The man was a rough and ready Pathan from Rohilkhand. He became really angry, then asked, 'What do you mean?' Khan Sahib replied, 'I was just asking. I mean, a stag doesn't come from its mother's womb with a full set of antlers.' One time he asked Basharat, 'You have a silk drawstring. Other than it's always coming undone, is there some reason you prefer it?' Another time he scolded Basharat very harshly in front of several friends, 'Please, yaraji, sorry, but I'm an ignorant man. Why do you go around all day saying, "Greetings! Greetings! Greetings!" Is a simple "hello" not good enough for you?'

Mistaking the Cave of Fear for the Cave of Hira

Actually, Basharat had never thought about this. Neither had I. Basharat had always heard his father say 'Greetings,' and he had always found this to be very sweet sounding and elegant. Khan Sahib scolded him like this one more time in front of others, and this made Basharat think about the past. One scene after another passed through his mind.

1. He sees the Mughal emperors take off their Timurid hats and Tashkent turbans and throw them to the ground. In their place, they tie Rajput turbans. The Shadow of God on Earth puts a tilak on his forehead and sits in the Prayer Hall in Fatehpur Sikri listening to Faizi recount chapters from the Persian Ramayana. Then, just a little while later, the Hindu pundits and Muslim mullahs create such a hullaballoo while arguing that it seems as though donkeys in heat have started to gnaw on wasp nests. Akbar the Great is so fed up with religion that he invents his own. In order to win over his Hindu subjects as quickly as possible, he expresses his disappointment with and rejection of his ancestral religion. The truth of the matter is that despite his great power he has turned his back on the sharia, is disappointed with mullahs, and is scared of the majority of his population. Gradually, the Shelter of All Religions mistakes his cave of fear for the Cave of Hira and declares himself a prophet,* although his own wife Jodha Bai and his advisor Mullah Do Piaza reject this claim. In

---

* In Islam, there are five pillars. In Akbar's religion, there were four professions of faith: the renunciation of wealth, the renunciation of life, the renunciation of religion, and the renunciation of honour. In this religion, there was no need for a fifth because after the fourth (that is, the renunciation of honour) there was nothing left to renounce.

order to please everyone, he makes a religious cocktail, which everyone rejects on the exact same grounds.

His Mastery of Flute Playing Did Nothing for Me

2. Then he sees that the Mughal warriors who have ridden bareback on their black stallions through the night and who have conquered one country after another are now sitting on kingly balconies made in the Rajputi style, or they are now on the banks of the Jamuna River sitting in their red howdahs on the backs of gigantic elephants, whose foreheads have been painted with five stripes. They have taken off their quilted cloaks because of the hot wind. Their chainmail is replaced by light angarkha coats. Gradually, the conquerors turn their backs on their mother tongues of Arabic, Turkish, and Persian and form a new language called Urdu, which is initially as strange to them as Turkish or Persian is to Hindus. After the complete military conquest of a country, new rulers abandon their language and so accept a sort of cultural defeat so that the conquered people don't think that they want to institute their mother tongue on a permanent basis along with their coinage. The doors and archways of mosques and shrines begin to be decorated with bas-relief of the Hindu holy flower, the lotus. Never again will the assemblies of warriors hear the clanking and clamoring of Tajikistani dancing, or the passionate songs of Samarkand and Bukhara; time not only changes the tunes but also the instruments used to play them. It's now been ages since the great musicians from beyond India and the extraordinarily gifted singers of distant Persia pressed their harps, cymbals, and rababs beneath their arms and left. But the heavens didn't cry at their departure. Nor did the Himalayas mourn. That's because the connoisseurs learned to enjoy the pleasures of Indian ragas played on the sitar, sarangi, and drums.

3. The finger turns to yet another page in the album of cultural compromise. On the banks of the beautiful Gomti River, the last king of Awadh, a great connoisseur of the dramatic arts, with bells tied to his ankles, is choreographing dance steps on stage to match a Hindi melody that he himself composed. Turn another page and, along the banks of the Jamuna, you see another bizarre scene. A few bearded, God-fearing elderly gentlemen are reclining against their bolsters while writing essays in Arabic and Persian on the decline of the Muslim community, the renaissance of religion, and the need for jihad; and when they greet each other, they bend down piously, express only the most appropriate sentiments, and regale each other with politeness, most respectfully. They avoid saying 'Assalam Alaikum' (which for twelve hundred years had been the way that Muslims greeted one another, just as 'Shalom' had been for Jews and 'Jai Ramji Ki' and 'Namaskar' had been for Hindus) because the custom has become painfully outdated. Things get so bad that even Hazrat Shah Walliullah's family stops saying it! The compiler of the *Amir-ur-rawayat* writes, 'When Hazrat Shah Walliullah's family members greeted someone they said, "Abdul Qadir* offers his greetings. Rafiuddin† offers his greetings." When Hazrat Syed Ahmad Barelvi came to take initiation rites as a disciple of Hazrat Shah Walliullah, he was the first person to ever greet him with "Assalam Alaikum!"'‡

---

* Hazrat Shah Abdul Qadir Dehlvi, may God have mercy upon him.
† Hazrat Shah Rafiuddin Dehlvi, may God have mercy upon him.
‡ Hazrat Shah Walliullah, may God have mercy upon him, was very happy to be greeted like this, and he ordered that in the future all greetings should be in accordance to the sunnat (*Amir-ur-rawayat*).

All these cultural compromises went on throughout the centuries winning over our hearts, but in the end they proved to be just wishful thinking. In the tumult that followed, cultural refinement and kingly designs couldn't save anyone's life or property (nor could they save Urdu itself, the very language of that compromise). Time drowned all this wishful thinking and fancy understanding in blood. After all, velvet sheets can't stop walls from crumbling. So what was going to happen happened. How could it possibly be that your beloved tongue is cut off at the root, the flag of sincere tolerance is lowered, and yet the culture left over would flourish?

Basharat often says that he will never forget how an illiterate Pathan from Peshawar made him give up his stilted style of greeting, which had been nurtured in his family for four generations.

12.

Karachiites Don't Let Chicks Grow into Roosters

Khan Sahib would normally ascribe two reasons for everything, and one was always quite absurd. For example, one day Basharat complained, 'Karachi mornings are always hazy and depressing. Even the sun doesn't want to get up. I don't want to get up. My body aches like a boxer was using me as a punching bag all night. In Kanpur, I got up as soon as the cock crowed. I would spring up out of day every day.' Khan Sahib pointed with his stubby, little index finger at his knees, 'There are two reasons for this. First, in Karachi, people don't let chicks grow into roosters. They slaughter them before they're big enough to crow. Second, your springs have arthritis. Eat fried fenugreek seeds for forty days, and apply a paste made from the plants that grow on the community well. One of our Pashto poets has said that every plant in a well is medicinal because they're always being touched by our damsels' scarves. Whenever I come to Karachi, I'm always surprised. Whoever

I meet, whoever I talk to, they're always complaining. I haven't met one person who was proud of the city. There are two reasons for this. First, there's nothing to be proud of. Second...'

Weeping Wall

He had raised his index finger toward the heavens and was about to tell us the second reason when Mirza Abdul Wadud Baig interrupted, 'Sir, the second reason is that muhajirs, Punjabis, Sindhis, Balochis, Pathans—they all came here looking for work. The sun was so hot. Like an affectionate mother, Karachi spread her torn, worn-out canopy over everyone's heads. It even embraced those who wanted no more than a little heap of sand to rest their heads on. Then they got greedy. Everyone's unhappy. Everyone's complaining. Everyone's upset. Take the muhajirs. They think of Lucknow, Bombay, Barabanki, Junagarh—even little Jhunjhunu—' (meaning, Jaipur, and here he pointed toward yours truly) '—and sigh and moan. They don't realize that the city that they miss, the city whose memory has left them in a permanently tearful state, well, it's not this place that they miss but their bygone youths, to which they can't ever return. So, sir, what they're crying over isn't geography but time's passage, and this poisons the life they know today. Punjabis, who Sir Syed Ahmad Khan nicknamed "the passionate Punjabis," will cry out, "O, Lahore, Lahore, where have you gone?" when they reach heaven. "There's no city in the world like Lahore!" they say. They don't like Karachi at all. Because they don't find the same taste of Multan's mangos and Montgomery's oranges in Sindh's spotted bananas, chikku fruit, and papayas, they get really sad. Gul Zaman Khan, the night watchman, is from the Frontier. He sits in his shack in Sher Shah Colony and longs for the mountains, forests, and rivers of his homeland!

Hey, no one brings the desert into the house!

'He eats Delhi's nihari stew for breakfast. Then, in the afternoon, he dreams a miraculous dream—in a forgotten corner of his boss's house, he lovingly waters his Frontier corn, which he's planted out of season.

> *Everyone is sad when in a foreign land*
> *But look—I've made my hometown flowers bloom even here!*

'All day long, he speaks Bombay Urdu with his Pashto accent, then in the evening he relaxes listening to Pashto songs on the transistor radio, then he falls asleep in his roadside shack fantasizing about Peshawar's railway station. All throughout the night motorcycles, rickshaws and trucks rumble by on the street, backfiring and making a ruckus, but he dreams of the drums, the surna, and the rabab playing his favourite hometown melodies. When Balochis come to Karachi, they look at the blue ocean, and tears well in their eyes as they remember their province's craggy mountains and the fat rams that they make into crispy sajji kebabs. And the old Sindhi man, the poor soul, sighs as he thinks back to the time before the coming of these four gentlemen.'

Then Khan Sahib hammered the last nail into this particular coffin. He said, 'Enough! There are two reasons for this. First, Shaikh Sadi said that if you're always dreaming about some other village, then you can be sure that your village is going to go to pot. Back home, if a woman gets married for a second time but starts talking about her first husband, then her new husband will cut off both their noses. Mullah Karam Ali said that women like this are cry babies. There's a real bad word in Pashto for the second husbands of women like this.'

Sometimes Khan Sahib solved thorny issues and life's riddles with his illiterate commonsense in such a way that you would have to say that

> *Where the books of knowledge were on the shelf, that's where*
> *they stayed.*

The Roosters of Principle and Fake Wars

Please excuse me. I've digressed again. But now it should be easier for you to understand the temperaments of Basharat and Khan Sahib and the nature of their disputes, which had gone on for so long that when they took up the argument again, they couldn't help but smile. It was no longer an ordinary business dispute. They were holding fast to their principles. It had become a cockfight, although they had agreed that whoever won, they would remain friends. Khan Sahib did like to say that whoever eats the cock killed in a cockfight will become such a sissy that they will think everything the government says is right. Sometimes it seemed that he was stretching things out because he was enjoying himself; otherwise, he was a happy, kind, sociable, and charitable man. Basharat knew this very well. He also knew that Khan Sahib loved him very much and really enjoyed his wit and humour. Two years before this, in Peshawar, he had told Basharat that he wanted to sit him down and listen to his stories for months on end. Basharat was fond of Khan Sahib, as well. He really enjoyed watching the sparks fly when he'd get heated up.

On the one hand, Khan Sahib was not willing to compromise on his accounting because it would undermine his Pakhtun honour, but, on the other hand, he was so loving and considerate that if anyone gave Basharat a hard time, he was eager to make them feel the heat. Four years previously, an excise inspector had bought on credit 10,000 rupees' worth of lumber at his store, but Basharat had never seen the money. One year after that, he wrote a promissory note. But now the inspector refused to pay. He said, 'I'm not going to pay. Go ahead, take me to court. The promissory note expired already.' Basharat mentioned this in the course of talking about his other problems. The very next evening after sunset prayers, Khan Sahib took a couple dozen of his commandos to the inspector's house. He knocked on the door. The inspector opened the door and asked why they had come. Khan Sahib said, 'We've come to rip out the windows and doors that were made from my friend Basharat's wood.' Then, in one brazen jerk, he pulled the door off its hinges. He put the whole kit and caboodle (door, hinges, screws, doorknob) under his arm like mischievous schoolboys who go around with their writing slates under their arms. Then he ripped out the framed photo of the inspector's dead grandfather—whose frame, he suspected, was made of Basharat's wood, as well—and handed it to one of his lieutenants. The inspector was a wily sort. He immediately understood how delicate the situation was. He said, 'Khan Sahib, your humble servant wants to make a request.' Khan Sahib said, 'Shut your trap. I'm no ass. Your time for making requests has expired. The rich always think they can get away with shit. Come to your senses. Go get the money.'

It was just a couple minutes before midnight when Khan Sahib brought to Basharat the 10,000 rupees in ten stacks of new notes. Seven of the stacks were stamped Valeka Textile Mills, which fell within the inspector's circle of bribery. But it wasn't just this money. He also extracted from the inspector rickshaw-fares for his commandos, as well as milk money, at the rate of one litre per person.

Khan Sahib became so close to members of Basharat's family that he started to bring sweets, clothes, and toys for the kids, who had started calling him 'uncle.' To entertain the youngest boy, Khan Sahib would lie down flat on the bed, have the boy sit on his belly, and then pump his belly like a bellows to throw the boy into the air. When the neighbour kids saw this, they started harassing their mothers, asking if they could go over to get the same treatment. Now Khan Sahib went with Basharat to his relatives' weddings, funerals, and birthdays. But then suddenly Basharat put an end to this when he learned from external sources that his relatives actually preferred Khan Sahib! One day Basharat was aghast when he learned that one conniving relative—with whom he had a strained, or, really, non-existent, relationship—had invited Khan Sahib without inviting him!

Then he learned from an informant that Khan Sahib had already secretly visited the police station a couple of times. And that he had given the SHO a karakul hat, a gunnysack of walnuts, a honeycomb, and a revolver made in Darra for which he didn't have a license. Basharat started to worry that some new torment was on the horizon. Perhaps that too would have two causes.

13.

The Clown Has to Earn His Bread by Hook or by Crook

Khan Sahib no longer bothered with his own shaving, nor did he have to re-string his shalwar's drawstring when it slipped out. Now he had Khalifa for that. As I mentioned previously, Khalifa was a jack of all trades: a groom, a driver of animal carts, a driver of vehicles, a cook, a waiter, a barber, a gardener, and a plumber; there wasn't anything he couldn't do. He was also extremely skilled in the most useful art of all—companionship and sycophancy. When all these peripheral jobs fell by the wayside, he retreated to his ancestral one. He often consoled his eldest son, who despised the barbering profession and was ashamed by his family's involvement in it, 'Son, barbers never have to look for work. The entire world always needs barbers. I mean, as long as the world doesn't convert to Sikhism! But Sikhs won't let that happen.' Khalifa was by Khan Sahib's side day and night. In the evening, when Khan Sahib's band of mountain men bedded down in front of the house, Khalifa brought out coffee and chillum pipes. Once, he brought them a biryani made from four purebred roosters that had just learned how to crow. According to him, when these young roosters puffed out their necks and crowed in the early morning, then all the mullahs and hens of the neighbourhood became restless and came out to see what was going on. He also claimed that when he was holding the position of gardener at the Governor General's house, he had seen Khwaja Nazimuddin eat the father (roasted) of these deceased roosters. After the prime minister Muhammad Ali Bogra married Alia (his second marriage), he had asked her to cook up an aphrodisiac halva made from the eggs of the deceased roosters' fathers' mourning widows. One day, to celebrate the resolution of a Kohat land-dispute, he roasted a whole sheep and brought it to the house. He brought a goat's tail too, so that Khan Sahib wouldn't guess that instead of a goat he had actually cooked up a cheap sheep. (He liked the rhyme that came out of this, as well.) Khan Sahib immediately said that it was impossible for such scrawny thighs to have come from an animal with such a big tail! Khalifa had never thought about that. He got up, with his hands folding together in supplication. Then he grabbed Khan Sahib's knees. Then he started to massage his legs with great energy up and down. Khan Sahib said, 'Hey, now, what's the big idea? Why are you grabbing my knees and touching my thighs?'

Khan Sahib liked Khalifa's tantalizing conversations more than his food. He said, 'When the speaker and the listener both know that everything's a lie, then there's no harm in it.' He encouraged Khalifa's bragging. Every second or third day, Khalifa massaged Khan Sahib's soles with almond oil. Khalifa used to say that it refreshed the mind. One day suddenly Khan Sahib thought of something. He said, 'Are you saying that my brain is in the soles of my feet?' But Khalifa had been right because after a couple of minutes he was snoring with his revolver tucked beneath his pillow. Every so often, he would startle awake, his snoring would modulate to another key, and then he would fall fast asleep again. One day he was snoring in his upper register and Khalifa was massaging his feet, when, who knows how, but Khalifa's hand reached into his waistcoat's pocket. Without opening his eyes, Khan Sahib said, 'Hey, now, my cash is in my jacket pocket!'

In fact, Khalifa had got on Khan Sahib's good side. Attendant, courtier, chillum filler, storyteller, chief cook, personal assistant, guide, informer, counsellor—he was everything to him. For three days or so they were locked in some intimate conversations. On some excuse or another, Khalifa came every evening to Basharat's. Basharat's wife kept saying that these visits weren't free of subterfuge and potential danger.

The Easy Way to Recognize a Man-eating Lion

One day, as soon as he woke up, Khan Sahib proposed to Basharat that he deduct the price of the vehicle that had been standing idle for so long from the amount that he was owed and then give the vehicle to him. Basharat said, 'Your wood wasn't worth a penny more than 7,000, and the vehicle, with its new body and new parts, isn't worth anything less than 9,000. Moreover, the British officer who had used to ride around in it was in line to be knighted.' Khan Sahib replied, 'At the very most, this vehicle's worth 5,000, whereas my wood was worth 9,000. You've added to the car's price the cost of gas, tire repairs, Khalifa's salary, and his wife's bride price.' After a lot of back and forth, after a lot of haggling, the amount that Khan Sahib was demanding was fixed at what it had first been, meaning 2,513 rupees, 9 annas, and 3 paisas. But now Khan Sahib wanted the vehicle and not the money.

'Khan Sahib, are you doing business or bartering?'

'What's that?'

'It's what you're doing.'

'There's a real bad word in Pashto for that.'

When he referred to Pashto, no one had the courage to ask what he really meant. He often said, 'Pashto isn't a language for pleading and lamenting. It's the language of real men.' He meant that it was the language to be used to spread your news far and wide, or if you want to go into a sleeping lion's den, pull on its whiskers, and engage it in dialogue. Back then Mirza used to say that Khan Sahib was one of those men who wasn't content to pull on the lion's whiskers but he also wanted to stick his head into its mouth to conduct the scholarly research into whether lions were vegetarians or man-eaters!

Arranged Marriages, Tribal Style

For Khan Sahib's ease of understanding, Basharat used the phrase 'exchange of goods and services' instead of 'barter.' Then he explained what he meant. After the long explanation, Khan Sahib said, 'Yaraji! Why don't you just call it an arranged marriage in which both parties think they've got the short end of the stick!'

This clumsy example had in it an irrefutable logic. They used this to seal the deal. Khan Sahib was very happy, even proud, to announce that he was ready for an 'exchange of goods and services.' Each congratulated the other, and they hugged like the sad folks whose sister's husband is also their wife's brother.

Basharat was secretly happy to get rid of the ramshackle vehicle for 7,000, and Khan Sahib was even happier to get a car worth 9,000 in exchange for a load of horrible wood. Each party considered the outcome a victory for truth, while if you ask me, I would say that lies defeated lies, and trash was exchanged for trash. Khan Sahib began to caress the car. He said, 'I'll take it on a drive through Torkham and Landi Kotal. I'll park it in the shade of walnut trees. In Kabul, I'll load it with karakul hats, carpets, and pine nuts and then drive it home. On my honour, I swear that one pine nut from the northern reaches of Kabul has the power of ten wedding dates!'

As soon as the matter was resolved, Khan Sahib threw off his newly acquired Lucknavi Urdu and Kanpuri accent. After defeating his eloquent enemy, he had no need for camouflage.

Since for Khan Sahib there was no better means of transport than a black stallion not only in this world but also on the Sirat Bridge leading to heaven and hell, he started calling his new car a black stallion as well.

The History of Balushahi Donuts

Basharat secretly offered two prayers of thanks, but Khan Sahib couldn't keep a lid on his happiness. Having received divine intervention, he had defeated Basharat, and now he was itching to do a victory lap around his house. From Basharat's shop on Harchandrai Road, he looked out greedily at all the horses pulling carts. It was the moment for riding dressage* around his enemy's house. When he couldn't control himself, he patted his black stallion's thigh—that is, the car's mudguards. He put his hand on its snout and praised it. He wanted to feed it grass and currycomb it. When a horse-drawn cart pulled up in front of Spencer Eye Hospital and the driver unyoked his horse, Khan Sahib raced over, leapt on the horse's back, and rode in circles around Basharat's shop two times. Then he asked none other than Basharat to give him a jug of cold water, which he poured over his own head, and then ordered seven kilos of balushahi donuts and distributed them to everyone. Khan Sahib set aside donuts for three of Basharat's relatives and went to deliver them himself. Basharat couldn't believe it. It was too much to take. Even in his most distrustful state of mind, he would never have imagined that the three men

* Dressage: My dear friend Mukhtar Masood, who in addition to being a writer with great style is also a great horseman, told me that 'dressage' is a dignified and ceremonial gait that horses use when carrying kings. (Their gait is so gentle that whatever water is in the king's stomach won't jiggle at all.) Whichever of my young readers hasn't seen a king, a royal horse, or the way that Mukhtar Masood walks should read his *Awaz-e-Dost* [*The Voice of a Friend*] because the grace of his writing leaves the reader trembling for hours.

would turn out to be such crafty hypocrites that they would secretly join forces with Khan Sahib. Anyway, it was the first example in the history of the exposure of hypocrisy through donuts. I mean, it was the first time in the history of donuts.

His followers from Bannu fired their rifles into the air to declare the war's end. A neighbour came running to Basharat's shop to congratulate him; he thought that Basharat had just had another boy.

A truck driver had come to Basharat's shop to pick up a delivery, and Khan Sahib asked him to drive him in the black stallion to Govardhan Das Market, where he would treat him to tea and snacks. When Khan Sahib got back, he was overjoyed with how the car had performed, 'I swear to God, it was just like my father's black stallion!'

That night he called over a painter and had him spray-paint the car black so that, in addition to how it drove, it also looked like a black stallion.

'Et tu, Brute!'

The next evening when Basharat was having the store closed, a truck pulled up. Sitting in the passenger seat was the secretary from the police station, and in the back were both the stolen wood and the wood he had given as a bribe. The same constable was sitting on the wood holding his rifle. Through a DSP who had grown up in Bannu (and who was his brother in arms), Khan Sahib had not only extracted the goods from the lion's very mouth but, as a souvenir, he had also extracted his teeth. A taxi pulled up behind the truck with the lawyer inside. (The taxi had just been ticketed for emitting from its muffler more than the legal limit of exhaust.) He was there to make sure both parties were satisfied in the result once and for all. Just a couple paces behind him came his criminal-looking client, carrying the lawyer's briefcase in one hand and several law books in the other. The lawyer was carrying two boxes of sweets, one which he presented to Khan Sahib and the other to Basharat, with the following words, 'Please give this to your wife and kids from me.'

The secretary asked, 'Where's our Khalifa?' Basharat was quite shocked to learn that after Khalifa's night in the lock-up, he had started going to the police station twice a month to cut the hair of everyone from the SHO down to the accused criminals who were locked up there! If in the house of one of the station's staff members, or in the home of any of the criminals, there was a baby expected in the near or remote future, or if he saw any woman from the shacks that surrounded the station walking heavily, then he made them promise that if it was a boy, they would call him to perform the circumcision. His deceased father had advised him, 'Son, even if you become a king, never give up being a barber. Secondly, make sure you win over everyone you meet, or you get into his good graces.' So the poor guy ended up being everyone's lackey.

Until two in the morning, Khan Sahib dealt with ordinary cases of debts, as well as disputes that had erupted over stealing irrigation water, both of which had become rather complicated because of the exchange of curses that had followed the actual offenses. While he was hearing the cases and giving his decisions, a stream of people came in to wish him goodbye. Khan Sahib would say, 'Welcome,' and give everyone some tea, a hit on the chillum, some pine nuts, and some donuts. Then at four in the morning, he started packing. After the call to the morning prayers, he turned a purebred rooster in the direction of Mecca and slaughtered it. He gave the head to the cat and the rest to Basharat's family for breakfast. He munched on the heart himself. He smiled and then said, 'In my tribe, it's a custom to slaughter a cow when we've defeated a dangerous adversary. If the enemy isn't much, then we slaughter a ram.' At breakfast he announced that he wouldn't send the black stallion on the goods' train but that he would go by road so he could show the car the Punjab and different things along the way. The kids were very sad to see him go. He admitted, 'I don't want to go. But what can I do? I'm in the lumber business. If there were forests in Karachi, then I swear to God I'd never leave you.' Then he consoled them, 'God willing, in two months I'll be back. I have to deal with a Bohri Seth. My business is just me. And I'm old. I can deal with only one swindler at a time.'

He saw Basharat smiling, and so he smiled. He said, 'Doing business on credit in Karachi is like playing kabaddi in a sugarcane field! The bigger the city, the bigger the mess. The bigger your roof is, the more snow will fall on it.' Then in order to entertain the youngest son, he lay down on the charpoy.

When he was about to go, he gave 500 rupees to Basharat's daughter Muniza, who had become his favourite. It was for her fifth birthday, which was to be celebrated in eight days.

He distributed 73 rupees, 9 annas, and 3 paisas among Basharat's servants. The night before he had given 2000 rupees to a Pathan youth named Gul Dawood Khan so that he could go home to Kohat and launch a criminal case against his uncle for illegally seizing his land and so teach the bastard (and all uncles, really) a lesson for trying to filch the property of orphans. All this money came to 2573 rupees, 9 annas, and 3 paisas. This happened to be the amount over which the dispute had started, and the amount for whose collection he had invaded, along with his commandos and all their military gear. According to Mirza, he had set up his bhangra dance party in the very heart of his enemy's fort.

Thirty years have passed. I've been an accountant my entire life, but even today I can't tell you who got what and how much from whom, or who won in the end. It was a great misunderstanding: who we thought was our opponent turned out to be our friend and supporter; friends don't haggle in their hearts.*

Khan Sahib had distributed money to the servants and was saying goodbye to Basharat's father, when what did Basharat see but a man approaching them whose face (but only his face) looked like Khalifa. Instead of his usual tight-fitting pyjamas, muslin kurta, and velvet hat, he wore a Malaysian shalwar and kurta, and, on his head, he had tied on top of a brocade hat a turban from Mashhad. He also wore an embroidered waistcoat and sandals whose bottoms were fashioned out of tires from Peshawar. His waistcoat was three sizes too big, and his hat was three sizes too small. A prayer coin was tied onto the right arm of his waistcoat. And he was holding Balban's reins. Khan Sahib announced that Balban was going in a truck to Bannu. He said, 'I've four or five horses standing around in my stables, so what's one more? Every animal has its provisions apportioned by God.'

Khan Sahib said that Khalifa was going to drive the black stallion to Peshawar and that he wouldn't return until Doomsday. There were two reasons for this. First, his ancestors had come to India from Kandahar via Peshawar. They had come with nothing but their steely swords, which, from constant use, had been worn down into razors! Second, he had hired him as his servant.

Basharat's jaw dropped several feet.

'Khalifa! You!'

'Boss!' Khalifa said this with his hands folded together in supplication and in such a piteous way that no further explanation was

---

* Mirza Abdul Wadud Baig, who has given loans to friends time and time again, and so has lost both money and friends time and time again, repeats this last phrase with a little change to it. He says, 'Friends only haggle—hearts or no hearts.'

needed. It spoke of humiliation. It spoke of pleading. It spoke of the courage of being ready to earn a living by any means necessary.

14.

When He Was About to Cash Out

It must have been about two months after Khan Sahib left that a dictated letter came from him. It read:

> By the grace of God, everything is all right here. But there is something. I didn't want to tell you while I was staying with you because it would have unnecessarily worried you, and I wouldn't have been able to enjoy your company. Three weeks before leaving Peshawar, I was diagnosed with cirrhosis. It was Stage 2, which is incurable. The doctors at Jinnah Hospital confirmed this. They said that I should keep myself entertained. They said that I should try to remain upbeat, and to surround myself with cheerful people whose company I enjoy. That's what their prescription for good living came down to. Yaraji, I could read between the lines. But a tabla player could have told me as much. You didn't need an MRP or FRCS degree, or to poke around with a stethoscope to say that much!
>
> I thought of all my friends, but I couldn't think of anyone as loving, cheerful, and intent on making others happy as you. So I bought a ticket and went to Karachi. Everything else was just to pass the time. All the days I spent with you were extra days added to my life. May God keep you so cheerful and attentive to me. Apologizing to you for the hardships I caused would be a type of Lucknavi grace, which is beyond the likes of unsophisticated men like me. These sorts of things happen between friends. My grandfather used to say, 'There's a saying in Persian that goes either don't make friends with mahouts, or build your house so strong that it can withstand the blows of elephants.'

I'm sending with a truck driver ten kilos of fresh jaggery from Mardan with newly harvested walnuts set in them like jewels, three organic honeycombs from Swat complete with their real wax and dead bees, and twenty quails in a thin-necked basket. For Yousufi Sahib, I'm sending in a delicate basket two kilos of his favourite paneer from Peshawar Cantt, along with Pindi's hunter beef. When I was leaving, he asked me to send a couple good artifacts from the Gandhara Civilization. I got caught up in the commotion of leaving, and forgot to ask him what exactly he wanted. I asked a couple of my ignorant friends here. They sent me to some Gandhara store. They said, 'We sell top-quality trucks and genuine parts. What are you looking for?' On Monday, the secretary of a construction foreman came back from the Takht Bhai Mardan site with four exquisite statues of black stone wrapped up in a sheet. But when I asked a big-time smuggler here who sends larger-than-life statues to America, he said that they weren't the Buddha but they were his lackeys (for them there's a real bad word in Pashto), yes men, and suck-ups because the Buddha was never so muscular. I've heard that the Buddha, after he reached nirvana, looked as bad as Yousufi does now—all skin and bones. Anyway, I'm still looking. Greet him for me, and then tell him it would be better to hang up a photo of the man from Kabul.*

To hell with this disease! The goblet of life is spilling over before it has been filled. Even in dictating this letter, I ran out of breath. I don't dare cough properly for fear it will make you-know-who start crying. She hides herself in a corner and cries and cries. I keep explaining to her, 'Hey, now, as long as I'm still conscious, I'm not going to let this disease beat me.' Basharat, my friend, there's a real bad word in Pashto for men like that. Last week, I started

---

* After thirty years, I'm finally taking his advice. He hung his picture in the picture gallery of my heart that long ago, and now I'm providing you with its dimmest outline.

construction on a new house on University Road. We'll be able to sit fifty poets from Peshawar, or one hundred from Karachi, on its verandah.

Everything else is going well. Khalifa begs to say hello. I've got him a job as a servant at Muslim Commercial Bank. He rides the black stallion in the evening and over the holidays. He's in great shape. He's learned how to curse out the stallion in Pashto. But he hasn't learned which nouns are masculine and which are feminine. People break out laughing when they hear him talk. Just yesterday, I gave him a good trick—that is to conjugate as feminine whatever nouns he thinks are masculine. Then it will be Pashto. Greetings, love, and chastisements to all, each as they deserve.

Yours, lovingly,
    The Man from Kabul

PS: When I returned, I saw that there were some miscellaneous accounts still to be settled. But I can't travel. Please find some time to come and set right your friend's accounts, and your man from Kabul will hang on for a couple more days.

PSS: Moreover, it's hard to wait patiently for the house and verandah to be completed! I've already arranged for one white sheet without holes and five poets—all for you—may you live in peace.

Basharat left for Peshawar on the morning's first train.

Two Tales of the City

1.

Lighting the Ruins

They were together for about forty-five years. Let's call it a half century. After his wife died, Basharat was numb for many days. It seemed like he hadn't lost someone but that he himself had died. His grown sons buried her. He stood watching stoically from the mound of fresh dirt to the side of the grave. He still carried around the small bag of cardamom she had made for him. The crocheted skullcap he was wearing was the one his dearly departed had made, staying up till two o'clock on consecutive nights so he would be able to go to the mosque for Eid. Everyone threw their handful of soil into the grave, and that was then covered with rose petals. Only then did he step forward, take from his kurta's pocket several jasmine buds grown on bushes planted by his wife, and throw these buds, which were several hours short of blooming, on top of the bright flowers. Then he looked blankly at his soiled hands.

It was so hard to believe that the woman with whom he'd lived with for so long was suddenly gone. No, if that life had been a dream, then this was too. He felt as though she was sure to pop her head around the corner to smile at him. Sometimes in the night's silence, he thought he heard her footsteps and the clinking of her bangles. This startled him. No one had ever seen him cry. Strangers and relatives alike praised

---

'Two Tales of the City' is the inverse of *A Tale of Two Cities*. Or, in other words, it is the story of a city of two stories.

his steely resolve. Then suddenly it hit him. His defenses failed. He started sobbing like a child.

But all miseries pass, just as all pleasures fade. Days clipped by, as they had before. Like La Rochefoucauld said, it's against our nature to stare at the sun, or at death, for too long. The shock gradually wore off; it was replaced by grief, which then turned to loneliness. When I returned from Miami to Karachi, I found him in this state. Desperately sad. Desperately lonely. Of course, he wasn't as alone as he thought, and yet it's also true that you're only as lonely as you feel. Loneliness makes you think. Wherever you turn, you find your reflection; you fear your own company, and you want to escape. Your loneliness takes you by the hand and leads you slowly back to every thoroughfare, footpath, alleyway, and intersection you've known. When you stop, thinking the road has changed course, you realize it isn't the road but you who have changed. Roads don't go anywhere. They remain right where they are. But people change. Roads don't get lost. People do.

According to an old saying, regardless of exactly how many defects old age has, it has one more burdensome than all the rest combined. And that's nostalgia. In old age, a person prefers to turn back from their unwanted, imminent end to recall the places they used to know. In old age, the past flashes all its dangerous charms. Old, lonely people live in sad houses where they have to have lights on even at noon; and when bedtime rolls around and they put out the lights, their minds are lit by the bright glow of memories. As this glow becomes brighter, so too their desolation becomes more pronounced.

So something like this happened to him as well.

His Imaginary Past and Purgatory

God had made Basharat's life in Karachi fuller than he could ever have wished. But after his wife's death, he experienced a sharp pang of nostalgia, and he began to miss Kanpur terribly. Before this, the past had never had any hold over him. But now he was living exclusively in the past. There wasn't anything particularly wrong with his present, except that, for an old man, the present has the sizeable shortcoming of not being the past.

For quite a while, I've wanted to be able to forget

The film of his life, with its every event, began to play backwards through his mind. It was a total reversal, as though a wizened banyan tree had turned upside down to sit in a yogic pose, sending its knotty limbs and deep roots into the sky. After thirty-five years, he decided to go back to Kanpur, his purgatory. He began to miss each and every thing—the lanes, marketplaces, neighbourhoods, and courtyards; the roofs that smouldered like young bodies in the summer heat; the desires that spread into the night's dreams, and the dreams that transformed into the day's desires. It got so bad that he even began to think of his grade school as a piece of heaven, the very one that as a boy he'd taken so much pleasure in avoiding. All the pleasures, all the memories washed over him. His friends smashed together on charpoys; the shade of neem trees heavy with fruit; the eastern breeze bursting with the sweet smell of mango blossoms and mahua fruit; the tamarind trees with ripe seedpods, and girls looking longingly at them, and boys looking longingly at the girls; forests full of deer; ducks shot from the sky falling three hundred feet to land with a thud; screens made of sweet-scented grass; ponds full of water chestnuts; velvety melted ice cream slipping down your throat; mulsari flower bracelets; the thin, flickering tongues of chameleons hidden in the jamun tree's dense leaves at the height of summer; the lone stag standing on an outcrop with his ears turned alertly into the wind; the surging forth of youth and the despair of first love; the lightly tanned arms that fuelled both waking dreams and those of the night; the smell of freshly starched scarves; friends laughing and carrying on. This cache of memories called out to him so strongly that

> At once he dug his heels into the ground
> And started to turn around.

But he wasn't a boy any longer. I mean, he was over seventy. It didn't occur to him for even a second that all these wonderful, romantic things (which Mirza Abdul Wadud Baig, riffing on the phrase 'the tools of cultivation,' calls 'the tools of rebellion,' and each of which caused him to emit a hundred-decibel sigh) were not only available in Pakistan but in certain cases were even better there. There was just one thing missing in Pakistan. His youth. It turned out that after a lot of searching, he couldn't find it in Kanpur either.

These Boys Are like Old Men, These Men Are like Boys

He'd planted a mulsari tree in front of his house in North Nazimabad, but the mulsari trees of his memories were so much better smelling and more elegant. He was experiencing the state of mind that comes right after old age's onslaught when suddenly you desperately want to see again your childhood home before you die. But he didn't know that in the time between childhood and old age an invisible hand interposes a powerful magnifying glass. The wise know not to remove this glass. If it's removed, everything looks like its own miniature. Yesterday's gods turn into midgets. If you've been away from your hometown for a long time, you should never return for a belated last look. Nevertheless, you go. The scenes pull you like a magical magnet, and so you go. You don't realize that as soon as you look with your mature eyes upon the wonderland of your youth, its spell will be completely broken. Dreamland's fairies disappear, and soot darkens The House of Mirrors. You find that the sacred aromas of youth no longer exist. Moreover, where's the familiar rainbow of the God of Love?

What is this smoke?
Where is the fire of my youth?

You can't believe what you're seeing. Why does it look so different? Why does it smell so different? Sound so different? These aren't the picturesque lanes and marketplaces where everything was fresh and new. What happened to everything? To everyone?

Was this the face that launch'd a thousand ships?
And burnt the topless towers of Ilium?

When the spell breaks, your imaginary past collapses. You're no longer counted among the young or the old. You become suddenly colourblind. A peacock might dance in front of you, but you see only its feet, and so you cry! Everything loses its colour; dejection reigns supreme.

Your world is insipid
And your religion is cast in doubt

Wherever He Lived, He Grew Sick of It

So this childish old man went to Kanpur and mourned. For thirty-five years, he had lamented why he had left heaven for Karachi, and now he gnashed his teeth, 'My God! Why didn't I leave earlier?' He regretted that for no reason he had wasted a good third of his precious life regretting the wrong thing! If he was looking for things to cry about, there were three hundred and sixty five great ones easily found, and that was because there were just that many disappointments (days) in a year. He left no stone unturned in his dreamland, but

Those pangs no longer excited his heart
Those feelings were no more.

Thirty-five years of nostalgia collapsed, and now everything looked desolate and rundown. The wide, crocodile-filled river into which he had fearlessly jumped from the crown of a mighty banyan tree? Well, when he went back, he saw only a seasonal creek full of frogs. And the gigantic tree itself? A bonsai specimen.

He couldn't recognize himself in what he'd left behind.

2.

One Big Pigeon Loft

But enough of my philosophizing. Let's hear the story from our hero, Basharat, as his storytelling leads to a different sort of pleasure.

Although this story is quickly told
It has all the charms of those of old

Sir, when I saw my house, I was shocked, 'My God! That's what we lived in? And, more than that, we loved it!' The most pitiful and incurable type of middle-class poverty is when people have nothing but feel as though they lack nothing. God be praised—we were nine brothers and four sisters born one after the other. I use the phrase 'one after the other' knowingly because, whether playing, eating, lying down, or sitting, it would be more appropriate to have said 'one on top of the other.' Everyone's name ended in the letter 't': Ishrat, Rahat, Farhat, Ismat, Iffat, and so on. My father designed the house himself on the small school slate of the brother immediately older than me. He also kept over a hundred pigeons, and each was of its own unique race, with its own unique heritage. He didn't let male pigeons mate with female pigeons of other breeds. He had a lumber store. He built all his pigeon lofts, bearing in mind the size, bad habits, and length of each pigeon's tail. Sir, now that I've seen it again, I can tell you his worthless hobby made the house look like one big pigeon loft. In fact, we should call the house a crude version of the same.

My father was very perspicacious as well as practical. He realized that after he passed, his children would argue over the division of property, so as soon as another child was born he built a separate room. The problems implicit in this construction strategy were many. For one, part of the plan was to make each subsequent son's room smaller than the previous. By the time I rolled around, my room was so small that I couldn't stand up straight. It took seven years to build the house. And in this time, three more sons were born. When the walls for the eighth son's room went up, no one could tell if it was going to be a bathroom or a bedroom. With the arrival of each newborn, he would sketch out on the slate the necessary amendments (the added room) to the house's blueprint. The courtyard slowly disappeared. It became the cells we were going to inherit.

Buzary Replaces Bourgeoisie

Sir, you can't compare our Karachi house with its air conditioner, carpets, and fresh paint with that ruin, in which, if you happened to cough, plaster would slough from the wall. It hadn't been whitewashed in over forty years. In my cousin's house in Kanpur, I saw a plastic tarp used as a ceiling covering. No one in Karachi or Lahore knows the proper words for this ceiling covering, or for 'awning.' On the ceiling covering, there were three spots marked with nail polish with big multiplication signs (X). This meant that you shouldn't sit underneath; the roof leaked there. In Kanpur and Lucknow, I found my friends and relatives fallen on hard times. Those who were white collar still were, but now their collars had faded to grey. They'd become proud of their

---

Translators' note: Buzary refers to Hazrat Abu Zar Ghaffari, a companion of the Prophet Muhammad, who shunned a life of extreme luxury in favour of poverty.

indigence; they'd turned self-sacrifice into an art. At a private gathering, I made some superficial remark about this, and a junior lecturer who taught economics at a local college got bent out of shape. He said, 'You owe your wealth to the United States and the UAE. Our poverty is our own.' (To this, a man recited in Quranic tones, 'Alhamdulillah …') 'I hope you're happy piling up debt! The Arabs aren't wrong when they say the Third World is full of beggars.' I was a guest. I wasn't in a position to argue. He went on for quite a while reciting couplets in praise of poverty, its noble mindset, and its coarse bread. He recited some couplets about Hazrat Abu Zar Ghaffari. I made sure to nod appreciatively. I was a guest, after all. Whether Indian or Pakistani, today's intellectuals have replaced the love of making money with the love of not making money.

There's nothing that Indians don't make. Not just Kanpur, but every city is bursting with factories. Textile mills, steel factories, car and airplane factories, even tanks are made there. They exploded an atom bomb a long time ago. They've sent satellites into space. It wouldn't be surprising if they go to the moon. There's that perspective. Then there's another perspective, which is the following. One day I was on my way to Inamullah the Loudmouth's.* I took a cycle rickshaw. My rickshaw guy looked like he had TB. I could see his ribs through his tank top. His breath reeked of syrupy Banaras paan. He scooped the sweat off his forehead with his index finger and flicked it out in an arc. His sweat made his face and hands gleam, and in the hot sun it looked like he'd applied Vaseline. He was barefoot. He wore a watch on his bony wrist whose face was bigger than his wrist. He had a sexy photo of Parveen Babi on his bike's handlebars. Pedalling made him double over, and so he kept prostrating himself before Babi. We went

---

* Inamullah was once very proud of being brutally honest, and that's why he was called the Loudmouth.

one mile, but guess how much he asked for? Sir, all of seventy-five paise! My God, seventy-five paise! When I gave him that and a tip of four rupees, twenty-five paise, he couldn't believe it. He started to smile. Gradually his smile spread so wide I could see all his paan-stained teeth, which looked like pumpkin seeds. He looked greedily at my coin purse and said, 'Sir, are you from Pakistan?' I answered, 'Yes. But for thirty-five years I lived over here in Hiraman.' He gave me back my money, 'Sir, how can I take money from you? You're my neighbour, after all. I'm from there too.'

Now the Poor Grumble

And the population? God help us! It's like a big fair. The earth spurts up people from everywhere. You can't take two steps into a shopping area without wielding your hands and elbows. You could call it doggie paddling on land! And where you don't have enough space even to wield your elbows, you get to where you're going simply on the force of the crowd's pushing. It seems like everyone sleeps on the sidewalks. They grow up there, and they die there. But these people can't be bullied or bossed around. No one even checks to see who's nearby before they start complaining about the government. In our day, the poor were humble. Now they grumble. They'll let a cycle rickshaw through, but they won't budge an inch when a car comes by. Azizuddin the lawyer was saying that our country is very politically aware, but God knows. What I've seen is that pig-headedness increases in direct proportion to poverty. There are many conmen there too, but no one dares flaunt their wealth. I've seen women of rich families at weddings wear cotton saris and flip-flops. If they didn't have vermilion in the parts of their hair, I swear to God, you would take them to be widows. They don't wear any make-up at all, but we won't touch a chicken leg until it's had rouge applied to it! Sir, you must have seen the violent red chicken tikka of Tariq Road? In Kanpur, I saw cane beds and sofa sets in rich people's houses, and some of those were the very ones we had used to lounge around on thirty-five years ago! Sir, you'll find that Hindus have a leg up on us when it comes to Islamic simplicity!

What Was Going to Happen Has Happened, My Bearers!

You'd have to say that Urdu speakers still speak Urdu, but I noticed a strange change. It's not just the common people, but it goes all the way up to professors and writers: they don't speak like we used to. The crisp tone is gone. It's slipped further and further, so now it sounds like Hindi. Singsong. You know what I mean? If you don't believe me, listen to the Urdu news on All India Radio and compare it to Radio Karachi, or to me. When I pointed this out to Inamullah the Loudmouth, he got really offended. Seriously, sir, he made it personal, 'Look, bub, what about your Punjabi accent? You don't notice, but I do. Don't forget that on August 3, 1947, I went with you to the train station to see you off. You were wearing a black Rampuri hat, white churidar pyjamas, and Jodhpuri slippers. You cupped your hand delicately to say, "Greetings!" Right or not? You had paan bulging from your cheek, kohl lined your eyes, and the scent of itr-e-gil* came from the folds of your muslin kurta! Right or not? Back then you said "cha" for "chai," "ghans" for "ghas," and "chanval" for "chaval." Right or not? And when the stationmaster blew the whistle, you had a jasmine garland around your throat, you were pouring hot "cha" from your cup into your saucer, which you then blew on before slurping it down. You used to call Karachi, *Karanchi*. Right, right? Now after three decades of decadence, you come from your Karachi concrete

---

* Itr-e-gil: The mild scent of the first drops of rain soaking into the earth was worn in late summer. Now only corpses are covered in the earth's sweet scent.

jungle with a head full of white hair, wearing a billowing, haji-style kurta that goes down to your ankles. You come on your little pilgrimage, and now we all look like Pandits and Pandeys? Have you forgotten?' Sir, I was a guest. I let him have his moment. Then I got up silently, found a rickshaw, and went home.

Pick up the palanquin
And take me home!

At Times I Kept Quiet, at Times I Laughed

Lucknow and Kanpur were Urdu centers. They had countless Urdu newspapers and magazines. Sir, I know you don't agree with me, but I'm telling you our language was pure. During my visit, I didn't see one Urdu sign in all of Kanpur, and not in Lucknow either! Whenever I mentioned this to someone, they sighed or turned away. It was my bad luck to mention this at a party. It really got under this one man's collar. I think his name was Zaheer. He was on the city commission—a lawyer. Who knows how long he had been storing up these feelings, 'For God's sake! Please have mercy on us Indian Muslims! Let us be. Whenever someone comes from Pakistan, as soon as they get off the plane and exchange their money, they start in with this refrain. Everyone's eyes fill with tears, and they start reciting elegies to the city's death. Sir, please! How can we show you the Kanpur of a half-century ago? Nonetheless, everyone weighs the present against the India of that time. When they're done with that, they compare it against contemporary Pakistan. They scare off the other person's horse and end up winning both races!' He kept on talking. I was a guest. What could I say? It was just like the old Sindhi saying, 'She went to get her horns cut and ended up cutting her ears as well.'

But one thing must be said: however miserable their lives, Indian

Muslims are sincere, as well as full of grace, self-respect, and confidence.

I had long chats with Nushoor Wahidi. He's the embodiment of love, sincerity, and feebleness. Poets and writers hang out at his house all the time. Intellectuals go too. (The word implies intelligence only, not wisdom.) Everyone agrees that Urdu is very stubborn, and intellectuals profess that its future is not bleak at all. They organize enormous poetry festivals. I heard that at one festival more than thirty thousand people came. Sir, I can't agree with you when you say that poetry can't be understood by five thousand people at once—if it is, it's not poetry but something else. They have numberless annual conferences and symposia. I heard that there are some Urdu writers who have won the Padma Shri and Padma Bhushan awards. I asked what the meanings of 'padma' and 'bhushan' were, and they answered by stating how much each prize was worth! Even today Indians use Urdu in film songs, double-entendres, qawwali, and when fighting. There's an emphasis on Sanskrit words. But you can't curse out the average Joe in Sanskrit. You can only do that if you're talking to a Sanskrit scholar. Sir, I heard someone say that cursing, counting, whispering, and dirty jokes are fun only in your mother tongue. Anyway, I was saying that the Urdu intelligentsia is hopeful. When Indira Gandhi has to use official Hindi, she often slips up, and this gives heart to Urdu lovers.

Who Can Hold Off Time?

Nushoor Wahidi was all warmth and love. Even after chatting for four hours, when I got up saying I should go, he took me by the hand and sat me back down. And I was glad he did. His memory is weak. One time he kept asking about you, 'How is he? I heard he's writing humour essays. Really, it's too much!' You know that he's always been thin and sickly. He weighed seventy-five pounds. He must have been just as old. His nose dominated his face. His sickly frame reminded me of Kanpur's chunia bananas; they had exactly the same shape. You can still get them, so I special-ordered some. I was disappointed: they're not even close to being as good as our Sindhi spotted bananas. One day I happened to say that our Sargodha oranges are better than those of Nagpur, and Nushoor whipped his head around, 'That's not possible!' So Nushoor is (God protect him) still nimble-witted and spry. He looks better than he used to. That's because he's lost all his teeth, which used to stick out of his mouth this way and that like garlic cloves. You must remember how well Suraiya Actress used to sing, but her big overbite ruined the moment. I heard that after going to Pakistan, she had her front teeth pulled. I looked at a current photo of her in a film magazine; then I cursed myself for doing so. I made sure not to listen to her records, for fear of remembering how she looked. Aijaz Hussain Qadri has all the records from that time along with a horn gramophone. Sir, it's amazing that this gramophone was the height of science, music, and luxury! He played a couple songs of that era's Emperor of Music, Saigal. Sir, I was shocked to realize that his nasal singing had released such romantic feelings in me. Moti Begum's face is a mess of wrinkles and looks like a raisin. Nushoor said, 'Now, why are you feeling so bad for others? Get out your passport from '47 and compare how you look now.'

Who can hold off time?
No mountain can, nor any blade of grass.

There wasn't a national poetry festival to which Nushoor was not invited. And there probably wasn't another poet who got as large a fee as he did. People really respected him. Now, through God's benevolence, he has furniture. But he still kept to his old ways. His health was as usual. Meaning, very bad. Whenever I arrived at his house, he sat up from where he'd been lying down on his woven-rope charpoy.

He never changed out of his undershirt, and he always squatted on top of a pillow. I could see the charpoy's imprint on his back. One day I mentioned that I'd been on the train platform when it was announced in official Hindi that 'the train, from its scheduled time, will be extenuated by two and a half hours' and, by God, I had no idea what the train was doing—whether it was coming or going or simply taking its own sweet time. Hearing my story, he lost his temper. In the heat of the moment, he kept slipping from his pillow, and in one such instance, he slipped with such force that his big toe slid through the charpoy's hold. He dug it in and lashed himself upright. Then he started talking, 'It's not easy to get rid of Urdu in India. In Pakistan you don't have as many poetry festivals in five years as we do in five months. Crowds of twenty thousand are nothing. A good poet can rake in seven thousand rupees. And that's not including all-expenses-paid transportation, food and lodging, and the adoration. Josh acted too quickly. He left for no reason. Now he regrets it.' I didn't think it was the right time to tell him that Josh was getting eight thousand a month (and a car) and that he was sponsored by two banks and an insurance company. Or that the government had given him a house and a monthly stipend, although the money was so little as to be an insult.

These days Nushoor loses his breath when he recites in tarannum. He recites haltingly. But his voice carries the same depth of feeling; it has the same resonance. His big eyes still flash brilliantly. His manner and attitude are bold and fearless in the way people get when they don't care about anything anymore. He recited a dozen new ghazals. Amazing. One time I was about to tell him to put on his dentures before reciting. You've heard him many times. Once he created a stir all over India with his ghazal, 'This is a secret, but the priest drinks too.' Now audiences ignore him for lines like 'Wealth never liked Islam, capital never wanted to be Muslim.' Audiences have changed. Their silence is a type of ridicule. If Master Dagh or Nawab Sayal Dehlvi recited today some of their poems that used to blow people out of the water seventy or eighty years ago, they quickly would be fed up with the tastelessness of the audience and then leave. But Nushoor has changed too. He still runs away with each poetry festival. He still walks to the beat of his own drum. But he said he doesn't have the same passion, the same desire. To me, he always seemed sick, weak, poor, and happy. Nothing has quelled his dignity and pride. He holds his head high in the company of the rich. Sir, that generation was a different breed. Those molds have been broken in which such rare characters were formed. Tell me—who could be more haughty and egotistical than Asghar Gondvi and Jigar Muradabadi? Their livelihood? Selling glasses! Not in a store, mind you, but wherever they wandered. I've been friends with Nushoor for just forty or forty-five years. At first, it wasn't that. At first, I learned Persian from him at the Madrasa Ziaul Islam in the butchers' neighbourhood. And, yes, butchers there don't wear long coats with glass buttons anymore, nor do they wear fancy red patent leather shoes. In those days, you had to wear the clothes that everyone in your community wore; otherwise, you would be excommunicated.

I Want to Pay the Bribe Again

You can no longer recognize the old shopping districts. But I've never met such polite shopkeepers. They made me feel good. As soon as I stepped inside, they would put a cold drink in my hand. I wasn't used to dealing with such ruthless salesmanship. It felt very rude to accept a soft drink, drink it, then leave empty-handed. So I ended up buying a lot of what the salesmen brought out, and I was left without money for the things I had set out to buy. You would never believe that a respectable shopping district—The Mall itself—had once existed before all this elbowing and jostling, screeching and crying, as well as the swirling noxious odors. Sir, the British made sure to build such a mall in each town—a fashionable mall with high-class stores. It seems like just yesterday, but there was a time when the mall's sidewalks were lined with acacia bark so that the police inspector's son could trot his horse without difficulty. A groom followed on each side so that the boy would not fall off. When they got winded, the boy would double over laughing. We got to know this boy well. Once he took fifteen or twenty of us friends for a hunting trip in his village near Bahraich. It was five people per tent. At the back, there were the servants' pup tents at a respectful distance. We slept in big tents. I can't tell you how much fun it was. One night there was a dance performance. The prostitute was so pretty that even her bad pronunciation seemed cute. Professional hunters would bring us meat, and cooks would roast it on an open fire. Our responsibilities were limited to digesting the food and telling them what kind of game we wanted to eat next. It was the first time I ever ate sambhar deer. On the last night, they placed onto the picnic blanket four whole roasted black deer. In each deer, there was a goose, and in each goose, a partridge, and in each partridge, a chicken egg. We stared in utter amazement: how could we eat all that? This police inspector was very capable, shrewd, extremely likeable, and utterly corrupt. Sir, conmen, rapists, and drunks will always seem well-mannered, friendly, and likeable; it's because they can't afford not to be. This boy didn't end up doing much with his life. He died of cirrhosis. His younger brother came to Pakistan. Somehow he got a teaching job in a school in Maripur. After a couple years, he found me. 'I don't have a Bachelor's,' he said. 'I can't get by on nothing. I live in Saudabad. I have to change buses twice to get to Maripur. Half my income is swallowed up in this. Please keep me here as your secretary.' He had three girls coming of age. One caught her clothes on fire and burned to death. There were all sorts of rumours. He himself had two heart attacks that he had covered up at school for fear of losing his shitty job.

Back in the day, the police chief used to rule the town, including the criminals. I mean, he could do anything to anyone. Sir, Mirza's right. After studying one hundred and fifty years of public records, he decided that three city departments have been corrupt since Day 1. First, the police. Second, the PWD [Public Welfare Department]. Third, the Income Tax Office. For my part, I'd add the Anti-Corruption Department. They accept bribes only from those who accept bribes. Corruption is rife in India as well, and I've a little experience with this. But, sir, even when a Hindu accepts a bribe, he does it with such humility and forbearance that, I swear to God, I feel like giving him another!

And, sir, no matter if an Indian is Hindu or Muslim, young or old, they are the epitome of humility when they fold their hands together in greeting. The most famous politicians do so before and after their speeches, just as the most respected musicians do before and after they play. Once at a poetry festival, I saw with my own eyes and heard with my own ears the great Ali Sardar Jafri recite a dozen or so long poems, put his hands together contritely, then leave the stage. (Well, in this case, I can understand why he begged for forgiveness.)

3.

What Happened to the Red-Light District

And, sir, when I saw Mool Ganj, I got very sad. There used to be a red-light district there. You must think I'm a strange character. I've done the hajj twice, I've a permanent tattoo on my forehead from praying

263

so much, and yet in every story I tell I'm sure to sing the praises of prostitutes. What can I do? Our generation suffered from all sorts of unrequited passions. In the old days, prostitutes ruled our bodies and minds. You couldn't tell a story without one, nor could you become a man without one. And bear in mind as well that a whore was the only woman you could look at for as long as you liked; women suitable for marriage always wore veils. I've noticed that today's prostitutes act and look like housewives. Someone needs to explain to them, 'You're well behaved, but good behavior was what drove miserable husbands to you in the first place!' The purity and monotony of the household bored them to the point that they came night after night to stay at the Exotic Body Inn. Now this refuge is no more.

So I was saying there used to be a red-light district in Mool Ganj. After being pushed further and further out, prostitutes are now hidden back in Bakers Alley. Mool Ganj is nothing more than a filthy gutter. I also went back to where Mian Tajammul Hussain and I used to eat kebabs right off the skewers as we hunkered in shame next to the wall. That was fifty years ago. I've never found kebabs as good as the spicy ones we got back then in the red-light district. Except in Lucknow's Maulvi Ganj. Mool Ganj had good flower bracelets too! Oh, and I've discovered an excellent kebab cook on Aslam Road. Before you leave for London, I'll get you some. Sir, I always went out to eat kebabs but chewed homemade paan. Have you ever eaten paan made by a prostitute? But you've said that you haven't seen a prostitute dance since your circumcision ceremony, and for years you remained under the impression that before watching anyone dance you would have to undergo the same trial! A prostitute's paan doesn't stain your lips. I've noticed that paan doesn't stain the lips of old people, babblers, and poets. But now you're looking at my lips! Thank you! Before going home, Mian Tajammul would vigorously wipe his lips and swallow some jintan pills to mask the odour of the kebabs and onions. Haji Sahib, his father, had recently come from Chiniot, and he considered kebabs and paan to be among the debaucheries of UP. He would say, 'Son, whatever you do, do it in front of me.' But, for the sake of argument, if Mian Tajammul had indulged in these things in front of him, his father would have split his head with an axe, and this would have been a piece of cake because for years he had held to an exercise regimen of chopping ten kilos of wood after morning prayers. If there was a storm, he would go to the men's section of the house and swing around his colourful, ten-kilo mace. When he left Chiniot to look for a job, his father, meaning Mian Tajammul's grand-father, gave him a thousand-bead rosary, a set of maces, an axe, and a wife to keep him from straying from the straight and narrow. And this was all well and good. Putting all these tools to use saved him from doing bad, even if they didn't amount to much good.

But for God's sake! Please don't take my words the wrong way. I keep bringing up prostitutes and brothels, and yet it's not like I be-lieve all your problems get solved at a whorehouse. With God as my witness, I never did anything more than eat paan and kebabs and stare with envy at the stream of men going inside. Mian Tajammul would say, sighing, 'Look how lucky these men are! Their ancestors are either dead or blind!'

It was another era altogether. As the young grew into their bodies, the old lost their minds. Everyone in town thought it was their duty to keep track of the bad behaviour of everyone else.

We watch over them, and they watch over us …

At each and every turn, the old generation was making sure that our youthfulness couldn't be put to use. I mean, all the old people spent their lives bent over like prayerful wicketkeepers trying to expose our missteps and mistakes. I couldn't figure out what the purpose of youth was if it had to be like that!

Sir, I spent my entire youth doing push-ups and drinking buffalo milk. If that's not madness, then what is?

Listening to Music with Eyes Wide Open

My father, God forgive him, was a connoisseur of the theatre and the music hall. And it wasn't a passing fancy. When the mood overcame him, and he pulled out the harmonium, people walking by in the street would stop to listen. He would play with his eyes closed. In those days, the true aficionados always listened to music with their eyes closed because that allowed them to concentrate solely on the melody. That said, it was considered permissible to listen to prostitutes' singing with eyes wide open. Like the great musician Bundhu Khan, my father would sometimes start singing spontaneously. It was very pleasing. In fact, he sang concerts too but only for singers. That was how the elite did things back then. Shahid Ahmad Dehlvi was also like this. You saw my father only when he was bed-ridden and clinging to life. When he was young, he loved Heera Bai's singing. She was a dadar kanthiya; she could cast a spell by singing two notes simultaneously. She would sing mujrai—I mean, she sang while seated. If she was going to sing within a hundred miles, he would leave work and go. If for any reason he wasn't able to get there, she wouldn't enjoy herself as much. She sang Rajasthani mand and bhairav thath only for him. When she sang dhyut and rakhab, her halting rendition was a beautiful rubato. She was as active in her singing as she was otherwise. When singing darbari, if she added a special flourish, the entire crowd erupted in delight. You know very well that my father wasn't rich. He had a lumber store a fourth the size of mine. It was just enough to get by. In the market, if someone's store remained closed for three days, it meant that there was a death in the family. If it remained closed for four days, it meant the merchant himself had died.

But if my father's store remained closed for a full week, no one worried. It meant that he'd gone to exchange loving glances with Heera Bai. That said, his customers bought only from him. They would wait for a week. In the end, he managed to get some hooked as well. They began to go with him to hear her sing. After they were thoroughly addicted, he made them arrange for everyone's transportation. He also entrusted to them the task of giving her a love-token when she sang a sehra, or some money when she sang a good couplet or murki. She would take the money from them and thank my father. I don't know if these unfortunate souls ever learned anything about music from all this, but they ended up without any money to buy lumber. After emerging from bankruptcy, one opened up a harmonium repair shop. Another couldn't even manage that. To save himself from his creditors, he fled to Bombay where he went to the theatre every day and took in Mukhtar Begum and Master Nisar concerts and yet never bought a ticket. I mean, he earned the honorary duty of opening and closing the stage-curtain. During the day he sold the tassels that hang from fez hats. I heard that Dawood Seth too sold tassels in Bombay back then, but, for his part, he had never heard Heera Bai sing.

My love and understanding of thumri, dadar, and khayal that you see here comes from my father. Even Iqbal Bano, Suraiya Multaniker, and Farida Khanum started to recognize me. Mian Tajammul likes to say that it's not my face they recognize but my white hair. Sir, last year there was a dance troupe that came and, God prevent me from lying, there must have been a thousand people in the audience. I had to buy a ticket for Mian Tajammul as well. After completing his third hajj, he decided to stop spending money on music and dance concerts, as well as movies. That night he said, 'There's not one person like you in this sinful mob.' I thanked him. Then he said, 'I meant there's not another old fool like you. Not another man whose hair has gone white like yours, even your eyebrows. You know, you ought to either dye your hair or give up going to concerts.' I said, 'Tajammul, as far as being disgraced goes, perambulating with you in this horrible alley is enough. I don't have to do anything further.'

He Never Forgot to Pray or to Go to Concerts

As you know, my father was very well mannered and pious. He prayed five times a day and kept his fasts. God be praised! All of us children still pray five times a day. This too is due to his good example. He never forgot to pray or to go to concerts. It was 1922 or 1923. A Parsi theater company came to town for the very first time, and he went to their show every day for a month, and each day it was like he was watching the show for the first time. After several days, he became so close to the company that he got them to change the dialogue in several places. In one place he replaced a ghazal by Dagh with one by Master Zauq and got them to sing it in aiman kaliyan. He explained to Bibbo, 'When you recite your lines, you bat your eyelashes and sway your hips. But, depending on the situation, you should choose the one deadly weapon that works best.' Three times he lent his clean pyjamas to the lead actor. He told the manager, 'The man you've chosen to play Laila's father is younger than Majnoon! The way he's looking at Laila from behind his fake beard is the farthest thing from paternal.' When one musician's bad kidney acted up, my father filled in on the harmonium. He tied a silk handkerchief doused with itr-e-henna around his head and thought that no one would be able to recognize him. He had a ruddy complexion, bright white teeth, and thin lips. He didn't laugh much, but when he did his cheeks lit up and tears came to his eyes. He looked good in anything, so when Shireen was talking to Farhad she stared at my father instead.

My mother didn't like his obsession with the theatre. When we had grown up, she told him, 'Please stop going to the theatre. The kids are now teenagers.' He said, 'My dear, you're really great. The kids are teenagers, and you're telling *me* to be on my best behavior!'

His interest in the theatre was too much. He thought that Agha Hashr Kashmiri was a better playwright than Shakespeare. It wasn't that he was intentionally prejudiced. He'd never read Shakespeare. Once he was arguing with his friend Pandit Suraj Narayan Shastri that Dagh Dehlvi was a greater poet than Kalidas. At one point he launched an unmentionable insult at Kalidas in order to strengthen his case, and this proved surprisingly effective. Not only did Panditji seem ready to agree that Dagh was better than Kalidas, but he went one step further to propose that Dagh's successor Nawab Sayal Dehlvi was too. His pocketwatch read ten in the morning when he learned of Agha Hashr Kashmiri's death. His store was busy, but he locked up and went home. He went to bed, hiding beneath the covers. When Panditji came to console him, he stuck out his head. 'Panditji, how is Mukhtar Begum* going to survive? How will she be able to slay the tedium of her youth?' After a significant pause, Panditji answered, 'Mr Khan, an axe-wielding Farhad will eventually come.' (Who knows why he always called my father Mr Khan.) 'Is art ever left without a champion? She'll find a man.' Earlier that day, with a downcast expression and heavy heart, he came home, closed the verandah's door, and said to my mother, 'We've been robbed. Today we won't eat cooked food.' He ate sweets at dusk and went straight to bed.

Panditji knew nothing about music, but he was very perceptive and sympathetic. The next day he came by at dawn. He looked worse than my father. He heaved and sighed. He hadn't shaven. He brought halva puri and a dish of fried pumpkin home. He fed my father. We started to worry that Panditji might be readying to perform bhadra† on him.

---

* She was Agha Hashr's favourite singer.
† The Hindu custom performed on the near relatives of the deceased: after the

Fallen from the Sky, Stuck in a Whorehouse

Please forgive me, but I might already have told this story. I hope you won't get bored. If the details happen to change, it's because of my memory. I don't mean to mislead you.

When we asked my father to let us go see a dance recital, he would write a note to the manager: 'Please reserve some seats in front.' In time, I would write the notes and forge my father's signature. He knew this. One day he erupted at me, 'If you're going to forge my signature, then go ahead. But could you please not disgrace me by making spelling mistakes? The phrase is *barah e karam*, not *bara e karam*.' He always sent us to a matinee. His reasoning was that the show's negative moral effect would be half, just like the price of admission. I was just a boy, but inside I was on fire. When Munni Bai sang, everyone was spellbound. This wasn't Dagh's Munni Bai Hijab about whom he wrote an entire masnavi. Ours had an exquisite voice and was just as beautiful. I didn't want to breathe, didn't want to blink, lest I should miss something. What is that couplet, you know the one? 'He's talking to me, he's right here ...'?

'Should I look at her, or should I talk to her?'

Yes, thanks. Sir, my memory's completely shot. When I'm at a poetry gathering, I forget couplets. And if I remember, I realize after reciting that they were completely inappropriate. Just like now. It makes the embarrassment twice as bad. Right now I wanted to recite the couplet that goes 'Just one blink ruins the spectacle.' Well, I'll get that one in later. What you said is right — after fifty-five, you should be happy to remember even one line. Sir, when Munni Bai sang Master Dagh's ghazals, everyone was lost in bliss, including her.

---

cremation ceremony, their hair, eyebrows, beard and moustache are shaved.

Passion lost itself in the overwhelming spectacle ...

I know that Dagh loved debauchery and that he preferred prostitutes. But his style wasn't depraved at all. He wrote in the high qila-e-muallah way, as though his words were bathed in the Jamuna River. Idioms and colloquialisms were his forte. His poetry was especially loved by prostitutes. Like your friend Mirza Abdul Wadud Baig says, 'Dagh's poetry fell from the sky to get stuck in a whorehouse, then danced into the night.' But Firaq Gorakhpuri went too far when he said that Dagh turned debauchery into a sort of genius. You weren't around then, but, well, even today, Dagh's ghazals work at any concert. For those who were around, they know that Dagh was so popular that when the renowned religious scholar Maulana Abdussalam Niyazi caught the poetry bug, he became Dagh's student. He was such a devotee that when anyone recited one of Dagh's couplets, he would cry, 'Subhan Allah!' and fall prostrate to the ground. I was saying that Munni Bai sang five of Dagh's ghazals in the film *The Poison of Love*. All five were tremendous, but each and every one was out of place. Sir, after '47, prostitutes disappeared—poof! Where are those sorts of prostitutes today? It's also true that the true connoisseurs are gone as well.

Silver Sex Powder and a Chillum from Chiniot

Oh, yes, it's come back to me! I knew a man named Mian Nazir Ahmad. He was somehow related to people in Chiniot. He went to Bombay frequently in connection with his leather business. There he got addicted to horseracing. He hardly had any money left after betting, and so he spent that very sparingly. He got hitched to a prostitute named Gulnar. After returning from the hajj, she renounced her bad ways and made Mian Nazir give up many of his vices. So he changed.

She didn't have the flat expression and raspy voice that many prostitutes get in middle age. She could really sing milad shareef. Her voice could be extraordinarily sad. When she sang Jami's na'ats or Anees' marsias, she would cover her head in a white scarf and sway gently, and a thousand shades of sweetness dissolved into a thousand shades of devotion. We listened to her on the sly. She looked good in black at Muharram. She moved to Pakistan. She lived in a little three-bedroom apartment on Burns Road near Adeeb Saharanpuri's place. Even in the winter Mian Sahib wore a muslin kurta, and every morning after taking an ice-cold bath, he would drink a lassi. It was rumoured that one day he had been overcome with a desire for instant strength and so had gulped a big dose of roop ras, or silver sex powder. Gulnar's two younger sisters Munni and Chunni were a real handful. You know black and green cardamom? Think of them like that. It's too bad that no one uses black cardamom anymore. It does taste different. I know you don't like black cardamom. But I really don't think it looks like a cockroach. Munni Begum's face and sumptuous arms made her look nude whatever she was wearing, you know what I mean? Chunni Begum sang Persian ghazals well. People were always asking her to sing more. She sang sitting down, but if she thought the audience wasn't appreciative enough, or if the mood suddenly struck her, then she would get up. The sarangi and tabla players* would tighten their golden turbans and get up to accompany her. She would go through the audience two or three times while dancing in circles then stop in the very centre of the crowd and spin quickly like a whirligig. Her long gold-embroidered dancing gown would rustle as she twirled, and with each revolution its hem would rise toward her waist. It was like a danc-

---

* In those days, the sarangi player and the tabla player were called the 'sarangia' and the 'tabalchi.' That is, to play the tabla was merely to play the tabla. They felt no need to justify their art. Calling a tabla player the 'tabla master' had not yet come into vogue.

ing show of lightning bugs. The music and the movement went from fast to faster, and the flashes of light would sparkle and flicker. Soon everyone lost track of the dancer, and all they saw was the dance.

Then I didn't see anything other than a restless hot flame …

And when she suddenly stopped, her dress would wrap around her shapely legs like a vine. The musicians would try to catch their breath, and the singed fingers of the tabla player resting on the khiran* seemed as though they were about to spit blood.

Look, I've returned again to god-forsaken brothels! But you've stopped taking notes. Are you bored? Or am I repeating myself? I promise that I won't let any other prostitute, no matter how ravishing, come between us. Sir, we enjoy these conversations, don't we?

You should remember these; you'll never find them again …

Two days from now you'll be on your way to London. It was Mir himself who spoke about the world's ephemerality when he called getting together with friends a 'floating party' because each friend is a traveller and company is fleeting. Anyway, I was talking about Mian Nazir Ahmad. He couldn't stand Kanpur's 40-degree weather, and so in May he fled to Chiniot to enjoy its 40 degrees. He claimed that Chiniot's summer wind was not as bad as that in Kanpur. We came up with a Shakespearean song:

> Blow, blow thou Chiniot 'loo'
> Thou art not so unkind
> As local specimens of mankind
> Who couldn't care who's who!

Mian Sahib often said that everything in nature has a purpose. In the Chiniot heat, the year's festering thoughts were purged in sweat. He

---

* Khiran: The black, round part of the tabla.

never let the racing season or sickness prevent him from fasting. In the summer, he always broke his fast by licking a lump of salt from Lahore and taking one deep drag on his hookah. First, he would test the hookah with three or four quick puffs, just like the sitar player tests the tightness of his strings with a pick, and the tabla player knocks on the sides of his instrument with a hammer. Then with one deadly drag he would suck the tobacco dry, and his life too would pass before his eyes—*soo-soo-soo-suh-suh-su-su-vu-vu-vu*. His entire body would go limp. A cold sweat would break out. His eyes would roll back in his head. First his spirit would pass from his body, then his senses, and that is how he remained until Gulnar served him pomegranate juice and stood him up for prayers. The hookah's hose was wrapped in jasmine garlands, and the stem was wrapped in sweet grass. He liked his tobacco strong, bitter, and raw. He ordered paan syrup from Lucknow. He ordered his silver mouthpieces from a goldsmith in Delhi. His clay chillums and chillum plates (the part between the coals and the tobacco) were always from Chiniot. He liked to exclaim, 'My lords! There's nothing like the sweet smell of dirt from Chiniot!'

It's Spring in Lahore

Mian Nazir Ahmad would stand on his rooftop wearing a muslin kurta without a cap on his head even in the depths of winter. And he would be flying a kite. He was so silly that he thought that wearing a thin kurta was proof of youth. A couple of us boys would steal some of his aphrodisiac pearls to satisfy our sweet tooth, but then for weeks afterwards we would wait in anticipation for their miraculous effects to take hold. Mian Sahib never used a blanket except when he had a bad fever. He was full of bitter contempt for the winters of UP. He said, 'My lords! You call this cold?' He respected only two sorts of cold—Lahore's and the type you get after catching malaria. Your friend Mirza Abdul Wadud Baig had this complaint—that people in UP don't know how to properly celebrate winter, just like Punjabis don't think so highly of summer. Sir, UP winters and Punjabi summers are put up with as yearly punishment. They also have their own opinions about the monsoon. Punjabis accept the rainy season because without it their crops wouldn't grow. But in UP the monsoon is made for tasty deep-fried treats, mangos that hang heavy from trees, and the swings where young girls play. In the Punjab, only parrots care whether mangos (or anything else for that matter) are hanging from trees.

You said that the English get their decency and good manners from how it rains for three hundred and forty five days a year, and the other twenty bring snow. I mean, they end up cursing out the weather instead of each other.

On Shankarat, Mian Nazir Ahmad would enter the kite competitions even though he wasn't very good. He would get six or seven of his kites cut, but he was happy and his losing made others happy as well. Whenever he lost a kite, he would immediately think back to Lahore's spring. Sir, what did he expect but to lose his kites? He would be flying his kite against others in Kanpur and telling stories about Lahore's wonderfully colourful spring skies. His eyesight had become quite weak as well, but he would grudgingly put on glasses only to count currency or to eat fish. One unintended consequence of his refusal to wear glasses was that the kite that he understood to be his opponent's and that he zealously 'cut' turned out to be none other than his own; as its string wore down, it would quiver and shake like a greedy person's mind. Only when the string suddenly snapped would he realize that he had ruined his own kite and the only thing left for him to do was to wind his spool. He often said that while there was no doubt that the kite-makers of Lucknow were the best, the wind in Lahore had no parallel. In truth, it's only in Lahore that the kites rise up into the wind so quickly to show their strength; it seems like the kites themselves are eating the string. It's only in Lahore where kites blossom into full colour pulling on the line in the wind. In Kanpur, people say 'it's cut' as though apologizing or consoling someone whose relative just died. But in Lahore, it's 'I cut it,' and this sounds like the cry of one wrestler who, having just thrown his opponent, sits on the loser's chest, with the arena's dirt coating their sweat-soaked bodies.

He got a lively fellow from Lahore to hold his spool. This man was a lecturer at Haleem College in Kanpur. His name was Abdul Qadir. He also wrote poetry. So when the two got together, their kites' strings were those of endless memories and the glass bits glued onto the strings were those of hyperbole; their strings seemed to unspool on their own, and soon their kites looked like stars high in the sky that would soon reach the city limits of Lahore.

> *The dust is pink, the water is colourful, the earth is red and the wind is fiery …**

This is where Basharat's narration ends and Mian Nazir Ahmad's daydream begins.

Daydream

Now please listen to the story of the high-flying kite that crossed the Ravi River, as told through the voices of those two lively gentlemen from Lahore, as well as Basharat, and your humble storyteller.

> Today it's spring in Lahore. The spring chases away the cold. As the cold leaves, it brushes pleasantly against the spring. The co-mingling of the last rosy cheeks of winter with spring clothes is a sight to behold. Mustard flowers in the fields in every which direction,

---

* 'The wind is draped in twilight, the desert garden has rings of roses' (Siraj Aurangabadi). About this, Mirza says that even zebras seem colourful to us in our youth.

and later, the late-blooming roses and chrysanthemums will have their moment. Mustard flowers, kites, butterflies, dresses, flowers, cheeks—it's a rose garden within a rose garden. Yes, today it's spring in Lahore. Colour rains from the sky to intoxicate the land. In the spring, like during the monsoon, you will never see a dull sky or a weak breeze in Lahore. Like a spoilt child, the spring cries out from all directions reminding you of its presence, begging for your attention, 'Hey! Look over here! I've something else for you.' Look at how it changes colour. Sometimes the sky is full of stars twinkling like children's eyes, sometimes the glow of the Milky Way in the distant heavens, and sometimes a shower of golden wires coming from the thick, purple clouds. As the days warm, from time to time the sky releases the water of life, soaking the dry fields and sad eyes. The sky changes moment by moment. It's perpetually restless. Sometimes it's kind, and sometimes it's merciless. In a second it changes from a volcano to a blue lake. For a while, it sits like an angry lover with the dust of deserts pent in its chest. Then its mood clears, and it returns to embrace the earth tightly. As though nothing had happened. The shape-shifting clouds look like the ocean's foamy waves and then like boats themselves swimming through the sky's molten sapphire. Yesterday evening the murky horizon bloomed with light as it swallowed the sun, and it seemed as though this new glow would stay for centuries to come. The warm breeze stopped at once. The horizon held its breath; nothing moved. Then clouds began to form, and the skies were lit for hours with flashes of lightning. But today at noon, I don't know how but the sky became as blue as a peacock's breast, and if you happened to glance at the sky, your eyes would be smudged with blue. Then, as the night wore on, the sky folded its limpid blue into the river's transparent sheen. There is only one thing more beautiful, more colourful, and more playful than Lahore's sky, and that is its verdant land. Four hundred years ago, its land was just as beautifully coloured. And that's the reason Noor Jahan said,

> In exchange for my life, I have bought Lahore.
> For my life, I have bought another paradise.

So, in exchange for her life, Noor Jahan bought two metres of Lahore's heavenly land. But the good people of Lahore didn't remember this woman (who so loved the city) as she deserved. Now Noor
Jahan's tomb is a roost for swallows! But, sirs! The heavenly city at
` the end of the rainbow has become the city of two tales, and look-
ing for the city, the prince chose the path that ended with him being
cleaved in two. Now the city's really changed! Now the land doesn't
reveal its old secrets, beauty, and charm to many. In order to see
these things, a person needs old eyes and a child's kaleidoscope.*
If he had that, then every city would seem like a wonderland …

His daydream ended.

Now listen to the rest of the story as told by Basharat in his circuitous
way. (The fun of it is not 'long story short' but 'short story long.') In
so far as my pen and my memory allows, I will try to recreate word
for word his special idioms, his way of talking, and his lilt and stutter.
Whenever he starts telling a story, his digressions and random asides
start telling their own story. He doesn't even let you catch your breath.
Mirza calls this torture 'the story stocks.' When Coleridge's Ancient
Mariner starts telling his ghost story, the wedding guest becomes so en-
tranced that he forgets everything about the wedding. Dumbfounded,
he stands listening. So that's sort of what happened to us as well:

> He holds him with his glittering eye
> The Wedding-Guest stood still,
> And listens like a three year's child:
> The Mariner hath his will.

* Kaleidoscope: Calling it a child's wonder wheel or rainbow maker would be
more appropriate than calling it a colourful telescope. Inside it, there are colourful pieces of glass that with each movement produce new colours, configurations,
and 'patterns.'

4.

I Am Ibn Battuta, This Is My Masterpiece

So, sir, I went to see Mian Nazir Ahmad's house, as well. I have a lot of memories in that house, but I couldn't recognize it. It had undergone a special facelift. Three air conditioners were running. On the verandah, an elderly Sikh man was tying up his topknot with a comb. This was the only house I saw that looked better than before. I introduced myself, and after I told him why I had come, he very warmly invited me inside. He treated me very well. For quite a while, he asked about his hometown, Gujranwala. I made things up as I went along. What was I supposed to do? I'd gone through Gujranwala last year in a minibus. So I took a mental snapshot, enlarged it, and turned it into a best-selling Urdu travel narrative. Well, you love those things. It's just like Aatish said,

> You must set out on a trip to find a welcoming land.
> Thousands of shade trees line the road.

But from the slobbering of writers of travel narratives what's most clear is that once a man leaves his wife at home and sets out on the open road, then life is one pleasure after another. Every step is on a tree-lined boulevard. Each tree has thousands of branches, and on each branch four virgins dangle, waiting for him, and just as this Don Juan passes underneath, these ladies fall into his bag.

> How many single ladies the open road holds!

It's as though his trip becomes an odyssey of assignations—not just from country to country and city to city, but from house to house, door to door, and alley to alley. The traveller crosses paths with women every day, and he remains unsatisfied until each woman has crawled onto his lap and so meets her comeuppance.

The daily offerings are always fresh
And head to foot full of new details

Professor Qazi Abdul Quddus, MA, BT, says that each and every pru-
rient story about these chaste women is ridiculous. (I should have
said ri-*dick*-ulous.)

And you've done very well. You've kept the thousands of pages
of notes from your own travels to, what, fifteen, twenty countries, in
your pile of abandoned manuscripts. Well, sir, there's a strange wind
blowing. As soon as they buy their plane ticket, whether they're just
going to Dubai or Sri Lanka, today's writers think they've become
Ibn Battuta, think their travel accounts are masterpieces, and think
their travel encounters with beautiful ladies are the sayings of saints.
I agree with your suggestion that just as the Pakistani government
makes each applicant for a passport swear that Mirza Ghulam Ahmad
Qadiani is a false prophet, they should also make each writer swear—
no, provide a written guarantee—that upon their return they will *not*
write a travel narrative and they will *not* accuse themselves of having
acted inappropriately while abroad.

Gujranwala Is Gujranwala

The elderly Sikh man kept on asking about his beloved city, and I
very confidently continued to make up things about Gujranwala. He
kept calling out to his sons, grandsons, and sisters-in-law, 'Come here.
Say "hello" to Basharatji. He was in Gujranwala in November.' My
problem was that, other than Lahore, my knowledge of the Punjab
was limited to one locale, I mean, Toba Tek Singh. Akkhan Auntie's
grandson worked there at the Agricultural Bank, though after three
months he was suspended and was left stranded there for eleven
months of waiting. From what I knew of that area, I constructed tall

tales of Gujranwala. The surprising thing was that the old man not only liked my rendition but also confirmed it to be true! I made up a story about the past and present of a canal where the old man used to jump off a bridge to swim with virgin lady water buffalos. When he asked, I confirmed that I had seen the same spot on the left bank of the canal where he used to leave his Hercules bicycle alongside his clothes. One time, thieves stole his clothes but left his bike. After this incident, as a precaution, he never brought his bike again. When I added the detail that the rosewood tree at that locale was as good as dead and soon its old limbs would fall upon the auction block, the old man got weepy, even though he wasn't in any better shape than this tree. The wife of his middle son, who was a lively, good-looking woman, said, 'Babuji had a heart attack last month. Please don't make him cry, Uncle!' I didn't like being called 'uncle' at all.

When the old man liked some witty remark of mine, he would slap me on my thigh and obstreperously order another glass of lassi to be brought from the kitchen. After the third glass, I asked to go to the bathroom. In order to protect my thigh from his slap-happy praise, I adopted a very reserved manner, lest in a thoughtless moment anything funny should slip from my mouth. He said, 'We have a very good transport business here. I've seen all of India. But Gujranwala is something else. The corn and mustard greens here don't have the same flavour, the same smell. And the jaggery here is worthless.' He went as far as to say that there was a lot of water in India's water, but in Gujranwala's water there was a hint of alcohol. (He meant that it was *strong* water. He compared everything that was good for you to alcohol.) As I was leaving, I said that if there was anything I could do for him, he should feel free to let me know. So he said, 'Then, if you could, make sure that someone travelling this way brings three or four big chunks of Lahori salt.' His great wish was that before dying, he would be able to take his sons and grandsons to Gujranwala and take a picture standing in front of his middle school. As a gift, he gave me a length of raw Indian silk. As I was leaving, the same daughter-in-law wished me goodbye. This time she didn't call me 'uncle.'

What Should I Call It—Torments or Dreams?

The old man showed me around the entire house. His daughters-in-law went ahead and hastily tried to tidy the messy house. Those things that they didn't have time to deal with were dumped onto a bed and covered with a clean sheet, so whenever I caught a glimpse of a clean sheet, I assumed that beneath it was trash. Sir, curiosity isn't necessarily a good thing. In one room, I stealthily pulled up the corner of a sheet. What appeared there was the old man's uncle with his hair down, wearing tight underwear! His white beard was so long and thick that there wasn't really any need for him to be so formal. The house had changed a lot. The arch-shaped windows through which Gulnar, wearing a glittery, silver-and-gold-threaded scarf, had used to look were now blocked off with bricks. Now, look, you've started smiling again, sir! What can I do? The old-time words and expressions still find their way out of my mouth! The courtyard had been paved. The jasmine vines were gone, as was the guava tree.

Back in the day, Mian Nazir would get two waterskins of water sprinkled onto the courtyard during the evening and then have wicker stools set out for everyone. For himself, he ordered a lathe-turned Chiniot charpoy with colourful legs. When Mian Nazir's nostalgia became too much, he fed us cubes of local sugarcane. But when he thought of Lyallpur's sugarcane, he couldn't swallow for his emotions. On moonlit nights, Mian Nazir would sing mirza sahiban in a voice that sounded like our gym teacher's as he played the jugni tongs. When he got emotional, we got emotional, although our crying was due only to his bad singing. After a while, when he realized how awful he sounded, he would throw the tongs contemptuously across the courtyard and say, 'My lords, the tongs of Kanpur aren't fit for singing. They're only suitable for filling a chillum.' Sir, once he had been a playboy. And yet, while he had lived in Kanpur for a long time, he had never eaten paan, never greeted others with high formality, and never recited poetry, not even at a brothel, where all of these things were the staples of culture.

After lying through my teeth, I left the house. My nostalgia immediately wore off. Then Inamullah The Loudmouth took me to see my old house. We stopped at the corner of an alley sweetshop. He said, 'You want to go see Ramesh Chander Advani, the lawyer? He's from Jacobabad. He's seventy. But he doesn't look it. He looks eighty. Hearing that someone has come from Karachi, he's dying to see who it is. He wants to ask about Jacobabad and Sukkur. Then he'll play kafiyan for you on the sitar. If you say you like it, he'll play more. And if you don't, even then he'll play more. He'll say, 'This one's better. Maybe you'll like it.' He remembers the poetry of Shah Abdul Latif Bhitai. He's learned Hindi, but when he gets excited, he starts talking in some strange, ghostly language. He's crazy, but you'll get a kick out of him.'

So, sir, I talked to Advani. Or not so much that as listened to his monologue. It was like being taken prisoner. He wanted to confirm that Jacobabad was as beautiful as it had been when he had left it as a young man. I mean, was the full moon as full as it had been? Do the palla fish still jump around in the Sindh River's waves, shining and glimmering in the sun? Is the weather still good? (Meaning, is it still 46 degrees in summer or has that declined as well?) Does the hot wind still blow from Khairpur with its sweet scent of dates? Was there still the yearly cattle fair in Sibi or not? What about the Sibi darbar? When I told him that at the fair there was now a poetry festival and poets came from great distances to participate, he went on for a long time lamenting the fair's deterioration. He asked, 'Have good cattle gotten so rare in Sindh?' He couldn't stand UP's fertile plains. He said, 'You see, we're rough, uncultured desert people. But we're warmhearted. We care about each other. You cultured people of the plains and swamps—what do you know about how the hot wind blows playful waves in the sand, making pictures that it erases then begins making again? You see, raging windstorms make our entire sandscape. The hot summer winds and their minaret-like dust devils churn through the desert. Today's sand valley was yesterday's sandstorm. Mountains of ember-hot sand blow up in the scorching afternoons. Before dawn, the gentle wind that blows over the cold, velvety sand sounds like a pakhavaj drum. The tossing and turning waves of sand look like strong, young, flexed biceps. No two waves are the same. No two hills are the same. No two nights. When the empty monsoon clouds pass winking over Sindh's sea of sand, the moon locks everything beneath its spell. Those who think the desert is all the same haven't yet learned how to see. You see, we're nothing compared to you. But we're the fish of this sandscape. We can dig our fingers into the sand in the middle of the night and tell you over which hill the sun rose in the morning, which way the wind was blowing in the afternoon, and what the clocks read at that very moment in the city. When the earth decides not to give us its bounty at harvest time, we take all the beautiful colours of the rainbow and sprinkle them over our block-printed clothes, our patchwork quilts, our scarves, our shaluka kurtas, our cholis, and our decorative tiles.'

Once his crying enema was over, I left. Outside I said to Inamullah, 'That was too much. What a strange Hindu—he's living on the banks of the Ganges but dreams of deserts!

He lives here, but his heart lives there
Imagine living in exile your whole life long

If it's so bad here, we should put him on a camel and send him to Bikaner where we'll have him sit on a mound of sand or on the stump of an acacia tree where above his head there won't be a cloud in the sky and beneath his feet there will be nowhere good to die. If you show me another person afflicted by nostalgia, I swear to God, I'll gather up a water pot, a water-drawing rope, a mat, Nazir Akbarabadi's *Complete Poems*, fruit salt, and head for the desert wilderness. So listen up. I don't want to have to shake hands with one more old person.'

Sir, my old age and wretchedness make me want to throw up. Your Mirza wasn't wrong when he said that each time you shake hands with another person as old as you, your life expectancy goes down by a year.

5.

Mullah Aasi, the Monk

I went all around Kanpur. I met everyone. Everything came back to me. But the best part of the trip was meeting Mullah Aasi Abdul Mannan. Zauq said this about meeting old friends:

> *It's better than meeting a messiah or Khizr himself.*

When sending letters, Abdul Mannan's grandfather adopted the habit of signing 'aasi' ('sinner') before his name. His grandson confiscated the name for himself, and, beginning in the seventh grade, he began to sign his name Aasi Abdul Mannan. He sprouted a beard the next year. By the time he was in the tenth grade, everyone called him Mullah Aasi. And the name stuck so that now he's known only by that name. AASI A. MANNAN is still written on his gate. He's a marvel. He's lean but muscular. He's light skinned. He's of average height. He has extraordinarily long, monkey-like arms. His shoulders slope down like coat hangers. His thick hair has gone white, but it retains its curls. His eyes protrude like those of fish. Since childhood, he has had a tic in the corner of his right eye that still twitches from time to time. He didn't touch his beard for the first ten years. And the truth is he looked better with it. He had a long neck and a small, round face. The day he came from the barber with his face clean-shaven, it looked like a chillum on top of a hookah's stem. He always got his throat shaved on the first day of the new moon, and afterwards he would say, 'I got my collar tightened.' (That's what they said there.) But Mushtaq Sahib, you used to have a moustache back then too; you ought to put a photo of it in your next book. Mullah Aasi liked to say, 'I haven't prayed since I stopped doing all childish things. At times in the past if I got stuck somewhere at prayer time and someone insisted, then I led prayers. This was my beard's big drawback. So I shaved it off.' When he started pretending to be Buddhist, people began calling him 'Mullah Monk.' He still can't pronounce 'r,' but the way he says it is pleasing. His tone of voice is very sweet. He's as carefree and eccentric as ever. In fact, more so. When I was face to face with him, I couldn't help but stare. I was surprised to see that someone could live like him. He left off everything and shadowed me everywhere. It was a real treat. What can I say? It was like a river of love. It was like a shower of affection.

Please believe me, he was just as we left him in '47. He must have been seventy-five or older. But he didn't look it. I asked him his secret, and he said, 'I never look in a mirror. I never exercise. I never think about tomorrow.' But he was underrating himself on the last claim. Let alone the next day, he didn't even think about that day. He hadn't changed a bit. He greeted me very warmly. In his embrace, I felt transported back into my twenties. I felt like I was meeting a long-lost twin. I agree with you that the embrace of some people always makes you feel ecstatic.

You'll find Mullah Aasi ready to help everyone and ready to do every sort of work, just so long as it's not his own. He knows every police officer in town. If someone needs him to speak on their behalf at midnight, he goes with them. If someone's sick or in a bad way, he'll hoof it himself to make sure they get medicine or whatever else they need. He's also a homeopath. Regardless of whether homeopathic medicine has any effect or not, his hands had the healing touch. There were always sick people hanging around him. He didn't charge anything for medicine or advice.

And this was no different in his youth. Like Aladdin's genie, he was always ready to be of service. He was a great organizer. Once during the summer of '41, Mian Tajammul Hussain had a great idea; his dad had gone to Calcutta. He said, 'Hey, Mullah, it's been ages since I've seen a prostitute dance. The last time was for the wedding of Mr Jamal's son. That was seven months ago. Let's get a dozen friends together to pool our money for a show. All you have to do is grab the bull by the horns and get her here. Then, by god, it'll be a blast!'

'Now why didn't you say anything before?' Mullah Aasi replied. 'You just get a carpet, and I'll do the rest. But there's one thing. When money's involved, there's always the chance of foul play. Infighting's OK—and expected—when everyone's trying to do good, but when bad things are involved, we need absolute confidence in one another and unanimity among ourselves. So, now, tell me one thing, who would a collectively hired prostitute pay her respects to?'

That Saturday after dinner, Mullah Aasi arrived on a horse-drawn cart with 'the rest.' (He himself was holding onto the cart's side—that part that extended out from the seat.) He brought down the betel-nut box, the tablas, the sarangi, the ankle-bells, and the old and infirm tabla player. He whispered to me that the prostitute hadn't wanted to come on account of his beard. As for money, we managed because we split the costs among ourselves. Everything else was his doing, and that included selecting and procuring the bungalow in the country-side where this party was to take place. He was friends with the deputy collector. He laid out the food on the picnic blanket by himself. He had bought Kanpur's special red-and-white rasgulla in big terracotta cups. He had gone to the trouble of having Lucknavi cream made for us to eat with zardah. He said the paan was folded by a comely, young Lucknavi woman. She packed it so tightly that if you should happen to throw it at someone, the victim would cry out in pain. The paan might break into pieces, but it would never unfold. Just before spreading out the picnic blanket, he supervised the sprinkling of jaggery and salt onto the tandoori bread. In Kanpur, these are called chinte ki roti. He made sure that newly plated fingerbowls filled with neem leaves and water were placed in the room's corner. Long story short, he did everything. Then after we all sat down on the picnic blanket, someone asked where he was. We sent out a search party, but he was nowhere to be found. The party took place, but it was joyless. The next day when I asked him about it, he got mad, 'When did you ever invite me? You asked me to arrange things, so I did.'

Do Lizards Breastfeed?

His mood was always like this. His obtuseness and eccentricity were the same as before, if not more. Which story should I choose? This is from his school days. He wasn't a preternaturally stupid person. I mean, he was an average sort of dunce. There were three months until exams. It was December and wickedly cold. He started study-ing on Christmas. To get ready for the test, he shaved his head and started applying oil. From a mile's distance, it was clear that this was pure mustard oil. The very first night, cold struck his vulnerability, meaning his head, and the second day he had a bright green cot-ton cap made, which when he wore it while eating paan made him look exactly like a parrot. The first thing the following Thursday, he bought the liver and head of a white goat. He had the head cooked, and then he served it to a few fakirs that evening. In those days because of purdah customs, no man could go on the roof. But he stood on the roof anyway calling out to the kites, 'Kite! Kite! Kite! Kite!' This went on for quite a while. Then he threw the liver scraps to the swooping birds as the men in the neighbouring houses rained insults upon him. In the afternoon, he took outside his rope-woven charpoy and doused it with boiling water to kill those bugs that for years he had been raising on his own blood. These were their last rites. He turned the charpoy upside down in the sun, and then he covered the dead and half-dead bugs in heaps of warm earth. Inside, he attached a broom to the end of a bamboo mosquito-net pole and removed wasp nests and spider webs from the ceiling. From time to time, he threw the light of his flashlight onto the ceiling to count the number of lizards and to investigate their nocturnal habits and sinful deeds. Among them all, there were probably three males. I'm forced to say 'probably,' because, as Mirza says, it's not within mortal limits to tell the gender of birds, lizards, fish, punks, or Urdu nouns. When birds, punks, fish, and lizards are overcome by their human urges,* they can tell their sexes apart and so put into action the lessons of the birds and the bees. But with Urdu nouns there's no such luck. The task of assigning their gender is left to the old and eloquent. Once Ustad Jaleel wrote a thoroughly researched paper on gender. After a medical examination of seven thousand words, he pronounced their gender, and he also made notes about those words whose gender still remained so contentious that the folks of Delhi and Lucknow were ready to crack heads.

* Mirza uses the phrase 'human urges' for the actions and behaviours of animals as well.

The three male lizards mentioned at the beginning of this account were chatterboxes. They rode double-decker across the ceiling all night long, and Mullah grew worried that this would disturb his studies and his peace of mind. So, in order to punish these evildoers for their evil ways, he got a Diana air rifle from a friend. And yet he never used it because, as he says, as soon as he put his finger on the trigger, he remembered that several of them had suckling babes!

I objected, 'No! Lizards don't breastfeed their young!' He retorted, 'Well, then, whatever it is she's feeding.'

After cleaning the ceiling, he turned to cleaning the wall. Above his writing desk, there were pictures of the actresses Madhuri, Kajjan, and Sulochana. He didn't remove them but turned them upside down. Then, to keep himself on the straight and narrow and to inspire in him a fear of God, he hung up a picture of his father, who was a great tyrant and flew off the handle at the slightest provocation. Like Dracula does, he hung a cloth over the mirror. Otherwise he would have gotten frightened by the look of terror on his face. His friend Hari Prakash Pandey urged him to be on his very best behaviour and to practice celibacy during the exam period, but this was completely unnecessary because for his and our generations, licentiousness wasn't a problem—we longed to be licentious! Pandey told him one trick: if any lustful thought slipped into his mind, he should prick his thumb with a pin and keep it in until the thought disappeared. But what happened was he screamed a lot, and the lustful thoughts remained. On the very first day he found there was no more room on his pincushions, that is, on his thumbs, and so he fell to using his big toes. The next day he couldn't even put on his shoes.

The Eraser Says, 'I'm the Emperor of the World.'

He renounced his bad habits. That is, he temporarily renounced talking behind friends' backs until late at night; cards; chess; looking into bioscopes; and keeping bad company, meaning, the very sort of friends he had. He renounced these from Christmas to the end of his exams, and he smiled when he said to himself that this counting would be 'both days inclusive.' Then, from his locked wardrobe, he took out copies of the sexy passages from *The Poison of Love*, which was then a banned book, as well as ten or so other excerpts from disreputable masnavis, all of which were at that time considered pornographic. He had written these out in his own hand, and, despite their mistakes in spelling, actually, on account of these mistakes, the pleasure was doubled: not only were some of these errors serious and embarrassing, but they were obscene as well. He took these manuscripts along with two packs of cards (one of which was brand-new) into the courtyard to set them on fire. He got oil from a kerosene lamp and set the old pack of cards on fire when he remembered a piece of advice of the old: regardless of the nature of the work, do everything slowly; quick work is Satan's work. So he cursed Satan's work and set aside the new pack of cards, as well as the sexy passages.

He bought two pencils and six erasers, as for every two pencils, he needed that many erasers. Then Mullah Aasi bought from the paper recyclers five kilos of railway receipts and bills of lading on which to do his 'rough work.' It cost one anna. In those days, frugal boys did their drafts on the backs of such paper. He bought a half kilo of saunf, and after letting a good-looking girl from the neighbourhood remove the stones from the mixture, he preserved these stones in a glass jar, just as some patients proudly display their kidney or gall stones after their surgeries. But that girl is another story. Let's leave it for later. Then he mixed the saunf with some coriander seeds and kept them in a porcelain jar. Hari Prakash Pandey said that if you drip just two drops of coriander juice into the mouth of a rutting bull or into an exploding volcano, then each will immediately become calm. Saunf increases the sparkle in your eyes and the freshness of your mind, and so he had a handful before drifting off to sleep, and then right after waking up.

Once the proper study environment was achieved, he asked the best students which books he should buy. He made a list and then bought them—most of them secondhand. This was not because they were cheaper but rather because among these books he found extremely rare editions in which two or three generations of failed students had highlighted all the important parts. These marks were like lighthouses pointing out the dangerous cliffs where disappointed generations of negligent students had ended up sinking their ships despite their best intentions. He even found one rare edition in which only the unimportant parts were underlined. He knew then to skip these parts. He felt certain that with these books in hand he had already won half the battle against the examiners. Then he went to see Hari Prakash Pandey, who always scored the highest at the government college. After much pleading, he managed to borrow all his books for two days. He loaded them onto a horse-drawn cart and took them home. Then he hired a poor sixth-grade boy at the wages of an anna a day to underline in his books all those sections of Hari's books that were underlined. Then he got two stamps made: one that said, IMPORTANT, and the other, MOST IMPORTANT. He took the entire stack to Hari and made his request: 'Would you stamp those sections you think I ought to pay attention to? Please—'

Types of Books and Shameless Enemies

With everything underlined, he developed another emergency technique in order to make sure he didn't study anything that was unnecessary or pointless. He called it, in English, 'selective study.' (I don't know it's Urdu synonym.) It went like this: he used scissors to cut out in their entirety those chapters that the previous year's exams had covered so that these sections would not distract him and in order to lessen the unnecessary terror with which the books' bulk filled him. And not just these chapters. He also cut out those associated passages that spread like cancer's secondary growths into other chapters. Moreover, he removed the chapters that his advisors and well-wishers promised would never come up. He also relied a little upon his intuition. Finally he built up the courage and removed those abstruse sections that he would never have a chance of understanding, even if he should read them ten times. After this surgical pruning, less than a quarter of his books remained. Of these, there were three that were in such a state of disrepair that he had to take what was left of them and clip them inside other books. One book had been pared down to its title page. He stuffed some unimportant pages back inside it for good luck and to give heart to his examiners. He decided that if he was still alive by the time the exams rolled around, and if he was still able to see, then he would throw a cursory glance upon select portions of these aforementioned pages. After all, no two books can be read the same way. And his God-given intelligence and intuitive understanding should be worth something, too. As for his fear of failing, well, that would be there no matter what. It is what it is. And, anyway, it was much better to study hard and fail with dignity than to cheat and pass. Someone quoted a maxim from Bacon that he quite liked. The funny thing was that it was from a Bacon essay that he had torn out because he thought it was worthless. You probably know the maxim: 'Some books are to be tasted, others to be swallowed, and some few to be chewed and digested.' Mullah Aasi had added, 'And some are to be read by a proxy who will tell you their gist.' He modified this maxim further by saying that most, if not all, books are such that they should be sniffed, and then left for those who have no noses.

Sir, the other day at the function for the luxury beach hotel, you read from an excellent poem on noses. Probably only a couple of people in the audience realized who you were talking about. Even though your enemies don't suffer from these attacks, I know you find them very pleasing. Do you remember any of the lines?

> They haven't got no noses
> The fallen sons of Eve.*

Laying Bare the Whole of History

He also made history into child's play. It went like this: he asked Hari Prakash Pandey to make a list of all the important dates so that he could deal with them in one fell swoop. But not more than twenty. Up till then, by hook or by crook, he had managed to deal with only five or six dates. Master Fakhir Hussain once said that history is no mystery, it's just a bunch of dates; whoever uses the most dates in their answer gets the best score. Mullah Aasi learned the Urdu plural of 'date' from this piece of advice. When Master Fakhir Hussain said that, for us, the year of a great person's death was more important than the year of their birth, Mullah Aasi felt as though something was amiss. He also learned from none other than Master Fakhir Hussain that 'to be propagated,' 'to be liquidated,' and 'to be ensconced' meant 'to be born,' 'to die,' and 'to sit on the throne,' respectively. He also gave this tip that the examiners form their impression of you from your first answer's first paragraph. After learning these tips of the trade, Mullah Aasi, in the midterm exams of the tenth grade, made sure to lay bare the whole of history in the very first answer. I mean, in the very first paragraph on the very first page, he ripped through all the dates that he had copied onto his palm and onto the bottom of his Swan Ink box. It didn't matter that none of these dates responded to the question, or that not even two of the dates went together. Threading all

---

* 'The Song of Quoodle,' G.K. Chesterton.

these dates together in such a way that Master Fakhir Hussain could see that the effect of his advice was something that only Mullah Aasi could have done.

The question was on Lord Dalhousie's policies. I don't remember it word for word, but in his first paragraph he constructed a complete chain of kingship that disregarded both religion and race. Then he killed them all. It went something like this:

> After the reign of Ashok the Great (liquidated 232 BC), the next big kingdom was that of Emperor Aurangzeb (liquidated 1680 AD) who tossed his father from the throne in 1658 AD and ensconced himself there. Meanwhile a ferocious battle took place in Panipat, and while anarchy could not be reigned in, still Aurangzeb treated his brothers fraternally, that is, he put them to death one after the other. If he hadn't, they would have done the same to him. Actually, as soon as Akbar the Great (propagated 1542, liquidated 1605) had died, there were signs of disintegration in the kingdom, and after many kings died, this resulted in the Battle of Plassey in 1757 AD and the Battle of Seringapatam in 1799 AD. And in Europe, Napoleon (liquidated 1821 AD) was beginning to lose control. [Here he suddenly remembered two more dates, so he threw them as offerings into the fire as well.] We shouldn't forget that Firoz Tughlaq (liquidated 1388 AD) and Balban (liquidated 1286 AD) also failed to bring stability to their kingdoms. And here we shouldn't forget that from 1757 to 1857 is a hundred years ...

He held tightly to Master Fakhir Hussain's advice that the way to defeat the examiners, as well as the correct approach to history, was through an assault of dates. He didn't know the year of his birth, and so in that column he had always written, with complete honesty, 'Unknown.' But when Master Fakhir Hussain scolded him, 'Look, here! The only thing we can claim not to know—and not to want to find out about—is who our father is,' so afterwards, he began to write 1908 as his date of birth and affixed AD lest any nincompoop get confused.

We also learned from Master Fakhir Hussain that we should use the words 'misappropriations' and 'misunderestimations' to characterize our own serious blunders, so as to give them a hint of scholarly eloquence. At the time Master Fakhir Hussain was losing his memory. If he couldn't remember something while trying to make a point or give an answer, he would say, 'I'm not presently at liberty' in such a way that we would become embarrassed at how ignorant we were not to have known better than to ask our question at such an inappropriate time. Teachers had a special way about them back then!

That reminds me of another bit of Master Fakhir Hussain's wisdom about exam trickery. He said that wherever you can use a difficult word, make sure not to use an easy one,* 'You are students. A simple style looks good only to scholars, and they are the only ones who lack it!' On this point, he also said that whenever we knew the plural of a Persian or Arabic word, we should use that over the singular. Thus, I learned from him how to call an enemy 'my accursed devils.' Its singular, 'cursed devil,' didn't have half the bite.

Mullah Abdul Mannan and Napoleon

Along these lines, a well-wisher once told him that if he prepared three essays in advance and memorized the details from three battles, then he would never fail an English or history exam, that is, if the examiners weren't total incompetents. This was back when he followed

---

* In 1989, there was an interesting reverse dictionary published that gave for every simple word a difficult, abstruse, and unknown synonym. This dictionary has become very popular in those ranks of society whose job it is to speak plainly and openly. I mean, among professors, critics, clerics, government spokesmen, and business executives. How happy Master Fakhir Hussain must be to see his advice being taken so seriously fifty years after his death!

the advice of anyone, and that down to its very last letter. So he would fail each time in a new way, and each time he found himself upset over the examiner's incompetence. Of the three battles whose details he memorized (along with the maps of the battles themselves), his favourite was the decisive Battle of Waterloo where his hero Napoleon met with overwhelming defeat. When he told his friends of his failings, he used this historical incident; instead of scholastic embarrassment, he spoke with a general's arrogance: 'I have met my Waterloo!'

Later, as he recounted his life's other failures, he would use the same historical words. But, sir, the difference between Napoleon's defeat and his was the difference between heaven and earth. Napoleon collapsed after one defeat, but Mullah Aasi consistently announced his defeat with an iron determination to fail yet again.

I Have Brainlock

By the time he had laid all his traps for the examiners and had constructed all his shortcuts, there were only four weeks left before the exams. A shortcut is actually the path that smart but lazy people take in order to travel the least possible distance in the most amount of time. Sir, you should never measure distance in feet but in minutes. Anyway, Mullah Aasi now busied himself with studying. At seven in the morning, he would eat a breakfast that consisted of eight puris, one pound of piping hot jalebis straight from the griddle, and fresh sherbet made from cucumber and ten almonds that had been soaked overnight in the shadow of the stars. Then he would give the lock he used on his door to someone outside, ask them to lock it behind him so that he couldn't get out even if he wanted to, and then shut himself inside. The lock would be opened at nine every night. He kept to this schedule for about two and a half weeks. But he didn't end up taking the test. He said, 'I have brainlock.'

Sir, what else is new? Just a few days before the exams, he fell into the habit of leaving on his bike at dusk and not returning until dawn. He was busy trying to unearth the test questions. He was cultivating relationships with the house servants, cooks, sweepers, suckling babes (along with their nurses) of those teachers that he suspected even slightly of having already made up their portions of the exams.* As soon as he got any lead, or when he laid his hands on something promising, he delivered this information during the night to the pertinent houses. Once these were in the possession of those worthy of them—meaning, all the miserable students of town—then he would set off on his bike to find more. One night I saw him outside a printing press. His special devotees were cramming whatever paper cuttings, proof scraps, and general paper waste that lay around into two big bags to cart off to his house where he would subject them to a microscopic inspection. Someone had shared the top-secret rumour that this press was printing one of the exams. His spies were at work all over the city. According to him, his agents had spread their nets in Agra, Meerut, Bareilly, as well as in the cities of Rajputana and central India—any city that had a branch of Agra University—and in these places no examiner would be able to save himself from dishonour. His agents were those who had failed for several years running in a particular discipline, and each agent was specialized in the subject that had tripped him up the previous year. When the leaks and secret information began to dry up, he didn't lose courage. He filled up

---

* In this, he was following the sage advice of his teacher and spiritual preceptor Master Fakhir Hussain who liked to say, in the words of Saadi, that if you feed partridges, pigeons, and other birds on a regular basis then one day you'll be able to entrap even a phoenix. The problem was that while Master Fakhir Hussain taught him how to lay out grain, he didn't teach him how to grab the bird. He himself fed birds but nothing more; in fact, he sacrificed his field's entire harvest to them. Hoping to catch a phoenix, he never managed to touch even the tail feathers of any bird.

any holes by using his intuition and singular methods. For two hours he sat on a bench outside the house of the examiner responsible for making up the first test, and, with his neck slung in one direction and his feet dangling in the air, he 'sniffed out' the questions. Three questions were thus revealed. He went home and added three more in the following fashion: he wrote out ten questions on pieces of paper that he then crumpled up into balls; then he asked the five-year-old brother of the young girl I mentioned before to choose three. The first part of the exam was to be on Monday morning. He delivered his question sheets to the houses of those students who had been failing year after year, and also to those students who struck him as possible future failures. He was done with this charity work by three thirty on Sunday morning. Once home, he took a cold bath. Then he went outside and stared at the morning's stars for quite some time. His Hindu neighbour was bathing near his well, and each time he doused himself with a bucket full of cold water, he cried out, 'Hari Om! Hari Om!' (The colder it was, the louder, his cry.) Mullah Aasi asked this man to lock his door from the outside. Then he went in and went to sleep. Why? Because he had brainlock.

Mullah Aasi's Intuition and His Miracles

If he had spent on studying even one-hundredth of the energy he spent on revealing the exam's questions for the benefit of the general population, he would have passed with flying colours. Anyway, the depressing thing is not the amount of time he spent on this worthless pursuit; rather, the thing that makes you want to cry is that out of the test's eight questions, five were ones that he himself had predicted. It seemed as though the examiner had used *his* question sheet as the basis for the test! The rumour spread that an investigation of the examiner was underway. Mullah Aasi went so far as to say that the examiner had removed the bench where he had had his revelation. Afterwards, and for a long time, slackers met there religiously. Well, God knows if that's true or not.

Suddenly he was famous all over town. The following day a huge crowd of test-takers gathered outside his house. The next portion of the test was in four days. In that interval, droves of students came from near and far (some by truck, some by train, some on foot) to camp out in front of his house. It felt like a fair. Never before and never afterwards has heaven witnessed such a singular gathering of the wasted youths of UP. The rumour spread that the police were investigating and that CID officers were wandering through the crowds disguised as fathers. Mullah Aasi said that there were two burqa-clad girls, as well. Shakeel Ahmad, the youngest and most handsome boy in our class, related how the taller girl had pinched his butt and how he had caught a glance behind her niqab and had seen that she had a man's curly mustache. God knows if that's true. While Mullah Aasi was still not going to take the tests, he did everything in his power for those who were. He said that if he took the test, he'd lose his intuitive abilities. The rumour spread like wildfire among the students that since Mullah Aasi's revelation he had renounced the world, become a Sufi, and was currently performing miracles right and left. When asked about this, he said, 'I can't deny it.' He had himself locked inside where all day he used his sixth sense to reveal the test questions. Then, at exactly midnight, and then at two thirty in the morning, he would step outside his exalted cell wearing the worn-out gown of his late maternal uncle, the lawyer Sajjad Ahmad, and announce the upcoming questions. This state of affairs went on for three days. I don't know anything about mysticism or whatever, but I can tell you that his face was full of the sort of deep peacefulness you associate with ascetics. His eyes were never more than a quarter open. He renounced meat, garlic, and lying. As soon as he rose in the morning, he bathed in icy cold water that forced him to gather all his strength so as not to start screaming. He became so pious that he never looked at women. If even a hen or female goat wandered by, he looked away like an embarrassed schoolgirl. He became so careful about avoiding the opposite sex that he began conjugating certain Urdu nouns as masculine even though a blind person could tell they were feminine. Long story short, in order to discern the coming questions, he used all his spiritual powers and mystical attainment.

But after the first test, not a single question of his ever appeared. He could no longer show his face in public. On his behalf, we can say that at least he had had a sincere heart when he tricked all of God's creatures. That year, every boy who had failed within a fifty- or sixty-mile radius of Kanpur claimed he had done so because he had used Mullah Aasi's test prep. The worst part was when these repeat failures—who every year were used to cursing out their fates as well as their examiners—set Mullah Aasi within their sights. When they started launching vituperative attacks against him, he secretly slinked off to his grandparents' house in Amroha. One boy's uncle even beat up Mullah Aasi's uncle in the busy market. For over a month, no old person in his family dared leave the house.

So, sir, this was our Mullah Aasi Abdul Mannan. Except these eccentricities, he was no different from any other youth of the time. The other day you quoted a singeing remark of Mirza Abdul Wadud Baig's. Really, what was the worst associated with youths back in those days?

- *Year-long loafing*
- *Ascetic practice implemented before exams*
- *Acne*
- *Rabblerousing at poetry festivals*
- *Agha Hashr Kashmiri's plays*

- *Reynold & Maulvi Abdul Halim Sharar's Islamic novels*
- *A half-litre boiled milk before going to bed*
- *Regular push-ups & onanism*
- *Bathing every Friday*
- *Conversations at night*
- *Solo goosestepping in front of the ladies' compartment at the train station*
- *Shouting slogans against the British while hoping they'll hire you*

Mullah Aasi died a bachelor. He never wore a bridegroom's garland, and he never heard the shehnai played for him; he never had dates distributed at his wedding, and in the end he shrivelled up like a date. I tried to get him to talk about it. He wouldn't touch it with a ten-foot pole. He would begin to talk in esoteric phrases that didn't sound like him: 'My whole life was so chaotic that I never had the time to consider matrimonials and other means of leisure and lechery.' (Yes, Mullah Aasi uses these choice phrases in place of 'marriage.' What pleasure you get from listening to him comes half from his way of talking.) 'Women or no women, I never thought my life was lacking anything. However, if women feel they were deprived of any of their rights, I have no knowledge of this. May God forgive me ...' He went on like this. He still lives in the room in which he was born. It was suffocating to realize he had lived his entire life — seventy or seventy-five years — in one neighbourhood, in one house, and in one room. In Karachi, you don't get even a grave for that long. When the grave-diggers notice that over the course of one year no one has come to recite the fatiha above such-n-such grave on Shab-e-barat, or Eid, or Bakrid, then they remove the skeleton in order to make room for a new corpse. When the trumpet is sounded at the end of the world, then one hundred and one corpses will arise from each grave. The last one will be the gravedigger's.

6.

This Was the Cure for the Old-Time Believers

Sir, the truth is that there are a lot of crackpots in the world, but Mullah Aasi was something altogether different. One of his acquaintances said that after one final Waterloo, he lost it. He belongs to the Malamatiyya Sufi sect. He prays in the same way that many Muslims drink alcohol, that is, on the sly. It's the same sect of which Hazrat Madhav Lal is said to be a member. One man said, 'It's been ages since he became an apostate.' Another replied, 'When was he ever a Muslim?' Haider Mehdi told me how he had once asked him, 'Mullah, is it true you've become Buddhist?' He laughed and then said, 'When I turned fifty, I realized you can't trust life. Why shouldn't I try to correct my bad faith? The night is wearing on, and I've tried out so few things.' One day he was in a fine mood, and so I asked, 'Maulana, so what's so good about Buddhism other than the fact that Mahatma Buddha slipped out of his house while his wife Yashodhra slept?' He smiled, then answered, 'I am my own Yashodhra. But that fortunate one will awake in my next life.'

One of his confidantes went so far to say that he had made clear in his will that his corpse should be taken to Tibet. The poor Tibetans! What had they done to deserve that? They had never hurt him in any way. But Professor Bilgrami, who teaches English at a local college, strongly refutes this. He says that Mullah Aasi asked for his uncleaned body to be consigned to the funeral pyre, just like that of the author of *Lady Chatterley's Lovers*, D. H. Lawrence. Lawrence's widow grew afraid that some of his fanatical devotees would steal his urn (with the ashes inside), and so instead she had his ashes mixed with cement to make a very heavy slab that people could come kiss before leaving. Long story short, everyone had something bad to say about him. As for me, I once saw a prayer rug positioned backwards on his mother's little wooden prayer stool that was set in the corner. I mean, the rug's

303

arch design was facing east not west. I heard that he sits on it in yogic poses and meditates. I also saw a beggar's bowl. A friend of his had remarked that should Mullah Aasi ever take a full-time job, then he would go beg with this bowl from house to house. There were five or six books on Buddhism on the table. I riffled through them. God knows who had underlined them for him. He kept only one decorative item. That was a human skull, which people joked was that of Gautama Buddha, before he reached nirvana.

There was a giant pair of tongs resting on a neatly folded maroon cloth. They looked like Alam Lohar's. One jealous man made fun of them by saying that when Mullah Aasi goes to Mount Sinai to fetch fire for his satak's* bowl, he will grab the Ten Commandments with these very tongs and then stomp his way home. Nearby there was a pair of wooden sandals like sadhus wear—the ones whose toe pieces were like the camel pieces in chess. On the little prayer stool, there was an earthen cup, iktara, withered tulsi leaves, and a Buddha statue. In short, it was a ready-made Buddhist museum, though its paraphernalia was covered in dust. To me, it seemed like it was all for show. Like he was spiting himself just to piss off others.

We Hold the Hell for Infidels in Our Chests

Some thought that he went to these lengths just to piss off Muslims. But that doesn't seem true. That's because Muslims have never opposed the idols of Hindus, Christians, or Buddhists; rather, thanks to

---

* Satak: The dictionary says that a 'satak' is a 'pechvan' or otherwise a slim lady. A pechvan is a hookah with a very long elastic pipe. If we combine these two meanings, then we realize that the elders of yesteryear looked for the traits of hookahs in women as well, and that, after much comparing and contrasting, they decided they liked hookahs and mysticism more than women. This was the cure for the old-time believers!

Islamic law, they are always on the lookout to insult each other over sectarian issues and to brand each other as infidels.

We hold the hell for infidels in our chests

Open Sesame!

Try to guess what he does for a living. I'll give you two minutes. (Then after just thirty seconds ...) Sir, he's a tutor! He helps underprivileged boys study for their final high-school exams. He gets home at midnight. Walking five or six miles is nothing to him. He said, 'Riding conveyances makes your ego swell. Except donkeys. That's why the Jewish prophets all rode donkeys.' But I heard he never accepts money. About this, he said, 'In the East, there is a long tradition that you shouldn't accept money for water, advice, or teaching. If you do, you won't feel good about it, and when you die you can't take money with you anyway. Education that you have to buy never results in spiritual growth; never has, never will. Real change only comes about through enlightenment, and that has no price.' God knows how he gets by. It can't be due to a hidden hand because Buddhists don't believe in God and His infinite benevolence. Buddhists prefer to beg. Actually, Mullah Aasi has fortified himself with philosophy. I didn't get it at all. You can call it craziness or nonsense, but that's just him. Who would have guessed that a boy who hated studying that much would turn to teaching as a route to nirvana. I don't remember if you said this or me, but, for us, those boys who suck at studying join the military, and those who are physically unfit for that end up as college teachers. Sir, nature finds a place for everyone. Once upon a time, Mushtaq Sahib, even you really wanted to be a professor. God had mercy upon you and made sure that never happened. And, as you know very well, I was a teacher for many years. If you ask the truth, that was the happiest time of my life. See,

After I left your place, I never found the same leisure.
Only in your company did I find such pleasure.

But there's another thing. Everyone says he's a great teacher. Apparently you don't have to be a scholar to be a good teacher. He even taught for a while at a government school. But when the Department of Education said he had to pass the BT test within three years or he would be demoted, he submitted his resignation, saying, 'I'm not a patient man. I can't wait three years. My teachers were all BT-certified, and I always failed!' After that, he never worked. He did, however, volunteer at a school for the blind. His voice is sweet, tender, and full of patience. It always was. Words communicate meaning, but the tone of voice carries this meaning to your heart. The magic isn't in the words but in the voice. Saying 'open sesame' won't open the treasure door in the *Arabian Nights* for every Tom, Dick, and Harry; it has to be Ali Baba's voice. The key to the heart's door isn't a word but a sound. If Mullah Aasi has to repeat himself, or if someone gets confused, his voice becomes even smoother. You feel like you're swallowing sugar cream. Inside every good teacher is a child sitting with hand raised and head bobbing, indicating whether he has understood or not. Any good teacher is addressing this child. He lets the child keep his innocence.

7.

That Room Talked

It Was Like Going Back In Time

My intense conversations with Mullah Aasi took place in the very room where forty-five years earlier I had said goodbye to him before leaving for Pakistan. Back in those days, everyone was going to

Pakistan, leaving behind land, property, houses, jobs, dear friends, and lovers. In that very room, he had hugged me and wished me safe travels, 'Go, my dear, go. I give you over to Koh-e-Nida.' To this very day, he cannot understand why any sane person would leave Kanpur. The same ceiling fan hangs from the same unsteady rafter, and it still screeches in the same manner. When I wanted to talk, I would switch off the fan. As soon as it was switched on, a whirlwind sprang up, and the dust that had settled on the books, walls, and carpet would rise into the air, asphyxiating the mosquitos. He uses the fan not to save himself from the heat but rather to save himself from mosquitos. But that's very infrequently. He's not worried about saving on electricity. He's worried about saving the fan. Using it shortens its lifespan. But, God be praised, that fan has grown up! By now it must be forty or forty-five years old! At this rate, it will live to be one hundred. Many sadhus and yogis believe that God has predetermined the exact number of breaths each person can take, and so Mullah Aasi usually sits holding his breath so as to lengthen his life. But from time to time he has no choice but to breathe. His fan lives on in similar fashion.

Stepping into his room made me feel as though I had travelled to another world. It was like going back in time. Everything was just as it had been. In fact, everything was still in the very same positions. By God, I felt as though the cobwebs were the same ones I had known so long ago! I saw only one change. He had shaved his beard again. When I asked about it, he dodged the question. Then he said, 'I could stand it just so long as it was black.' Mr Inam winked at me, 'Mahatma Buddha also shaved.' The room's layout was the same as in '47. The walls were grease-stained; only where the plaster had recently fallen off did they look clean. On the left wall, two feet above the bed, forty-five years ago I had written out in pencil an itemized list for a picnic. Now its first four lines remained. Sir, in those days there were 192 pai in a rupee, and one pai was equal to one rupee

of today. I was surprised to see that before I had done the accounting, I had written the number 786! Like your Mirza Abdul Wadud
Baig says, back then, Muslim boys considered their failing in math
to be the heavenly confirmation of being Muslims! Back then, every
job that involved accounting, business, and that brought profits was
considered the province of moneylenders, corner-store owners, and
Jews. But I had memorized the Chakravarty math tables, and I still
know how to multiply by ¼, ¾, and 2½—whatever good that is. It
was a good ruse for controlling boys' passions—no, for controlling
them and their passions. Thinking of Muslims brings back another
memory. You see this bruise on my forehead that I've got from banging my head on the floor five times a day? By the grace of God, I got
this when I was twenty-five or so. Even Mian Tajammul's company
and Niaz Fatehpuri's books couldn't distract me from my prayers. You
won't believe me, but two-thirds of my hair went white at that age.
Anyway, I was about to say that on the wall above the rosewood table,
there were his high-school graduation photos. All five years of them.
In the fifth year, he managed to steer his ship home when a former
classmate passed his BA and started to teach English at the school.
In the fifth photo, he stands behind the principal, gripping tightly the
back of his chair. It was rumoured that he didn't want to pass because
then he would have to give up being the class monitor. Who has ever
heard of a class monitor in college? One photo was sepia. When I saw
myself, I was shocked. My God, that's what we looked like when we
were young? How sad we all looked! We promised to be friends forever, work for the welfare of humanity, and write letters to everyone
every third day till the end of time. The table was covered with the
same green tablecloth. Ninety percent of it had turned blue from ink
stains. I could barely control myself from pouring ink on the remaining ten percent so as to get rid of its leucoderma. Back then servants
wore uniforms made of the same material as the tablecloth. Some-

times on very cold days, Basheer, the school servant, would scold us and send us back home, 'Boys, coats and kisses won't work today! Go home, put on a kamri and a mirzai [cotton-stuffed vest] and then come back.' He himself came from home in a threadbare mirzai that was so old that there was only one little wad of cotton in each of the vest's lozenge-shaped patches. But he never went home in his work clothes. It was free of wrinkles and stains. He rang the bell to announce the end of the day in such a way that the bell seemed to giggle.

Big Cause, Small Men

The killer poem that Maulana Shibli wrote after the destruction of the Fish Market Mosque ('We, the slain, the martyrs of Kanpur') is still hanging from the very nail that got bent in half while being hammered into the wall. Sir, the man who has never mistakenly hammered his thumb is one to watch out for. You have to be on your guard against clever devils like that. Khwaja Hasan Nizami wrote about this mosque, 'This is the mosque where our elders fell writhing to the ground, where their white beards grew red with blood.'

The glass that covers the poem was broken in the middle so that it looked like a spider's web. After fifty years, I read the poem in its entirety, as well as the poem that goes 'Muhammad Ali's mother said, "My son, give your life for Khilafat."' How should I put it? It didn't move me. The causes of that era and the one before it, for example, the Silk Handkerchief Movement; the Khilafat Movement; the Balkan Wars ('If you want to die well, let's go to the Balkans, let's go'); opposition to women's education and science education (where Akbar Illahabadi was in the vanguard); Muslim protests, including those of Maulana Muhammad Ali Jauhar against the Sharda Act (the act prohibiting child marriage); these and many other causes that we were ready to lay down our lives for, now they just seemed odd.

Take the Khilafat Movement. Gandhiji also supported it. You can't imagine a more passionate, national, organized, and pointless, futile movement. But people then were larger than life. Today, causes are well thought-out and meaningful. But people aren't half of what they used to be. Nushoor recited Sauda's couplet, which, even though it's two hundred years old, feels contemporary today:

> Laments feel insipid, souls have lost their strength.
> O God, where have the lions of yesteryear gone?

Those were strangely emotional days. I remember how Badri Narayan once called Mahmood of Ghazni a 'pilfering tyrant,' and so Abdul Muqeet Khan retorted that Shivaji was a 'mountain rat.' Things escalated, and Badri Narayan began to slander the Mughal emperors one by one. He said extremely offensive things about Aurangzeb's daughter, the Princess Zaib-un-Nisa, penname Makhfi [Hidden]. So Abdul Muqeet Khan laid waste to Prithviraj Chauhan, Maharana Pratap, and Raja Sawai Man Singh. But when he turned to Maharaja Ranjeet Singh, Badri Narayan lost control, even though he wasn't a Sikh. (He was a Gaur Brahmin.) They fell to fighting right then and there. Muqeet Khan broke his thumb, and Badri Narayan broke the bridge of his nose. Actually, this was all an excuse: they were in love with the same boy.

In the Company of Birds

The walls were adorned with the same decorative tughras and the same calligraphic texts, and the bed was the very one on which Muqeet Khan had used a knife to carve the name of this boy. It was on one of the legs near the bed's head. Then he had used this knife to cut his finger, and he dabbed blood into the carving of the boy's name. You too must really think that I'm strange. If, through some miracle, I stop talking about prostitutes, then I start talking about good-looking young boys! Sir, what can I do? I can only tell the stories that these sinful eyes have seen. But look at Mir's poetry. Or his autobiography. Or look at Mushafi's poetry. In all of them, you'll see clear references. Sir, we had enough courage to talk about women only after we went to college. I really don't want to tell his name. He became an important politician for Congress, but then he was ousted from the party on corruption charges. He married the former wife of a deputy secretary. But then she ran away with a Sikh businessman just three months after he was dismissed. You can't guess how we used to suffer from the claustrophobia of sexual deprivation back in those days—you weren't old enough then. Majaz wasn't lying when he said,

Sleeping with death is bearable
Because she'll lie down with you.

Sir, the fact is that back then if you showed even an X-ray of a woman to a boy, he would fall head over heels in love.

Where once had been a glass skylight was now a piece of cardboard. Through a hole in that, a bird was coming and going quite contentedly. She had made a nest nearby. Her chicks were chirping constantly. Mullah Aasi said that once the chicks grew up and left the nest, the house would feel empty. Dust covered his rug. The hole in the rug that Mian Tajammul Hussain's cigarette had burnt forty or forty-five years earlier remained, except that it had grown so large that now you could pass a watermelon through it. Around the hole, frayed threads hung loosely. You could see through the hole that awful red shade of cement that used to be in all the railway waiting rooms and government bungalows.

In those days, Mian Tajammul Hussain must have been around thirty years old. He had three kids already. But he was so scared of Haji Sahib (his father) that he went to his friends' houses to smoke.

Haji Sahib considered smoking cigarettes immoral. He smoked a hookah. He also considered bioscopes depraved. Therefore, he never let Mian Tajammul go to the movies by himself. Rather, he went with him.

So I see you're smiling because I used the word 'therefore.' Sir, people from Lucknow and Kanpur are fond of saying 'therefore.' To us, 'hence' sounds clunky. But, sir, back in those days, I heard even ordinary people using a lot of big words like 'hence,' 'howsoever,' 'notwithstanding,' and 'so much so.'

A Lizard's Severed Tail

The ceiling was completely rotten, and termites had eaten through the rafter. The ring that secured the fan to the rafter had been worn down to almost nothing. I'm not an astrologer, so it's hard to say which one of these would collapse first. He seated his guests right underneath the fan, and this poor soul spent his entire visit looking up. The ding in the ceiling where I had once shot an air rifle at the lizards was exactly as it had been. Oh, speaking of lizards reminds me of your friend with the wife and the note she wrote that the hostel boys stole and read. What was it she wrote? I think it was in Hindi. Jagat Narayan Srivastava was his name. They had just got married. The note read, 'I swear to Ram! These nights without you, I writhe like a lizard's severed tail.'

Wow! This makes a fish writhing on a dock seem like nothing. You use the phrase 'a fish out of water' as a symbol for nostalgic people, but that's not fair to them.

I've already told you that Mullah Aasi has no source of income. He never has had one. But he has never lacked for things to do. He might be unemployed, but he has never been idle. It must have been '50 or '51. His mother went for the second time to Ajmer to pray for him to get a job and to lose interest in Buddhism. Someone there told her to go to Hazrat Data Gunj Bakhsh's shrine because Khwaja Ajmeri himself had gone there for a forty-day chilla retreat. So she went to Lahore to pray for six months. God knows how it happened, but the embroidered silk sheet she brought to lay in offering on top of the saint's grave caught fire one evening. People said that her powerful prayer turned back on her. If God's door is closed, no offering is accepted. She cried all through the night. Then in the morning, while she was prostrating herself in prayer, she joined the Answerer of All Prayers. She suffered from chronic heart problems and asthma. She was buried right there in Lahore's Miani Sahib Graveyard.

After his mother died, no one ever cooked in his house. He rents out half of the house. For fifteen years, the renter hasn't paid rent. Recently I heard that the renter is filing a suit in order to kick Mullah Aasi out of the house. Sometimes he says he's seventy-two, and sometimes he says seventy-five. Then he says 'by the solar calendar,' just in case. Saying 'solar' reminds me of something that happened when I was in the sixth grade. In front of the entire class, I read 'qumri' [dove] instead of 'qamri' [lunar], and 'lardeeture' instead of 'literature.' Master Fakhir Hussain roared in laughter, and afterwards he started calling me 'Basharat Lardeeture.'

8.

The Servant's Golden Age of Service

I went to see Basheer, the school's servant. He's completely old and worn down, and yet he holds himself as straight as a gun's barrel. When he gets riled up even a little, his voice turns into a bark. He said, 'It's a shame I'm still alive. The only reason I'm alive is to bear my children to the grave, those I used to sit on my lap. Well, I had my time. But these days I don't break a sweat or dream. Once every six months

I dream of ringing the school bell, and the next day I'm full of vim and vigour. Thank God my hands and feet still work. Master Samee-ul-Haq is twelve years younger than me. But his memory is faltering, and his digestion is worse. He finds himself standing with a little pot in his hand, and he can't remember whether he's going to the bathroom or just went: if he's just gone, then why is his stomach upset; and if he's on the way there, then why isn't there any water in his pot?

'I remember every boy's face and his behaviour. Sir, you were considered good-looking, even though you used to shave your head. Mullah Aasi parted his hair in the middle like ladies do. Your friend Aasim wore a silver amulet around his neck. His father died the morning of the very first day of the final high-school exams. Throughout the test, I stood in the corner reciting, "God be praised," as well as the aiyat-al-kursi. Twice I gave Aasim half-full glasses of milk. The year of the earthquake in Quetta your friend Ghazanfar committed suicide by running in front of an oncoming train. He was his father's only son. But I have hundreds. What bastard says I'm childless?'

Those Who Cursed Politely

He started up again, 'Son, it's due to God's kindness that I retired when I did. Otherwise, how much indignity would I have had to suffer? Thank God I'm still active. In old age, sickness is pure torture. But being too healthy is an even bigger pain. You don't know how to burn off the extra energy. An active old man has no place in the world. He likes to wander around aimlessly near the banks of rivers. Last year I dragged myself all the way back to school. I stopped short in amazement. The school servants were gambolling about, and they weren't wearing their name badges, coats, hats, or turbans. To this day, I've never gone even to the bathroom without a hat on. And I've never bathed without a loincloth. One day Hamiduddin came wearing nothing more than a kurta because he had left his coat with the darner for mending. He set out on his tasks when the principal intercepted him, 'You're going to appear before the kids with your family jewels showing?' In our day, servants were like kings. The principal always greeted us before we greeted him. You've witnessed that no teacher has ever addressed me by my first name or without respect. And I've always addressed each and every boy with respect. A foul-mouthed policeman once spoke rudely to me in a busy market, 'Hey, you, out of my way!' At the time I was wearing my official uniform. I grabbed him by the ears and lifted him into the air. He weighed one hundred kilos. I've set straight my fair share of cocky men.

'Today's servants look like chicken farmers. In our day, people knew etiquette and were well-mannered. The upper classes never spoke down to people. Even if they were cursing you out, they did so politely. Your grandfather was very hotheaded, but he insulted people with grace and according to their rank: bhondu [idiot], bhatiyara [inn-keeper], bhardbhoonja [someone who roasts chickpeas], bhand [buffoon], and if someone stooped really far, then bhardu bhardva [pimp]. The school's Urdu teacher said that he was a great scholar: he didn't swear, but rather he conjugated the sound 'bh.' Well, I'm an uneducated man, but that day I learned what 'conjugate' means. They were excellent teachers. Whatever they said lodged itself in our hearts like a bucket dropped into a well. Why? Because they knew how to respect ignorant people like me. Today's scholars are so arrogant that they think of themselves as wisdom incarnate. New things cramp their style, like new shoes. But even though they've swallowed the entire ocean with all the oysters in it, they still can't spit out even one pearl.'

The Day's Last Bell

For a while, Basheer Chacha sat laughing through his toothless grin. His gums have receded, but he still has that twinkle in his eyes. Then he sat down pompously on top of a battered stool. Although his bragging had lasted just a little while, it had calmed his shaky head, hands, and voice. He started up again, 'Believe me, hearing them hit the bell disgusted me. Now anyone at all is allowed to ring the bell. These idiots act like they drank too much on Holi and are banging on drums. How on earth are the kids supposed to focus on studying? I got through five bells, but then, before it was too late, I took to my heels. Why? Because I wasn't going to be able to stand hearing it again. Once an old guy gets worked up, it's more than hard to get him to cool down. I earned the right to strike the bell after fifteen hard years. Back then the servant who rang the bell was respected and powerful. One day, news came from the principal's house that his wife was about to deliver. Leaving quickly, he forgot the year-end exams on his desk. That night I didn't go home. I sat on top of the test all night like a coiled snake. Another time, the geography teacher and I were on the outs for seemingly no reason. I'll tell you something I learned the hard way. Enmity without reason and loving an ugly woman are the purest and most dangerous types of hatred and love. That's because they both start at the point right after thinking has stopped. I mean, I went out of my mind for no reason. And his mind's light was squelched by an ugly woman from my neighbourhood. Love is blind. It's not necessary for a woman to be beautiful. It's enough for the man to be blind.'

Basheer Chacha hereby fell into a laughing fit that bent him in two. Then he began again, 'In our day, ladies as black as coal weren't called black. They called them "milk chocolate." Black was reserved for opium and Shakti Ma. So I was about to say that when the geography teacher had the ninth and tenth grade classes, I started ringing the bell ten minutes late. On the third day, he surrendered. The other teachers were complaining as well. They sat me down in the staff room and said, "Mr Basheer, forgive and forget. Don't throw out the baby with the bathwater."

'I never listened to anyone. I did as I pleased. I rang the bell when I knew it was time. This slave of yours has never been enslaved by a watch. My internal clock has never been wrong. I was my own boss. No one dared interfere with my work. When I heard the news of Kanpur's Maulana Hasrat Mohani's death, I swear to God, without asking anyone's permission, I struck the bell and closed down the entire school. Ghulam Rasool Daftari was a real coward. He said, "Basheer, you know, you're in for it now. The Director of Education is going to want a word with you." I said, "I'll tell him, 'Be rest assured, my ever-abiding lord, when you expire, I'll be sure to do the same.'" But when news of Vallabh Bhai Patel's death arrived, the principal said, "Basheer, ring the bell, send everyone home." He said it twice, but I ignored him. He insisted a third time, and so I drew a long face and hit the bell as weakly as I could. Some heard; some didn't. After '47, call it "independence," I started using the shadow on the compound-wall as an indication of the hour. The neighbourhood set their watches to my bell. It's been fifteen years since I retired, but my right hand starts tingling at the time when I used to ring the first and last bells. It starts to throb compulsively. The last day on the job is really hard on everyone. It was my last day. I was on my way to ring the bell for the last time when suddenly I became overwhelmed with emotion. I sat down right there. I handed the mallet to Majeed and said, "Son, I can't do it. Take charge of things from here. Ring the bell of my departure." Then I went to see the principal. He said, "Mr Basheer, the teachers want to give you the gift of a very fine watch." I said, "Sir, what on earth will I do with a watch? I don't care about time anymore. I struck the bell without ever looking at a watch, so why would I want one now? If you want to give me something, give me my name badge. I've worn it for forty years." I must say that he was very generous. Without the slightest hesitation, he said, "Take it." It's hanging over there on a peg. Every three or four months, I use lemon

317

to polish its brass to a high gleam. But my hands aren't as strong as they used to be. Without the badge, I feel like my shoulders are bare and lopsided. Sometimes after I'm done polishing it, I put it on. Then I sit up straight again. For a little while, I feel as young as I ever did.

'Son, it was '55. Hundreds of rowdy students bent on a strike bum-rushed the school, trying to get it to shut down. They were trying to incite violence. The innocent kids were terror-stricken. The teachers were frozen in place. The principal was worried. I couldn't stand to see them like this. I challenged the goons, "Which son of a bitch thinks he can get the school to close without me ringing the bell? Stupid fools, get out of here, or I'll ring *your* bell!" The principal called the cops. The cop said, "I can't make out what you're saying …" I became furious. I grabbed the receiver and yanked out its one-metre-long cord. Then I picked up a long-bladed paper-cutting knife in one hand, and with the receiver in the other, I sprang upon the goons in my school uniform, waving my weapons about helter-skelter in the air and shouting a battle cry. The crowd dispersed. Death was hovering about them. Some fell here; some fell there. And I took care of those that didn't fall.'

Basheer Chacha's eyes began to twinkle. He got this from being around mischievous boys all his life. They had taught him how to daydream.

The Man Who Sits at the Foot of the Charpoy

He related some of the finer points of the art of bell ringing, which I had never before considered. For instance, the first time each day, he would hit the bell with full force right in its centre. This was done emphatically and regally. He announced recess by striking a high note along the bell's rim that would resound in a jingling fashion. The grave clangs of Monday were completely different from the giggling chimes of Saturday. He said, 'The new line of servants doesn't know the difference in moods between morning and afternoon.' Although he didn't say this, I began to feel that while ringing the morning prayer bell, he must have imagined that he was performing raag bhairavi.

As long as I was there, he kept coming back to his official duties. If he hadn't been a school servant but something else, he still would have carried out his duties with not only the same diligence but also the same humble devotion. When a man stops taking pride in his work, he quickly becomes apathetic. He turns his job into something dishonourable and worthless.

Basheer Chacha said, 'One month before being laid off…' (he uses this detested word instead of 'retirement') '… the principal recommended that special consideration be taken and my salary increased since I'd been a loyal employee. The answer that came back was exactly the opposite: that I should retire immediately. It's like the saying that goes, "The husband wants to cut off his wife's nose, and she insists on a nose ring." The reason I was laid off then was because a sycophant inspector wrote me up in his report as being too old. And bent over. And having a limp. But, glory be to God, six months later this hunchbacked, lame old man hoisted this fool onto his shoulders and took him to his final resting place. May God's name be praised!

'In our day, we would hold court from our charpoys. Our elders had always instructed us to never sit near the head of any bed. Always sit at the foot of the bed. That way if someone older shows up, you won't have to give up your seat for them. So we spent our entire lives sitting at the foot of the bed. Son, now the boat's reaching life's far shore. I was born poor, and I'll die poor, but, by the grace of God, I was never anyone's punching bag. I always wore my name badge with pride and considered my uniform a robe of honour.' He also said that each year a new crop of boys would show up, and yet he took the time to advise each and every one. Moreover, in the golden age of his service, he saw nine principals come and go, as well as thirteen inspectors. They flitted in, then flitted out. He put many of these superiors in their place. As he recounted this, his head stopped quivering, and he puffed out his chest. Quelling his cough, he said, 'The principal said many times that he wanted to promote me to supervisor of all the school's servants, water carriers, sweepers, and snack peddlers. I pointed out that there is only one Lord, and He is God. In my life, I've seen a supervisor or two. They're all about themselves. Your humble servant doesn't give a damn about them.' After telling the same stories for so long, Basheer Chacha had begun to believe them. In old age, you begin mistaking tall tales for the truth.

Even Today, Friends, a Boy Is Nothing to Scare Me

To make him happy, I told him he was as strong as he had been back then. 'What do you eat?' I asked. Hearing this, he flung down his cane and stood up with his chest—no, his *ribs*—puffed out.

He said, 'In the morning, I drink four glasses of water on an empty stomach. This is a fakir's secret charm. A few days ago a delegation of neighbourhood folks came by. They started whispering among themselves. They didn't have the courage to speak to me. I said to them, "My dears, speak up. There's no shame in asking for a favour." They said, "Chacha, you're still childless. Please remarry. You're still in fine shape. Wink at any passing beauty, and she'll make a beeline for you. We'll take your message to whomever you please." I said, "I respect what you all think. But it will ruin my youthfulness. I'll think about it and then give you an answer. The problem is I've already had one wife die. If another dies, I won't be able to handle that." See their presumptuousness? One glib-tongued boy said, "Chacha, if that's the case, then marry someone who'll outlive you. Bilqees is a widow twice over." I said, "Watch your mouth! How well you treat your elders!"'

I teased him, 'Chacha, now with you in old age, it will be difficult for you to control a wife of the new generation of independent-minded women.'

He said, 'You haven't heard the old saying that goes, "So what if the stick is broken, you can still use it to keep things in order at home?"'

Then he leaned his head against his cane and laughed so hard that he fell into an asthmatic fit. For ten minutes, he wheezed and wheezed. I was scared that he might not ever catch his breath again.

9.

Gautama Buddha Cum Paperweight!

Mullah Aasi and I decided to go to Lucknow, the city of lovers, famous for its beautiful evenings. (The city's eloquent spokesman and a true lover of the city, Maulana Abdul Halim Sharar, has written about this chapter of Awadh's cultural history in the red ink of the setting sun.) I had to convince Mullah Aasi to go with me. I didn't have the guts to see it alone after forty years. People had warned me how that spectacle of life and liveliness—Hazrat Ganj—the pinnacle of splendour and grace—was no longer what it had been. That it was now a ghost town. Sir, I don't know if Lucknow is haunted, but my mind was. One man scared me when he said that the Char Bagh Railway Station sign was written only in Hindi, and that there wasn't one Urdu sign to be found anywhere in the city; that said, the inscriptions on tombs were still done in an exquisite Urdu script—you couldn't find such pure and silky smooth calligraphy in all of Pakistan. I was a guest. I said nothing. Two days ago I was speaking with a man from Delhi and mentioned that Karachi's nihari and gole kebabs are much better than the ones that Delhi is famous for, and, sir, he went crazy. I'll never do that again!

Mullah Aasi didn't show up on time. At first I was mad. Then I got worried. I got a rickshaw and went to his charming abode. Musty papers, files, and thirty years' worth of bills and receipts were spread across his carpet, and he was sitting on his haunches in the very middle of it. He hopped to and fro like a frog looking at his papers. When he found something that he wanted to look at later, he put a Buddha statue on it. He had three statues: one of a smiling Buddha with eyes closed; another of a young Buddha from the time he left his sleeping wife at home for good; and the third was of a skeletal Buddha deep in a month-long fast. He was using them as paperweights. I had raced over. I was covered in sweat. My muslin kurta clung to me like an onion peel. As soon as I entered the room, I flipped on the switch for the fan, but the switch gave me a shock, and I fell onto the floor. Well, sir, at that point a storm broke in the room and hundreds of paper airplanes took flight. We couldn't see each other. His 30-year-old filing system took to wing. He quickly put on his wooden sandals and shut off the fan. If you weren't wearing wooden sandals, the forty or 45-year-old copper switch shocked you so bad you would think you were about to die. He ran here and there grabbing his papers just like boys run after kites. He said, 'I'm sorry, but I can't go to Lucknow today. Something unexpected came up.'

The Good Points of the Chicken Pose

Sir, the unexpected thing was this. The water bill he received the day before had his father's name not as Aijaz Hussain but Aijaz Ali. He'd never noticed this before. And so he was going through the bills from the last thirty years to see when this mistake first appeared, and if this mistake was limited to the water bill or had spread to other offices.

Why the Water Department was interested in his father's name was also something that he wanted to resolve. I said, 'Maulana, just pay the bill. What difference does it make?' He said, 'Of course it makes a difference. If your father's name doesn't matter, then what in this world matters? When I was in the fifth grade, I said that Emperor Shah Jahan's father was Humayun and so Master Fakhir Hussain made me stand in the corner in the chicken pose. He thought I was fooling around. But if it hadn't been that, it would have been something else. For the most part, that's how my school days went. I was allowed back to the bench only when he ordered me to stand on it. When I dream about those days, it's either me in the chicken pose or me finding out that I failed a test. Master Dwarika Das Chaturvedi, the director of education, has just returned from a trip to Europe and America. I heard that his report says that no other country in the world has discovered the chicken pose. At one point, I stopped wearing a fez. That was because when I was in the chicken pose, its tassel would dangle one inch in front of my eyes like a pendulum. Right, then left. Then, by the end of the class period, when my legs were about to give out, the tassel would start swaying front to back. It also seemed to denigrate the Turks, which my belief in Muslim brotherhood couldn't stand. So I gave up wearing hats altogether.'

I quipped that Mahatma Buddha never wore a hat. He didn't dignify my quip with a response. Instead he said, 'Have you ever noticed that since the chicken pose was banned in school, both educational and moral standards have gone down? I tolerate all sorts of stupidity in my students, but if they mispronounce words, I immediately make them stand in the chicken pose. And I don't allow them to wear tight jeans. Because then it's hard for them to pronounce Persian words, to clean their butts, and to stand in the chicken pose. But that pose makes today's boys start wobbling in just five minutes. Back in our time, I knew boys who could stomach twenty lashes of the cane without so much as wincing. One became a superintendent of police; he's retired. Another was a director in the Department of Rural Uplift. Now where are such mischievous, courageous boys! There was not a question of character back then. Think of it like this: back in the day, we failed in chemistry because we didn't have Bunsen burners, but today they fail because they've never felt the cane.'

A Silver Bowl

It was extremely hot. For the first time in almost a half-century, I scooped water with a coconut shell to fill his famous engraved bowl. Inside, the entire chapter of the 'soora-e-yasin' is engraved. It's pure silver. Have you heard the expression 'bowl-like eyes'? Sir, I've seen them! When we used to come back in the evening after soccer, we would wedge the bowl's thin edge between our lips, and immediately we felt the water's coolness spread through our bodies. Immediately after his birth, Mullah Aasi had drunk his mother's milk mixed with honey from this very bowl. As his grandfather and then his father lay dying, they were given drops of aab-e-Zamzam from this very bowl. Even today people often borrow it to fill it with water to give to the sick. I drank water from it but felt a little uncomfortable doing so—there was grime deep in the grooves of the engraving. But, sir, the truth is that even today the water might be the same cold water, the bowl is the same as well, the drinker, the same too; but where has the old-time thirst gone?

He also had a steel cup with Muradabadi engraving. It must be just about as old as he is. The first time I went to see him, he sent a student out on an errand. He brought back a little packet of sugar. Mullah Aasi then turned a pencil upside down and used it to stir the sugar into the water to make a sugary drink. I had completely forgotten how good a sugary sherbet tasted! In our childhoods, we often served this to guests. Soda water and ginger drinks were used only for indigestion and for their bottles during Hindu–Muslim riots.

Sher (Shah) Is inside the Iron Cage

Now what was I talking about? Yes, it was about his bills. After he got all his bills in order, I wanted to turn on the fan again. But he stopped me. He said, 'I'm sorry, but Sher Shah is under the weather. The fan will only increase his fever.' I looked around. I couldn't see anyone of that or any other name, sick or otherwise. But I shouldn't have been looking for a person. Sher Shah was, in fact, the name of his sick pigeon that sat in the corner in a big mesh locker, the type that people used to call a 'ganjeena' and use as a refrigerator. It had a wooden frame of three tiers covered by a thin wire mesh, whose secondary purpose was to let air in, but whose primary purpose was to keep flies, cats, rats, and children out of the food. Beneath each of the frame's four legs, people used to put bowls of water for ants. When those ants that would try to cross these moats to reach the banned delicacies above got to the water, they drowned. (So therein floated the bodies of greedy ants.) These lockers were better than refrigerators and freezers because leftovers would rot within half a day, and this would save everyone from having to eat them over and over ad infinitum. These lockers were in every wealthy family's house back then. Lower middle-class households had another system where they hung things from the ceiling. And in the homes of the poor, even today the safest place to store food is in the stomach.

The aforementioned locker had been the intensive care unit of Mullah Aasi's pigeons since 1953. Another reason he couldn't go to Lucknow that day was that he didn't want to leave his sick pigeon alone while he went on a pleasure outing. Once, he had a female pigeon named Noor Jahan that died, and he didn't leave the house for two weeks. She had chicks, and they weren't used to caring for themselves. He fledged them. When a female anara pigeon (the ones with red eyes) named Draupadi broke her beak, he fed her from his hand for months on end. He named each and every pigeon. When I was there, we saw through the open door a fan-tailed pigeon named Ranjeet Singh that was walking in front of other breeds' female coops with his chest and tail feathers puffed out. He was walking in circles in such a fashion that had he been a man he would have been killed in communal violence long ago. For him, there would have been neither funeral nor memorial service.

A Pigeon Coop

He had always loved pigeon flying. His father had, as well. My father did too, for that matter. Even your Mirza Abdul Wadud Baig is convinced of the virtues of pigeons. Hobbies—real hobbies—should be completely worthless and without redeeming value. Usually people raise animals for some self-gain or self-interest. For instance, those miserable people who keep dogs do so because they can't afford an aide-de-camp or courtier. Some people pet dogs under the mistaken notion that they must have the virtues of younger brothers. They raise goats with the idea of dropping their faeces into milk and serving that to Urdu critics. Elephants were usually raised by those nobles who had fallen out of favour with a king; the king had in fact given the elephant, along with a silver howdah, so that the nobleman would be forced to keep stuffing food into the animal for as long as it lived. People raise parrots so that when they get old and forget their pet phrases, the parrot will continue to repeat whatever they have taught it. Mullahs put up with rooster calls only because they want chicken for dinner. And, Mushtaq Sahib, in 1963 you kept a monkey because you wanted an animal you could call 'Darwin'!

Sir, pigeons are kept only because they're pigeons, and that's it. But one of Mullah Aasi's neighbours, Sadullah Khan Ashufta, swore to God the following was true: 'One day, it was bitterly cold, I prepared a cup of Kashmiri tea, then went to his house. It was six in the morning. Inside it was freezing cold. He was sitting deep in meditation in front of a Bodhisattva statue, and, to keep warm, he held a pigeon in each hand.' If anything about this is off, then blame Ashufta.

One day we happened to start talking about pigeons. He said, 'I've heard, but can't believe, that you don't have a single pigeon coop in all of Karachi. What kind of city are you building? I wouldn't want to look at the sky if it didn't have pigeons, sunsets, kites, or stars. My friend Abrar Hussain was in Karachi in December 1973. He must have stayed two months. A haze hung over the city the whole time. He saw a star only once, and that with binoculars. It was actually a comet! He said that unlike in Lucknow, people in Karachi don't conduct kite, partridge, chicken, or ram duels. Instead they fight themselves. But the truth is there aren't any kite contests or pigeon contests in this neighbourhood too. Only this one coop remains. Lucknow is even worse off. Once upon a time, after you left, in December '47, Alim-uddin—you know, our Shaikh Chilli Laddan—had packed to go to Pakistan when at the last minute he changed his mind. That was because Master Abdus Shakoor, BA, BT, told him that he couldn't take his pigeon coop on the train. And if he managed to sneak it on board, then at the Wagah border, the Pakistani customs official might arrest him on some suspicion. My brother Basharat! You immigrated to Pakistan and so became a muhajir. But without going anywhere we became foreigners in our own country. This is not the city that it was; that's become something of storybooks. It's different now. This neighbourhood is now 95 percent vegetarian. The street-cats are dying for meat, and so they hang around my pigeon coop all day long. Do you remember the boss at Allen Cooper? What was his name? Sir Arthur

Inskap? When his wife brought a Siamese cat from England, her husband neutered all the cats of Kanpur so that their cat would remain unsullied. Ajmal, the lawyer, lived two doors down. People liked to say that one night Sir Arthur got Ajmal's dog neutered as well, just as a precaution. That was in '41, just before the Quit India Movement.'

We laughed about this for quite a while. Even these days when he laughs, he laughs like a child. Then he wiped his tears and suddenly turned serious. He said, 'I'm not strong enough anymore to go up on the roof to close the pigeon coops. At dusk, the well-trained pigeons return to their coops on their own. My students make sure the rest get in. Then they feed them. The noble pastimes of old are no more. You can't find millet in town anymore. I have to order it from a village fifty miles away. The village registrar was my student. But nowadays just ask any college graduate what's the difference between finger millet, pearl millet, and foxtail millet. If he knows the difference, I'll shave my eyebrows using his piss for shaving water. Ninety-nine percent of everyone has never seen barley. Tell me, is it the same in Karachi? Three years ago a well-wisher came from Karachi, and bearing in mind my long dedication to this pastime ...' (look, here, again, Master Fakhir Hussain is speaking through the mouth of Mullah Aasi) '... as a gift he brought the novel *Twilight in Delhi*. Its author is the venerable scholar Ahmad Ali. He writes so well. He knows everything about Delhi. The Urdu translation was entirely idiomatic. By God, it was very good. Each and every page was filled with idioms related to women and pigeons. If he has another book about pigeons, please send it along with someone.'

The Black Pigeon and the Handsome Young Girl's Cat

There isn't any one story that can sum up his eccentricities. I'll tell you about one of his annual routines. He finally passed his final high-school exams when he was twenty-two; yet even before this, he had stopped looking in the newspaper for any test results. During the month the results were printed, he didn't buy newspapers, read newspapers, or meet with people who read newspapers. It might have just been indifference, but it also might have been fear. Mirza thinks that he couldn't face his yearly good-for-nothingness in printed form. In any event, a week before test results were to be printed, he would go over to his close friend Imdad Hussain Zaidi's house to give him a black male carrier pigeon and white male tumbler pigeon. Then he would go home, lock the door, and begin meditating. He instructed Imdad Hussain to immediately release the white pigeon if he passed, and the black one, if he failed. Then from time to time Mullah Aasi would stick his head out the window to look up at the sky and go onto the roof to see if the results were in yet.

Each year that the black pigeon came back, he would slaughter it and give it to Merjina (the good-looking neighbour girl's cat). In ancient times, kings had killed the bearers of bad news, and so he carried on this kingly tradition until he had earned his BA. On the day the results were released, there would be intervals of crying and carrying on in the house, and that was because whenever his mother and sisters saw a black pigeon, they would assume the worst, even though just as many white pigeons landed on the coops as well. After every three or four years, that day would at last come again when

It came, headlong, tumbling, thrashing, writhing...

Meaning, the white tumbler came. He was so happy that he fed all his seventy or eighty pigeons wheat instead of millet and released them to fly together. The next day he put a tiny silver painjani* on the white pigeon's feet and then placed ten female taftah pigeons in front of his coop.† I said pigeon coop without thinking about it. What I should

* Painjani: ankle bells for pigeons.
† Taftah: resplendent white pigeon, male or female.

have said was that by the time he graduated from college, he had gone through this three times—middle school, high school, and then college—and so his white female pigeons had increased by thirty, and his entire house had been transformed into a harem of good-news-bringing birds—meaning, tumbler pigeons. With this, the people of the house were reduced to being nothing more than the servants and shit-picker-ups of said pigeons.

That's One Army That's Apparently Short on Arms

The day when he wasn't able to go to Lucknow because of his ailing pigeon Sher Shah, I said, somewhat annoyed, 'My God, look at you. The world's advanced, but you're still messing around with pigeons. Can't you give up them already?'

He replied, 'Your father was a great adept at pigeon rearing. In comparison, I'm nothing. People think it's a despicable hobby, but it used to be the best of the best. I read somewhere that when Bahadur Shah Zafar's party would set out, a flock of two hundred pigeons flew overhead, creating shade for the Protector of the World. When Wajid Ali Shah was exiled to Matiya Burj, even in that wretched state he brought more than twenty-four thousand pigeons and the hundreds of caretakers required for them.'

'And people still don't understand why the empire declined!' I said. 'Their ancestors had been brought up in the shadows of swords, but they were brought up under the shadows of pigeons! No wonder the royal trains ended up in Matiya Burj and Rangoon! If Bahadur Shah had spent on artillery even a tenth of what he spent on pigeon coops, and if Wajid Ali Shah had spent on guns even a tenth of what he spent on girls and pigeon coops, then their conquering armies, no, their *pigeon* armies, wouldn't have come to that sad pass where, leave alone fighting, they didn't even have guns to give up during their surrender, my God—

That's one army that's apparently short on arms!'

Mullah Aasi shouted, 'So you're saying the Mughal Empire declined because of pigeons? Even Jadu Nath Sarkar never said this!
Mr Chaturvedi was saying that there are seven lakh and fifty thousand pet dogs in England. In France, there are thirty million pets.
According to government figures, every third child in England is a
bastard! And in the last ten years, there were more than two and a
half million abortions! In our country, a man has many children, but
in their country, a child has many fathers. So why the hell aren't they
in decline?'

10.

Crazy

There's one story in particular about Mullah Aasi's odd behaviour
that I want to share with you. A neighbour complained several times
that Mullah Aasi's renter had put in a new window that looked onto
his property and exposed the ladies of the house. When Mullah Aasi
did nothing, the neighbour came over to threaten him, 'If you don't
have that window filled in, I'm going to take you to court. I swear on
my mother's grave that I'll bankrupt you! Your Buddhism won't be
worth anything then!' Poor Mullah Aasi, the renter was a thorn in
his side, as well. His renter was impossible to deal with. So instead
he lectured his neighbour on the negative aspects of keeping purdah,
but this only made the neighbour more upset. A couple days later the
neighbour came over with a court order saying that if Mullah Aasi
didn't remove the window in under a month, he would be brought
to trial. Mullah Aasi read this, then tore it up. He had up till November 30. At five o'clock in the morning on December 1, Mullah Aasi
knocked on his neighbour's door. His neighbour looked frazzled; he

answered the door barefoot and rubbing his eyes. Mullah Aasi said, 'Sir, so sorry to wake you this early. I just wanted to remind you that today you have to take me to court. Goodbye.'

The way that people in Karachi say 'crazy,' well, that's always applied to him, but now he's totally intolerable. He keeps in one wardrobe all his schoolbooks that he read—no, that he *didn't* read—from the eighth grade up till graduating from college. (He keeps separately a file for all test papers.) The silver cup in which saffron had been dissolved during his childhood Bismillah reading ceremony, the gold-embroidered hat he had to wear to Muslim circumcision ceremonies, and all sorts of other relics are stored safely in another wardrobe. Just be thankful that he wasn't able to dictate actions at his own birth otherwise he would have kept his umbilical cord with the other keepsakes in his collection. There isn't enough time to tell you in detail about all his stuff. Just think of it like this: collecting everything in one place was his attempt to reduce the painstaking labour that historians and biographers usually have to go through when picking through the lives of famous people. My God, I've never met anyone like him. I think he was incapable of throwing anything out, other than his religion. Even his trash became 'antiques.' You couldn't call it a room; it was a debris field of memories, and if you happened to dig with a spade to its very bottom you would find him himself.

In the Name of the Younger Wife

Likewise, he has impaled on darning needles all the letters that his friends and family have written him over the last thirty or forty years, and these are organized chronologically. Mostly, it's postcards. In those days, 95 percent of people wrote postcards. If a postcard's corner was cut, this rang the alarm that the card contained news of someone's death. Just by seeing the corner cut, the women of illiterate households would start enumerating the supposed attributes of the unknown dead person and then start crying and carrying on. If a neighbour read aloud the postcard, the women would add the name of the dead person to their lamentations and subtract some of the attributes. I've seen postcards with thirty or more lines written on them that the writer had probably used a watchmaker's loupe to write and that had to be read in the very same way. I knew a leather merchant named Sheikh Ata Muhammad who, when he went to Calcutta to buy goods, would write postcards to his beautiful youngest wife (whom everyone in the neighbourhood just called 'The Little One') in order to save money, and yet he had no ability to express his personal feelings so parsimoniously. Back then people loved reading others' letters on the sly. The postman would let us—meaning, Mian Tajammul Hussain, Mullah Aasi, and me—read Ata Muhammad's postcards. We fed the postman meatballs (made out of deer) in exchange. Sir, once he developed a taste for meatballs, he was hooked. When I was working at a school in Etawah, I wrote a letter home to my new bride that the postman let Mullah Aasi and Mian Tajammul read. Its contents spread through town like a cholera outbreak. From the leather merchant's postcards, I had stolen wholesale several passionate exclamations and even some full sentences. Although he sold rawhide, and, actually, his very ornate writing skills went beyond what you would expect not only from someone in his job but also from a husband in general, his letters conformed entirely to the ideal set out by Chaudhuri Muhammad Ali Rudaulvi concerning how to write letters to your wife. I mean, she couldn't show it to anyone! Some jackanapes told Sheikh Ata Muhammad about what was in my letter. He said that if some man wanted to copy his most intimate words to his own wife, then his was a happy fate. When my wife learned that I had plagiarized, for quite a long while even my extremely original letters smelled to her like rawhide! It was a big mess. My wife and 'The Little One' started thinking of each other as co-wives, and this ashamed both of us men. When I went back to Kanpur over the December holidays, I confronted the postman about his misdeeds and threatened to report him to the postmaster and get him fired. I was so upset I was beside myself. I yelled at him, 'You worthless scoundrel! Now those two are feeding you deer meatballs!' Getting up, he begged for mercy with his hands folded together. Then he said, 'I swear on the Quran. Since you've left, I haven't had any. You might as well accuse me of eating pork!' I took off my shoe and chased after him, and then the rascal admitted that they had served him meatballs made from nilgai.

Black Box

Yes, so what was I saying? Oh, yes, I was talking about the letters that he impaled on darning needles. On each needle, there was five years' worth of correspondence. These needles were nailed onto a round base of wood. They were the filing cabinets of yesteryear. For the letters of the dead, he had a black piece of wood that served as the base. He said, 'When I hear that someone has died, I have to go around to all the needles, remove that person's letters, and then stick them on the one reserved for the dead. And I kept in this black box my important papers and those of a highly personal nature. I've drawn up my will specifically so that when I die my remains will be fed to the sacrificial fire. I mean, these papers will be.'

The black box that he was pointing to underneath his bed was ac-

Black box: That strong, fireproof, waterproof, shockproof box that houses a device that tells you the reason for an airplane's falling from the sky and killing all its passengers. Or, in the words of the honourable Mr Majid Ali, whether the passengers fell and then died, or died and then fell.

tually a cashbox. After his father's bankruptcy and subsequent death, he was left only with this fortune as his inheritance. Even now he often brags that it's big enough to hold a hundred thousand rupees. People say that his will is in this box, and the will spells out what exactly he wants done to his corpse. I mean, if he wants to be buried in the Muslim way, fed to the vultures and crows like the Parsis, or taken care of according to Buddhist traditions. Because he was so confused about religion, this sort of clarification was very much needed. It's like Ghalib wrote, 'Drag my corpse through the alleyways.' But, against his wishes, his Sunni devotees buried him in accordance with Sunni tradition, even though the poor soul was an Imamia Shia. Sir, I just remembered. Ghalib really said it best, 'O, God! Save me from dying like an unbeliever and living like a Muslim!' He put all that into a seven-word line.

The Truth That You Remember after Death

According to his good friend Sayyid Hamiduddin, the will makes clear that he was a Muslim, that he would die a Muslim, and that everything else was a hoax that he put on to irritate his brethren. So his blasphemy was just trickery. I've heard that he instructed others to read his will only on that very day that those unprinted parts of Maulana Abul Kalam Azad's book are taken from their safety deposit box. About this, one troublemaker insinuated that in his will, Mullah Aasi wrote all sorts of heedless opinions about Maulana Azad that he never expressed during his lifetime for fear of offending mankind. Just think what slings and arrows he must have launched! The very worst you can say about Mullah Aasi is that he spoke the truth. But, Mushtaq Sahib, what kind of truth is it, if you don't have the courage to utter it during your lifetime? Each moment has its truth, crucifix, and crown. The expression of truth is appropriate in its moment and only in its moment. Those who remain silent are degrading not only the moment but themselves as well. According to your Mirza Abdul Wadud Baig, after a person has lived a happy life, indulging without remit in the convenience of expedient lies, then when this person is dead and buried, that's hardly the time to suddenly yell the truth from the top of your lungs!

Love Letters and Gautama Buddha's Teeth

It was also rumoured that the box held the letters and photos of a Punjabi refugee girl that he tutored. God knows if that's true. That was before he turned Buddhist. At that time, I had already come to Karachi. Everyone was curious about the box. But his box had an enormous brass lock whose key he always kept tied to his drawstring. But who can stop people from talking? Someone said the girl had committed suicide by slitting her wrists. Someone said it was on account of something unspeakable. It was also rumoured that this girl had another tutor. Other rumourmongers said that her blood fell drip by steamy drip on the road as her corpse was carried to the funeral ghat. That night her father swallowed thirty or forty sleeping pills and was dead by morning. But if you think about it, neither the girl nor her father died. Actually, the wife and her six kids were the ones who died. Three or four days later, someone stabbed Mullah Aasi in the stomach as he was entering an alley. His intestines spilled out. He lay in the hospital for four months, stuck between disgrace and an anonymous death. I heard that it was the day he got discharged that he became an ascetic. But, sir, he was an ascetic from birth. It's said that if an ascetic's boy plays at all, it will be with snakes. And if it hadn't been this one snake, it would have been another. Oh goodness, sir, when a boat gets stuck in a whirlpool, even the Prophet Khizr will make a hole in its hull to drown you!

I don't know if it's supposed to be a joke or not, but Inamullah The Loudmouth said that Mullah Aasi kept four broken teeth in the box that he meant to leave as relics for his worshippers and descendants. After all, Mahatma Buddha too left at least a hundred teeth (now under heavy guard) in various holy places where people frequently visit.

Only one thing in the entire room looked new. That was the latest edition of the magazine *Irfan*. Who knows if someone had sent it to him by mail, or whether some prankster had left it there. I skimmed parts. Sir, this magazine is the highest example of faithfulness. There was no difference between the edition published fifty years ago and the one of today: it had the same table of contents, the same font, and the same look. Thank God for that! It seemed as though the publication house hadn't changed a whit either! The contents were also exactly the same as they had been in Sir Syed and Shibli's time. If only this edition had been published seventy or eighty years earlier, it would have been entirely up to date! If Maulana Shibli Nomani and Deputy Shams-ul-ulama Nazir Ahmed LLDS could see it, just think how happy they would have been!

11.

The Deer Antlers

The deer head is still hung there. In that house of torment, only it retains its life-like look. It looks like it's going to spring off the wall and run off into the forest. Beneath it, there is an oval sepia photograph of his grandfather. Sir, in those days, everyone's grandfathers looked the same. In a standing pose, they had a big beard, turban, a flowery gown, a flower in one hand, and a sword in the other! Not just after 1857 but in fact well before, noblemen used swords as walking sticks and poets used them as a metaphor for the murder weapon that the beloved will use to kill the poet (and he will enjoy it). This was the period of deterioration and anarchy in South Asia when the daf drum of the war poets lost its status and tablas replaced the war gong. To prove their nation's greatness, people pointed to their splendid ruins.

The deer must have been seventy or eighty years old. His grandfather had shot it in the marshes of Nepal. He had cut off one horn for the good (healing) of the public. Rubbing a little of its powder helped relieve kidney pain. People came from quite a distance asking for the horn. One dishonest patient went so far as cutting off an entire inch before he returned it. (He said he had pain in both kidneys.) Now Mullah Aasi personally supervises the grinding down of the horn on the whetstone. These sorts of ignorant, magical practices still flourish in India. When he started praising his special ointment, I made fun of him, 'But, Mullah, the kidneys are inside the body.' He said, 'Yes, your father had three or four treatments before he left for Pakistan. He wanted to take a horn with him. I didn't let him.'

Natraja and Dead Partridges

Mullah Aasi showed me another beloved photo. This one was of Mian Tajammul Hussain in Natraja's victory pose. That is, he stood smiling with his foot on the head of a nilgai and displaying the stock of his 22-gauge rifle. I'm standing to the side, pulling a long face, with an old-time zinc-plated flask hanging around my neck, and a mallard in each hand. Mian Tajammul claimed that the nilgai measured from chin to tail the same as a man-eating Bengal tiger. For a long time, hunting nilgai was illegal in India. But now you can. Once they started being a nuisance in the fields, people started calling them horses and killing them became OK. Like in England where they no longer call blacks 'black' but instead call them 'ethnic' and then kill them without any qualms.

Chaudhuri Gulzar Muhammad, the photographer, used his Mint camera to take this photo on Mian Tajammul Hussain's property. When they were having their photos taken, people back then had to hold their breaths for so long that their faces looked funny. So only the dead nilgai ended up looking real. Gulzar Muhammad often tagged along when we went hunting. I never had any interest in hunting—I mean, not in the actual hunt. But I liked the eating part. Mian Tajammul always travelled with his assistant (me). God forbid but if he is sent to hell, then I'm sure he won't go alone. He'll send me first to set up his welcoming committee. There was good hunting seven or eight miles from town. Usually we went by horse-drawn cart. The horse had to transport the nilgai back despite its being exactly the same weight. One poor soul (me) was responsible for everything that had to do with the trip, except for pulling the trigger. For instance, not only did I have to carry around stuffed tiffins for everyone, but I had to get up at four in the morning to have parathas and kebabs made, before schlepping them hot off the griddle back to stuff everyone to the gills. In the freezing cold December air, I had to retrieve the wounded ducks from the pond. If he missed while shooting at a deer (which often happened), I would have to swear to God that a bullet must have found its mark. The deer was definitely limping. And once the wound cooled, the shameless deer would suddenly collapse into a lifeless heap. If a partridge should happen to die before the sacrificial ceremony, one sin of my office was that I had to daub halal partridge blood on its neck because if it died before the knife could touch its neck, he would insult me for weeks. I prayed for the long life of the wounded animal so that it would last long enough for me to kill it halal style. He sent the non-Muslim birds to Sir Arthur Inskap's house. Well, we didn't send them. Actually, I had to take them over on his bicycle. He would sit on the back carrier with the meat in his lap so that everything wouldn't weigh too much! He weighed two hundred and thirty pounds on an empty stomach. Despite this, I pedalled very fast. If I didn't, the smell of the meat would attract the street dogs. He would say that the gun was his, the bullets his, the aiming his, the kill his, the butchering his, the bike his, and he even said that he had filled the bike's tires with his own air. Then he would say, 'If I drive, what's there left for you to do?'

If the beloved is also faithful, then why are you here?

You understand? What should I say? I can't express how much humiliation this friendship has caused me. How should I say that Mian Tajammul always rested his gun on my shoulders when he took aim? Sir, how could he have used my shoulder when I was not only carrying his gun but him as well? By God, not only did I have to bear with his insults, but I actually had to bear his body.

I Was Punished for the Horny Camel's Misdeeds

I've probably already told you that old Haji Sahib, I mean Tajammul's father, considered horse-drawn carts and cars the height of arrogance and laziness. But he had no problem with bikes and camels. That's because he considered these among the tools for ego-killing. He often said, 'Up till I was twenty-five, I had only ever seen eunuchs dance. And that was at my son Tajammul's birth. When I was twenty-six, back in Lyallpur, I snuck into a prostitute's dance show at a wedding. When my father found out, he was livid. He threatened to disinherit me, although all I was scheduled to inherit were his debts! He said, 'The boy's turned bad. I'm the first of the Chiniot clan who's been shamed by his own son.' And so by way of punishment, I was sent from Chiniot to Jhang to buy cotton on credit on the back of a horny camel whose forehead was oozing very bad-smelling pus. It hardly moved. Instead, it cried its guttural cry. But in the dying light of the setting sun, when we caught sight of the trees of Sargodha along the village's edge, suddenly he stopped in his tracks. He had seen a female camel. In giving chase to her, he passed through Sargodha, and then for five miles he flung me up and down, this way and that, on top of his hump. After the first mile, I lost track of her. (I'm not a male camel.) But he was hot on her scent's trail. I was riding on a time bomb. Then the camel blindly stepped (with me on his back) into a swamp. He quickly got stuck. I could neither sit on top nor jump to safety. The villagers brought a rope, a ladder, and gravediggers, and they saved me. The saddle on the camel's back had been a metre wide. For a week, my legs were splayed apart. They looked like a sling-shot's arms. I walked like a dangerous murderer with fetters on. Or like a boy after being circumcised. I asked the Mehter toilet-cleaner to put the Turkish toilet's footrests a little wider. I was punished for the horny camel's misdeeds. My father said that from seeing how I walked, camels must have learned a lesson too.'

Aligarh Pyjamas and Arhar Lentils

In 1907, Mr Haji Sahib started working at four rupees a month for a Hindu businessman in Kanpur. He was a completely honest man. He was also very tall and muscular. The businessman must have thought how easy it was going to be for him to collect his debts. After World War II, Haji Sahib became a millionaire, but he didn't change at all. I mean, by his masochistic stinginess, by the way he dressed and acted, by his humility, and by the way he talked, anyone would have thought he was still earning just four rupees a month. He wore a coarse muslin kurta, and he tied his square-patterned lungi above his ankles. He wore a shalwar only when he had to go to court or to a funeral. He never sold anything on credit to those who wore sunglasses, pants, and churidar pyjamas. He must have lived in UP for forty or forty-five years, but he had never eaten smoked firni, nihari, and arhar lentils. Also, he never wore his dopalli hat and pyjamas. But in 1938 he had an operation, and when he was unconscious the nurses dressed him in pyjamas. When he came to, he immediately took them off. Like the poet says,

> It was good to be unconscious
> Too bad I came to.

He would often say that if tongs had to wear something to conform to sharia or to some other law, then Aligarh pyjamas would look best. (This sounded very funny in Punjabi. We asked him to say it often.)

The Nilgai and the Doll-Faced Naseem

I goaded Mullah Aasi, 'Do you still hunt?' He said, 'I don't have the time or the taste for it anymore. You find deer only at the zoo. I don't even use down pillows.' He took down a tattered undershirt from a clothesline. He smelled it, then took down a wooden frame and began rubbing it with the undershirt so that the glass was revealed, and then beneath that, a photo.

This photo was taken by Chaudhuri Gulzar Muhammad in the forest during a hunt. In it, a Chamar untouchable and yours truly were carrying a black buck on a hunting pole back to a horse-drawn cart. The good thing about the photo was that the crows and kites hovering overhead were nowhere to be seen. What should I say, sir? My friend made me do a lot of things for free. But I didn't mind. I would have done anything for him. It was a very beautiful and muscular antelope. Its huge eyes were filled with sorrow. I remember that I looked the other way when its throat was being cut. A good hunter will usually not kill a black buck. The entire herd scatters, not knowing what to do. You must have heard the saying, 'Kill a black buck, and seventy female deer will become widows.'

Chaudhuri Gulzar Muhammad was from Pindi Bhattian but had lived unhappily in Kanpur for twenty years or so. At his studio, he also sold photos of the Taj Mahal and the Qutb Minar, which he himself had taken. He decorated the walls of his house with photographs of Pindi Bhattian, including one of his house with a thatched roof and ridge-gourd vines climbing over it. In front of the door, an old man with a saintly face was sitting on a beaten-up charpoy and smoking a hookah. Nearby, a goat with udders as full as balloons was tied to a stake. Every photograph was an example of Laila's beauty as seen through Majnoon's lovestruck eyes. We all laughed when he said 'de-chagi' instead of 'degchi' and 'taghmah' instead of 'tamghah.'*

He was well built. He could cut through the largest bone with only one stroke of a cleaver. He could skin a nilgai weighing two men, then butcher the meat all neat and proper, and all in under a half hour. His kebabs were the best. He always dreamed of Bombay. When he was skinning an animal, he would say, 'The only thing worth anything in Kanpur is its nilgai. Just you wait and see, one of these days I'm going to become a cameraman for Minerva Movietone, and I'll shoot close-ups of Madhuri and Mehtab and send you prints.' He would start to dance and make sexy poses, and instead of wrapping a black cloth around his head he would put on top of it a bloody mop, and with a fake camera he would take a close-up of himself. One time, while he was taking a picture of the doll-faced Naseem, his knife slipped and he cut through the nilgai's skin. Mian Tajammul Hussain shrieked, 'To hell with the doll-faced Naseem! You've cut her for the third time! What were you thinking? You're ruining the hide.' There was

---

* Taghmah: In the North-West Frontier Provinence and in Punjab, when people say 'taghmah' instead of 'tamghah,' they chalk it up as a mispronunciation. In reality, the real word is actually 'taghmah,' from the Turkish, and the correct spelling is 'taghma.'

an excellent taxidermist in Kanpur. But he had to send lion heads to Bangalore. The rich had lion skins on their floors, the middle-class houses had deer skins, and the women in poor houses made designs with colour-fast dyes on their cow-dung-coated floors that looked like carpet designs.

The Story of the Deerskin

Even now the hide of the doe that Nisar Ahmad Khan killed is spread out on Mullah Aasi's floor. There was a fierce edge to Khan Sahib's countenance, demeanour, and way of speaking. And his beliefs were always extreme. He was known as a Wahhabi, God knows if he was or not. He was addicted to hunting. He was very kind to me. Mian Tajammul Hussain used to say that the reason he liked me was because of my shaved head and ankle-high pyjamas. The bullet wound in the hide was exactly as it had been. While dying, she had delivered a full-term yearling. No one ate the doe's meat. Nisar Ahmad couldn't sleep for two nights. It affected him more than the time he was out partridge hunting and accidently shot a farmer who was standing behind some bushes and in the process blinded the man. He spent two hundred rupees to get out of that. Within three months of this affair with the doe, his only son, who was studying for his BA, chased a wounded duck into a pond and drowned. People said, 'He lost his son because of the pregnant doe's curse.' When they brought the body to the verandah of the women's quarters, the women started wailing and carrying on. Then there came a choked, heartrending cry. Nisar Ahmad said to his wife in a grief-afflicted voice, 'My dear, patience, patience, patience. God's prophet prohibited people from crying loudly.' His wife stopped crying but went over to the window and started banging her head on its bars until her head bled. Her hair's part was splattered with blood. They lowered the corpse into the ground, and when people were throwing dirt into the grave, Nisar Ahmad took dirt in both hands and started smearing it over his head and white hair. People stepped forward and grabbed his hands. No more than six months later, the man who had tried to calm his wife then wrapped himself in a shroud and stepped into his grave. According to his will, he was buried next to his son. (His wife's grave was at his foot.)

So I went to the cemetery to pray the fatiha. I had a hard time finding it. While it was still possible to recognize some things about the city, the cemetery had completely changed. It used to be that everyone knew every grave because no one forgot a person once they died. Sir, a cemetery is also a place to learn things about life. When you go to the cemetery, when you see each grave, you remember the day the person died, how much lamenting went on, and how the mourners moaned and wailed. You remember how these mourners then died and so caused others to cry for them, and how they became one with the earth. Sir, when this is going to happen, then why all the sadness, why the distress, why all the crying?

I went and prayed the fatiha at Master Fakhir Hussain's grave as well. Please don't ask about all the things I remembered there. His gravestone had fallen over. On it is engraved a Persian couplet that he often read to us. Thirty-five years of rain had made the letters difficult to make out.

After I die, don't look for my grave on earth
In the heart of the divine my tomb is lodged

His recitation style was a special mixture of straight recitation, a bashful tarannum singsong, and a sort of musicality, which he himself had invented and that died with him. Before reciting the couplet, he would open the third button of his shervani. As soon as he finished, he would take off his tassel-free fez and set it on the table. Since he read each and every couplet with the same rhythm and metre, those that had pauses or gaps he filled with the exclamations, 'Oh, yes!' and 'My lords!' or he emitted a very pregnant cough. While reciting the couplet mentioned above, when he got to the part that went 'the heart of the divine,' he would gesture three or four times knowingly toward his chest. But when he got to 'my tomb,' he would open his hands toward us bad students and pretend to dig his own grave.

Look, I've entered into the labyrinth of memories! The poor Sahir said about this—or perhaps it was someone else—

> O, God, memories of the past are torture
> Please wipe away my memory bank.

But I've got away from the story of the deerskin. One day, out of carelessness I knocked over a penholder. The ink from the pens is still on the hide. I noticed that Aasi never steps foot on the pelt. It's the most expensive thing in the entire room. He walks on the patches of the open floor in a zigzag as though he were sliding down a chute in Chutes and Ladders.

Two Tales of the City

Nisar Ahmad Khan gave Mullah Aasi his unlucky rifle because he was his son's close friend. During a riot, the police rounded up all the neighbourhood's guns, and they took this gun too. He never saw it again. He had only a stamped receipt to show for it. He tried everything. He even hired a lawyer. But a policeman at the station said that the DIG had taken a liking to it: 'If you keep complaining, you'll get your gun. But the police will come to your house and plant a liquor still, as well. All your relatives have left for Pakistan. Your house too can be registered as evacuee property. Think about it.' So he thought about it and didn't say anything. God, oh, God! It used to be that the city's top cop would come meet his father every three days or so. A Purdey was a great gun. They say it would cost twelve thousand dollars today. But, sir, if you ask me, such a valuable gun can only be used for killing a man-eating lion, a dictator, or oneself. Anything else would be an insult to it. While showing everyone his gun license and his stamped receipt for his impounded gun, Mullah Aasi still likes to say, 'Even from a half mile away, if it just grazes a black buck, it will die right then and there.'

12.

Crass Ways of Dying

Sometimes when old friends meet again, there comes a painful lull in conversation. There's so much to say that you end up saying nothing. A thousand memories, a thousand things crowd out each other. They elbow each other, they grab each other by the shoulder, and they stop each other from advancing. *First, me ... First, me ...* So, sir, in that moment when I saw his desperation and felt so bad for him, I was thinking that if he had come with me to Pakistan, things would have been better. Suddenly he broke the silence, 'Why don't you come back? When we heard about your heart attack, it was an occasion of great mourning. How did you get this rich person's disease? I've heard that medical science doesn't yet know its real cause. But my belief is that one day soon a magnifying glass will be invented that will discover that money carries the germs of this disease. My friend, why the hell did you go to Pakistan? What was lacking here? See, you had a heart attack there. Mian Tajammul Hussain did too. Muneer Ahmad had a bypass. Zaheer Siddiqi got a pacemaker. They found a hole in Manzoor Alam's heart. I'm sure these are all the result of living in Pakistan. Everyone was healthy when they left. Khalid Ali was in London having an angiogram when God took him right there on the table. They packed the corpse in a splendid teak casket and flew him to Karachi. On top of this, our withered, skinny friend Ehtasham died in Lahore of a heart attack. Sibtain and the crippled inspector Malik Ghulam Rasool had heart attacks. Maulana Mahir-ul-Qadri too. If you think about it, who didn't have a heart attack? My dear friend! There's peace of mind here. Contentment. Trust in God. No one has heart attacks. Although of course you hear that it happens a lot with Hindus.'

What was his point of emphasis? It was on the fact that everyone in Kanpur dies a natural death. No one dies of heartless heart attacks. I mean, sir, he made my heart attack a peg upon which he hung the exhumed corpses of all our friends. I don't even remember all their names. After my second heart attack, I gave up trying to contradict people. Now I just assume my opinion is always wrong. This makes everyone happy. So I sat silently listening. And he continued naming all those lucky men who didn't die of a heart attack but of something else: 'Our Maulvi Mohtashim died of TB. Hameedullah Senior Clerk, the grandson of Khan Bahadur Azmatullah Khan, died of throat cancer. Shahnaz's husband, Abid Hussain the lawyer, died a martyr in Hindu–Muslim riots. Abdul Wahab Khan from Qaimganj battled typhoid for a full twenty-five days, but none of the doctor's medicine worked. He remained conscious and aware of everything right up till the end. Just two minutes before he died, he cursed out the doctor, using his full name. Munshi Faiz Muhammad died from cholera in less than a day. Hafiz Fakhruddin had a stroke and died. But God is great! No one has died of a heart attack. No one has died of such crass ways! I don't know one well-off person in Pakistan who hasn't had a bypass. If things continue like this, the day's not far off when the rich will perform circumcisions and bypasses in one ceremony!'

He started lecturing me on reincarnation and nirvana, but he interrupted himself when he remembered another person. He left off talking about Mahatma Buddha dozing beneath the Bodhi tree and said, 'Even Khwaja Faheem-ud-din didn't die of a heart attack. After his wife died, he still had his two daughters. They were his life. But one day he couldn't pee. The doctor said it was his prostate. They immediately performed an emergency operation, but something went wrong. After three or four bad months, he got better. But his eldest daughter suddenly married a Hindu lawyer, and his youngest married a Sikh contractor, and this ruined him. He was an old-fashioned man in words and deeds. He returned to bed to bewail his state, and he stayed there until he married the Christian nurse who had helped clean him during his convalescence. That whore stayed by his side waiting for him to ask for her hand. But he was reluctant.

Come, you snake charmer, what are you waiting for?

When the disinherited daughters heard that he had gotten married, both sent word that they considered him reprehensible. He screamed, "You unlucky ones! At least I did this strictly according to sharia law!" Sir, while all this did really happen, Khwaja Faheem-ud-din didn't have a heart attack. When he heard about your heart attack, he was sad for a long time. He said, "Why doesn't he come here?"'

Sir, I couldn't stop myself. I said that if I got prostate cancer, I'd be sure to come back.

Pindola's Cup

During his school days, he was a very picky eater. He was repulsed by do piyaza, garlic chutney, head-and-foot meat dishes, liver, kidneys, udder-meat, and brain. If any of these were served, he would leave. During my visit, I was invited to one dinner held in my honour where among the dishes served there was pan-fried brain. Sir, to make this, you first have to sprinkle the brain with minced garlic, then once it

congeals into little balls, crush it, and all of its bad odour will disappear, as long as you sprinkle in a lot of garam masala and chilli pepper.
When I saw this, I was amazed that he too ate everything and was not
repulsed. I asked him about this lapse in his dietary regimen, and he
said, 'Whatever comes to my plate was given to me by God. Who am
I to refuse it?'

He said, 'You haven't heard the story of the monk? Monks begged
for food for seven years in order to crush their egos once and for
all. Without doing that, a man can't hope for much understanding.
Mahatma Buddha called the beggar's bowl the king's crown. Even
if someone wants to give a monk more than he can eat at any one
time, he can't accept. And whatever's put in his bowl, he must eat it,
whether he wants to or not. There's a Pali story about a monk named
Pindola. One day a leper put some chunks of bread into his bowl.
But when the leper was putting them in, his rotten thumb also fell
in. Pindola said they tasted the same. Not good, not bad.' Sir, after he
told this story, he bowed his head and continued eating. As far as I
was concerned, not just the brain, but the entire dinner had turned
toxic. Sir, now his mind is like Pindola's cup.

Mullah Monk

People say that the girl he liked committed suicide in 1953. I heard
that after that, all his desires went away and he stopped accepting
money for his tutoring. That was thirty years ago. If someone feeds
him, he eats. Otherwise he scrunches a pillow to his stomach, draws
in his knees, clasps his hands and puts them under his right cheek,
and goes to sleep. What do you call that? Yes, the fetal position. But
I don't at all agree with the Freudian theory that you like. You sleep
in the fetal position too. But it's not because you're renouncing anything; it's due to your ulcer. Mullah Aasi, the monk, says that the

Buddha also tucked his left foot on top of his right foot and put his hands under his head as he slept on his right side; this is called the lion position. The lecherous and debauched sleep on their left side; this is called the sex position. I learned from no one else but him that you can spot someone with a bad character simply by seeing how they sleep. In any event, his world is such that whatever anyone gives him to wear, he puts it on. He eats whatever. From whomever. Whenever it's given. Whenever he gets tired, he sleeps right there. Wherever he is, that's his inn. His body is his pillow; his mind is at ease. For four days he might not make it home. But what's the difference? If a good-for-nothing husband stays out or comes home, it's all the same. May God reward his disciples. They're the ones who take care of him. I've never seen such loving, helpful students. One day Mullah cupped his hands like a bowl and said, 'Just for a handful of grain, think how much effort the gypsy puts in. If everyone knew that life could be so easy, then the machine of the world would grind to a halt. All this show, all this hypocrisy, would end at once. Inside everyone lives a personal Satan. Desire is this Satan's other name. As each person breeds desire and gives it free rein, their heart turns that much harder and their life gets that much more difficult. When the dinosaurs got so big that they had to eat 24/7 in order to stay alive, that's when they went extinct. You should eat only as much as you need to keep your spirit and your body on the same plane. If your body gets fat, your mind will too. I've never met a skinny preacher. It's not possible to pray and meditate with a full stomach, and it's not possible to be debauched on an empty stomach.'

Then he picked up from his desk his handwritten compilation of Buddhist mantras, and he began reading excerpts from its introduction in a singsong voice, as though he were reading out loud Sanskrit shlokas: 'Boddhisatva said to Bhagvan Sachak, "O Agivesan! When I clenched my teeth, blocked my throat by pressing my uvula against my tongue, and tried to control my mind, suddenly my underarms started sweating. Just like a burly man would press down on a weakling's head or shoulders, that's how I pressed down on my mind. O Agivesan! Then I started meditating by holding my breath for long periods. I could hear the sound of breathing coming from my ears. It sounded like air being expelled sharply from an ironsmith's bellows. O Agivesan! Then I started covering my ears with my hands. This made me feel as though a sword's sharp point was piercing my forehead. But, O Agivesan, I didn't stop meditating!"

'"O Agivesan! From meditating and fasting, my body grew weak. You could plainly see my joints through my skin. My hips lost weight and started looking like a camel's foot. My spine started looking like a spindle. Like the beams of a dilapidated house show through the old structure, so too did my ribs. My eyes drew inward like stars reflected in a deep well. As the pieces of raw, bitter pumpkin dry out in the sun, so too did the skin on my head. When I put my hand on my stomach, I touched my spine. And when I put my hand on my back, I touched my stomach. I was all skin and bones. When I ran my hands over my body, my hair fell out."'

He's No Friend of Mine! He's No Friend of Mine!

After reading this, he paused for a moment. He closed his eyes. I assumed he had started meditating. After a while, he opened his eyes just so the lashes no longer touched. He was engrossed in the seventh step of meditation. He cupped his hands and said, 'There's one sort of thirst that a drop or two of water can quench. And there's another sort that for however much water you drink, your thirst only grows worse. After every drop, it feels like there're thorns digging into your tongue. It depends on the man. Some want sex, some want wealth, some want land. Some people have a thirst for knowledge and fame. Some want to lord it over people. Some get obsessed with women. But the biggest source of restlessness is the false thirst that people inflict upon themselves. It swallows rivers, clouds, and glaciers, and it still isn't satisfied. It takes people from one river to another, from one mirage to another, but the thirst still isn't quenched. *Water! Water! Get me water!* And slowly this unquenchable thirst melts humans and drinks them up. The Quran says, "When he left with his army, Taloot said, 'God will test you with a river. Whoever drinks its water is no friend of mine. My friends are those who don't fully quench their thirst. So if you want a handful, that's fine.' Aside from a small group, everyone drank to their heart's content. So when Taloot and his close companions crossed the river and approached the enemy, his forces told him that they were too weak to meet Jaloot and his army in battle" (Surat Al-Baqarah 33). Everyone has a river like this. Whoever drinks its water won't have enough courage to fight against evil. *He's no friend of mine! He's no friend of mine!* Victory and liberation are for those who wade through the river without drinking.'

This is why he was called Mullah Monk. The way he spoke was thornier than his matted hair, and his beliefs were more colourful. As he spoke on in his Sufi-like way, he looked like a sadhu. Suddenly his turban fell off and you saw a sadhu with matted hair springing free upon every word, every mantra. He had done his ablutions in aab-e-Zamzam, and yet he had smeared his body with ashes. Sometimes you would think he was one thing, sometimes you think he was something else. And sometimes you would feel as though you have wandered far into unknown lands:

> With a tilak on his forehead, he sits in a temple
> He renounced Islam a long time ago.

And sometimes he would make you feel as though Gautama Buddha renounced his deep meditative trance under the Bodhi tree to don the haji's robes. Sometimes he jumped from topic to topic without making a point. He jumped like a locust from one thing to another, and then from that to yet another. One day I goaded him, 'Maulana, many Muslim jurists think that the appropriate punishment for an apostate is death.' He got my drift. He smiled. Then he said, 'It's something to think about. What point is there to crucify someone who has already committed suicide?'

Everyone's Face Is My Face, Everyone's Eyes Are My Eyes

Despite his warmhearted reception, I still felt that he was holding back. He had a sort of dervish-like indifference. With people, too. One day he said that being attached, whether to a thing or a person, is the real cause of sadness. People like that will never be able to breathe deeply; they will never achieve enlightenment. If people could harden their hearts and break from everything, then they would be freed from the endless circle of the emotions. Then they would never be happy or sad, never satisfied or disappointed. Ghalib writes in a Persian couplet,

> Neither bliss nor loss stays in our heart for long
> In our sieve, liquor and blood are the same

His spiritual attainment repudiated the famous line 'his dispassion held neither wisdom nor pleasure.' Two days before I was to leave for Pakistan, I teased him, 'Maulana, you've lived here a long time. You have no ties except to the city itself. Come with me to Pakistan. All our friends, all our brothers, are there.'

He said, 'Our ancestors are buried here.'

'But you don't even pray the fatiha above their graves, you don't make offerings at their graves on Thursday nights either, so what's the difference?'

Just then a spotted cat came into the room carrying a kitten in its mouth. A pigeon got scared and went to hide in the corner of its cage. Then a neighbour girl came in holding a caged myna in one hand, and her doll stuffed underneath her armpit. She said, 'Neither of them has eaten since morning. They aren't talking to me. Please give them some medicine.' Mullah Aasi took the sick doll's pulse, and he chirped and warbled to the bird. The bird answered. Mullah Aasi took a lemon drop from a box and gave it to the neighbour girl. She started to suck on it, and the doll seemed to feel better. He smiled.

We picked up the conversation from where it had been interrupted by the cat, the neighbour girl, and the bird. He said to me, 'Here I share everyone's pain. Who will need me there? Who's as poor as me there? Here there are people even poorer than me.'

> *Those dear to me all have broken wings and are miserable*
> *O, Compassionate One! It doesn't suit me to be unlike them*

'For God's sake, try it once and see. You think Pakistan is different from how it really is. People's lives suck there too! Come for my sake. At least for a week.'

'Who will ask about me over there?'

'Then think of it like this—in a crowd of people wearing crowns, the crownless person coated with dust stands out.'

Who knows if he really was convinced or just felt defeated, but he said, 'Brother, I was just throwing some grain your way, but now you invite me to your perch. I'd love to go, but God knows what would happen to my pigeons.'

'Their fate doesn't rely upon God's wishes, but the cat's. But, look, since when did you believe in God?'

'It's a figure of speech. The jamun tree you see there was planted by my grandfather. After the morning star has just set, or at dusk when the evening is growing deeper, you can see through this window hundreds of birds on this tree chattering because they're so happy. It does something to you. Who's going to take care of this tree?'

'First of all, this old jamun tree isn't tied to you. It doesn't need you, and it doesn't need Buddhism. It needs cow-dung. Second, you're confusing things. Mahatma Buddha became enlightened not under a jamun tree but a pipal tree. But, for the sake of argument, if you can't live without taking care of birds and trees, then you can look after Karachi's emaciated donkeys and, in Lahore, the Upper Mall's jamun trees—and that to your heart's content. We put up ladders before the jamun fruits ripen. The good folks of Lahore don't throw stones at the fruit on other people's trees like they do in Kanpur. We carefully climb the trees, eat the fruits there, and serve them to the orchard keepers as well.'

'I'll go. One day I'll go for sure. But some other time.'

'What's the harm in coming with me now?'

'What will happen to these kids?'

'What usually happens. They'll grow up. No one will miss you. You'll die, and then what?'

'So what? These kids, and their kids, they'll live on. They fill my heart with joy. When I die, I'll speak through their mouths. I'll see through their eyes.'

(This is where Basharat's narration ends.)

Postscript

So He Too Had A Heart Attack

On December 3, 1985, just before the sun rose, and just as he had said, when birds were chattering playfully in the jamun tree as though they were ready to die themselves, Mullah Abdul Mannan Aasi had a heart attack and died. The neighbourhood mosque's imam declared that there was no need for a funeral prayer for the infidel. When the deceased didn't believe in God, what would be the point of asking for forgiveness and mercy? The procession lingered for quite a while underneath the jamun tree. In the end, one of his students played the part of the imam. Hundreds of people were in attendance. Before the ritual rites were performed, his black box was opened in front of the neighbourhood dignitaries. Inside, there was a note left on a piece of paper from a school copybook. It was written in pencil, but it didn't have either date or signature. It read:

To Whom It May Concern:

All my assets should be sold at auction so that a trust can be established for my pigeons. Care should be taken that no trustee eats meat. Also, please don't bury me in Kanpur. Lay me next to my mother in Lahore.

The First Memorable Poetry Festival of Dhiraj Ganj

1.

The Benefits of Failing

Basharat says that after taking his BA test, he got worried about what would happen should he fail. By the grace of God, this fear disappeared entirely after praying, but he started worrying about something even more distressing. If, God forbid, he should pass, then what? It would be difficult to find a job. His friends would leave to get on with their lives. His father would stop giving him an allowance. With nothing to do, no job, no means of supporting himself, nothing to busy himself . . . life would turn into pure torture. He would be forced to buy English newspapers for their 'help wanted' ads. Then he would have to shape his resume for each stupid job in such a way that it appeared that he had been born into this glorious world just for it. He would have to do this one hundred times. Then he would have to suffer the disgrace of going from office to office until he finally got a job somewhere. Although it was very likely that he had failed, he had a sneaking suspicion that he had passed.

> *Let's wait and see what happens*
> *If this doubt is borne out or not*

In order to postpone this humiliation for two more years, many boys applied to MA or LLB programs. All the Muslim boys that Basharat knew, who three years previously—meaning, in 1933—had got their

BAs, were now jobless and loafing around, except for the one lucky soul who came in first (among Muslims) and was now a PE teacher at the Muslim middle school. The frightening worldwide economic slump and unemployment of 1930 was still not over. For a rupee, you could have got fifteen kilos of wheat and a kilo of pure ghee, but who had a rupee?

Sometimes despite himself, he would truly hope he had failed. It would be better that way. That way he would be able to live for another year without worry. As Mirza says, 'After you fail, you have to suffer people's disrespect for only one day. Then everything's fine. What happens is this: it's just like at Eid when each and every old person in your family comes to your house, only in this case they will take out their years of pent anger in explaining your failure, and hence the family's disgrace, according to their own sense of things.' In those days, whatever a young person did would bring disgrace upon the family. Things weren't like they are today: for one, now you can't find a family that's worried about shame. I've also noticed on many occasions how a family's elders, both those nearby and far away, would, according to their relationship and strength, take the time to beat the boys with their own two hands when they failed. This lasted up to the sixth or seventh grade. But when the boys' hands and feet started growing, and they had grown so much that they cried in two voices at once (meaning, when they were thirteen or fourteen years old), then the elders didn't beat them. That was because they feared they would hurt their hands and sprain their wrists. So they satisfied themselves with scolding and gnashing their teeth. Each of the elderly would weigh the certified and authentic worthlessness of the boy in question against their own supposed educational achievements, and seeing only wreck and ruin in the new generation, the old fogies would come to the welcome conclusion that the world still needed them. They would say to themselves, 'How on earth can we turn over control to this worthless generation!' Mirza says that they always spoke to the young as though they themselves were prophets, 'When you grow up, you're not going to be anything!' Sir, even idiots like me could tell that was going to be true! For this sort of prophecy, it wasn't even necessary to be a white-bearded mullah or an astrologer. In any event, this farce would take only one day. If he passed, he would enter into an age of trial and tribulation with one misery following hard on the heels of another.

Basharat and Shah Jahan's One Desire

In the end, his second suspicion proved true. He passed. This pleased him, surprised his teachers, and absolutely floored his family. That day he took the time to write out BA after his name and to stare at it from different angles, in the way that artists stand back and look at their paintings. Then once he even wrote in parentheses 'first attempt' after BA. But there seemed something boastful and arrogant about that. Soon afterwards he found a piece of cardboard and wrote his name in blue ink, 'BA' in red ink, and stuck that on his door. A couple weeks later he saw in a local Urdu newspaper an ad for the Dhiraj Ganj Muslim School—they were starting a ninth grade the next year and were looking for an Urdu teacher. The ad also promised that it was a permanent position, that the work environment was chaste and peaceful, and that the monthly salary was reasonable. To explain what 'reasonable' meant, the ad had in parentheses the following: '25 rupees, with allowance, per month, and a quarter rupee raise per year.' When the crown prince Zafar made Muhammad Ibrahim Zauq his teacher, he set his salary at four rupees a month. Maulana Muhammad Hussain Azad writes, 'When Zauq's father saw the salary, he forbade his only son from taking the job. But fate called out, "Don't think just about the four rupees. They're four pillars in the hall of the Kingship of Poetry that's now within your reach. Don't let this opportunity slip by."'

361

But what he liked was the promise of the peaceful work environment. Dhiraj Ganj was a small town between Lucknow and Kanpur. It was so small that everyone knew each and every family's dirty business, and that, going back generations. Not only did they know the contents of each clay pot cooking on each stove, but they also knew which houses were frying with oil. People were so nosey that no one could do anything interesting at all. And, when it came to nitpicking, the town put to use every ounce of its collective talent.

For a long time, Basharat had hoped that fate would be kind and grant him his wish to become a teacher. People respected teachers a lot. His father had a lumber store in Kanpur, but in comparison to his father's business, every other profession on the face of the earth seemed more interesting and less disgraceful. As soon as the news came that he had earned his BA, his father, to please Basharat, changed the name of his shop to Educational Timber Depot. Against his will, Basharat worked at the store for a couple of days. He showed no interest in it at all. He used to say, 'Just to sell something, you have to tell lies from morning till night. If you try to be honest, you don't sell anything. The store was full of sawdust, and customers had to yell to be heard.' As a young boy, he had wanted to drive trains, and after he grew up, he changed that to wanting to be a teacher. A classroom is nothing less than a kingdom. A teacher is another kind of sovereign. That's why Aurangzeb hadn't allowed Shah Jahan to teach kids while under house arrest. Basharat considered himself luckier than the king, especially since he was to get twenty-five rupees as a salary.

There's no doubt that back then teaching was a dignified, honourable profession. There were two important things for your life and career. First, respect. Second, peace of mind and freedom from worry. Never in the history of the world has honour been so prized as it used to be in the subcontinent. There is no real synonym in English for this term. When English journalists and famous writers use this word in English, they often use the word 'izzat' without bothering to translate it. Even today when the older generation blesses someone, whether or not they mention health, personal safety, the blessing of having a lot of children, being well off, or seeing their faith grow stronger as they age, they are sure to ask God that He protect the honour of the younger and older generations, in that order, and, when it comes time to die, that He take from the world (with honour) the younger and then the older generation, in the same order. Even when it comes to jobs, we don't pray that we perform well, or that we have means of advancement, but rather our only wish is that we retire with 'honour.' This wish doesn't exist in any other language or country in the world. The reason for this is that we have more, and more various, opportunities to be disgraced than people anywhere else in the world. Working people consider disgrace a professional hazard and so bear with it. The habits and hells of the feudal system don't disappear overnight. In those days, servants called themselves 'salt-eaters' and considered themselves loyal. (In ancient Rome, the soldiers were paid in salt in lieu of currency, and slaves were bought for salt.) A salary wasn't the just recompense for hard work; any money exchanged was charity, or just a tip.

A Neon Sign of Good Behavior

In the ad, Maulvi Sayyid Muhammad Muzaffar — the school's founder, manager, chief administrator, guiding light, accountant, and embezzler — stated that applicants need not apply by mail, but rather they should come in person at eight in the morning with their degree and documented proof of good behaviour. Basharat couldn't understand what would constitute proof of good behaviour. Proof of bad behaviour was easy to come by. For example, traffic tickets, a restraining order, a warrant for arrest, a notarized copy of a conviction order, or a copy of a registered list of offenders, on which the names of the biggest troublemakers are listed. A man can prove his bad behaviour in five minutes, but he can never prove his good behaviour. But his anxiety was pointless. That was because his appearance (a shaved head; kohl-rimmed eyes; high-water pyjamas; a black, velvet Rampuri hat; wooden sandals that you wear around the house, to the mosque, or in the neighbourhood) meant that even if he wanted to look like anything but a goody two-shoes it was impossible. Good behavior was his destiny; there was no choice in the matter. And his appearance wasn't just its proof; it was its neon sign.

This was the very appearance of all lower middle-class boys of the neighbourhood's respectable households. 'Respectable households' meant those people who never personally had to do anything in order to be, remain, and be called 'respectable.' The stamp of respectability, property, and the abovementioned appearance was bestowed one generation after another as a matter of legacy within those houses in the same way that genes and hereditary diseases come to everyone else. If the great grandson was the spitting image of his great grandfather in beliefs, in the limits of his knowledge, and in his appearance, then this was considered proof of this family's nobility, respectability, and authenticity.

For his interview, Basharat wore his best clothes. He had his achkan coat washed. It had grown discoloured, so he told the washerman to apply a little extra starch. The previous Friday, he had gone to the barber's to get his head shaved with clippers. Then he had it shaved again, but this time with a razor. After that, he had the stone from a raw mango rubbed over his head, and then he had his scalp massaged with amla oil. It stung for quite a while. Then he put on his hat. As he looked in the mirror, he saw that his shaven head had started to sweat as it would after he applied Vicks or balm. He started fanning himself. When he took off his hat, the fan's motion made him feel as though the wind was mixed with mint. (It's probably not inappropriate for me to admit that when we left our Asian confines and for the first time saw with our own eyes the bright colours of Europe, our entire existence stung the same way.) Then Basharat spit-shined his shoes as soldiers do and so put the finishing touch on his get-up. The chairman of the selection committee was the County Treasurer. He had heard that his was the voice that really counted. He was a free-spirited, witty man, elegant and literary; he was sociable, fearless, and he accepted bribes. He rode a horse to work. His penname was Nadim [Ashamed]. He was a crafty, clever man.

To win him to his side, Basharat bought a ream of almond paper and a half dozen reed pens, and all night long he prepared a manuscript of poetry, that is, he copied out twenty-seven ghazals. He wrote under the pen name Makhmur [Drunken], which his teacher Jauhar Illahabadi had given to him. He named his not-yet-fully-fermented wine, I mean, his incomplete poetry collection, *The Winehouse of Makhmur from Kanpur and Lucknow*. (His only tie to Lucknow was that five years before this happened, he had lain half-unconscious in a hospital bed for five days after his gall bladder had been removed.) Then he added a bulky appendix as well.

The story of this appendix was that while selecting poetry for the volume proper, he had to be so self-critical that it was painful; it was like having to carry a mountain on his back. No matter how worthless and weak a poem is, it is as hard to set it aside as it would be to call your own offspring ugly or to remove your own loose tooth by yourself. Even Ghalib hated this, and so he had handed over the task of cutting down his poetry to Maulana Fazal-e-Haq Khairabadi; he had sat with his face turned away, exactly as many people do when getting a shot. Although Basharat set aside some things, he wasn't satisfied. And so he ended up making an appendix of all his excised poems. These poems were mostly from the period when he was without a teacher and went by the pen name of Fareftah [Lover]. The defining quality of this pen name was that it always ruined his closing couplets, and so his ghazals usually didn't have them. In the several closing couplets he did write, in accordance with the rules of poetry, he used the synonyms Shaidah and Dildadah (and he marked them as such), but that only caused other problems. Actually, the thing was that it was beyond the power of any human to put into verse all the myriad things that he was thinking about in the hollow recesses of his mind.

Yaganah (the Poet) Thought He Was God; By God, He Wasn't

On the first page of his *Collected Poems*, he drew an arch, and on top of it he wrote in Arabic, 'Some poetry is indeed pure wisdom, and some eloquence is pure magic.' And beneath that, 'The Winehouse of Makhmur from Kanpur and Lucknow.' And then, 'Updated Table of Contents.' Then on the next two lines, 'Published by Munshi Nawal Kishore Press, Lucknow, Under the Auspices of Kesari Das Seth, Superintendent.' Then he carefully added in very faint letters 'To be' before 'Published,' so that at first glance you wouldn't see these words. Then, on the last line, he wrote, 'First Edition, December 1937.' Underneath the title, he wrote his name in letters twice as large, 'Basharat Ali Farooqi of Kanpur and Lucknow, BA (Agra University), Successor to the First Officer of Poetry, the Most Eloquent, God's Beloved, Hazrat Jauhar Chughtai Illahabadi.'

If any reader doubts this, then I would like them to know that even Krishan Chander wrote MA after his name until 1947, and, that without it, his name seemed so painfully naked that he didn't recognize it as his own. This tradition went back many years. Whenever his work appeared in a book or magazine, Akbar Illahabadi's name was written in the following fashion: 'The New Voice of the Times, Khan

Bahadur Akbar Hussain Sahib, Retired Sessions Judge, Allahabad.'

And Basharat's favourite poet, Yaganah Changezi—who called himself 'the Wizard of Ghazals, the Father of Meaning, Yaganah Alaihis-Salam (Peace Be Upon Him)'—dedicated his second book to his hero and spiritual preceptor Genghis Khan with the following words of limitless worship and praise: 'A Humble Gift to Hazrat Changez, the Great Lord, Scourge of God, the Fountain of Fear, the Prophet of Wrath and Punishment, the Emperor of Human Beings, who Surpassed Alexander and Jamshed, from Mirza Yaganah Changezi of Lucknow.'

But Basharat unwittingly let one error slip in. He had copied everything from the title page of a book from Nawal Kishore Press in exactly the same diction and with the same honorific tone (including the same price), and while introducing his teacher Jauhar Chughtai Illahabadi, he had also copied down 'Beloved of God' after his name as a courtesy and hadn't thought about how the man was presently living, and not only living, but young and healthy, and that he would still have to wait a long time to secure his place in the hereafter.

Yaganah had published his volume of *Collected Poems* with checkmarks indicating which of his poems he liked best. Some he had marked great; some he had marked double great; and those that sent him straight into ecstasy he had marked triple great. This was so that an absentminded reader in the years to come couldn't complain that no one had indicated a hierarchy of greatness! So Basharat followed in his teacher's footsteps, but instead of the outmoded system his teacher had used, he put a red tick mark in both the right- and left-hand margins.

He had only one complaint about the job in Dhiraj Ganj: writing 'Dhiraj Ganjvi' after Makhmur not only ruined his pen name, but it also ruined everything fine about his ghazals. But when he thought about those poor poets who lived in places with even more stupid-sounding names—like Phaphund, Bahraich, Gonda, Barabanki, Chiraiyakot, Jalandhar, Loharu, Ludhiana, Macchali Shahar—and how they had to put up with those names, then, according to him, it wasn't that he grew more patient, but that he grew to understand the quandary. One day as he lay in bed, he suddenly thought how the great poet Nizami wrote after his name, 'Ganjvi.' So his disgust for the term went away. If God wished it, he thought, He would reveal to him how to stomach the 'Dhiraj' part, as well.

From Maulvi Mujjan to Tana Shah

No difficulties presented themselves in getting a recommendation letter to the County Treasurer. But whomever he asked about Maulvi Muzaffar (whom everyone called Moli Mujjan, whether out of contempt, laziness, or love), presented him with a new problem. One person said, 'He feels for his community. He has access to higher-ups. But he's mean and malicious. Watch out for him.' Another person said, 'Moli Mujjan also runs an orphanage, the Light of Islam. He makes the orphans give him leg massages, and he makes them sweep the school. He sends the teachers out with the kids to Kanpur and Lucknow to ask for donations. But he doesn't pay for their transport. There's no doubt he doesn't give up easily. He's really helped the Muslims of Dhiraj Ganj. Those Muslims there that are educated and employed have his school to thank.' Sometimes it seemed that people were sick of him for no reason at all. Basharat started to kind of feel sorry for him. Just as Master Fakhir Hussain had once told him that the secret to doing good work was to avoid trying to correct your elders, your bosses, or those who aren't as misbehaved as you, even if you see them going down the wrong path; like the three wise monkeys, turn blind, deaf, and dumb. Then you will get what you want.

One bitter old man, the calligrapher of the magazine *Zamanah*, said the following: 'He's not just a miscreant, he's also a miser. He'll make sure to shortchange you. First he'll look you up and down. He'll appraise your character. Then he'll hound you till you die. He learned to sign his name when he had to start writing fake receipts for his charity collection. And now? He's Sir Syed! I saw with my own two eyes that he signed his marriage certificate with his thumbprint! He's completely illiterate. But he's clever as hell. And underhanded. And sly. He's not your ordinary brown-noser. He's a rogue, a rake, and a huckster!' The abovementioned gentleman delineated Moli Mujjan's different shades of baseness with such craft that, in order not to miss the finer points of his worthlessness, you had to have a dictionary on hand or, like me, to have spent your entire life in the painful company of wordsmiths.

Sayyid Aijaz Husain Wafa said, 'Moli Mujjan is sure to pray five times a day. His knees, forehead, and conscience all have big calluses on them. He controls the police chief and the County Treasurer through his good manners, feelings of Islamic fraternity, hospitality, and bribes. He's also asthmatic. He wipes his nose on his sleeve ten times in five minutes.' The old guy didn't have so much a problem with that as with his pronouncing 'aasteen' as 'asteen,' 'yakhni' as 'akhni,' and 'hauslah' as 'haunslah.' He had heard for himself Moli Mujjan say 'Mijaz Sharif' for Mizaj Sharif and 'Shubrat' for 'Shab-e-barat' [the Night of Salvation]. Like fools, brown-nosers, and goats, Moli Mujjan was always saying 'me, me, me.' (In order to save themselves from appearing pretentious, the elite of Lucknow have always referred to themselves in the first person plural, 'we.') A skinny old man added, 'He's a butcher or grocer by caste. And he's from Delhi. So he hugs you three times. The upper classes from Awadh do it just once.'

But this is absolutely an injustice for those who live in Awadh because hugging just once isn't so much about their high status as about their hoity-toityness. You also have to keep in mind that the tradition was for repining wives to use dry rice and dew as the tools of suicide:

they threatened to eat the dry rice and fall asleep for good in the morning dew. They were only housewives, and Tana Shah far surpassed them. It's famously recounted that when he was led in chains into the court, the question was raised how he should be put to death. The courtiers made their own suggestions. For instance, one said that the reprobate should be tied to the leg of an elephant in rut and toured through town. A second paid his respects and then said, 'But who's going to do this? An elephant in rut is horny for elephants. He won't want to have anything to do with people. But if you want to punish the elephant for Tana Shah's debauchery, that's another matter.' A third courtier spoke, 'For a degenerate like Tana Shah, the best punishment would be to castrate him, then throw him into his harem.' Another courtier suggested, 'You should pour copper sulfate powder into his eyes to blind him. Then lock him in Gwalior Fort, and for two years make him drink opium on an empty stomach so that his body wastes away and he sees himself for who he is.' A historian objected, 'Tana Shah isn't Your Majesty's blood relative, and this treatment's reserved for real brothers.' One callous man said, 'Throw him over the castle's parapets.' But an objection was raised here that on the way down his fearful soul would leave his body, and if real suffering was the goal, then it would never come to pass. In the end, the vizier solved this problem and so proved his own wisdom. He said that if both mental anguish and physical pain were the goals, then send a woman cowherd his way. For those readers who haven't seen a debauched nobleman or a woman cowherd, then you should know that from just one whiff of butter and raw milk, from one sniff of a skirt that's been in a foul-smelling cattle herd, from just one nose-tickle of a black waistcoat that has turned white from the alkalinity of sweat, a nobleman will lose consciousness. To bring him back you must then remove the musk gland from a deer, distill it into incense, and force him to inhale.

2.

The Sweetshop and a Dog's Breakfast

Basharat left at three in the morning to get to the interview. When he arrived at Maulvi Muzaffar's, it was seven and Maulvi Muzaffar was sitting on his chaise lounge eating jalebis. Basharat introduced himself.

'Come in, come in, the man from Kanpur!' Maulvi Muzaffar exclaimed. 'Kanpur's like Lucknow's kissing cousin. Since everyone knows people in Lucknow are hoity-toity, I won't even bother asking you to share my breakfast. Oh, Zauq, standing on formality is kind of like standing on glass!' (Yes, he said 'kind of' when he meant 'exactly.') 'You must already have eaten. The selection committee's going to convene in an hour in my office. We'll meet there, OK? And, hey, that loser you used for a reference? He's not only a tremendous miser, he's also dumb as a rock.'

This conversation transpired in under two minutes. Maulvi Muzaffar hadn't even asked Basharat to sit down—he'd had to stand there like a servant.

Since Basharat had left home in pitch darkness, when he saw Maulvi Muzaffar eating warm jalebis he realized how hungry he was. In the words of Muhammad Hussain Azad, when you're hungry, anything tastes good. So, after wandering around for a while, he asked where he could find the sweetshop, and when he got there he ordered two-thirds of a pound of jalebis hot from the fryer. He had just picked up the first jalebi from his leaf-cup when suddenly the sweetshop owner's dog came up to him, stuck its snout up the leg of his wide-bottomed, Lucknow-style pyjamas, and started licking his calf with amazing devotion. Basharat stood motionless for a while, letting the dog do whatever it liked. This was because he'd heard that if a dog starts following you or starts licking your hands or feet, it's best not to run away or make a fuss because then the dog will get angry and really give it to you. Basharat gave the dog a jalebi; immediately the dog lost interest in his calf, and so Basharat managed to eat a jalebi himself. But once the dog finished the treat, it went straight back to licking Basharat's leg without even cleaning the remaining tidbits off its tongue!

Now this became the pattern. Basharat would give the dog a jalebi and then quickly stuff one into his own mouth. But if there was any delay, the dog would go back to licking Basharat's calf with the same feverish intensity as before, apparently trying to get at the bone inside. Basharat was no longer scared, and he began to notice the dog's cold nose tickling him. Right there and then, he made two important decisions. One, never again would he stop to eat jalebis in the middle of the street like some country bumpkin from Kanpur. And two, never again would he try to imitate the fine folks from Lucknow by wearing wide-bottomed pyjamas. He resolved to observe these rules until death.

Having finished feeding the dog, Basharat put the leaf cup on the ground, and the dog fell to licking out the syrup. Basharat went back to the sweetshop and bought a cup of milk for himself plus a little extra for the dog, hoping that he would be able to slip away while the dog drank its fill. Basharat swallowed his milk in one gulp and set off to see the town. Noticing Basharat leave, the dog pricked up its ears in alarm, left the milk, and started following him. This confused Basharat: what on earth could this lowly creature want? Three or four times he tried to slow down a little to catch his breath, or he made as though he wanted to turn around, but the dog wouldn't let him do anything.

At every turn in the road, dogs rushed out from the alleys to shepherd Basharat and the dog toward the next deployment of yipping canines—a veritable inter-alley canine task force. The dog fought off the others quite bravely. As long as the battle raged, as long as the ceasefire was still unsigned, as long as the skirmish with the next alley's Lion Brigade was still imminent, Basharat stood peacefully in the middle of the action watching the goings-on like an impartial UN observer. He was trying his best to stop the village boys from throwing stones at the dogs because, in fact, their stones were only hitting him. The dog lashed out at any other dog that tried to get to Basharat, who, truth be told, found himself rooting for the dog—his dog. Just a few minutes ago it was just a dog, but now things were different, and he was suddenly worried about coming up with a good name for it.

He realized suddenly that the arrival of a stranger in a village is announced by three things—dogs, peacocks, and kids. But once the hue and cry is over, every house in the village treats you as their guest.

Dogs Named Tipu

It upset Basharat that the sweetshop owner and the village boys called the dog 'Tipu.' After the British martyred Tipu Sultan in the bloody battle of Seringapatam, they began calling their dogs by this name. There was even a time throughout north India when this name was so common that everyone referred to any stray dog as Tipu—'Scram, Tipu!'—without even knowing why stray dogs were called this. Other than Napoleon and Tipu, the British treated none of their enemies so badly, and this was because none made their hearts fill with such awful dread. A hundred years have passed in South Asia with the name of the martyred sultan on everyone's lips! 'Get lost, Tipu!' 'Take that, Tipu!' The trials and tribulations—the sanctifying sorrows—and great sacrifices—of only a few select martyrs are not forgotten after they die. These are the few that God Almighty blesses with eternal martyrdom!

Sole/Soul Reader

Although Maulvi Muzaffar had spared no expense in building his own house (out of brick) and in building the school (half out of brick), he had decided to have his office in a room with a corrugated tin roof in order to exhibit the model of simplicity set by the true Muslims (those of the first generation). This is where the selection committee was to meet. There were three candidates including Basharat, and the following guidelines were written in chalk on a blackboard to the right of the door: (1) Candidates are asked to wait patiently for their turn. (2) Under no circumstances will candidates be reimbursed for travel expenses. A meal will be provided at the Light of Islam Orphanage after noon prayers. (3) Before the interview begins, each candidate will be asked to present proof of their having given a one-rupee donation to the orphanage. (4) It is kindly requested that candidates extinguish their cigarettes before entering.

When Basharat arrived in the foyer (meaning, the shady skirt of a neem tree), the dog was by his side. He motioned suggestively several times, trying to get it to leave, but the dog had no such intentions. Basharat sat down on a boulder, and the dog stationed itself right by his feet, wagging its tail happily and casting appreciative glances up at its new friend. This pleased Basharat—not only was he beginning to feel attached to the poor thing, but the dog's presence felt kind of reassuring.

The candidate who introduced himself as LT from Allahabad was squatting in the shade drawing a good-luck mandala in the sand with a little twig. Whichever way you added up the digits of the mandala, the total was twenty—this was the very mandala considered to be a surefire way to get a woman or to win over a superior. In the intricate curlicue folds of his ear, he had stuffed a cotton ball doused in a sweet-straw cologne, and the Bengal Locks hair oil that he had profusely slathered on had begun to flow down his forehead.

The second candidate came from Kalpi and announced that he had both a BA and a BT from Aligarh. He wore sunglasses, which made sense since the sun was blazing, but he also wore a red silk scarf whose only purpose seemed to be to gather the copious amounts of sweat streaming down his face. As far as his suit, well, it would have fit just right if he had been a hundred pounds lighter—the two bottom buttons of his shirt and the two top buttons of his pants were left undone. His sun hat was the only thing that fit. It appeared as though his turquoise ring had become too tight as well, because when his name was called, he took it from his pocket and installed it on his pinkie. His shoelaces were untied, but when standing up, he couldn't see them anyway. He said he used to be a goalie, and despite his hulking body, he was able to cinch himself between two branches in such a fashion that from a distance he looked like a big sideways 'V': shoes on one end, and hat on the other. He joined in the conversation from his perch, and from there he spat out his paan spittle and flicked ash from his Passing Show cigarette.

After a while, a fakir showed up and sat down near Basharat. This was the type of fakir with matted hair, a walking stick, and chains around his ankles—the type that wanders around with a little gong that he strikes from time to time. He raised his walking stick to Basharat's forehead and said, 'I tell fortunes by reading the soles of feet . . . so take off your shoes, or I'll mess you the fuck up.'

Basharat thought the man must be crazy, so he turned away. But then the man said quietly, 'Son, you have a mole on your pelvis and a wart in your right armpit.' This sent shivers down Basharat's spine, and he immediately took off his shoes because what the man had said was true.

A short distance away the third-grade boys were exercising beneath a banyan tree. They were doing push-ups. When they extended their arms the very first time, they cried out in pain, and after they dropped back to the ground only two boys had enough strength to do it a second time. The rest lay there like lizards sunning on a rock. They turned their heads and looked helplessly toward the PE teacher who barked at them, 'What? Does your mamma give you watered-down milk?'

The lower half of the reed mat covering the doorway was in tatters, leaving its coarse threads hanging limply. The first candidate was the guy from Aligarh, and they called out his name the way they summon plaintiffs and defendants in a court case—I mean, by surname first, and so loud you would have thought there were as many as two hundred candidates sitting in a line extending two miles into the distance. The candidate jumped down from the tree as though sprung from a catapult. He landed with a thud. He readjusted his sun hat and was about to enter when the servant stopped him. He asked for proof that he had donated to the orphanage, then had him hand over his pack of Passing Show cigarettes, of which only two remained. Then he had him take off his shoes, and they entered as though approaching the Almighty Himself. After fifty minutes, they came out. The servant went over to a gong that hung from a rocking horse next to the door, and he struck it so that everyone in town (as well as the three candidates) would know that the first interview was finished. The boys milling around outside clapped loudly. Then the candidate from Allahabad was called in; he erased his mandala from the sand and rushed inside. After fifty minutes, the servant came out and struck the gong twice with such force that all the peacocks in town began crying out. (Each interview lasted the same fifty minutes as a class period.) The servant winked at Basharat and motioned for him to enter.

3.

The Black Hole of Dhiraj Ganj

When Basharat went inside, he couldn't make out anything. Since there was neither a window nor a skylight, the only way light got into the room was through a little round hole in the wall. Gradually outlines appeared from out of the darkness, and he could see the walls, whose plaster was made from both yellow mud and fresh cow dung into which dried mustard stalks and chaff had been mixed to strengthen the compound. The plaster's natural golden varnish sparkled in the dim light. In the corner to his right there were two beads of light. Suddenly they began moving toward him, and this frightened him until he realized it was a cat in search of some mouse. To his left, there was a really strange cot: it was four feet high, its legs were so thick they looked like the trunks of trees, and whoever had made it hadn't even bothered to shear off the bark. This is where three of the selection committee's members sat with their legs dangling. Nearby, another member was sitting on a reed stool with no backrest. Maulvi Muzaffar was sitting with his back toward the door on a reed chair that had no padding left on the armrests, and so its bare reed fibers were showing through. A very cheerful-looking man was sitting on an iron chair. He had turned it around so he could sit with his chest pressed against the back and his chin propped on top of it. His skin was so dark that the only thing Basharat could see were his teeth. This man was the County Treasurer and the chairman of the committee.

One member hung his fez on top of one of the cot's legs, but when the cat came over to bat its dangling tassels, the man put the hat back on. Everyone was cooling themselves with fans made of date palm branches. Moli Mujjan pushed the stem of his fan down the neck of his shervani to scratch his back and when he brought it back out he sniffed it to see if it smelled. The County Treasurer's fan was fringed with red lace and had a small mirror in the middle.

For the candidates, there was a stool with a kidney-shaped hole — the standard type in those days. For the longest time, I couldn't figure out the purpose of this hole. In the summer, some people put an earthenware water pitcher or flask on it so that the beads of evaporation oozing from the pitcher would seep through the hole and cool the pitcher's bottom. Throughout the interview, Basharat couldn't decide whether he was shaking from being nervous or whether it was the stool itself that was shaking.

The County Treasurer was sipping a sweet lassi, and the rest of the men were smoking hookahs. Everyone had taken off their shoes, and if Basharat had been informed about this state of affairs, he certainly would have made sure to wear clean socks. The man on the reed stool sat with his left foot resting on his right knee and had interwoven the fingers of his right hand among the toes of his left foot and was playing a game of push-em-pull-em. A tarnished spittoon was being passed around. The room smelled of a curious combination of the hookah-smoke, the Benares tobacco in the paan, the earthenware water pitcher, the watermelon rinds tossed into the corner, the previous candidate's sweet-straw cologne, and the wall-plaster's cow dung. A smell wafted over this that you couldn't be too sure about: was it that of the homemade shoes worn into everyone's feet, or the rotten stench of their feet coming from their shoes?

The small round hole in the wall was of an uncertain nature as well. It was difficult to decide whether it was there to supply light or just to supply a little contrast to the shades of darkness that shrouded the room; whether it was there to let the room's trapped smoke out or to let the dust outside in; whether it was there to provide a means to look out at the world or to provide a means for all the Peeping Toms to look in. Skylight, ventilator, spy-hole, chimney, window, and port-hole—Basharat thought it was the most multipurpose hole in all of Asia, and so overworked that it suffered from ontological confusion, which in turn led to its not being able to do anything well.

Every five minutes a new face was at the hole. Outside, one boy bent over so that his buddy could climb onto his shoulders and look in. They remained in this position until the boy giving support got tired. When his legs gave out and his waist started to wobble, he would yell out to his friend, 'Hey! Get down! It's my turn now. Let me see!'

The hole was also a passage for oxygen and insults. Long story short, Moli Mujjan suffered from asthma. When a coughing fit overtook him, and he felt as though he couldn't breathe, he rushed over

378

and stuck his mouth against the hole. Once he refreshed his lungs, he intoned majestically, 'God be praised!' then launched into a cursing rampage against the boys.

A little while later the sun changed its position in the sky, and a bright beam of light shot straight through the hole into the room and illuminated the smoke dervishes and dancing dust motes. What a vision! On the left, on a shelf set into the wall, there were balls that the theology students had made for drying the piss off the ends of their penises. These were arranged one on top of the other so neatly that they would have looked like peda sweets from the market in Badayun if only they had flies swarming all over them!

On the right wall, there was a framed photo of King George V, over which hung a shrivelled marigold garland. Beneath this were two more photos—one of Mustafa Kamal Pasha and the other of Maulana Muhammand Ali Jauhar, who was wearing a loose, long-sleeved robe and a sable-fur cap decorated with the moon and stars. Between these was a large photo of Moli Mujjan with a framed appreciation certificate beneath it from all the teachers and staff congratulating him on making it through a bout of cholera and wishing him the best for all times, a certificate that earned them the pay he had withheld for the five previous months.

I forgot to mention that the dog went in with Basharat for the interview. Basharat had tried his best to get it to stay away, but to no avail. The servant told him he couldn't take the unclean thing in, and this gave Basharat the opportunity to say that the dog wasn't his. 'Then why have you two been acting like bosom buddies for the past two hours?' the servant asked.

Picking up a clump of dirt, the servant made like he was going to strike the dog, but the dog sprang upon his calf. The servant began screaming. Basharat called off the dog, and it obeyed. The servant didn't thank him.

'You're still going to insist it isn't yours?'

So he went in, and the dog with him. Forget barring the way, the servant didn't have enough courage even to look at the dog.

As soon as they got inside, chaos erupted. The committee members started yelling and screaming at the top of their lungs, but when the dog barked even louder, they all got scared and shut up, making sure they raised their legs up onto their chairs.

'Gentlemen,' Basharat said, 'if you remain quiet and motionless, the dog won't bark.'

'Why did you bring this dog in?' someone asked.

'I swear it's not mine.'

'But if it isn't yours,' the man replied, 'how come you know the ins and outs of its shameless behaviour?'

Basharat sat down on the stool, and the dog took up residence at his feet. Basharat didn't want him to move because his presence was reassuring. Twice during the interview, Moli Mujjan laughed contemptuously at Basharat, and the dog started barking over him. He became frightened and immediately switched off his cackling. How much Basharat loved that dog!

What's There to Say about Me?

The interview began. The County Treasurer cleared his throat to quiet everyone, and the silence that spread through the room was so deep they could hear not only the tick-tock of the wall clock but also Maulvi Muzaffar's rasping breath. The barrage of questions was just about to begin when the clock struck eleven, and everyone again fell silent: living in Dhiraj Ganj would soon teach Basharat that whenever the clock struck the hour, then according to a countryside custom, everyone would sit in respectful silence to consider whether the clock had struck the right hour or not.

The interview began in earnest. The man he had thought was the servant went and sat on the edge of the cot. It turned out he was the theology teacher who was temporarily doubling as the Urdu teacher. This man ended up being the one who grilled him, whereas Maulvi Muzaffar and another man, a retired reader for a circuit court judge, ended up blabbering nonsense. The country treasurer, on the other hand, gave small bits of encouragement and supported Basharat's candidacy throughout the interview. Here's a sample Q&A, so you can get a sense of the strengths of the respective speakers.

MAULVI MUZAFFAR: (caressing the *The Winehouse of Makhmur from Kanpur and Lucknow*) Please explain the benefits of poetry.

BASHARAT: (with an expression that implied the question was out-of-line) Poetry? I mean couplets. Or I mean its meaning … its devotees … actually, I like poetry …

MAULVI MUZAFFAR: Excellent! Recite something from *Khaliq-e-Bari*.

BASHARAT: God alone is the Creator. / And He is the Actor Supreme.

COURT READER: Your father and grandfathers did what sort of work?

BASHARAT: Nothing, really.

COURT READER: Then how can you be fit to work? It takes four generations of gut-wrenching labour to create a man capable of holding a job!

BASHARAT: (naively) Sir, I've already had a hernia operation!

THEOLOGY TEACHER: Please show us the scar.

COUNTY TREASURER: Have you ever caned anyone?

BASHARAT: No, sir.

COUNTY TREASURER: Has anyone ever caned you?

BASHARAT: Regularly.

COUNTY TREASURER: Good, then you'll be able to maintain discipline.

COURT READER: So tell us—why is the Earth round?

(Basharat looks at the court reader with the defeated look of a wrestler pinned to the mat.)

COUNTY TREASURER: (to the court reader) Sir, we asked him here because we need an Urdu teacher. The interviews for the geography teacher are on Thursday.

THEOLOGY TEACHER: Please write something on the blackboard to demonstrate your good penmanship.

COURT READER: Why are you against beards?

BASHARAT: I'm not.

COURT READER: Then why don't you have one?

THEOLOGY TEACHER: Do you love your maternal or paternal uncle more?

BASHARAT: I've never thought about it.

THEOLOGY TEACHER: Please answer the question.

BASHARAT: I don't have a paternal uncle.

THEOLOGY TEACHER: You know how to pray, right? Please recite your father's funeral prayer.

BASHARAT: He's still living.

THEOLOGY TEACHER: God have mercy on me! Your face seemed so sad, I just assumed ... then please recite your grandfather's, or is he too drawing breath?

BASHARAT: (in a sad whisper) He's passed away.

MAULVI MUZAFFAR: Please recite something from Hali's *Musaddas*.

BASHARAT: I can't recall anything at the moment, but I can recite some couplets from his poem 'The Supplication of the Widow.' *

---

* When they heard this, the selection committee members who were seated on the cot smiled knowingly, the County Treasurer winked at Basharat, and Moli Mujjan's face turned white. The reasons? Just recently he had married the math teacher's sister, so the math teacher got four extra rupees a month—something

382

COUNTY TREASURER: Fine, then recite some of your favourite couplets that have nothing to do with widowhood.

BASHARAT:

Ripped apart—all our ties—strangled in death's straightjacket.
On the tomb's throw cushions lies the wrestler—he's nothing now at all.

COUNTY TREASURER: Whose poetry is that?

BASHARAT: It's Urdu poetry!

COUNTY TREASURER: That's amazing! Simply brilliant! What wonderful wordplay! The bonds of life are ripped apart, and then the ties of death's straightjacket strangle you. So the word 'throw' could be both the wrestling move and then the soft pillows of death's eternal rest—as though God has 'thrown you' in a wrestling match! Then the world's impermanence is summed up in a short phrase, 'he's nothing now at all.' It's a marvel that so many things could be hidden in just two lines of poetry! Only a true master is capable of composing a throwaway couplet like this.

MAULVI MUZAFFAR: Are your tastes simple or extravagant?

BASHARAT: Simple.

MAULVI MUZAFFAR: Are you married or still footloose and fancy-free?

BASHARAT: I haven't married yet.

MAULVI MUZAFFAR: Then what are you going to do with your whole salary?! How much will you give each month to the orphanage?

COUNTY TREASURER: When did you first become interested in poetry? Please recite the first couplet you ever wrote.

---

no other senior teacher could do because they didn't have any widows to marry off. Everyone in town was talking about Moli Mujjan's quick wedding, lengthy reception, and the promotion of his brother-in-law. But his brother-in-law wasn't satisfied with the four extra rupees and ended up bitching and taunting all the time, "You don't really love me, you love my sister!"

BASHARAT:

Watching and waiting, I saw the corpse jumping for joy.
And yet the Alley of the Beloved is still so far.

COUNTY TREASURER: Bravo! To turn the couplet on 'and yet' is a stroke of genius! My God! The corpse was happy too soon! And 'still so far' … it hardly says anything and yet it says so much!

BASHARAT: Thank you very much. Truly.

COUNTY TREASURER: Such a great couplet from such an unexpected place? Besides economy in language, the couplet also shows parsimony in thought!

BASHARAT: Thank you.

COUNTY TREASURER: (The dog starts to bark.) I'm sorry to interrupt your dog's barking, but what is your goal in life?

BASHARAT: To get this job.

COUNTY TREASURER: Well, then, consider it yours. Tomorrow morning bring all your stuff. I'll need your paperwork completed on my desk by eleven thirty. Your salary will be forty rupees a month.

* * *

Maulvi Muzaffar stamped his feet on the floor and protested, 'Hey, new employees get only twenty-five!' The County Treasurer shot him a fiery glance that shut him up. Then he wrote a note in English on Basharat's file indicating that, in this candidate, he had found all the lofty qualities of an ambitious young man who could become a successful accountant or schoolteacher, if placed under the proper supervision. And that even though he had no free time to speak of, he was personally ready to give him some time and attention. Last of all, he wrote that he had given the candidate an eighty out of hundred, but that he was willing to up the score five points considering his good handwriting. That being said, he would also need to deduct five points due to his bad poetry.

The Virtues of Radishes and a Good Name

Basharat didn't eat lunch at the orphanage but at the house of Maulvi Badal (Ibadullah), the Persian teacher at the school. The buttery bread, mashed potatoes, and garlic chutney really hit the spot. Maulvi Badal assured him of his affection and that he was willing to help him, 'Son, I'm going to teach you how to darn, how to knead dough, and how to make every type of gravy under the sun. I swear to God, you won't miss having a wife at all!' His recipe for fried radishes was quite complicated and dangerous. That was because it began with having to go into the radish fields before dawn. He explained that, contrary to the countryside's customs, Basharat shouldn't cavalierly enter the green fields in the early morning but rather he should stop on the field's edge and clear his throat in the way that people do when approaching a doorless outhouse or one with just a ratty piece of cloth for a door. Then he instructed him in the proper manner for asking the owner of the field, Dhapan, who wore skirts one hand's length above the ankles and blouses with necklines that hung one hand's length beneath the collarbone, as to where in the field he could find the freshest, most round, and most tender radishes, and how to ask this in such a way that he shouldn't seem to be looking at those parts of her body that were worth looking at. He also advanced the notion that vegetables that look like bats are the source of vitality and relieve flatulence. By these 'bat-like' vegetables, he meant those plants whose feet face heaven, for example, carrots, cabbage, and turnips. Then he showed him radish greens and instructed him in how to tell which is bitter-tasting; and which is plump, but tasteless; and which is firm but stringy—as these will be so acidic that you will pucker your lips as you eat them and afterwards your stomach too will pucker. But some are so well-shaped and sweet that you will wish they were three-feet long. He also said that if you happen to pull up an acidic radish by mistake, don't throw it away. Rather, make it into juice and put it in a camel-hide flask. Then, after forty days, use a cotton ball to apply it to your eczema or herpes. If God wishes it to be so, your skin will clear up, and it will look like the skin of a newborn babe. And afterwards when Basharat used cotton balls to dab this distillation onto the boils of his uncle's eczema, the old man did actually scream just like a newborn babe!

The dog followed him to Maulvi Badal's house, as well. Basharat considered the dog to have been the source of the miracle that had happened during the interview. When it was time to board the pickup back to Kanpur, the dog leapt into the truck, and all the passengers there shrank back in fear. The driver's assistant picked up the engine crank and raised it to hit the dog. Basharat lunged forward and grabbed his wrist. The dog rode on the roof of the truck all the way. At this point, calling such a loyal dog just a dog made him feel guilty; he started calling him Lord Wellesley after the general who had turned Tipu Sultan into a martyr.

Once back in Kanpur, he petted him for the first time. He had had no idea that a dog's body was that hot. The dog had wounds all over his body from the stones boys had thrown at him. He bought a pretty collar and chain for the dog.

4.

In the Presence of the Great Man, the Munificent County Treasurer

The next day Basharat packed his entire world into a trunk and left for Dhiraj Ganj. He paid a painter four annas to paint in white his name, degree, and pen name—which the painter was able to stretch out to only two lines. This trunk was older than Basharat himself, and he attached to it a new four-lever brass lock. He had so few articles of clothing that during the journey his small, Muradabadi water pitcher kept clanking around inside. (Another reason why it made so much noise might have been that this freshly plated tin pitcher was the most expensive thing he owned.) After arriving, Basharat didn't even have the chance to freshen up before the County Treasurer's servant came in carrying a stick and a message that the most respected and august County Treasurer wanted to see him. Basharat asked, 'Right now?' The servant responded, 'When else? He wants you there already! In person!' Hearing this surprised and yet pleased Basharat. But his happiness quickly vanished when this man demanded in the same officious tone that the price for bringing the message was lunch money and provisions for his return journey. He said, 'This is how things are done in the countryside. Yours truly is a mere wage-earner.'* As Basharat was considering these demands, the servant obsessively spit-shined the silver ferrule of his stick with his cotton scarf.

In the brutal afternoon heat, Basharat walked two miles to the County Treasurer's house, where, still huffing and puffing, he learned that the County Treasurer was taking a nap. After an hour or so, he was called inside. The pleasing chill of the sweet-scented grass screen permeated his body. His eyes, which had been burning from the hot wind, were suddenly filled with a cool light. The punkah fan hanging from the roof was moving like an elephant's ear. The white cool of the sheet that was spread on the floor felt very pleasant against his burning palms. And when the heat of his palms warmed the white sheet, then he placed his palms elsewhere. The County Treasurer

* This man was a courier whose wages, as well as travel, food, and lodging expenses, were borne by the subordinate to whom he delivered the government order. This was a kind of punishment. In some areas, notices were sent only by these couriers, so that it served as a lesson to the one receiving it.

welcomed him warmly. He offered him a piece of watermelon that had been kept in ice and some peeled water chestnuts, as well. He said, 'Please recite some of your poems—some of the ones that aren't absurd, ones that have long lines, that keep to a metre, and that aren't indecent.' After he recited a couple of poems to warm applause, the County Treasurer recited his own new poem, 'The Particles of Earth Have Turned into Moon and Stars Tonight,' which he had written for the deputy collector's recent visit to Dhiraj Ganj. After he handed the poem to Basharat, he said that the deputy collector's brother-in-law's wedding was on the twenty-seventh and that Basharat was to write a lively wedding poem, according to his example, and show it to him. Then he winked at him and said that the metre could be that of 'The Supplication of the Widow.'

Everyone Gets His Due (Especially the County Treasurer)

During all this, the County Treasurer had been scratching his thigh. Somehow a black fly had got into his skintight churidar pyjamas. He had tried over and over to kill the bug by pinching it.

Then a good-looking, young servant named Nazo brought a glass of fresh falsa-berry sherbet. The County Treasurer watched Basharat from the corner of his eyes to see if he looked at her or not. She was a knockout in her coarse, white muslin kurta. When she bent down to hand the glass to Basharat, the delightful scent of her sweat wafted from her body. She bent so far down that he touched the little bells hanging from her neckline's silver buttons. Her frilled pyjamas were flush against her thighs, and the patches that had been sewn on had, in one or two places, opened at their seams and so he could see her enticing skin, which seemed to be giggling at him. After Basharat drank the sherbet, the County Treasurer said, 'Well, you must be tired. You can start teaching Urdu to my kids tomorrow. They're real rascals.

The littlest of the three has just started.' When Basharat hesitated, the County Treasurer's manner suddenly changed. He turned cold, 'As you must have known—and do know now—and will know in the future—your real salary is only twenty-five rupees. The fifteen rupees that I personally tacked on to make it forty, well, that's for tutoring my kids. You think I'm crazy enough to waste fifteen rupees of the hard-earned money of a Muslim charity on a young buck like you? After all, a trustee has some duties to uphold. You should know that the school's principal only makes forty rupees! And, on top of it, he has a BA and a BT from Aligarh, for which he was second division. He's from Amroha, but he's extremely honourable. He's a Sayyid. Also, he doesn't compose love poetry with a shaved head.' And with that phrase, he struck Basharat to the very core. Basharat was speechless.

Then Basharat asked in a voice of entreaty, 'Do you see any alternative?' The County Treasurer roared with laughter. He teased him, 'Of course. The alternative would be for you to earn twenty-five rupees and tutor my kids for free. What does my nobleman think about that? My son, you don't know anything about the world. If I placed a pigeon in each of your hands, you wouldn't be able to tell which is male, and which is female!'

Basharat wanted to retort, 'Mr Columbus, if this is what you mean by "seeing the world," then a pigeon would have a much better method of "discovering" the truth!' But the County Treasurer coughed several times very loudly, and one of his revenue department underlings (who had been down the hall crouching in some corner and was covered in dust) jumped up and approached Basharat. He got up in Basharat's face and said, 'How can you talk to the director in such a childish way? This is a great honour for you. If he so much as winks in their direction, every single professor from Lucknow University will drop what they are doing and head straight here. He's already been offered the post of the deputy collector three times. But each time, he spurned them coldly: if he became selfish and took the job, then what would happen to the staff at the Dhiraj Ganj county offices, and what would happen to the county's people? How could he have left us in the lurch?'

Basharat was dumbstruck. In these situations, real men kill some-one, and the cowardly take the easy way out and commit suicide. But he didn't do either of these things. He took the job, which was more difficult than both.

How Lucky He Is Who Achieved This High Rank!

The County Treasurer had his little princes come out from the women's quarters. He said, 'Say hello to Uncle. He's going to start coming tomorrow to teach you.' The biggest and smallest boys said hello. The middle one cupped his hand, bowed twice, and said hello. But while he bowed for the third time, he made a funny face.

The County Treasurer's mood changed. The boys formed a line and then left. He turned to Basharat, 'Tomorrow there are interviews for the open geography teacher position. I nominate you to sit on the selection committee. The theology teacher isn't suitable for the committee. I'll go ahead and tell Moli Mujjan.' Hearing this made Basharat tingle all over. If someone had right then nominated him Viceroy, he wouldn't have been any happier. Now he would have the chance to eviscerate the candidates. He would make sure to ask, 'Sir, you stick your degrees underneath your arm and walk around like a big shot, but please tell me, why is the world round?' He was going to love it. How sweet it was that right after he was put to shame for no reason at all, he would be able to put to shame others for absolutely no reason at all! His wounded ego was healed in under a second.

He was so happy he forgot to tell him that he refused to be the one to call in candidates and to strike the gong. As Basharat got up to leave, the County Treasurer winked at his wretched assistant, and this man gave him a fifteen-kilo bag of wheat and a pot of the cream-like milk from a cow that had just given birth. The County Treasurer also instructed his assistant to deliver a cart of thatching straw the next day to him; and to send a conscripted labourer to immediately make a bamboo fence. In those days, people who couldn't afford sweet-scented grass to make screens to put in their windows used thatching straw instead. And those people who couldn't afford straw used to sprinkle water (taken from little pitchers) on their sweet-scented-grass hand-fans. When overcome by drowsiness while fanning themselves, they descended into the dreamy chills of an imaginary sweet-grass house.

5.

The Unexpected Duties of the Urdu Teacher

Basharat's duties started early the next morning. Maulvi Muzaffar made him sign a declaration that he, the humble servant, had officially received his supplies. 'Supplies' is a very comprehensive and misleading word. The truth was that the things deemed supplies weren't things that anyone needed to ask for at all:

- *homespun cotton rag (chalk eraser) – one and a half items*
- *handheld fan – one item*
- *attendance register– one item*
- *terracotta inkpot – two items*

In handing over the blackboard eraser, Maulvi Muzaffar told Basharat that he had seen how teachers wasted chalk and so the school's Executive Committee had decided that from then on they would have to buy their own. He informed Basharat that he would get a date-palm fan in the summer. He knew for a fact that teachers were careless. In just two weeks, the fan's woven fronds would unravel. Teachers were notorious for taking the school-fan home over breaks. And some were lazy. They would beat the boys with the fan's handle even though there was a neem tree available just outside. Maulvi Muzaffar also gave him a small wooden stick that his predecessors had probably used as a toothbrush. It gave that impression because its upper end, which the previous scholars had chewed on absentmindedly when deep in thought, had broken off. Basharat was upset by its improper use because now there wasn't any way he could use it to restring his pyjamas.

After he had got his supplies, Basharat asked for his course books. At this, Maulvi Muzaffar informed him that as per the Executive Committee's Resolution 5, dated February 3, 1935, all teachers would have to buy their own. Basharat grew hot under the collar, 'All of them? From the first grade to eighth grade?' Maulvi Muzaffar answered, 'Unless you think we should test those going to middle school on a first grader's book ...'

Maulvi Muzaffar also informed him that in an attempt to cut out all unnecessary expenses the executive committee had laid off the PE teacher. He said, 'What do you plan to do with your free time? The staff room isn't there for bored teachers to lollygag and take naps. In your free time, why don't you lead exercises?' With this he pointed to his stomach. 'You'll fart less. Young men should take care of themselves.' Basharat replied curtly, 'I don't know any exercises.' Maulvi Muzaffar responded very sweetly, 'No problem. No one pops out of their mother's womb doing exercises. Ask absolutely any student to teach you. Thanks be to God, you're a bright man. You'll learn quickly since you admire Tipu Sultan and Tariq, the Conqueror of Spain.'

Basharat had been teaching the boys Urdu with great zeal for two weeks or so when Maulvi Muzaffar called him into his office. Then he said, 'By the grace of God, you're Muslim, or at least you indicated so in your application. Now, can you please learn as quickly as possible how to recite the funeral prayer and how to make offerings to your ancestors? We're a small village, here. They'll come in handy from time to time. The funeral prayer is actually part of the curriculum. Back when I was in school, learning how to wash a corpse was compulsory. Over in Barabanki, a djinn has again possessed the theology teacher's wife. On moonless nights, he flips her charpoy. The theology teacher has gone to cure her. Last year, he accosted his neighbour and broke his jaw. Two teeth, too. Then he came back. You're going to have to fill in for him. It's obvious that an angel isn't going to descend from heaven to fill in for the asshole.'

Then after several days, he started up again, 'Son, what do you do on Sundays?' Basharat answered, 'Nothing at all.' Maulvi Muzaffar replied, 'So you're just sucking in air, is it? That's most improper. Sir Muhammad Iqbal once said, "O, Muslim youths, have you ever thought about this?" A young man shouldn't sit around idle like that. School gets out early on Friday. After Friday prayers, why don't you take care of the orphanage's correspondence? You're like family. Why should I keep things from you? Your salary actually comes from the collection for the orphans. For three months, you haven't been paid. I don't have a lamp like Aladdin. Actually, the orphans don't generate as many expenses as you teachers do! Why don't you take your bike and go collect donations for the orphans on Sundays? It's good work. It'll also save you from the sin of idleness. Thanks be to God, there are plenty of Muslim families in the countryside around here. Work hard, and you'll find God. What's the problem in finding a couple stupid donors?'

Basharat was thinking about how in the world he would be able to recognize potential 'donors' when Maulvi Muzaffar dropped the second bomb. He told him not only to bring back donations from the surrounding countryside but also to find eligible orphans as well!

The Ideal Orphan's Mugshot

It seemed to Basharat that finding orphans would be even more difficult than soliciting charitable donations. That was because Moli Mujjan set in place firm limits: the orphans shouldn't be the healthy, muscular types; rather, they should look a little pathetic. They shouldn't be gluttons; they also shouldn't be so young that they have to be spoon-fed. They shouldn't be such big eaters that they gobble up one piece of bread after another and don't even burp afterwards. They shouldn't be so pampered that if one mosquito should land on the prince's rosy cheek, then he would fall ill with malaria and so gulp down bucket after bucket of milk like there was no tomorrow. So many boys have hollow legs. They should be skinny on the outside, but healthy on the inside. They shouldn't be so feeble that if you ask the little princes to get some water from the well, then they fall in with the bucket. Or that as soon as you put a bucket brimming with water on their heads, then their hips start swaying like kathak dancers, or dirty dancers. Like this, they will break a bucket every day and then bring its rim as proof of their misdeed. As though they were right there in front of him, Maulvi Muzaffar suddenly started scolding the boys, 'Hey, what is that? Is that a necklace? Is it your mother's or sister's? Get it out of here.' Then his recitation continued. They should be average height and not too old. They shouldn't be so big or brash that if you slap them, your hand will sting for hours and the bastards' cheeks will escape unscathed. In the winter, they shouldn't be too affected by the cold. If the weather gets a little cool, they shouldn't go wandering throughout the countryside shivering and shuddering and shaking, and so giving a bad name to the orphanage for no reason at all. Basharat was told to make sure they didn't wet their beds. And that the family had no reported cases of lice and no congenital diseases. As for their growing, Moli Mujjan made clear that they should be not just slow growers but actually permanently stunted so that every year they wouldn't create a stir about needing new clothes and shoes. One-eyed, crippled, blind, deaf, and dumb — yes, but they should only *seem* to be. The boys should never be good-looking. They shouldn't have pimply faces or long noses. Boys with long noses will eventually become gay. While he was describing the mugshot of the ideal orphan, he kept turning to look at Basharat in the same way that portrait painters inspect the model's face while making an outline on the canvas. He kept on talking. But Basharat's attention had strayed. One after another despicable portrait passed through his mind. But he never once thought of himself.

Maulana Rumi's Masnavi and the Orphanage Band

First scene: The train's guard waves his green flag and whistles. As the train starts to move, six boys leap into a third-class compartment, from which a man selling kohl and luxurious salajeet ointment descends. The boys are wearing knickers and shirts. Only one boy's shirt has any buttons left on it, but his sleeve had been ripped clean off from the shoulder during a scuffle. None wears shoes. All wear hats. One boy carries a large picture frame with a certificate signed by some unknown local politician. As soon as they enter the compartment, they elbow and push their way in further to secure their spots. Once the train leaves the station, the biggest of the boys gets out a tin can filled with loose change and starts rattling it like a tambourine. The compartment falls silent. Then the babies crying in their mothers' laps startle from fright and start suckling, and the babies that were suckling suddenly start crying. The men stop staring at the women sitting in front of them, and these ladies' husbands stop yawning. And when all the passengers stop doing what they had been doing and turn in the boys' direction, then the boy with the tin can stops rattling it. His companions turn their faces toward heaven, and, in a sign that they have established contact with the divine, they simultaneously roll their eyes back so far that all you can see are the whites of their eyes. Then they all start singing the chorus of a very foreboding song: 'Please listen to our pleas too / Once we too had mothers and fathers.'

All the orphanage's boys who entered the third-class compartment had adult voices except one, and he led the chorus in his shrill voice. Back in those days, there was not even one passenger from Peshawar to Travancore, or from Calcutta to Karachi, who didn't know these foreboding songs. Since the time that trains and orphanages came to South Asia, this has been the only song they have sung. It reminds me how five hundred years ago, somewhere in South Asia, a misanthrope set some of Maulana Rumi's *Masnavi* to music in an ustu khuddus* style, and, like this orphan's song, that song too hasn't changed in over five hundred years. This misanthrope's setting of Rumi's poetry must be sung with a nasal intonation, and only those imams can sing it that truly believe that singing is forbidden. If you want to turn someone off to singing, mysticism, Persian, and mullahs (and all at the same time), then just listen to a little of this song.. (I didn't write 'Please sing yourself' because this song can be sung by only those men who have never heard Persian spoken by an Iranian and who never eat chicken except when it's free.)

Second scene: The orphanage band is playing. The bandmaster walks in front, swaying his head from side to side. The bandmaster

---

* Ustu khuddus: While the literal definition of this phrase is quite different, Mirza, because of this style's ugliness and disgusting pronunciation, uses this word often—and this word is used here only because no other word would work. If you don't believe me, go ahead and try another word. But, in the dictionary, you'll find this meaning: a cure for headcolds and craziness that doctors call the 'broom of the mind'!

is walking with his stomach jutting out, and so quite the opposite of weightlifters, army soldiers, and scandalous women. Some of the boys are holding horns that look like jalebis, or like the writhing of angry young men. Even though the boys have put the mouthpieces to their lips, the poor souls don't have enough wind to blow through them. And so, for the most part, you hear the drums and the flutes. Sometimes you don't even hear the flutes as they gasp for breath, and so the drums are all you can hear. Mirza says that you wouldn't wish a wedding band like that upon even your worst enemy. Wherever you went in South Asia, it was exactly the same melody. Yet there were several interesting differences between Hindu and Muslim bands. For one, Muslim bands almost never had cymbals. And the drummers in Muslim orphanage-bands played with such fervour that while they spun around, with each time they struck the drum, their fez's tassel spun 360 degrees around their heads. Instead of tassels, Hindu orphans used their religious rat-tails. Secondly, for Hindus, only orphanage bands played this song. But, for Muslims, being an orphan was neither here nor there. In Karachi, I've heard school marching bands play this tune on their sports day: 'Once we too had mothers and fathers / Once we too had mothers and fathers.'

O, Emperor of Ghazals, Is There Any Cure for It or Not?

The great thing about that line is that in its seven words there are four sequential parts and each functions like a key to its meaning: 'Once / we too / had / mothers and fathers.' Whichever part you empha-size will be newly foreboding or will shed new light on helplessness. If you lay special stress on 'had'—*haaaaaaaaaaaaaaad*—then the whole line's feeling will change. Such multivalent lines rarely come even to the best poets. But Mehdi Hasan's a different case; he can make whichever word he wants into such a 'keyword.' He's a man of endless talent, and yet he has developed one bad habit: in order to prove his poetic mastery, he often chooses a couplet with a word that he thinks he can spin. He cuts short the alap's introduction and so gives notice to the listeners that there are some surprises in store for them, which will come about when he reveals the wonderland of the word's meaning. Then he spends half an hour twisting and bending and pressing on the word. He takes a crack at it from all sorts of angles just to prove that all of the line's ambiguity resides in it. All the other words are merely for the tabla player, meaning, they are only for rounding out the sound and giving things a solid footing. The point is to show that he isn't just singing the line, but that he's explaining the line while singing. Now other singers have started copying him: although they themselves don't understand the meaning of the words, they sing and 'explain' at the same time.

Sometimes Mehdi Hasan drives this keyword into the raga's no man's land. And sometimes he shouts out 'Kabaddi, Kabaddi!' and brings the keyword onto his side of the field. Then he continues on, as though freestyle wrestling, twisting and turning, pruning and primping the line, and so tests not only the limits of his poetic powers but also the patience of the audience. When the keyword gives out, it finally reveals its meaning. Then, after a long gulp of air, he makes a funny face, begins to gnaw on the word, and closes his eyes in a show of intense enjoyment. Then after sucking the marrow from it, he spits it out right in front of the tabla player, as though saying, 'Ustad, let's play some duets now.' Sometimes he shakes the keyword's limbs until they're about to snap off; then he sits on its chest in his silk-embroidered kurta and delicate waistcoat, and plops his harmonium on top as well. When it tries to get up, he kisses it, licks it, and makes it lie down again, 'Stay close to my side, the night has just begun.' And finally the rare moment comes when this lover of music puts his tongue in the word's mouth in such a way that the raga begins to scream, 'You put your tongue in my mouth / and pull my soul back from hell!' Then, finally, after many hours of manhandling it, he slaps it and lets it go, saying, 'Go away. This time I'm letting you go. Next time don't show your face around here.'

If you care for your heart and soul, don't come into my throat.

Oh, You Mean from That Perspective ...

Basharat was hired as the Urdu teacher, but because of a shortage of teachers he was forced to teach just about every subject except theology, and that was because the head imam at the main mosque in Dhiraj Ganj had issued a religious decree stating that if the theology teacher happened to have a dog at home then the entire class would have to wash themselves properly after class! Basharat was very weak in mathematics, geometry, and English, but he wasn't worried at all because he had learned how to teach from his own teacher Master Fakhir Hussain. Master Fakhir Hussain's self-professed subject was history, but he would often have to teach Master Mendi Lal's English class. Master Mendi Lal's kidneys gave him fits, as well as his grammar. It was noticeable that he never made it to school whenever he was scheduled to teach grammar to the ninth- or tenth-grade classes. Apparently his kidneys were suffering from grammar! All the teachers were anxious about teaching any subject but their own. Master Fakhir Hussain was the only teacher always ready to tackle anything. He had got his BA on the 'Bhatinda,' or Munshi Fazil, track, which is to say he didn't know English grammar at all. If he'd wanted, he could have spent the entire hour cracking jokes or dispensing life lessons. But his conscience wouldn't let him waste time. Or, like the other teachers, he could have busied the students by giving dictations. But doing that was beneath the dignity of his oceanic knowledge and the duties of scholarship.

So the heavy stone that others kissed and moved on from, he put on his back and jumped with it into the ocean of knowledge. First, he lectured on the importance of grammar; he emphasized that just as the tabla is the basis for Hindustani vocal music, and curse words are the basis of conversation, thus grammar is the basis of the English language: if the students wanted to excel, then they would have to master grammar. Master Fakhir Hussain's English was like a building, a unique specimen of architectural art, and one of the seven Wonders of the Ancient World. I mean, there was no foundation at all. And for the most part there was no roof. Where there was a roof, he was holding it up with his legs like a bat hanging upside down. In those days, English was taught in Urdu, and so where Master Fakhir Hussain's English was collapsing, he propped it up with Urdu couplets. He was a very skilled, experienced teacher. He got through the most problematic situations without it affecting him at all. For instance, he might ask the students to parse something. Or he might resolve to ask them only the simplest possible questions. Once he wrote 'TO GO' on the blackboard and then asked the boys, 'OK, then, someone tell me—what is this?' One boy raised his hand, 'A simple infinitive!' He nodded his head approvingly, 'Exactly right.' But then he saw that another boy still had his hand up. He asked, 'Is there anything wrong?' The boy answered, 'No, sir. It's a noun infinitive.' Master Fakhir Hussain answered, 'Oh, you mean from that perspective.' But then he saw that the smartest boy in class still had his hand raised. He said, 'You still haven't put down your hand. What is it? Please speak up.' He said, 'It's a gerundial infinitive, but not a reflexive verb. Nesfield's grammar says so.' And with this, it was clear to him that

He was voyaging across uncharted waters.

He said in a calm and understanding way, 'Oh, you mean from that perspective.' Then he saw that the fluent English-speaking boy who had gone to an English-medium school had his hand up. He said, 'Well? Well? Well?' The boy said, 'Sir, I am afraid this is an intransitive verb.' So he said, 'Oh, you mean from that perspective.' But he didn't understand the idiomatic expression 'I am afraid,' and so he said to the boy in a tone full of love, 'But, my dear, what's there to be afraid of?'

He always said that the door to knowledge should be left propped open. But he himself had never gone through it! Find me a teacher nowadays for whose ignorance you feel any love!

Master Fakhir Hussain was the last specimen of our simple-hearted ancestors and their generations of witty teachers. Although his knowledge was never 'presently at liberty' to be divulged, he was always up for any challenge.

Basharat often says, 'Master Fakhir Hussain couldn't hide his ignorance from even no-good students like me. I've met important intellectuals, but if you give me the choice, I'd prefer to learn from Master Fakhir Hussain. Sir, he was a real man. He wasn't a book. He taught you about life.'

6.

People Say You're a Sayyid, but I've Never Met a Sayyid like You

I will leave it to you to imagine all the disgraces that Basharat underwent. In these circumstances, Basharat got through things as best he could. Soon enough it was nearing time for the school's annual December function, and the preparations were so time-consuming and rigorous that not only could Moli Mujjan not find the time to present the teachers with their back pay but he also didn't bother lying about it. December was the season for yearly community functions;

duck hunting; sending Christmas fruit-baskets to important officials; kite-flying; eating heat-giving, aphrodisiac foods; and becoming disappointed in their results. On the thirtieth of November, when Moli Mujjan sent for him, Basharat thought that perhaps the meeting was contrived to give him his back pay in private so that the other teachers wouldn't find out. But as soon as he got there, Moli Mujjan said, 'In your poetry, why don't you write on the behalf of your community instead of declaring what you want to do with others' wives and daughters? What did our Maulana Hali of Panipat* say about poetry like that?' (He snapped his fingers trying to remember.) 'What was that couplet? The one about toilets?'

Basharat recited reluctantly, 'Those filthy, sullied couplets and qasidahs / Even a stinking toilet smells better.'

His Wife and Maulana Hali's Shared Faults

When Basharat recited the couplet, Moli Mujjan shouted, 'God bless you! God gave you the ability to write poetry. Please use it. For the

---

* *Our Maulana Hali*: He called Hali and Sir Syed Ahmed Khan 'our Maulana Hali' and 'our Sir Syed.' There was a reason. He pronounced Sir Syed's name with an izafat, so, 'Sir-e-Syed.' He considered Hali to be one of his own, and Sir Syed to be his peer and equal. When the teachers, or someone with ulterior motives, called him Dhiraj Ganj's Sir Syed, Moli Mujjan felt that Sir Syed would have been honoured by this comparison. He also had the following edge over Sir Syed: whereas in the case of Sir Syed's college fund, his treasurer embezzled money because of Sir Syed's negligence, in the case of Moli Mujjan, his control was so strict that he wouldn't allow anyone but himself to embezzle. And in the case of Maulana Hali, he saw three connections. One, Hali, like him, wore a scarf. Two, Hali, like him, felt his people's suffering. Three, Hali, like his first wife, was from Panipat. And it seemed true as well because after his second marriage, a civil war had broken out inside his family and his life itself became the Battle of Panipat (one long battle) in which the female elephants (the women) always won!

annual function, can't you write a good poem for the orphans? You should mention the insensitivity of the Muslim community, the contributions of Muslims to science, Sir-e-Syed's legacy, the peace and tranquility brought about by British rule, the importance of charity, the conquest of Spain, and the County Treasurer's good work. Let me hear you recite it beforehand. There's not much time.'

Basharat answered, 'I'm sorry. I only write ghazals. You can't write about all that in a ghazal.'

Moli Mujjan got irritated, 'I'm sorry—are ghazals good only for declaring what you want to do with others' wives and daughters? Listen here. Last year, the Urdu teacher was fired just because of this. Like you, he too wrote poetry. I told him that important folks were coming for the awards ceremony. Upon the arrival of each donor or VIP, the orphanage band was going to play for five minutes. I wanted him to come up with something stirring to illuminate the orphans' dire straits, as well as the orphanage's social benefits and its good work. I said, "You have a good voice. Sing the poem." The very day of the awards ceremony, he came to me whining and full of excuses. He said, "I tried and tried, but I couldn't think of anything. These days I'm not feeling it." I asked, "What the hell do you mean?" He said, "I'm not feeling inspired." I said, "What? This is too much. Are you telling me that I'm going to have to start keeping tabs on each and every good-for-nothing employee?" He said, "I'm very embarrassed. I'll find something appropriate to read from another poet's work." I said, "OK, no problem. That will work." But, my God! He really went too far. In front of the entire audience, he read almost every single godforsaken line of our Maulana Hali of Panipat's "The Supplication of the Widow." He was standing next to me on the dais. I tried everything to get him to stop—I winked at him, I nudged him with my elbow, I cleared my throat loudly, I tried everything. In the end, I pinched his right hip, but he turned his left hip toward me and went on. It was very embarrassing for the school. Everyone was laughing behind their hankies. But he was turned toward the heavens and crying on the behalf of the souls of widows! One itinerate singer, through whom I had delivered the invitations, said that the asshole had actually added two or three modulations in raag malkauns. People must have thought that I was about to open up a home for widows and so was using Maulana Hali as an excuse. Afterwards, I scolded him, and he said, "I looked through every single poetry book I had, but there was nothing on orphans. The odd thing was that even Mir Taqi Mir, who was orphaned as a boy, had written masnavis in praise of a dog's mother, and even for a cat named Mohini, but nothing, not a single line, for poor orphans! So too Mirza Ghalib has written qasidahs, sehras, and couplets in praise of bread made from chickpea flour, as well as a domni dancer, and betel nuts (he went so far as to compare worthless betel nuts to the "tits of a fairy"), but he didn't write even one couplet on orphans, or at least in *Nuskha-e-Hamidia*. When I had read through all my books, I realized suddenly that orphans and widows are exactly the same. Their problem is the same, their suffering is the same. With these things in mind, I humbly chose to read 'The Supplication of the Widow.' It's a masterpiece. For three years running, there were questions on it on the entrance exam." And so, with these things in mind, I fired this masterpiece. But then the bastard filed a report against me with the inspector of schools, saying that I thought that Hali was obscene, and, moreover, that on five occasions I had made him bring me bathwater in a bucket. It was a total falsehood! I must have done that fifteen or twenty times! And it was also a lie that I always asked for it in a bucket. He brought the water sloshing over the sides of a terracotta water pot. And about my bathing, he jealously cast aspersions upon its innocence. Anyway, such feeble blows amounted to nothing. But now the Department of Education has written to me, asking for a reply mail: "What objection could you have to Maulana Hali's *Musaddas* and his 'The Supplication of the Widow' when the government has made them a part of the curriculum? Please highlight the sections you find objectionable." But now that you've come, you can write back to them for me. But the objections should be written in such a way that it will be impossible for them to respond. And please find a couple errors in his language. After all, he was from Panipat. You can't cure him of that. My wife is also from there. If you talk to her, you'll see through all his linguistic pretensions.'

By Hook or by Crook

Maulvi Muzaffar's weaknesses were as clear as day, and his strengths were hidden from view. He was much smarter, and much craftier, than Basharat could have guessed and, in the end, could stomach. He wasn't a total idiot. He was an experienced man, he could read people's faces, he was connected with the rich and powerful, and he was strict. His daily life was simple, and in this simplicity there was a sort of craftiness. Except for a second marriage, he indulged in nothing. He was gullible; he didn't keep his promises. But he never gave up. For ten years or more, he had found a way to keep the school running. His code of conduct allowed every sort of cheating. To see the problems in his way of running things, you didn't have to be an oracle or a savant. They were obvious. But most people wouldn't have been able to get done what he got done. He often said, 'Son, sometimes you have to bend the rules.' But the problem with people like this is that once you bend the rules, you never stop. And, if you ask me, I would say that these people like bending the rules more than anything else. Even when these men point to heaven, there's something crooked about it.

7.

Widow's Curry

The teachers were told that the school's finances were in a bad way. They were implored to open their hearts and give donations to the school so that they could collect their salary. In his half year of work, Basharat had got exactly sixty rupees, which had been entered in the school's accounting books as a no-interest loan. Now he was reluctant to ask for his salary because he didn't want his loan to grow. But while his back salary grew, Moli Mujjan's tone of voice grew more silken and his conversations, more circumlocutious. One day, Basharat halt-ingly asked about the money, and Moli Mujjan said, 'Son, think of me like your dad. I can't figure out what you'd do with so much money in a little hayseed town like this. You're a bachelor. Having so much cash lying around while you live alone is risky business. At night I'm scared for you. Sultana Daku is wreaking havoc around here.'

Anyway, his demand had one result and that was that every day Moli Mujjan started sending over a pot of watery yogurt.

The County Treasurer never paid him, but from time to time he gave him a basket of spinach or chickpeas, or a piece of deer meat, or sometimes a big jar of rasawal pudding or some lumps of fresh jaggery. On Eid, he gave Basharat a pot of Sandela laddoos, and on Bakrid, the head of a goat buck in heat. At the end of the summer, he gave him four watermelons in a worn-down gunnysack, and, as Basharat was taking them home, they kept spilling out upon his each and every step. When he tried to catch one, the others rolled away. By the time he had got halfway there, they had all split open, and so he left the gunnysack next to a roadside well and went home. A bull freed onto the open road by Pundit Jugal Kishore in the memory of his father started licking the watermelon juice with great relish until a sexy young cow came by and turned his attention from something good to something better.

During the January rains, when Basharat's thatched roof started to leak, the County Treasurer arranged for two bullock carts of small bundles of thatching straw, reed mats for lining the ceiling, and he conscripted four thatchers as well—and all, free of charge. The entire region's thatched roofs had gone black from the sun, fire-smoke, and rain. Only Basharat's thatch was golden. After it rained, the sun's rays seemed to be showering gold coins on top of it. Also, the County Treasurer sent a gunnysack of finely carded cotton for a blanket, and a pillow stuffed with down on whose cover Nazo had embroidered a rose. (Basharat slept on this pillow upside down—facedown, with his nose and lips on top of the flower.) The County Treasurer had impounded a rebellious farmer's milch goat in the Kanji House for two weeks under the pretext that it was a stray. When the price of feeding it surpassed its actual price, Basharat was handed its leash and told it was his. But he didn't accept for two reasons. One, he said that he had drunk so much watery yogurt and eaten so much widow's curry* that his eyes had grown yellow and his poetry, weak. He couldn't have any more liquidy food. Two, while he could produce poetry and fulfil his teaching duties without bread or money, a goat wouldn't be able to produce milk in that condition, and it would be hard pressed to produce even goat droppings.

The King of Flab

When Basharat complained that he had to walk three miles in the bright sun to reach school, the County Treasurer ordered that he be given a mule for transport. He had bought a stubborn mule at an army auction. Now, in its old age, it was good only for humiliating head-strong Jats, Chamar leather-workers who refused to work for free, and farmers who didn't give free milk and cuts of their harvests: they would

---

* Widow's curry: A sort of curry without little doughballs in it.

have their faces smeared with soot, and then they would be planted on the mule's back to parade through town. Trailing after them would be a rabble of drums and cymbals so that the mule would buck and startle. Once, a hated grass-cutter—who hemmed and hawed about handing over his weekly supply of grass—fell from it, broke his back, and was left completely paralysed. Basharat thought it was more dignified and safer to walk. It would have been a real pain in the ass to walk the three miles if Lord Wellesley hadn't been there to accompany him. He would talk to the dog on the way to and from school. And he would reply on the dog's behalf. But as soon as he thought of Nazo, his fatigue and irritation disappeared. His stride automatically grew longer.

He continued teaching the County Treasurer's naughty sons up till the incident that I'll recount later. He was known as Mr Teacher throughout town. And, in this role, he was welcomed everywhere. When people came to the County Treasurer's hoping for his help, they would even pet Lord Wellesley. From eating the milk and jelabis that the County Treasurer had received as a bribe, the dog had become so fat and lazy that now he only wagged his tail. He had grown scared to bark. His fur had become as shiny as the coats of racehorses. Throughout town, he was now called the King of Flab. But those jealous of Basharat called him the County Treasurer's Tipu! In the winter, Nazo styled a coat for Lord Wellesley from an old waistcoat of hers, and so people stroked the dog's new coat and treated him very well. Moli Mujjan had the bad habit of barging into people's classrooms while they were teaching to see if they were teaching well or not, but he never went into Basharat's classroom because Lord Wellesley was always standing watch outside.

As Basharat grew more experienced, he was asked to be the County Treasurer's helper on hunting trips, and so Lord Wellesley learned how to swim out and retrieve wounded ducks from lakes. The County Treasurer had asked on several occasions to be given the dog. Each time, Basharat motioned to himself and the dog, 'This dog of yours, along with my dog, is your slave. Why would you want to bother with walking him and dealing with his pee and poop?' When the County Treasurer had a special collar ordered from Lucknow and placed around the dog's neck, the dog started to be treated as though he were among the king's elect, and Basharat started to walk around town with an air of pride. But there was no doubt that the dog was a good breed because his grandfather, Tipu the Elder, had been a pointer raised by a judge on the Allahabad High Court. When he had left for England, he had given his dog to his reader. Lord Wellesley was his offspring, but in Dhiraj Ganj he was suffering humiliation and disgrace in each and every alley.

Moli Mujjan hated Lord Wellesley. He said, 'First of all, he's a dog. Even if he was Ashab-e-Kahaf's dog, he'd still be a dog. Also, he's been trained to bite only respectable people!' There's no doubt that he seemed much more dear when he was barking at Moli Mujjan. He had been trained so well that on Basharat's command he would bring his ruler from the staff room. Moli Mujjan said that once he had seen the filthy beast carrying the attendance register in his mouth! (But he probably didn't say anything at the time because he was scared of the County Treasurer, rabies too. A Chinese sage once said that before you throw anything at a dog, find out who its owner is.)

With respect to manners and habits, Lord Wellesley was entirely unlike other dogs. When a stranger came to the house, he didn't bark at all. But when this person got up to leave, the dog wouldn't let him go. He would grab the man's leg in his vice-like jaws and not let go.

The Teachers Have Eaten Up the Orphanage!

Gradually Moli Mujjan stopped offering even no-interest loans. He started avoiding people. One day, covered in chalk, carrying his eraser, and with his attendance register underneath his arm, Basharat was leaving his classroom when Moli Mujjan pulled him by the sleeve into his office and started in on him. Probably it was an instance of 'the best defense is a good offense.' He said, 'Basharat, son, it's been a while since you've not got your salary, and yet you don't seem bothered. The school has fallen into dire straits. Think of something. The teachers are paid out of the orphanage's charity fund. The teachers have eaten up the orphanage! I'm scared that you all will suffer the wrath of God.' This lit a fire under Basharat. He said, 'It's almost been eight months since I started here. I've got all of sixty or seventy rupees. I've had to ask for a money order twice from home. After all this, if there's still some risk of incurring God's wrath, then you can have this job back.' And right then and there he handed over his supplies. I mean, he gave Moli Mujjan the eraser and the attendance register.

Moli Mujjan suddenly changed tactics. He gave the eraser back to Basharat, wiped his hands, and said, 'The sixty or seventy rupees that you're telling me you've got has come straight from the charity and alms fund, and so the orphans have had to eat less. And this is how you're paying me back? Sir-e-Syed also had to go through such trials near the end of his life, but he couldn't survive them. I won't go easily. Well, anyway, try to have some patience. God willing, I'll put everything right by selling off the Bakrid hides. You know how things are going for the orphanage. The poor souls climb onto each other's shoulders to steal a little bit of kerosene from the city streetlights so that they can read at night. The city workers have hung the lanterns from poles as high as palm trees so that no one can use them to read. Someone should ask them, "Have you hung up lanterns or the sun? Do you expect the innocent boys to stitch your fathers' shrouds in such dim light?" Three or four years ago there was an orphan who fell from a pole. The bones in his hands and in his legs snapped like a raw cucumber. Abdus Salam, the bonesetter, tried his best to put them in place, but they started to suppurate. I took him to Kanpur, and his leg was amputated right here above the knee. His right hand was fixed, but only in the way that relatives patch up their relations after a fight. It bent like a bow. If he'd attached strings from both ends, he could have played it like a sarangi. The crippled boy gradually fell in with the wrong crowd. When I took him by the ear and threw him out, he went to Kanpur and joined up with a band of beggars. When he came back, he tried to lead the other boys astray, "Hey, you should jump off a light pole too. Life's so fun now. I don't have to clean dishes. I don't have to shout my lessons from the top of my lungs. I don't have to massage anyone's feet at night. I don't have to recite every day the ninety-nine names of God on chickpeas for someone's funeral, and then eat them myself. I don't have to brush my teeth with charcoal every morning. To smoke a cigarette, I don't have to go over and over to the outhouse. I can smoke as much as I want, and I can go around puffing smoke like a train. In short, it's heaven here. If you do something bad, no one's going to say anything." The elderly say that his manners marked him as a bastard. Anyway, I was saying that this is your school. Your orphanage. I'm not blind. Even a blind person could see how much of yourself you're putting into your job. You'll go far in life. If you continue to work hard like this, then, God willing, you'll become the principal in twenty-five years or so. I'm not an educated man. I can't become principal. You see what shape the school's in. The number of donors has fallen so low that if Sir-e-Syed were alive he would slap both himself and Nawab Mohsin-ul-Mulk on the forehead. But you all spill your bile on me. What can one man do alone? No man is an island. What we need to do now is to get the nobility, the rich folks, the landowners, and the surrounding towns to know about us. We need to get them all here. Showing just one orphan's face to them is better than a thousand sermons and a hundred thousand ads. We're a virtuous institution. We're not like a circus or

411

one of Agha Hashr's plays. People don't care about us. Please believe me, since the teachers haven't been paid, I haven't had one night of solid sleep. I've been talking nonstop with people to get their advice. I've asked you several times to figure out how I can pay you ASAP. After thinking about it a lot, I've decided to act on your advice alone. To put us on the map, it's absolutely vital that we host a terrific poetry festival. People still call Dhiraj Ganj a village. Just yesterday I got a postcard. It was addressed to "Dhiraj Ganj Village." Dhiraj Ganj Village! God! I couldn't stand it. For the longest time, people thought Aligarh was a village until the bioscope showed up, and traffic accidents claimed their first victim.'

About the division of labour, he clarified that Basharat would be in charge only of bringing the poets, seeing them off, arranging for their food and lodging, doing the publicity, and arranging for a venue. The rest he would do. That is, he would be the Master of Ceremonies!

8.

Dhiraj Ganj's First and Last Poetry Festival

The date of the poetry festival was set. Basharat was entrusted with all sorts of responsibilities, which were actually different types of punishment: inviting the noteworthy citizens of Dhiraj Ganj; setting the misra-e-tarah; choosing the poets themselves; making sure all the poets got on the last train from Kanpur (and taking care of them on the trip); getting them back to the station for the first train immediately after the festival; arranging for the poets to be well taken care of (for free) from before the official beginning up to when they recited their ghazals; and other types of responsibilities like these. Moli Mujjan gave Basharat ten rupees for train and horse-drawn cart round-trip fares for the poets and for himself, for food and lodging in Dhiraj Ganj, and for paan, cigarettes, and miscellaneous expenses; and he urged him to return all the unused money, as well as all receipts and an itemized list of expenses, the day after the festival. He also instructed him in no uncertain terms that he himself was to buy the poets each a fifty-paise ticket and that he was not to give them cash to purchase their own tickets. Basharat was about to ask about pocket money and gifts for the poets when Moli Mujjan solved this problem. He told Basharat, 'Make sure to ask them to give a charitable donation to the school and orphanage. If they're not embarrassed to recite poetry, then why would they hesitate to give money to a good cause? If you don't screw things up, we should get some money from each. But whatever we're going to get has to come before the start of the festival. After they've recited their ghazals, they'll never give anything. The early bird gets the worm. And if any poet says they can't afford fifty paise, then, by God, he should be admitted to the orphanage too. Why is he sitting around doing nothing in Kanpur?'

Readers will wonder why there is no mention of the principal in this talk of the preparations underway. There's a very good reason for this. When Moli Mujjan was hiring a principal, he did so upon one condition: that the principal should in no way interfere in the school's business.

Call it vanity or inexperience, but the misra-e-tarah that Basharat chose for the festival was from one of his own new ghazals. The largest advantage of this was that he would become famous from no effort on his own part. The second benefit was that he wouldn't have to rack his brains to come up with another ghazal for the festival. It tickled him pink to think that many famous poets would have to write ghazals based upon his own line. He thought, 'They'll toil for hours. From time to time, they'll stamp their feet. They'll grab at their hearts. They'll grab at their hair. And then as soon as they finish, they'll get together and start reciting.' He invited eighteen poets, including Jauhar

Chughtai of Allahabad, Kashif Kanpuri, and Nushoor Wahidi. They agreed out of love for Basharat and their desire to encourage him, but also because Basharat's job was on the line. Nushoor Wahidi and Jauhar Illahabadi had also been Basharat's teachers. He didn't give his line to them. Instead, he asked them to write anything they wished. It seemed that the only criteria he had used to select the rest of the poets was that he shouldn't suspect that they were better poets than him.

Who Invented the Ikka?

He scrunched all eighteen poets into two horse-drawn carts and brought them to the railway station in Kanpur. Upon reading that eighteen poets were packed like sardines into two horse-drawn carts, whichever readers think I'm exaggerating have probably never seen a horse-drawn cart or a poet. (This was in Kanpur. In Aligarh, one horse-drawn cart would have been enough.) For the sake of readers, I'll describe the construction of this unique and amazing conveyance. First, take a board on which you clean the bodies of dead people and cut it into a rectangle. Then stick onto it two different sizes of rectangular wheels, hoping that the wheels will render Aligarh's streets smooth and the wheels themselves will become round. The board should be about six feet or so above the street's potholes so that the passengers' dangling feet and the passers-by's heads will be at the same level. The diameter of the small wheel should be five feet. The spokes used for the wheel should look like the sun's rays, and they should be strong enough so that a passenger can use them to boost himself onto the main seating area. (This will also set the wheel in motion.) Then, there should be a yoke of two pieces of bamboo from which you attach an old, starving horse whose ribs the passengers can count even from a distance so as to satisfy themselves that it has a complete set. There's your ikka. Its four hazardous parts will be mentioned again later.

Like nihari, rasawal, smoked rice firni, idioms, monsoon dishes, swings in mango groves, arhar dal, silk comforters, long, pleated skirts, dopalli hats, the folk heroes Alha and Udal, witty poems, so too ikkas are part of the special patrimony of UP. During my stay in Aligarh from 1943 to 1945, I also rode in ikkas (and suffered disgrace doing so). I think a horse must have invented them. That's because the ikka has this one design trick: the passengers have to work harder than the horse; the weight of the extra passengers doesn't rest on the horse but rather on the other passengers on whose laps they are sitting.* You must have seen how in Western ballet, there are many delicate moments when the ballerinas stand balanced on their tiptoes. All of their weight rests on their big toes, but on their faces, instead of a grimace, there is a smile. I saw such a happy spectacle, or spectacular happiness, in Aligarh when the university's boys would use their thumbs to pad themselves against the ikka's exposed nails as they sat between heaven and earth going in circles around the girls' college. It's said that the secret to happiness in life is that once you've found a space big enough to stick in your thumb, you should stuff in your entire body.

Collision with a Road-grater

The passengers sat coiled amidst one another's curves. When the ikka, complete with horse and passengers, got stuck in an open manhole, then, according to folks from Delhi, 'the fruit got all squished.' The passengers' limbs were entangled and strung together like shirtsleeves and drawstrings in a washing machine. When someone had to

---

* Hazrat Josh Malihabadi says about ikkas that 'the whole lot of them is so bad that if you put Alexander the Great in one, he would look like a countryside pimp.' Setting aside this exaggerated way of talking, we see that the sticking point and ultimate object of contempt is not the pimp nor the prostitute, but the countryside!

get out, everyone else had to unfasten their locks and chains, and only then did this adventurous soul become freed enough from that bony vicegrip that he could jump six feet down while still cross-legged. Body parts got so mixed up that if someone's calf itched, they would scratch it till it bled without remit, and yet the itch would still remain. And that was because it was someone else's calf. If an ikka got into an accident, nothing and no one was the worse for wear. That's because, for one, the ikka didn't have any parts whose breaking or losing would matter at all. And, second, the offending car or bike would slide beneath the ikka's bottom so smoothly that not even the horse would notice anything amiss. Sometimes the entire mass of passengers would fall to hit the ground with a thud like in one big rugby scrum. I saw something like this with my own eyes. It was Aligarh, 1944. It was during World War II. I had to go out to find a razorblade, which was rare in those days. I went from store to store asking in vain. Suddenly in the middle of the road I saw seven or eight black parachutes landing. I was told that an ikka carrying girls from the girls' college had had a head-on collision with a road-grater, and, with the help of their air-filled burqas, the girls were descending safely from the ikka's great height. Moreover, boys wearing fezzes and shervanis buttoned up to their Adam's apples were standing there, ready to lift up the wounded, perform first (non-)medical aid, offer human sympathy and service to fallen humanity, and proffer themselves as potential lovers.

To Start with a 100-Horsepower Curse

In the back of an ikka, there were so many passengers crammed in together that should the horse have tripped or passed out from fatigue, even then the horse wouldn't have fallen to the ground: the weight at the back-end of the cart was so great that it would keep him propped up. There was no custom of putting cushions inside the ikka. The wood inside the cart shone more brilliantly than any of the most expensive pieces of wood because there was a very different method of polishing. Every day, for at least ten or eleven hours, the wood had been polished by the asses of graduate students. (Undergraduates sat on the laps of graduate students.) If anyone had used cushions, at the very first jerk the passengers would have slid out of the ikka as though on a flying carpet and then land on the heads of the passers-by. Passengers weren't allowed to grab ahold of the ikka from outside and so get carried along. This would have slowed it down. It would be wrong to say that the ikka was powered by the horse's strength because what happened was that the ikka driver would get down, push from behind, and issue a 100-horsepower curse to start it; only from this would it wobble into action. The horse had no ability to stop this at all.

'Khushamdeed!' ['Welcome!'] … Correct Spelling

The Dhiraj Ganj school-kids had decorated the train platform with colourful little flags in the same way that a careless mother ties a bright ribbon in her girl's hair without first washing her face. As soon as each poet descended from the train, a marigold garland was draped around his neck, and he was handed a single rose and a glass of boiled milk, which, once it was in hand, he gasped, 'Where should I put it?' The greeters would ask the newcomers, who had come from Kanpur, which was twenty-five miles and one hour away, 'How was the journey? How's the weather in Kanpur? After you wash up and rest, you'll feel better.' In reply, the guests would say, 'What time is the evening prayer here? Dhiraj Ganj is famous for its hospitality. What souvenirs are good? How many chickens can you get for a rupee? Are Muslims here as poor as they are in the rest of India?'

The two o'clock train had brought to Dhiraj Ganj the eighteen poets and five groupies, whom one poet had brought with him. The

Light of Islam Orphanage Band had started playing three hours before the train's arrival, but as soon as it arrived, sometimes the drummers would stop, sometimes the flute players, sometimes the trumpeters (whose instruments looked like elephant trunks), and sometimes all three sections would stop at once. Only the bandmaster continued waving his baton. The reason was that these instrumentalists had never before seen a train engine up close. Seeing it, they fell into a trance during which they forgot to play their instruments. With the engine stopped so close to them, they could see its each and every mysterious detail: the whistle; the coal shovel; the sharp odour, like that of Western medicine, coming from the sizzling, crackling coals in the boiler; then next to the fire's flames, the Anglo-Indian driver's beet-red face and the blue tattoo of his wife on his wrist; the black handkerchief wrapped around the Muslim coal-stoker's head and the coal's zebra lines on his face; and the long iron rods that connected the wheels to the engine that looked exactly like the boys' arms did when they played, moving them back and making the 'chuk chuk' sounds of the train. Steam sprayed across the boys' faces. The boys saw the milky smoke released from the engine's chimney turn to the colour of ashes and then to a thick black. They liked the smoke's bitter taste in their throats. The hissing black dragon of curling smoke passed beyond the last compartment and rose into the sky with a restless quivering motion. The band's boys were silent, completely silent, as they wanted to see up close, as up close as possible, the train's whistle as it released its steam. When they had to go, they wanted to leave their eyes at the station. If you had wanted a band of boys to play music, it would have been best to get a train without an engine.

The poets were picked up at the station in two bullock carts. Every ten minutes, they asked the drivers why they were still so far from town. The bullocks' horns were adorned with decorative silver caps, and bells hung from their necks. One had the word 'khushamad-eed' [flattery] written in henna on its side. It was being punished for this incorrect spelling. I mean, the driver was repeatedly poking the bullock with a cattle prod on the first letter of this word. In my opinion, all banners, welcome gates, and processional arches made to greet politicians and VIPs should have this spelling because that's the real reason behind all the fuss. Behind the carts, the PE teacher led the teachers en masse with the fathers of the schoolboys right behind them. Then in front of this group the band was playing, and in front of the band there was a boy holding the Light of Islam Orphanage's black flag that read, 'O, heaven, we're not scared of evil,' and also something to the effect that the people of the earth should start worrying about their souls and give generously to the orphanage. This was the first flag in the history of flags to scold and beg at the same time. Otherwise, the ignorant are content to decorate flags with several colourful stripes and patterns. At the very back of the procession, Lord Wellesley was leading a running throng of all the town's butt-naked children and dogs. When several music connoisseurs among the poets objected to the band's music, the PE teacher told them that without the music, the dogs would be sure to set upon them.

O, Samdhin, Your Mare Is in the Chickpea Field!

One week previous to this, Basharat had instructed the bandmaster in the following manner: 'For God's sake! Don't play your foreboding, mournful crap. It's a celebration. Play something cheerful. You still have a week.' So they first played a song made famous on the gramophone of 1925:

My son, my son Jumma, please bring me some hot coals
Bring me some hot coals, and bring me tobacco
Bring me a little water
My son, my son Jumma, please bring me some hot coals

Then they played an even more cheerful tune from a famous record of His Majesty's Voice. It was a hit song in 1930 that everybody sang, including me:

> O, samdhin, your mare is in the chickpea field!

After providing this information, the next line had the abovementioned person being invited to the abovementioned place, that is, the chickpea field. I heard this song about fifty years ago when not only did I not have the foggiest notion what a samdhin was, but I had never even seen a chickpea field. It's clear that the unbridled mare went to the chickpea field because she was hungry for fresh green chickpeas, but it has remained a mystery to me what the man was doing in someone else's field. I still can't say with confidence who the song's main character is—the mare or the samdhin. The song's lines about rowdiness and moral conduct were such that it wasn't clear if they were intended for the mare or the samdhin. Other lines were so rough and ready that it seemed like the author was none other than some horse. But please keep in mind that although the mare had been missing since the morning, the samdhin was being called into the field in the evening. It wasn't clear whether the man was calling her there so that the two could ride together on the mare's back, or so that the three of them could eat chickpeas together.

Walk on These Very Rocks

When the procession of the eighteen poets passed in front of the school, a small cannon fired eighteen rounds to honour them. This was a small community cannon that was normally fired on the occasion of someone's birth or circumcision. As soon as it was fired, a raucous chorus of all the town's dogs, kids, crows, chickens, and peacocks rose up. And the old women said, startled, 'May religion awake, and apostasy abate.' The little cannon itself was so surprised by its firing that it kept recoiling back and forth for a while. The poets were being put up in well-off farmers' houses, and so the farmers came to the school to pick up their guests. One farmer brought a pony for transport and a little coconut hookah to pass the time on the way back. The handful of wealthy citizens in town didn't get along with Moli Mujjan, and so the poets' accommodations were at the houses of these well-off farmers, and these lodgings were sure to ruin their sleep for the night. It's one thing to romanticize country life in poems and novels and to praise its sincerity, simplicity, contentment, and natural beauty; but it's really not possible for a city intellectual to stay in a farmer's half-made house or some mud hut. Before you hug a farmer, you have to hug a bunch of things at once: their livestock; their drinking glasses smudged with his ghee-greasy fingerprints; the bread that they have cooked with the very hands that they just used to form dung cakes; their rough hands used to handling ploughs, sickles, and dirt; their hands smelling of love and onions; and their butter-greased moustaches.

If you can walk on these rocks, then you're invited.

9.

A Short Treatise in Praise and Condemnation of Prostitutes, or His Self-Defense

An Account Of The Origins Of Poetry And Children

For this countrified poetry festival—which, for Dhiraj Ganj, proved to be both quite memorable and its last—eighteen out-of-town poets were invited, and, in addition to those, thirty-three local poets showed up, invited or not. Among the out-of-towners, there were those who came despite the lack of money it promised because, after all, it was a village, and so they expected the festival organizers to give them some vegetables, baskets of dried fruits and harvest products, and a half dozen or so chickens in a leather bag. In Dhiraj Ganj, there were some mischievous young men who were notorious for having ruined a number of poetry festivals in the vicinity. Basharat had an unusual method for disciplining them. He had an old friend who after failing the final high-school exams for a handful of years had gotten sick of the examiners' stubborn unwillingness to acknowledge that he was a true gem and so had got a job in the Income Tax Department. He wanted to work there not just for its cathartic possibilities but also to punish the notorious department. He found the department's atmosphere just right for composing poetry. He liked his job so much that he wanted to keep it until he retired. He had a lot of children. He composed poetry anywhere and much too often. The birth of his poetry and his children was inspired by the same thing. I mean, he blamed the Fountain of Plenty (the Grace of God) for the arrival and abundance of both. He couldn't even write a simple sentence without adding rhyme and metre. Prose made him as uptight as poetry makes everyone else.

He wrote poetry, but he hated poetry festivals. He said, 'These days poetry and poetry appreciation are practiced in the same fashion. I mean, without understanding. I'm not even talking about the proper way to praise someone. Today people don't even know how to hoot properly. Poetry isn't fit for festivals. It's something to be read in solitude, then understood, repeated to oneself, and suffered through. If poetry is in a book, then no one can hurt the poet. I can show you not just one or two couplets but a couple hundred from Mir's *Collected Poems* that would result in the loss of his honour and his turban if he read them at a poetry festival today. He would also be lucky to return home with his head on his shoulders.' He remembered only these couplets of Mir. He remembered only those couplets of the other masters in which he perceived some flaw or another. Basharat got this friend to write a half dozen random lines that were then distributed to those notorious youths; they were asked to get ready to recite during the festival as well. And the trick worked. It's been observed that a poet who is expecting to get praised by other talentless poets will never hoot them off the stage. It's been said that the best way to stop thefts is to make the thief the police chief. In this, I see that in addition to the virtue that he won't let others steal, there's one more difference: the things that he had obtained with great difficulty through burglary in the middle of the night would now be brought (happily and willingly) as bribes to the police station by the homeowners themselves.

From Between the Lines to Between the Loins

Under the same ruse, Basharat had got Hakim Ahsanullah Tasleem to write five random ghazals on the promise that in the winter he, Basharat, would get the good doctor fifty starlings, twenty partridges, five green pigeons, and two geese for his witch's broth. And that on Bakrid, he would get him five castrated goats for half price in Dhiraj Ganj and send them on, as well as the brains of a hundred debauched male sparrows for his sparrow halva, and one dozen live black desert scorpions (which he would catch himself) for the doctor's aphrodisiac for the rulers and nobility of the princely states.* Hakim Ahsanullah Tasleem was not only the special doctor for the prostitutes of Mool

---

* I asked Basharat, 'Man, why did you ever agree to catch alive so many different animals, including birds and poisonous insects, for him?' He said, 'When I didn't intend to look for any of them, the more the merrier.' Then he reassured me that he hadn't lied by mistake, but rather, by habit.

Ganj, but he was also a poet who wrote ghazals for them to sing. When a prostitute was pregnant, he would write smoothly flowing ghazals so that at no point would she have to stop abruptly and shake her hips. In any case, back in those days, prostitutes mostly sung the verses of Dagh, and beggars sang those of Bahadur Shah Zafar. If he took a fancy to a particular prostitute, he would fill in her name in the ghazal's last, signatory couplet and give her the poem in full. Some prostitutes, for example, Mushtari, Dulari, and Zehra, would get famous poets to write them ghazals, and they received praise not just for their singing but for writing the ghazals themselves. Hakim Sahib also corrected their pronunciation. The rest went beyond what he could correct; I mean, all those things couldn't be helped. In those days, it was a literary fashion to try to reform prostitutes and their worshippers. Actually, society wasn't obsessed with this; it was just writers: whether these works purged society of this evil or not, the writers themselves enjoyed writing about these women. The recounting of sin is more delicious than the act itself, as long as the narration is longwinded and the narrator himself is weak in both body and mind. Émile Zola's *Nana*, Ruswa's *Umrao Jan Ada*, Toulouse-Lautrec and Degas' paintings of prostitutes and brothels are the first moments of sexual realism; whereas Qari Sarfaraz Hussain's *The Beautiful Beloved* [*Shahid-e-Rana*] was the first example of preachy exoticism that was then taken up by Qazi Abdul Ghaffar in his grandiloquent but totally ignorant romance *Laila's Letters*, which was furthered by the affected simplicity of Ghulam Abbas' *Anandy*, and then Manto's apparently rough realism.*

Yet these are all inverted romanticism. For us, stories about prostitutes

---

* Well, Manto was a boozer. That poor soul had neither the time nor the energy, neither the body nor the mind, to circumambulate that alley of sin. He had as much personal experience with brothels as Riyaz Khairabadi had with booze. Maybe for us personal experience isn't that important.

are usually ones about *special* prostitutes. About them, childish wonderment, fanciful thoughts, rumours, and romantic notions (picked up from anyone, anywhere, and in whatever amounts) are lumped together and dumped onto the reader so that you start seeing parrots and mynas hopping around and chirping happily; and you can't find a real prostitute anywhere. Under the romantic debris, you can't even hear one prostitute's ankle-bells. The immature sentimentality of the acned faces of youth gives life to these myths and will keep the blood running warm in the veins of scholars for many years to come. The prostitute born in this City of Desire has thrown her chastity belt into the river and fears no one, not even the writer, not even herself.

From her head to the tips of her toes, good heavens, she's pure ice—

This started sixty or seventy years ago, but it's equally true today. The middle class considered prostitutes despicable and worth hating, but at the same time their mention gave rise to a vicarious pleasure. Using social reform and the issue of prostitution as an excuse, writers satisfied these contradictory bourgeois impulses. The poetry and fiction, but especially the fiction, of the first half of this century is a reflection of this changing love-hate relationship with prostitutes. It gave birth to a double meaning in which even reproach became an excuse for pleasure. Under the banner of social realism, the amount of praise that prostitutes got from Urdu fiction writers surpassed what they got from their nightly customers. But in the last thirty years, English fiction has stopped writing between the lines and now writes openly between the loins.

When the Gentleman Grew Old

In Mool Ganj, Waheedan Bai had a brothel where you could always find an old man passionately grinding spices on a slab. People said that thirty years ago he had come to the brothel after Friday prayers in order to tell Waheedan Bai to mend her ways. But back then this dish was at her spiciest, and so his mission continues unabated today:

My mission is endless, O wait for me!

By the time Waheedan Bai retired (she wasn't fit for her line of work anymore, anyway) and renounced her chronic sin, this gentleman's beard had grown white and extended to his belly button. Now he helped her daughters in the kitchen and in selecting their customers and their ghazals. The gentleman had grown old. Well, in 1931 when she went to Mecca on pilgrimage, he was the only representative of the nine hundred rats to accompany her.*

When a Daughter Was Born in a House

Hakim Ahsanullah Tasleem claimed that he had inherited his wealth, medical practice, and poetic talents. But he freely admitted that the first was much reduced. His father Hakim Ahtesham Hussain Rana had such a large estate in Kannauj that it couldn't fit onto one map! He mentioned this with great pride and exaggeration. Now he was in possession of the map, and moneylenders were in possession of the land. Hakim Ahsanullah Tasleem treated debauched royals, as well. He could tell which magnate it was just by looking at his pee. And as soon as he felt his pulse, he could tell from which brothel the magnate had caught which bug. It's understandable that if a boy was born at a brothel, his entire household would cry and carry on. Hakim Tasleem had a family recipe that ensured a baby girl would be born. This pow-

---

* Translators' note: A play on the idiom 'the cat went on pilgrimage after she ate ninety-nine rats.' This phrase is used when you have been sinning all your life, and then at the end of your life, you renounce sin and do something virtuous.

426

der was wrapped in the paan that was given to nightly VIPs. You can guess the efficacy of this powder by the fact that in Kanpur whenever a woman gave birth to a girl she began to pester her husband that he must have eaten paan at one of the hakim's brothels.

However beautiful and seductive a prostitute may be, Hakim Sahib was tempted only by her money. The prostitutes respected him a lot. The rumour was that they were eagerly awaiting his death so that they could build him a marble shrine where they would go every year to celebrate his anniversary in great style.

Monks' Fantasies

So again Mool Ganj. And prostitutes. This was Basharat's favourite topic of conversation, which our readers must already be thoroughly familiar with (and disgusted by). He always brings them up in even the most serious conversations, thereby ruining them. But it's certainly true that he's another sort of man:

He walks through the market, but buys nothing.

Just like some people with allergies suddenly come down with hives, prostitutes pop up with their ankle-bells jingling in his conversations, and that without regard to situation or circumstance. He prays tahajjud at three in the morning. Long ago he became a grandfather, but prostitutes haunt him. Once I scolded him, 'In the old tales, the souls of heroes and monsters would hide in the bodies of parrots. But, for you, in every story, every character's soul hides inside a prostitute!' He said, 'Forget about my stories. Have you seen any movie heroes praying nafils these days? Books are the same. It's no longer necessary to put in a prostitute if you want to talk about sex. A girl from a respectable family will do fine. Yet prostitutes still make fiction-readers and cinemagoers perk up like patients going for the big raisins in the hakim's witch's brew! Actually, you have to understand Unani medicine if you hope to understand prostitutes. And the opposite is also true. For us, Unani medicine and prostitutes are as necessary as they are reviled.'

And Basharat was right. Perhaps it's difficult to understand today. But, like forbidden pleasures are wont to do, prostitutes used to possess the minds of rich men. And that wasn't true just of that one age. It's said that the great emperor Aurangzeb wanted to get rid of the world's oldest profession and so announced that if prostitutes hadn't married by a certain date they would be forced into a boat and then sunk in the Jamuna. Most prostitutes preferred drowning over the trials of the kitchen, and they preferred the jaws of crocodiles over husbands whose lovemaking was like an obligatory prayer session. I mean, compulsorily, and with no passion and love! Only a few prostitutes reluctantly married.

> *All calamities are now passed, O Ghalib!*
> *Now only a hasty marriage remains ...*

Now just take a look, two hundred years later, at the *Tazkira-e-Ghausiya*. Its compiler, Maulvi Ismail Meruthi, quotes a true story about his most respected spiritual master and guru: 'One day, he said, "When I was staying in Zinat-ul-Masjid in Delhi, one dervish friend of mine—Yusuf Khan Kambalposh who wrote *The History of Yusuf, or, The Wonders of the West*, the first Urdu travel narrative about England—invited me to dinner. We left after the evening prayer. He took me to a brothel in Chandni Chowk and then disappeared. At first I thought that perhaps the food was being prepared. But then I thought that he had taken me there for no reason and then simply left. I thought, 'Why the hell did that good-for-nothing bring me here?' After a couple hours, he came back laughing, 'Sir, I left you here so you could overcome your qualms!' After that, he took me to his house and fed me."'

Please bear in mind that Kambalposh was a very free-spirited and whimsical person. This story is from the time when, in the company of his spiritual master, he experienced a transformation of heart. Just imagine—if this was his autumn, then how fun the spring of his life must have been!

Then, look at a thumbnail version of what came after this by one hundred and fifty years. When a poet like Josh—skilled, of noble birth, and of refined, nay, exquisite, taste—sketches a picture of the pleasures of life and its infinite happiness, then look at what magic his graceful pen gives rise to—

Life put her hands on her hips and started to sway and dance.

There's no harm in putting your hands on hips and starting to sway and dance, provided the hips are your own. Also, dancing like this should be part of your job description. It shouldn't be just for fun. I mean, what's objectionable to in someone putting your hands on your hips and dancing? But, if you dance like this, people will know your caste.

So Mool Ganj was the red-light district. People back then had just as bad morals as they do now, but their eyesight wasn't as bad, and so they didn't call the area with prostitutes the 'beauty market.' They called a whorehouse a whorehouse. Nowhere else in the world have the horrid cells of ugly prostitutes, who sell STDs along with their nasty bodies, been so glamorized. Later on, the phrase 'the beauty market' was popularized by writers who would never have touched a prostitute with a ten-foot pole. But personal experience was probably not needed. Riyaz Khairabadi wrote poems praising alcohol his whole life long, but his drinking never advanced past sherbet and fresh-squeezed lime juice. But it wasn't just then. Poets today write romantically about gallows, gibbets, hangmen, and nooses; you don't have to be hung to write about it. If you don't have the courage or the wherewithal to praise debauchery and to wander the alleys of the night, then 'lust sears its secret images into your heart.'

And the truth is that the images are much better. Why? Simply because they're imaginary! The frescoes and statues of Ajanta and Ellora's caves are their classical examples. The artists made such sexy, erotic bodies. And once they decided to make them sexy, they didn't stop at anything. The voluptuous bodies are carved with sensuous lines, so much so that it's hard to find one straight line anywhere on them. In fact, the noses aren't even straight! The sculptures of these sexy women and nymphs reveal the obsessions of the sculptors: lips as plump as orange slices; full breasts that made the sculptors themselves horny; curvaceous hips sporting a water pitcher that at every curvy step threatens to overspill its water—like the on-lookers' hearts that threaten to leap out of their bodies; waists that curl and twist amidst all these zigs and zags; bellies that look like the ocean's receding waves; and legs, which Sanskrit poets compared to the trunks of banana plants. Their knowing and shameless bodies, their desirable, exaggerated curves, and their beckoning breasts were all made by (and for) those horny celibate monks for whom sexuality was forbidden and who saw women only in their dreams. While they were dreaming, when a woman came close by, and they felt their blood begin to boil, then they immediately awoke, rubbed their eyes with the palms of their hands, and began to carve their dreams into the stone.

Dream-catchers

Compared to the art of these monks, the entire tradition of Western porn and erotic art seems childish and insipid. The bodacious narphal breasts* of these hourglass bodies—which ripened on the very

---

* Narphal: This word had been very common in Urdu for women's breasts, bodies, and beauty, but like many other beautiful words it also became a victim of

branches of desire and in the heat of the imagination—could only have been made by monks who, leaving their Yashodharas asleep, had come in search of truth and nirvana. But in the damp and dark caves where they spent their entire lives, and where they could only see their dreams, they cut into the stone to give life to their dreams, I mean, women! This wasn't the work of a couple years, or even a couple eons; rather, these enlightened ones spent a full thousand years making this very mithun kala art.* When all the statues were done, and each statue had achieved its dreamy form, then the sculptors stepped confidently outside the dark caves only to find that the sun of religion and truth had long since set and now there was nothing left but layer after layer of darkness. So, frightened by the darkness outside and its tumult, they put their hands over their eyes and rushed back to the familiar darkness.

The ascetics who were lost for centuries within the labyrinth of form and eroticism were made of dust, and to dust they returned. But their dreams remain. You won't find such dreamers, such wanderers and kidnappers of the soul, anywhere today.

> *Now there is no one in the world, O Ghalib,*
> *To mix reality with dreams…*

But look at what nonsense I've written! I started with Hakim Ahsanullah Tasleem, weaved my way through the brothels, and ended up in Ajanta and Ellora. But what can I do? This is how my elegant friend talks. He weaves seamless stories from the rays of the sun and moon.

Wahhabian puritanism and surly Nasikhism.
* Mithun kala: Readers shouldn't look up 'mithun' in the dictionary but instead read Rajender Singh Bedi's masterpiece of the same name. In that story, Bedi has cut through an entire flint mountain to sculpt an idol, and he has carved it with such skill and with such powerful blows that he never had to use his adze on the same spot twice. (I don't know the Urdu synonym for 'erotic art,' so I was forced to forge this new term.)

In this section, I've tried as far as possible to retain his words and his ADD style, with no additions or subtractions. He says to me, 'You can't guess how bad it was in my time—the suffocating atmosphere, the pious deprivations, and the horny piety. Between us, there lies a gap of a generation. Twenty years.'

And he's right: between our generations lies a prostitute.

10.

Who Stole the Show?

Setting aside Jauhar Illahabadi, Kashif Kanpuri and Nushoor Wahidi, it was very difficult to determine who should read first and who last, because of all the other poets, invited and local, everyone thought themselves equal to everyone else, and it was such a fierce tug-of-war that it was hard to say who was spouting the least absurd poetry, and so who would be asked to read last. But it was solved in the following manner: poets would recite in reverse alphabetical order. That meant that Yawar Naginvi would be hooted off the stage first. The problem with the correct alphabetical order was that Basharat's revered teacher, Jauhar Illahabadi, would then have to recite before him.

At the venue, there was a lot of confusion. Contrary to all expectation and forecast, scads of people came from the surrounding countryside. There weren't enough rugs or water. Later, people wondered whether it had been Moli Mujjan's enemies who had spread the rumour that at the end of the festival, laddoos and dates were to be given out as benediction gifts, as well as small packets of medicine for malaria and ranikhet (a deadly chicken disease). One country bumpkin brought his dozen chickens in a big bag because he was fearful they might not make it till morning. Similarly, a farmer, full of hope, washed his water buffalo and brought her along. She only had boys, never girls. Someone had said that Hakim Ahsanullah Tasleem, of prostitute fame, was coming. The majority of the audience had never been to a poetry festival and never seen a poet. The festival started quite late, which is to say, ten o'clock, which was like two in the morning for the country crowd. The young men serving as volunteers (and who the local crowd called 'young quails') were in charge of the lights, but, full of zeal, they had lit the kerosene lanterns at six and by nine they had gone dark. Then it took an hour to refill the kerosene in the lanterns because, as this took place, the naughty boys wandering through the festival had to be told off, each according to their age and degree of naughtiness. But the festival crowd was so loud that no one could hear these curses. That day, the district magistrate had called the County Treasurer to his office. And so, in his absence, the naughty boys felt emboldened. By midnight, only twenty-seven poets had read. Some wiseacre had taught the master of ceremonies, Moli Mujjan, a unique way of praising the poets, so instead of saying, 'God be praised! Wow,' Moli Mujjan said, 'Encore! Encore!' This meant that the twenty-seven poets took the time of fifty-two! The hooting also was doubled in effect. Qadir Barabankvi had read only his first couplet when the audience started hooting and hollering. He was so frustrated that he said, 'My dear friends, please listen! That was a couplet not a curse!' But the crowd only grew more restless. Yet Qadir Barabankvi didn't relent. He asked a man for a bidi, lit it without the slightest rush, and said, 'My dear friends, once you calm down a little, I'll recite the second couplet.' According to Mirza, this was the first poetry festival in the history of Urdu poetry where the audience stole the show.

Saghar Jalaunvi

It must have been midnight. The crowd of four hundred was unruly. Scared of the din, the jackals at the village's edge didn't dare make a sound. A local poet, whose each and every couplet had earned him hoots and hollers, was now going back to his seat with his head bowed low, when a man, approaching on his knees over the stage's white sheet, came up to the master of ceremonies. He greeted him with his right hand, while his left hand was twirling the ends of his mutton chop moustache, which was peppered with grey. He spoke, 'I'm a poor man, and a stranger here.* Please let me recite my humble poetry, as well.' (Someone shouted from the side, 'Let Mr Humble recite some too.') The man said that if there was any delay in letting him on stage, his status would rise on its own accord and soon he would be thought of as equal to the great masters. He was given permission. He rose to standing and greeted the audience to the left, right, and centre. His cream-coloured achkan coat of tussore silk was so long that it wasn't at all easy to tell if he was wearing anything underneath or not.

Earlier on, when the crowd had knocked straight his black velvet hat, which had been placed at a rakish angle, he took it off, blew into it, and set it back on his head at an even more rakish angle. During the festival, this man had sat in the sixth row praising the poets in a strange way, shouting, 'God be praised! Wow! God be praised! Wow!' After everyone else stopped clapping, he would start, and he clapped in such a way that it seemed as though he was slapping together some chapatis.

He bowed very deeply from the waist to show his thanks, and as he made his way back to his seat to pick up his notebook, he raised his achkan coat so high that it was like in the rainy season when snotty, well-dressed ladies, being lavished with men's steady regard, lift up their pant legs so as to avoid puddles that even an ant couldn't drown

---

* His 'homeland' was in Jalaun (the Lesser), only eighteen miles away. But back in those days as soon as a man passed outside his town, he considered himself a stranger in a strange land. And by 'homeland,' people meant only their town and its vicinity; no one considered the county or state their homeland.

in. They walk around with a fussy sort of contentment that makes the onlookers pray that

Please, God, let it rain for two more days!

From his seat, he picked up his notebook, which was actually an old school attendance register in which he kept his ghazals, which he had written on old test-booklet paper. Hugging this to his chest, he took it to the master of ceremonies, as he was ready to begin reciting. There was a lot of hooting; it wouldn't stop. It was a strange type of hooting: it started before each poet got on stage and continued after he had left. He looked very closely at his broken pocketwatch once before he sat down and once afterwards. Then he tapped on it like on a small kettledrum and put it to his ear to see if it still wasn't working or if the drubbing had caused it to start up. Then he turned to the audience and said, 'My dear friends! Your shouting has made my throat go dry.'

He addressed the master of ceremonies and the audience, 'For a special reason, I want to recite a ghazal without the misra-e-tarah that we were asked to use. But I don't want to tell you the reason!' Hearing this, the audience shouted, 'Tell us the reason, tell us the reason! If not, hang him for treason!' When the demand grew, the man unbuttoned one of his coat's buttons and said, 'There's an error in the line that was given out.' He scanned the line to prove his point. The word 'maraz' [illness] was shortened to 'marz' to match the metre of 'farz' [duty]. He said that the festival would be remembered forever because that night the poets of Kanpur had made immortal a common linguistic error. Then, from the last row in the crowd, a bearded elderly man stood up not only to confirm this but also to throw another spark into the fire in saying that the letter 'alif' didn't scan either!

Thus, the letter 'alif' fell on top of the poets like a lightning bolt. Everything came to a halt. The audience members lifted the sky, the misra-e-tarah, and the poets on their horns. Moli Mujjan motioned with his finger to Maulvi Badal (the Persian teacher), and whispered into his ear, 'How does alif scan?' Maulvi Badal was at first at a loss for words, but then he recited the misra-e-tarah. Now there was a growing fracas. Jauhar Illahabadi wanted to say something, but the time for the poets to speak was now over. All that could be heard were sarcastic jibes, gripes, and curses. Things had deteriorated so quickly that if the earth had suddenly cleaved in front of them, Basharat would happily have consented to being buried inside, along with the Kanpur School poets, and Moli Mujjan (along with his bolster pillow).

This poet and faultfinder gave his nom de plume as Saghar Jalaunvi.

How the Poetry Festival Was Stolen

People had been sitting bored for quite a while when Saghar Jalaunvi's explosive objection not only breathed life into the dead festival but also led to a great ruckus. No one was in the right frame of mind to consider the validity of the objection. For us, singing and dancing performances, politics, and poetry festivals are selfish arts. All of their pleasure (indeed, their very justification for existing) is that of the solo performance. That's why shouting slogans in politics, just like shouting praise and insults while marching in a parade or during a poetry festival, has become a necessity, a tradition, and a safety valve. For us, these are the only acceptable forms of audience participation.

The oil in two kerosene lanterns had run out fifteen minutes earlier. And some others had never been set up properly, so they too gave up the ghost. After Saghar Jalaunvi's moment, some mischiefmaker had shaken all the other lamps so that their mantles fell off. Everything went dark. Scuffles broke out. It was so dark that the poets couldn't be found, and so some innocent audience members started getting hit. Some were cursing out the poets by their names—no, by their pen names. Then someone shouted very loudly, 'Everyone!

Run! Flee! Save yourselves! The Hakim Sahib's water buffalo is on the loose!' This incited a melee. No one could see the black buffalo in the dark night, and so those frightened villagers equipped with sticks started beating their neighbours, thinking they were the buffalo. I still can't figure out how the thieves were able to locate all the new shoes in the pitch-black night. And it wasn't just shoes; everything that was worth stealing was stolen: a silver tray for serving paan; a dozen hand-towels; Saghar Jalaunvi's double-sized achkan coat, underneath which there was no kurta or undershirt; one printed linen carpet; all of the white party sheets; the orphanage's little, wooden donation box with steel lock; the orphanage's black flag; the master of ceremonies' silk bolster pillow and eyeglasses (which he was wearing); the silver toothpick and ear swabs that the village revenue officer had been wearing around his neck; and from the pocket of Khwaja Qamruddin, eight rupees, a silk handkerchief smelling of perfume, and a love letter he had written to his neighbour's wife.* Indeed, one impudent man reached into Basharat's skin-tight churidar pyjamas and snatched his silk drawstring in one brazen jerk. Another carried off a kerosene lantern on his head—granted no one could have seen someone carry off a kerosene lantern in that dark, but that was the only possible way. Only a couple feathers remained of the sick chickens. According to Saghar Jalaunvi, some wretch even tried to rip off his moustache, and only his timely scream scared him off. Long story short: whether something was useful or not, if anyone laid a hand on it, it got lifted, snatched, pilfered, or ripped off; it got stolen. And that included the County Treasurer's assistant secretary Banwari Lal Mathur's dentures! There was only one thing that no one

---

* Out of all the items pilfered that day, only this last was recovered the next day. But it was not only recovered; it was copied out and distributed to every house in town.

437

touched: the poets' notebooks were in exactly the same spots where they had been abandoned in the scrum the day before.

The villagers who had come to the poetry festival thought that perhaps these were the festival's closing ceremonies, so they took enthusiastic part in the fighting and stealing. And for many days afterwards, they enquired eagerly to everyone they came across when the next festival was to be held.

The Essence of Many Generations of Worthlessness

The poet who brought about this earthquake, no, who uprooted the entire poetry festival by his moustache, was none other than Basharat's cook.* He had received his uniform—an old hat and a cast-off achkan—on the previous Eid. He had the habit of grabbing strangers off the street to recite his poetry to them. If the stranger praised his poem, then he would pull him to his chest and hug him tightly. If he didn't praise him, then he stepped forward to hug him. He had no doubt that his poetry was inspired. Others also had no doubt that it was very intuitive because no knowledgeable intellectual would be able to write such worthless poetry. In two lines of poetry, it's hard to fit in so many artistic flaws and blemishes without divine intervention. It often happened that he had not yet completed his couplet when the

---

* It's possible that some readers will think I'm exaggerating because this book's every third character is a poet, or, at least, he calls himself one. In my defense, I think copying down Hazrat Rais Ahmad of Amroha's seminal statement ought to be enough: 'In our society, it was considered a necessity to have a pen name and to write doggerel. In our society, a nobleman without a pen name was considered a male water buffalo without a tail, or an ox without horns. The reign of wealth and the life of luxury and fortune ended quite some time ago. And now, for the older generation, only playing chess and playing at verse remain as remnants of the high life of refinement.'

stove caught on fire and his sauce burned. He had gone to school up to the fifth grade, which was more than enough for his own personal needs. He couldn't resist using his tiny English vocabulary and writing new poems. If you were in a conversation with him for just ten minutes, he would be sure to weaponize all the English he knew. He had people call him Saghar Sahib, but when he was busy in the kitchen, he went by his real name, Abdul Qaiyum. If you called him Saghar then, he didn't like it at all. He said, 'I've sold my hands into service, not my pen name.' Even in the kitchen, he heaped fatuous praise on himself. He said he descended from the family of the top chef of Wajid Ali Shah, King of Awadh. He said that he cooked from 150-year-old family recipes written in Persian. In fact, his tasteless sauces were the essence of many generations of accumulated worthlessness.

But It Requires More Hard Work

He claimed he could cook one hundred and one types of pulao. And this wasn't wrong in the least. Basharat had him cook pulao every Sunday. In a year, he must have cooked it fifty-two times. And each time he ruined it in a new way. He could cook well only those foods that lay beyond the reach of the ordinary man to ruin, or which look bad to begin with. For example, khichri, mashed potatoes, smoked firni, slow-cooked meat and turnip stew, arhar lentils, khichra, and sweet-and-sour mutanjan rice, in which, along with the sweet rice, he would add meat and lemon juice. Like wives without a knack for housework, he would cover up all the food's problems with chilli powder. (He removed all the errors of his poetry by reciting them in the tarannum singing style.) He couldn't cook sweets to save his life; that was because there was no scope to add chilli powder. On moonlit nights, he would sing his ghazals to the geography teacher while strumming on that man's banjo, and the teacher would remember his beloved, who had married a brass-spittoon maker from Murad-abad, and then break down crying. The style of singing that Saghar had unwittingly invented made it quite easy for him to start sobbing.

One day, Basharat teased him, 'You know, you write such good poems in such demanding metres. How did you ever become a cook?' He said, 'That question strikes very close to my heart. I don't get the same exhilaration after writing poetry as I do after cooking good food. In cooking, you have to make sure that everything's delicately balanced. If the person eating says it's bad, you have to accept this. And cooking is harder work. That's why no poet has ever agreed to work in a kitchen.'

Saghar Jalaunvi never thought of poetry as a way to gain people's respect, and one reason for this was probably that poetry had been for him a consistent source of humiliation. As proud as he was of his cooking, he was equally humble about his poetry. He openly admitted that Ghalib wrote better Persian poetry in Urdu and that Mir got a much better salary. Then he made sure to add, 'Sir, those days were different. The Urdu masters only had to write poetry and correct that of their disciples. Not one of them had to make chapatis.'

Who Is This Guy Who Speaks the Same Language as Hazrat Aatish?

There's no doubt that he cooked up some great poems. There were even some that Mir and Aatish would have praised, and that's because they were theirs! He claimed to be one among the disciples of God and that his poetry was intuitive. So his disciples kept up the brave front that it wasn't plagiarism so much as a happy coincidence of inspiration. Once he was reciting a new ghazal in Rudauli when some brat stood up in the middle of the packed festival to say that the poem was Na-sikh's, 'It's plagiarism! Pure plagiarism!' But he wasn't fazed. He smiled coolly. Then he said, 'Wrong! You're completely wrong! It's Aatish's!'

Then he took his manuscript to the MC. He said, 'Sir, please look at this. This verse is in quotation marks in my manuscript and afterwards I've written Aatish's name.' The MC verified this, and the man who had raised an objection was shamefully silenced.

Because his 'homeland' was Jalaun (the Lesser), he was affectionately called Saghar the Lesser. But he claimed connection to the Lucknow School of poets, and, when it came to matters of language, he absolutely hated people from Delhi and Punjab. Thus, he only plagiarized Lucknavi poets.

11.

I Left Your Alley

After the hullaballoo, no one thought about the guest poets. They were left to their own devices. And those that had no devices were left at the mercy of others. In part because of the disgrace of the night's commotion, and in part because of the lack of proper arrangements due to the lack of money, Basharat was in no mood to show his face to the poets the next morning. The ten rupees of 'off-the-books' money that Moli Mujjan had given him had already evaporated, and Basharat himself had had to spend seventy-two rupees out of his own pocket, and so now he couldn't afford to buy the poets train tickets home. He covered his head with a hand-towel and slipped off into the empty house of the theology teacher. Wellesley went with him. Basharat broke the lock and stayed in hiding all day. In the afternoon, he unchained Wellesley and pushed him outside, saying, 'Go, son, go enjoy yourself today, wherever you please.' At first, the furious poets of Kanpur banded together and went door-to-door looking for him. But then they grew tired and so headed off by foot to the station. After they had hardly started, others fell in with them, and soon they had a proper parade. All the area's half-naked boys, one completely naked crazy man (whom everyone at that time assumed to be a divine and so asked questions of personal and financial fortune), and all the area's bite-happy dogs dropped the poets off at the station. Rounding out the parade was an ash-smeared sadhu high on opium, and three biting ducks walking like stiff soldiers in a ceremonial goose-step. When the parade came by, the women at home—who had been kneading dough, preparing livestock fodder, stuffing their breasts into their crying babies' mouths, and cleaning and re-plastering the mud floors— came to the windows to watch, holding their dirty hands in the shape of parrots. Even a juggler, holding the rope on which he had tied his male and female monkeys, stood up to watch the spectacle. The boys and the monkeys made faces, and, hooting and hissing, lunged at one another. It was hard to say who was imitating whom.

The fragile poets who had grumbled on the way to town that they were being given a ride in a bullock cart now complained that they were being chased from town by foot. While boarding the moving train, Hairat Kanpuri told a coolie, 'Go tell that idiot loser, "Just try to leave Dhiraj Ganj. Come to Kanpur and see what happens."' All the poets paid for their return tickets out of their own pockets, except for the poet who had brought along five groupies. These six men were kicked off the train in the middle of the voyage for travelling without tickets. A group of charitable Muslims on the train platform collected donations and gave this to the ticket checker as a bribe, and so the men were forgiven for their sin. Luckily, the ticket checker was Muslim, otherwise the six of them would have been handcuffed and led away.

The Story of One Night

Not only the disgraced poets but the entire poetic community of Kanpur was after Basharat's blood. They spread such propaganda against him that even some prose writers were ready to eat him raw. In Kanpur, the news of the festival was on everyone's tongues. The poets who had gone to Dhiraj Ganj told such tales about their humiliation and disgrace that even if they weren't totally true the listeners wished they were because the poets deserved such treatment. People wanted all the details, but the problems were too many to count. Take food, for instance. Each poet complained that they were served dinner in broad daylight at four in the afternoon at the farmer's house where they had been put up. It's clear that the farmers served different sorts of food, and so for as many types of food that were served, the poets experienced different varieties of upset stomachs. Hairat Kanpuri complained, 'When I asked for some hot water for bathing, the lady of the house lifted her veil and pointed out the path to the nearest well. She assured me that I could find there cold water in the summer and hot water in the winter! The man of the house even indirectly enquired why I would want to bathe.' (This was a very common and ugly joke of that time.) 'And so when I put on my achkan without bathing and made to leave for the festival, he brought out his two-month-old stark naked son, sat him on my lap, and asked me to confirm for him that there was a paternal likeness. What was it to me? I said yes, and then very fondly I patted the boy on his head. This provoked the boy, and he peed on my coat. That was the coat I wore when I hugged the local poets.'

Then he said, 'I swear, on my honour, I returned from the festival at one. Until three, insects and mice were gambolling about above and beneath the charpoy. At three, a hue and cry was raised, "It's morning! It's morning!"' Each poet complained that they were forced out of bed at four o'clock, given a little pot of water, and told the bathroom was the other side of the wild-berry bushes. Hairat Kanpuri protested, and so the swaddling of a newborn baby was ripped from beneath it and given to him. He was told, 'If you're shy, then cover yourself!' The poets claimed to have awoken the roosters and asked them to crow in their sleep-drunk state the day's beginning!

Some complained that they weren't given solid food for breakfast. They were given a salty yogurt drink in a gigantic glass to wolf down on an empty stomach and then told to go on their way. One poet said that there had been a goat tied to the foot of his cot, and it had taken a shit all night long. Then when it was still dark, it had been milked, and this milk had been presented to him. He thought that even a buck goat couldn't take such treatment! Kharosh Shahjahanpuri said that they had started up the hand mill near the head of his bed at two thirty in the morning. It had been two girls, and they had giggled while singing a song about the flirting of in-laws, and this had ruined his sleep and aroused his libido. Aijaz Amrohvi said all sorts of birds had started to make a racket at four in the morning, and that with such noise, no respectable man could sleep.

Majzoob Mathuravi complained that he had been asked to sleep in the mud-plastered courtyard beneath a jamun tree and a cloud of mosquitos. All night long, with each delightful gust of the east wind, jamuns rained down on top of his head. When he complained the next morning, the son of the man of the house who had failed his final high-school exams said, 'You're wrong. They aren't jamun. They're phalainda. I've heard them called "phalainda" in Lucknow.' Majzoob Mathuravi said that there was a female water buffalo tied to a stake near his charpoy and that it had bellowed all night. Then, early the next morning, it had given birth, and the calf would have fallen right on top of his chest if he hadn't thought quickly and grabbed it as it came out. Even in his state of disgrace, Shaida Jarchavi found something to brag about. He claimed that the humiliation he had suffered was without precedent for a poet anywhere in Asia. Rana Sitapuri and Kakorvi had a doozy, too. He said that the house at which he had been sleeping—or, rather, staying awake—a stubborn baby kept crying out for his mother's milk all night long, and the baby's father kept crying out for his wife. Akhgar Kanpuri, the successor to Mayal Dehlvi, said that his farmer-host kept getting up every half hour to ask, 'Sir, is everything all right? Are you sleeping OK?'

Long story short, their complaints outstripped the number of poets by far. Each poet complained as though he had been personally tortured due to an organized conspiracy. But the truth of the matter was nothing like that. What happened was only that these city-dwelling disciples of God had seen country life for the first time (and that just for a couple of hours) and they had started whimpering. For the first time, they had seen how people lived just several miles beyond the city limits. And, if they had to live like that, they couldn't figure out why they bothered living at all.

Remove the Caesurae!

After a few days, the rumour was going around that those who had stuck to the misra-e-tarah that Basharat had given had resolved that if they couldn't find the line in the work of a classical poet, they would never again use any preordained line as the basis for their own versifying. Two poets started consulting Saghar Jalaunvi for poetry help. On the other hand, the poetic practice of Akhgar Kanpuri, the successor to Mayal Dehlvi, thrived. Now dozens of new students arrived every day to sit respectfully at his feet and absorb his special way of correcting their poetry. All he did was get rid of the hitches in the middle of their lines in the way that a weightlifter might help you get rid of your lower back pain by kicking you there straight on, or in the way that you ask the neighbour boys to jump up and down on the rope charpoy after it has gotten twisted out of shape due to the rain. (If it does get straightened out, you've also given the boys a taste for jumping up and down on others' charpoys.)

My Dear Maulvi Mujjan!

Somehow the day passed for Basharat. That evening he made off for a nearby village where he went underground at the house of an acquaintance who had helped him find an orphan several months previously.

He hadn't even made himself comfortable when he began to plan how he would inform his friends about his undisclosed, extremely secret location. He had spent fifteen hard months in Dhiraj Ganj. In the countryside, time itself rides in a bullock cart. His stick-to-itiveness had surprised him. When all avenues to advancement are blocked, gradually the unacceptable becomes acceptable. There wasn't one school that he was familiar with in all of north India where he didn't write to enquire about jobs. He even wrote unsuccessfully to a Muslim school in Assam about an open PE teacher job. He went for a handful of interviews that resulted in nothing. With each failure, he saw new flaws in society—ones that could be set right only by a bloody revolution. A friend had intervened on his behalf at Sandela High School, and when he got a letter announcing that he had won a job there, then he suddenly thought, 'Hey,

What's so bad about this bad world?'

After reading the letter a dozen times (and finding a new pleasure each time), he wrote his resignation letter on four-lined paper in fancy cursive and sent it to Moli Mujjan. He flung his fetters to the ground in one bold stroke. When writing the letter, he was out of his mind with the explosive intoxication of freedom, and so the 'r' in the word 'arz' [request] arrogantly punctured the following 'z,' and in the word 'istifa' [resignation] the final letter swung its leg back like a bully. After earning his BA, he had begun to sign his name quite floridly. But now, by the grace of God, its bouquet grew even headier. Moli Mujjan wouldn't need to read the letter to discover its contents because its every flourish spouted rebellion, its every dot dripped arrogance, and its every circle spoke of resignation. Basharat sealed the envelope with his bitter saliva in such a way that it seemed he was spitting on Moli Mujjan's face. After he signed the letter, he broke his inkpot in two. Instead of addressing his benefactor and boss Maulvi Sayyid Muzaffar as 'Your Honour, Munificent, Dear and Exalted Sir,' he addressed him in his Urdu letter in English as 'My Dear Maulvi Mujjan,' and with this, the bile that had been lodged in his soul for over a year rose into his gorge and then suddenly was gone. Now he was surprised that he had put up with such an abominable man for so long! What had come over him? Probably Moli Mujjan felt this as well. Because when he went to entrust him to God's care, which is to say, to say goodbye to him, Moli Mujjan shook his hand but couldn't look him in the eye. For his part, Basharat's 'goodbye' was filled with a thousand curses.

Basharat had thought a lot about one thing. He didn't have anything to give Nazo. He couldn't think of anything, but when it came time to leave, he took off his gold ring and gave it to her. She said, 'My God! What will I do with this?' Then she went into her room, and when she came out several minutes later, there was a lock of her curly hair tied to the ring, which she gave back to Basharat. She was crying silently.

You're Not Even as Tall as a Sword!

Everything at Sandela High School was good, except for the several problem boys in the tenth grade who were a little older than Basharat. These boys had been taking a several-year breather between each year of high school, and yet they weren't half as embarrassed about their age as Basharat was. As soon as he overcame his initial fear, and he began to feel at home, he sent a legal notice through his friend (who had just earned an LLB from Lucknow) to Maulvi Muzaffar stating that his client should be paid his ten months' worth of unpaid salary by money order, otherwise legal action would be taken in which all the school's irregularities and illegalities would be inevitably exposed.

Maulvi Muzaffar's response came two weeks later via registered mail in the form of a notice from his lawyer, stating, 'You fled without clearing the accounts of the "off-the-books" money and miscellaneous amounts given to you over time in connection with the poetry festival. Deduct your back pay from this and send the rest back to my client by money order. Send the accounts for the poetry festival, as well as all receipts, by mail. Please include all receipts for the poets' stipends, daily allowances, and travel expenses. Otherwise, please explain why a case against you shouldn't be filed in the appropriate court. You will be responsible for all fees. Also, during the welcome ceremony for the poets, you instructed the orphanage band to play a ghazal of yours that has several obscene couplets. Moreover, because you selected a line with a broken metre, the school's reputation, as well as the moveable property of the citizens of Dhiraj Ganj, has suffered harm, and so the executive committee reserves the right to collect full and just compensation.' The notice also threatened that if the money was not returned, he would be forced to tell Sandela High School, as well as the Department of Education, the full details of Basharat's criminal breach of trust.

Three days before receiving this notice, Basharat got an oral message from him that went like this, 'Son, you're still a child. Why are you messing with a badass like me? May God preserve you from all harm. You're still playing with marbles and pick-up-sticks. You're still sitting on my lap to ask for Eid money. If you mess with me, I'll tear you to pieces.'

The Man-Afflicted Dog

To destroy the last defenses of Basharat's crumbling fort, Moli Mujjan had put a time bomb in the notice's last paragraph. It said that when Basharat had sent a copy of his letter to the Department of Education, he should also have brought to their attention that Basharat had named his dog Lord Wellesley in order to mock and humiliate the

British Governor General. It said that Moli Mujjan had warned him plenty of times, but that he had stubbornly fanned the flames of hatred and rebellion through the vessel of one measly dog, and that every child in the area was ready to bear witness to this fact. Moreover, it said that he was so lost in the madness of revolution and opposition to the British that Basharat himself liked to be openly called Tipu!

Basharat was shocked. He thought, 'Oh God, what's going to happen to me now?'

He remained sad and worried for quite a while. Wellesley rested his head on Basharat's feet and lay there with half-closed eyes. From time to time, he opened his eyes and looked at Basharat. When he felt a little calmer, Basharat stroked his head over and over. It was more out of gratefulness than love. There wasn't a single area on his body where he didn't have bruises incurred by stones.

Behold—She Also Says I'm a Worthless Character!

As a courtesy, Moli Mujjan sent copies of this notice to all the poets who participated in that memorable poetry festival. Except for a couple, all the poets took to pestering Basharat about their money. One mean-spirited poet even put a hex on him. He said, 'Let the one who has put the knife to the throats of all my brother poets and embezzled their money find that God has filled his grave with insects and his poetry with awkward halts.' Now who was willing to listen to Basharat say that he had been given only ten rupees for the entire festival? One black-hearted poet went too far. He sent a satire written in the metre of the misra-e-tarah to Basharat's former cook Saghar Jalaunvi and asked him to correct it. But that faithful soul returned the poem, saying that for several generations his family had boasted of being the master chef of the Beloved, the Emperor Wajid Ali Shah, King of Awadh, and the Darling of the World; and that it was their principle that once in a person's employ, they won't speak a single word against them, even if they have embezzled more than anyone could imagine.

Tapish Dabaivi spread the rumour that Basharat's father had used the money to buy a new harmonium, which he played so loudly that people in the next neighbourhood could hear him; and that the instrument's very keys sang the song of embezzlement! His teacher, Hazrat Jauhar Illahabadi, didn't openly accuse him of a criminal breach of trust, but he did give him an hour-long lecture on the virtues of honesty.

The Ignominy of Advice

If you ask me the truth, I think it was none other than Jauhar Illahabadi who taught him his first lesson on the literal and metaphorical meanings of honesty. I'm pointing toward Maulvi Mohammad Ismail Meruthi's poem 'The Honest Boy.' This poem is a paean to an honest boy; I was taught it in my childhood. Its story goes like this. One day a boy saw a basket of ber fruit at his neighbour's when they were away. He really wanted to eat them, but then he remembered the advice of his elders about honesty, and he no longer wanted to steal the fruit. The brave child didn't even touch them. The poem ends with this couplet:

Wow, wow! Way to go, my boy!
You've trumped the heroes of old!

Indeed, how good were those days when, to tell stories about stealing and dishonesty, people couldn't imagine anything more valuable or enticing than some ber fruit! And there wasn't any temptation bigger and worse in our day than that sweet and sour fruit. One day when I was sitting around I thought about what example I'd give to the younger generation to teach them about stealing and dishonesty, an example that would go straight to their hearts. Just now, I've thought of a modern example, with which I'll end this story.

Example: An honest boy finds a cabinet full of porn flicks and pot. He knows very well what they are. That's because he's seen both many times in the schoolbags of his classmates. He knows very well about his friends' tastes. But then he's overcome by his father's advice, so he takes only a whiff, and then leaves.

Clarification: There were actually three reasons for this. First, his daddy had told him never to steal. Second, his daddy had told him, 'Son, never go near sex and drugs. Always keep your eyes on the ground. The most intoxicating drug is that of the eyes. And the dirtiest sin is that of the eyes. Because this is the only sin in which both cowardice and unmanliness are present. If ever a bad thought creeps into your mind, then think of your spiritual guru, and if you don't have one of those, then think about one of the old men in your family.' And so, the honest boy thought of his father.

Third, the honest boy found these two forbidden fruit in his father's cabinet!

Wow, wow! Way to go, my boy!
You've trumped the old heroes!

Author's afterword

Waking Dreams

'Ahsan Bhai! Munawwar Hussain's dead too, you know. Before he died ...'

'Before who died?' Mian Ahsan Hussain Ilahi asked, looking blindly at the ceiling fan and lifting his one paralysed hand with the other to place it on top of his chest. He wheezed and puffed and feared he was having a heart attack.

This was January 1987. I was having a tough time telling him what I wanted to say. Mian Ahsan Hussain Ilahi had been bedridden for five years. After his stroke, he lay in a coma in a heart specialty hospital for about two weeks. When he awoke, he discovered that half his body was paralysed, that he was going blind, and that he had lost control of his voice. Then his memory was patchy; he seemed to remember only bad things.

If you had seen him then for the first time, you would never have believed that this man had once been a rugged six foot four and two hundred and ten pounds, and how even at the age of seventy-two he would get up at four in the morning to work out for an hour and a half before playing tennis, and then, during the course of the day, he would walk four or five miles. After his first health scare in 1960, his taste for food, fun, and friends only grew. On a trip to London, he raced up every flight of stairs like Ibne Hasan Burney. He said, 'It's good for the heart, and it keeps old age at bay. Sixty years ago when I was a boy there wasn't a tree in all of Chiniot that I didn't climb.'

Upon doctor's orders, he was to watch what he ate. He gave up sending to Chiniot for its special pure ghee, as well as its mango pickle, but he continued to eat Chiniot kunna,* Sindhi biryani, ghee-slathered taftan bread from Burns Road, sajji kebabs from Quetta, almond sweets from Hyderabad, and Multan's anwar ratol mangos—in short, the perfect prescription for suicide for someone with heart problems. But he wouldn't listen to anyone.

He didn't indulge in food on the sly but would call over his doctors and serve them these delicacies with great joy and fuss. He would say that rich food gave the sick the courage to carry on. He stuck to his anti-health regimen without deviation. He also continued to fast as he figured he had fasted since childhood and so why stop now. Moreover, he didn't start praying five times a day because he didn't want to give anybody reason to say, 'Oh, just one heart attack, and Mian's got pious!'

He also got diabetes. That said, before going to bed, he would eat a big dish of full-cream ice cream. As smart as he was, he was even more headstrong. This was about everything, and health matters weren't any different. He had peculiar perspectives on things, including ice cream: 'Ice cream cools the heart and keeps blood pressure in check, just so long as you don't eat it in moderation. When I go to my in-laws in Sargodha or Sahiwal, I refuse ice cream out of politeness, but all night I toss and turn. Each night I don't eat ice cream, mosquitos massacre me. In 1970, I went on that trip to Europe, right? When I couldn't eat biryani for a couple days, I had to have a hernia operation in Vienna! But you're making fun of my love for food! Look at Ghalib. All his life, especially right before he died, he complained about his poverty and how no one appreciated his poetry. But notice what he got on his deathbed: in the morning, butter pressed from seven almonds along with a sugary sherbet; in the afternoon, broth boiled off

---

* Kunna: Tasty gravy baked in an earthen container—Chiniot's special dish.

a kilo of meat and three shami kebabs; and, as soon as it was nine at night, five rupees' worth of homebrewed liquor to go with the same amount of antacid.* My friend, God has given me everything except a lover who's fond of tormenting me! I might not be dying, but at the same time I don't get such treats. And, oh, when it comes to liquor, why is it that he drank the homemade stuff rather than Portuguese wine? You know, he drank the strong stuff so he wouldn't have to drink so much. He had to match his alcohol intake ounce for ounce with the foul antacid. My friend, just get me my full-cream ice cream, and I'll slam it down the hatch. I'm never going on a diet.'

After getting X-rayed and diagnosed by doctors, he often prepared his own concoctions to treat whatever it was he had. Doctors don't get mad at patients with so much initiative; they actually begin loving them. When he would start talking with his friends, his spirits improved—a smile would spread across his face, revealing his dimples, and each word seemed to carry its own charming wink. But, in the end, his food and fuzzy logic ended up leading to a severe stroke.

I had to walk through his living room and verandah to get to his room, and in doing so, I saw a lock on the door to his music room (in which he had nine or ten loudspeakers surreptitiously hidden). His personal library had been locked for four years: it held hundreds of expensive books whose covers he had had done by the Nizam of Hyderabad's bookbinder. In that very room he had introduced me to Niyaz Fatehpuri, Maulana Muhammad Ayub of Delhi, Muhammad Hasan Askari, and Salim Ahmad. From there he had held up the phone for a half hour so that I could listen to Ustad Bundhu Khan play the sarangi because he knew that when his friends enjoyed the same pleasures as he did, his own pleasure doubled.

This sarangi story is that his beloved late father Mr Haji Muhammad

---

* Curdled milk was given to patients with chronically upset stomachs. It's not too far-fetched to think that Ghalib used it to counteract the effects of his drinking.

Yaqub forbade several activities in his house: playing cards, keeping the photos of unfamiliar women (meaning, those of actresses), and eating paan. Music parties were also out. He would say, 'Son, music is not only forbidden, it's also bad luck. If you hear the sound of a tabla or ankle-bells coming from inside a house, you can be sure you'll soon hear the beating of the drum of bankruptcy and foreclosure. Music has wrecked many a house. Believe me, this is God's honest truth.' In respect for his father's solemn counsel, Mian Ahsan Ilahi thus arranged for the playing of whatever inauspicious melodies at the house of yours truly. But thank God the deceased's augury never came true! Not once did the drum of foreclosure sound in front of the nine houses (in which we'd rented rooms) during those days! Mian Ahsan Ilahi himself allowed music in the house on only three conditions. One, the songstress was not alive, which meant you were listening to a record. Two, the singer (male) must sing alone (without a tabla accompaniment), the audience must be only one person (just him), and the words must be totally incomprehensible and so the music limited to classical ragas. Lastly, the singer (male) must content himself with compliments as payment and so must sing only with the thought of getting his reward in heaven. Mirza says that with these pious rules and regulations in place, just as Mian Ahsan Ilahi's deceased father had predicted, you might well go bankrupt, but you'll never experience real music.

My friend was lying groggy in a raised-up hospital bed with a new silk comforter over him. On the wall to his right there hung two pictures from his youth. In one, he was standing next to Maulana Hasrat Mohani. In the other, he was smiling as he held the butt of a gun against a dead nilgai's snout. Beneath these pictures stood his new wheelchair, and on a tall stool there were arrayed all those expensive medicines of whose inefficacy he lay as half-dead advertisement. And yet his memory was still impressive: he had ordered my favourite jalebis still warm from Fresco and gulab jamun from Mullah Halwai in Nazimabad. To the right of his bed there stood a king-sized teak bed without any pillows on it, as his wife had died two months previously. On the windowsill directly in front of the door there was a small cassette player and next to it were the tapes of all the poetry festivals that had taken place on his lawn over the past thirty-five years. (He had ordered the grass from Dhaka and the roses and palm trees from Rawalpindi and Sri Lanka, respectively.) Due to his condition, a lot of things were prohibited—fans, air conditioning, bad news, and children. I thought maybe his hearing was going too.

* * *

'Our dear friend Munawwar Hussain has passed away,' I said, raising my voice a little.

'Yes, someone told me.'

His speech was so slurred that I had a hard time figuring out what he was saying. And then I had the feeling that he didn't want to talk about death.

He could focus on my words for only half a minute, and so it was very difficult to get across all of what I wanted to say during his short flashes of lucidity.

After living in Karachi for twenty-eight years, I had left for London in January 1979, and before leaving, I had tape-recorded the musings and reflections of two friends. (Why don't we say their names were Mian Ahsan Ilahi and Munawwar Hussain. What's in a name anyway? A friend's name will always sound good in your ears.*) I also took detailed notes. When I got to London, I quickly set to work on ten biographical sketches, which I set aside to settle for a couple years,

---

* Translators' note:
   What's in a name? That which we call a rose
   By any other name would smell as sweet.
                          Romeo and Juliet 2.2. l. 1–2

as I usually do with new work. Before rereading the manuscript, I first wanted to get permission to publish from Mian Ahsan Ilahi and Munawwar Hussain, and both gave it to me happily and without precondition. When I pulled out the manuscript to see if there wasn't some life in it yet, I felt very strange. It was as though someone else had written it. I also realized that it was the fodder for two books. I was separating the manuscript in two when I got a brief note from Munawwar Hussain, in which he said that while he had no personal objection to the sketches, at the same time, he was hesitant because some of his friends and family might not like to see certain things published. So he asked me not to use his name. Unfortunately, before I had a chance to go to Karachi and sort things out, he died, and that just two or three months after I got his note.

After listening to my update, Mian Ahsan Ilahi said in his broken manner that he had no problems with anything and that I should do as I saw fit. Then he said, 'But it's been so long. Come back to Pakistan. What's the point in coming back after I've died? I can hardly see anymore. Sometimes I can't even remember your face.' Then he broke down and started sobbing. It was the second time in thirty-seven years that I had witnessed him crying.

Actually, I was at a crossroads and didn't know what to do. The narratives of my two friends had blended so much so that their stories were like Siamese twins, and performing surgery to separate them was now impossible. It also seemed impossible to reveal the name, places of residence, and personal quirks of the one but not the other. So I was left with only one thing to do: I had to throw out the entire manuscript and rewrite it not just with aliases and such but also with an entirely fictionalized framework so that they would both have no connection to it. And that's what I did.

So in this book's five story-like sketches, if you begin searching for the events of the lives of my two friends or for any mention of their loved ones and families, you'll leave disappointed. I humbly request you to read them as nothing other than fiction. If any event or character seems real, then please consider it a bad coincidence. All the events and characters are made up. That being said, if any celebrity should happen to be criticized or spoken of harshly, then take that at face value. It's the absolute truth that I tried to the best of my ability to capture Munawwar Hussain and Mian Ahsan Ilahi's unique way of talking, as well as their witty repartee—how the sparks flew when the two got going!

Anyway, what does it matter if it's real or fake or exactly that combination that nowadays goes as 'faction'—fact plus fiction? A Chinese sage once said that it didn't matter to him whether the cat was black or white but whether it caught mice or not.

I wanted to give you this background to make clear my debt to my two friends and to dedicate this book to their memory: they are its inspiration, and they are the reason for its existence. The friendship and years of conversation I enjoyed in their company is very precious to me. They lived life to its fullest, and each moment I spent with them was a joy. It would be remiss of me not to acknowledge the blessing of their friendship.

* * *

Mian Ahsan Ilahi died several days after I visited him in Pakistan, and our country was left that much the poorer.

Now I am getting ready to return to my country after having lived in London for eleven years under the pretext of working at an international finance company. And now all his apprehensions have come true, and all his complaints have borne out.

In hindsight, the past decade was one of loss on all fronts—personal, literary, professional, political, and national. Everything lost and nothing gained. And yet one clear benefit of travelling and spending time away from your country is that your love for it and its people not only grows but becomes both undemanding and unconditional.

Sojourne did I through contre far and wide
Your pulchritude shined too brihte in my eie.*

The problem with living so far from home is that each bit of news (and each rumour) makes your heart pound and your blood run fast. The biggest problem with rumours from Pakistan is that they turn out to be true. Living like this for ten years or so means that if you're the sensitive sort, your spirits jump up and down like the lines on a seismograph during an earthquake. The lifeblood of politics? For us, it's molten lava.

All day and night my insides boil like a volcano.

When a country's leaders are self-interested, scholars overly political, ordinary people frightened and resigned to their ruler's will, intellectuals sycophantic, and institutions hollow (as for us who are in business, well, 'no one's innocent here'), then the road to dictatorship opens up, and a tyrant starts casting angry, sideward glances your way. Look at any Third World country. Dictators don't just appear out of nowhere. They're ushered in; they're called for—and with them comes Doomsday (Type 1 Calamity). They kick the Bedouins out of camp like yesterday's camels. Then the Bedouins start bickering with one another and go off in search of some unattainable and, in fact, non-existent rarity. They set their minds on finding a camel (a sucker) more stupid and more obedient than they are, so they can hop on and ride back to camp, and then, once there, curse out their old master (i.e. the old, too savvy camel). In fact, it's true that no one's more sincere than a dictator insomuch as a dictator thinks that no one can love his country and its people more than he does, and no

---

* Meaning, I wandered through many countries and cities, but spoiled by your elegance and beauty, I saw nothing.

one can help it as much as he can. He truly believes that not only does he know the pain of the country but that he also has its cure. Moreover, he thinks that from him alone springs the universe, and that he alone is the fountainhead of righteousness. It logically follows that his every command is tantamount to a heavenly decree.

Don't blame me, blame God

There's no doubt that he knows how to resolve to his satisfaction the specious problems that he (dis)ingenuously creates. You might say that like the person in charge of coming up with crosswords for a newspaper, he jots down all the possible solutions and then through his own brand of doublecross reverse-engineering comes up with the problems.

Hopped up on his absolute power and incontrovertible opinion, he addresses his nation as though its citizens were Stone Age savages: God has appointed him to raise them from the darkness and bring them into his non-divine rule—to make them human and then to make them civilized. But at the same time as he's miming to the sycophantic mirror, he can't see the very large writing right there on the wall. In fact, absolutism comes from egotism. You wait on pins and needles trying to please a despot's every whim. On his rigged balance of justice (crafted by his own hands), a despot sets his sword on this side for a time and then on that side in order to make things look even.

Each man styles justice to his own taste

Instead of a government you ought to call it a puppet show. 'If anything's wrong, don't shoot the messenger,' (i.e. me). But Mirza Abdul Wadud Baig, who always supports a new government with every ounce of conviction, and then, when it has run its course, always criticizes it with the same amount of conviction, well, he used to say (grabbing his ears in a show of piety), 'God forbid, but when I say

461

auzo billah-i-minashshaitanir rajim ['I seek refuge in God from Sa-tan, the accursed one'], I think that "rajim" really means "this very regime." God forbid! God forbid!'

As state affairs gradually become dominated by pomp and circum-stance, as well as a lust for power, then the dictator begins to treat his rivals as heretics, and the critics of his coterie of brown nosers as traitors and blasphemers. And for those who refuse to rush to kiss his iron hand, he is pleased to announce that God's country is closed to them—never will they enjoy the shade of its trees, or the moonlight of its night sky. He feeds rich biryani cooked in his own royal kitchen to 'God's disciples' (i.e. poets), instructs them on what their duties are, and then parses the meaning of the word 'disloyalty.' He knows quite well that when it comes to the fields of literature and journal-ism, there is a cabal more useful than that of the moment's opportun-ists, and that is the epistemological spin doctors. He compels them to confirm that censorship doesn't exist under his rule. That is, peo-ple can write their encomiums to him in whichever metre and with whichever rhyme scheme they like! Censorship? What censorship? It doesn't even matter if your paean has no sign of any skill—balance, intellectual depth, metre—just so long as it's full of praise. As per orders, a new trash-heap of odes—

Each day a new ode with a new first line.

As any age passes, so too does this one. And yet some folks have become so scared and so used to worshipping the reigning sun that even when that sun sets, they're still bent in prayer because you never know when the sun might rise up or from where. Sometimes you're trying to force someone to stand up straight when you realize they can't—their joints have lost their flexibility, and now, hobbled and hunched over, they go through the motions of living.

These naives fall flat when now it's time to stand up.

Whether it's Argentina or Dubai, Turkey or Bangladesh, Iraq or Egypt or Syria, you can find this sort of drama being enacted in practically every Third World country—just with changes of set, dialogue, and costume, contingent upon time and place.

* * *

These ten sketches—more like montages in their structure, flow and ornateness, and more like a novel in their breadth and scope—are the bitter distillation of Zia's Lost Decade. Only five are included in this book. After the French Revolution, someone asked Emmanuel Joseph Sieyès what noble work they could thank him for, and the three words he offered have become part of historical legend, 'J'ai vécu.' Meaning, I survived. But I don't know if I could save myself even from myself. In this book, you will discover here and there the hints of what eleven years of living away from my home and my friends did to my spirit. At the same time, London is a very interesting place, and its only defect is that it's located in the wrong place. But there are little things. Like how the weather is always overcast and foggy. You can't make out whether it's morning or evening, and so everyone has to wear watches that indicate a.m. and p.m. It almost seems like the weather is out to get you. The houses are so small and hot that it feels like each room is an enormous heating pad wrapped around you. In the words of the English Poet Laureate Philip Larkin,

Nowhere to go but indoors!

On the plus side of things, you can't find a people more polite, liberal, and patient than the British. Discussing religion, politics, and sex at social gatherings is considered the worst manners and a breach of etiquette—except at the pub. For delicate topics and serious discussions, the British first get drunk.

Also, the British are extremely well-mannered and sympathetic. Drivers are so well-behaved that should a single pedestrian indicate that he would like to cross the street, drivers would rather create a mini traffic jam than not let this soul cross. Yes, Mirza Abdul Wadud Baig is the height of sentimentality. When he sees someone stop for him, he feels so honoured that he has to restrain himself from rushing into the crosswalk and bowing to each and every car before crossing the street. In short, my corner of the cage is comfortable enough.

O, Hunter, I'm OK in this cage
Except how I want to fly away.

* * *

No writer can create a vivid piece of writing—one that comes out of the pulsing crucible of lived experience—when they are cut off from their loved ones and fellow writers, as well as the life and times of their country and its popular traditions and culture. Ninety-nine out of a hundred Asians living in Britain can't tell you the names of the beautiful trees standing right outside their houses (the other one didn't even notice the trees), and they can't tell you the names of the colourful birds that sing at dawn and dusk in these trees. They stay up all night yakking their heads off in broken English with their British girlfriends, and yet they don't know the words for the colour of these ladies' hair—golden auburn, copper brown, ash blond, chestnut brown, hazel brown, burgundy brown? Right. Don't ask.

They look around dazzled at everything and swear they are beautiful without knowing what in fact they are. A foreigner's understanding of a nation's cultural life, as well as the problems facing its society, is so facile and superficial that they never get beyond what they glean from museums, art galleries, theatres, and nightclubs; from wandering the bright night-streets of Soho; from suffering an inglorious mugging in the East End; or from getting quickies from the prostitutes of Charing Cross. If they manage to perform the impossible and get British citizenship, then they lose the modicum of respect they had as tourists or guest workers. Or if they marry some British lady in order to get a British passport and 'avenge the helplessness of their homeland,' then they think that they have all of Britain by the balls.

The British racial stock is very good. Their physique and colour, as well as their chiselled features, make them beautiful. Mirza says that an ugly British woman is rare indeed—you'll find but one in a thousand, but leave it to an Indian or a Pakistani to marry just that one! At the same time, marrying a British woman won't result either in fitting in or in understanding the country. Moreover, in time you'll realize that you don't even understand your wife. So an exiled writer (whether they have chosen exile for more salutary pay but less salubrious environs, or they went abroad to live the life of Riley under the excuse of personal or political reasons) ends up writing about a bygone era that the passage of time, psychic disconnect, and physical distance have rendered out of focus and steeped in glamorous nostalgia. Exile White Russian authors are the best example of this. But Urdu writers living (short- or long-term) in London aren't far behind:

> No one willingly leaves her elegant party.
> Forced away, he keeps looking back.

I haven't recounted what happened to me in London—I mean what befell this poor soul, and what doors to enlightenment were opened to me, a story that involves some shady characters that dance in and out of the shadows. If it is God's will, I will soon compile that in another book. The fact of the matter is that after the publication of *Zarguzasht* [*My Long Flirtation with Banking*], I had meant to start a new book from where I had ended my disgraceful story in the Alley of the Usurers. But, in the meantime, several things got in the way: London, a new banking job, back pain, and this book. Some other nettlesome issues cropped up: specifically, I got worried that my colleagues might think that my banking career was nothing but camouflage or some type of excuse. (Actually, when I got my first job on January 1, 1950, I was up to no good. My sole intention in involving myself with that forbidden occupation was to experience some things that I could transform into humorous pieces of autobiography.) The second reason I got so discouraged that I never started the second volume of *Zarguzasht* was that we live in the golden age of Urdu fiction. That is, these days the best Urdu fiction is being written as autobiography or travel narratives, and short stories and novels lag far behind. Too bad I've experienced so few things that the most important event of my life was my birth (and the most important event of my childhood was that I grew out of it). You see how hard it would be for me to reproduce this as a racy three-act play! The third reason that I didn't deign dip my pen into the ready-and-waiting inkwell was that I happened along the way to read the memoirs of Lord Contin, the president of Trinity College, Oxford, and the chairman of the board of British Libraries—a man well respected by the British intelligentsia and a man in whose personal library you can find more than twenty thousand books. He says that he never puts autobiography on the same shelf as biography, but instead puts them with humour! For weeks I admired how he had been able to arrive at this perspicacious nugget without reading my own offerings! Thank God wit survives yet today!

Most of the characters in this book are lost. They live in the past and avoid people at all costs. They suffer from nostalgia for a different time and place, and they suffer from this individually and collectively. When someone falls in love with the past and stops anticipating the future, they get old fast. (Bear in mind that anyone can age before their time—even the young.) If they can't get drugs, then the depressed and defeated can find their last refuge in the intoxication of memories and fantasy: just as the determined and diligent use their iron will to shape their future, the dead-to-the-world use their imagination to lose themselves in visions of their past, the heady rivers of memory descend into the mirages of the mind. Winding underground and then aboveground, irrigation canals water fields, and so too does the act of memory keep alive its dervish (the imagination) before suddenly it splits through the time-fabric and people are resuscitated.

Sometimes countries get stuck in their past. If you look carefully, you'll realize that this obsession is the real villain in Asia's problems. The nations that are the most backward, sluggish, and altogether miserable are the very ones that in an inverse ratio find their respective pasts glorious and worthy of endless trumpeting. As soon as anything bad happens, they bury their heads in the past. And this isn't the past that really happened, but the one that they fashioned to suit their whim and taste—a fantasy past. In the background of this reconstructive history project, it's worth watching the peacock dance of the injured ego: a peacock not only creates his own dance but his own forest as well, and there comes a magical moment when the entire jungle begins to dance, and the peacock stands still to watch.

Nostalgia is the story of that moment.

How and where the defeated ego finds solace depends upon a number of things—your taste, your skills, your ability to put up with failure (your patience), and the available means of escape:

- *Mysticism*
- *Renunciation*
- *Meditation*
- *Liquor*
- *Humour*
- *Sex*
- *Heroin*
- *Valium*
- *The Fantasy Past*
- *Daydreaming*

Whichever form of intoxication you prefer. At the moment of imminent colonization, Arnold wrote about the ability of the navel-gazing East to withstand defeat:

> The East bow'd low before the blast
> In patient, deep disdain
> She let the legions thunder past
> And plunged in thought again.

And in this arrogant meditation, centuries slip by. The most hypnotic and deepest form of intoxication available to humankind—the one that makes you indifferent to your surroundings—takes place through an admixture and imbrication of your thoughts and dreams. If you know this high, then everything else is A-okay.

A thousand miseries will dissolve into one great dream

The story goes in the *Mirat-ul-Khayal* [*The Mirror of Thoughts*] that when Sarmad was sentenced for heresy and public indecency and led in chains to the slaughterhouse, he saw the executioner with his drawn sword, smiled, and then said, 'I sacrifice my life to you, God! Come on, and come fast. In whatever disguise you come, I'll recognize you.' Then he recited the following Persian couplet, put his head beneath the waiting sword, and departed for the eternal rest:

> *A noise woke me from the dream of non-existence*
> *Still the night of tribulations! I closed my eyes again.*

An ancient Chinese custom for making fun of someone was to smear white paint on the person's nose so that he would look like a fool, regardless of how profound were his words. This is more or less the same fate that humour writers suffer. If he takes off his dunce's cap and throws it to the ground, then someone is sure to pick it up, dust it off, and put it back on his head. I don't know how I fared in the

Alley of the Usurers—I mean whether *Zarguzasht* was a success or not—but in any event, here you will have found the subject, tone, and treatment different. A subject—that is, the experiences to be recounted—determines its own manner of expression. Iqbal couldn't very well have presented to God his 'Complaints' in his teacher Fasihul Mulk Dagh Dehlvi's racy and flirtatious language. If you translate Ruswa's *Umrao Jan Ada* and Manto's short stories about prostitutes in Maulana Abul Kalam Azad's gnarled language* and force prostitutes to listen, then, believe me, it will take no more than a page to get them to abandon their profession. But not just them, me too! I would abandon my writing career because today it might be them, but tomorrow it will be me. In any event, the matter, mood, and modulations of this book are quite different. I wrote what I saw—a mystic witnesses, and then talks.

A storyteller of the old style, meaning a storytelling mystic, may be proud of his art and forthrightness, and he may take great pains to shave off every last hair on his head, and yet it's an old habit of the weavers of words that in the course of telling the story—in the course of interposing the warp and woof of the story—they suddenly change its tone, plot, and pleasures. It's also possible that in the course of storytelling, the storyteller himself changes: he's no longer the same man. Something like that happened to this sinful storyteller.†

> *Take this instrument away from me*
> *Because I'm done*
> *My song has turned into blood*
> *And flows from the harp's strings*

---

* You can find an example of this in the third part of 'The Mansion.'
† 'And only He makes you laugh and makes you cry' (Quran, Qala Fama Khatbakum 27, An-Najm 53).

This is neither a boast nor an excuse but rather a statement of fact.

Praise be to God that I'm at that point in my physical and literary life where I'm so indifferent to gold stars and black marks that I wouldn't even mind admitting to errors I haven't committed. Despite my insistence that 'if they don't get the joke, they're not from around here,' I'm not embarrassed to admit that I'm a gloomy and quite feeble person by temperament, habit, and principle. Perhaps pessimism is the fate of humour writers. Jonathan Swift, the father of humour writers, used to experience bouts of madness: his gloomy moods were so deep that he would decree that his birth was a tragedy, and so for his birthday he would dress in black mourning clothes and fast. Mark Twain also got depressed in his old age. Mirza says that I resemble these celebrities only in mood, but in any event one advantage I've found to premature despondency is that it eliminates the fear and sting of failure. In fact, it's tradition in many famous wrestling families that the fathers mangle the ears of boys who show pugilistic promise so that when the boys face off with nefarious opponents and these good-for-nothings tear at their ears, the boys will feel nothing. I think of humour as a defense mechanism. It's not the sword but the chainmail that you put on after being horribly wounded. Zen Buddhism says that laughter is a rung on the way to enlightenment. But a more telling demonstration of the difference between high and low comes when you climb a pole and someone takes away the ladder you used to get there. There's another saying I've heard: when a monkey falls from the top of a tree and lands on the ground, it's still a monkey.

* * *

'The Mansion' tells the story of a dilapidated, abandoned mansion and its hot-tempered owner. 'A Schoolteacher's Dream' is about a depressed horse, a barber, and a secretary. 'Two Tales of the City' is the story of a small room and the eccentric man who lived there for seventy-five years. 'The First Memorable Poetry Festival of Dhiraj Ganj' presents caricatures of one teacher and the founder of an infamous country school. 'The Car, The Man from Kabul, and The Lampless Aladdin' is a long-winded series of anecdotal sketches about a ramshackle car, an illiterate Pathan lumber merchant, and a lying braggart of a driver. In all, the characters, whether they be central, secondary, or merely to fill out the scenes, are all by definition 'common,' and when it comes to social status, ordinary; for this reason, they deserve extra attention and consideration. All that I've seen, learned, and loved about life has come through such people. It's been my bad luck that the 'great' or 'successful' people I've happened to run across have been entirely second-rate, rancorous, and superficial. Some wise man once said that if you look at how God made the common people in such great number, you can see that it must have given him pleasure or else why would he have made so many? Why would he have kept on making them eon after eon? When we begin to love them and hold them dear, then we finally begin to accept ourselves. The Arabian Nights of their lives doesn't end at the thousand and first night. *Every person is like an unread page.* How can we read them all?

It's possible that some readers won't take to the minutely detailed nature of this book and its scarcity of what you might call plot. I've already stated in some other context that plot is the purview of films, drama, novels, and conspiracies; if you look for it in the everyday, you'll be looking for quite some time. But details and close observations are neither some disease nor something to celebrate. If they aren't extraneous and pedantic, but rather are true and interesting, then they tell their own story; there's no need to force-fit them into some fictional frame or to push them into whatever ideal form you have in mind. Gogol, Chekhov, and Claude Simon all threw random details onto their literary canvases, and Proust made a novel out of his extremely detailed memories of a single dinner party (this is perhaps the best literary example of total recall).* The greatest example in English of a plotless novel is *Ulysses*—the story from eight in the morning till the end of the day, June 14, 1940. Eugene O'Neill's *Long Day's Journey into Night* is also kind of like this. I mention all these masterpieces only to point out that if my book stumbles, it's not the technique's fault but entirely my own. If I get lost counting the trees and miss out on the forest's beautiful sweep, it's all on me. In order to appreciate the magnitude and awe of Niagara Falls, you need to go beneath it and look up. Every time I look up, my jaunty hat (stuffed with my ego) falls at my feet.

* * *

Here I feel like I need to clarify and apologize for one heretical literary innovation and example of bad taste. The reasons I've given glosses to the Persian poetry are two: for one, the new generation of readers can't understand Persian; and, secondly, neither do I. Long story short, the inglorious truth of the matter is that yours truly officially studied Persian for only four days when in the fourth grade. Memorizing the Amad Namah terrorized me so much that I gave up and switched to drawing class. Although in drawing class there was no need for memorizing verb declensions, there was still ample room for sighing and crying out in disappointment because up till the tenth grade, my drawing skills hadn't advanced beyond a parrot and a goblet, which were the only two things I could draw even before dedicating myself to that craft. My drawing teacher used to remark that

---

* I didn't mention *Yadon ki barat* [*The Marriage Procession of Memories*] because, in it, the bridegroom rides on the shoulders of the members of the procession and has to throw dates to them as well as play the shehnai by himself. Then, when he's introduced to the bride during Arsi Mashaf (sitting together with the bride and the Quran in front of a mirror), he doesn't look at her but instead falls in love with his reflection. And yet many of its characters are so memorable that their exploits ought to be written in the ink of wine.

I signed my name with such love and attention, and that my cursive was so beautiful, that he didn't have the heart to fail me: 'Don't label it a grapevine, and you'll get a perfect score for drawing a water pitcher.'

Three of my well-wishers know very well that I don't know any Persian. So naturally whenever they write or we have an occasion to speak, they take out their quills of Persian poetry and use me for target practice. For about a dozen years, I put up with this in a state of profound wonderment, friendly indulgence, and respectful incomprehension. Then I finally came to my senses and realized that I had a number of friends who knew just as much Persian as I did (meaning, zilch), and I could torment them in just the same way! Doing this increased tenfold others' awe of my Persian erudition and proportionately cut down on their letters and the pleasure of their company. So wherever Persian poetry appears in this book, it's through the graces of these three well-wishers. One is my dear friend, the beardless straight-shooter Manzur Ilahi Sheikh (the author of *Dar-e-dilkusha* [*The Beautiful Door*] and *Silsilah-e-roz o shab* [*The Hours of the Day and Night*]) who calls from Lahore to enquire about my health, and yet the first things out of his mouth are lines of Persian poetry! I have to ask him to translate what he's just recited and subsequently interpret it, and, in the meantime, his money has run out and the operator disconnects us. The next day he writes a letter filled with apologies and yet more Persian poetry: 'I'm sorry that yesterday all our time on the phone was wasted on translating. In fact, what I had meant to ask was about your operation. What was it for? And how are you doing now? When I heard about it, I was very worried. Actually, on the subject of wasting time, Sadi said something very wonderful ... But Bedil—now he really raises the bar—O, does he ever!—when he says ...'

My second well-wisher is Dr Ziauddin Shakeb. Every time he goes to the British Library, he first drops by a bookstore and buys a post-card of a beautiful, recognizable scene and then proceeds to ruin it by scribbling all over it verses from Faizi, Bedil, or Talib Amli. Then he addresses it to me and drops it in the mail. The third is my dear and most wise friend, the inimitable Mukhtar Masood, who has wasted a quarter of a century trying to fill in the gaps of my impoverished store of knowledge. For hours on end he can hold forth on topics near and dear to his heart (and his alone), and in the course of this, he works himself up into a real-life state of ecstasy. Several times I've asked him, 'My dear sir, pardon me, but how do you know that I don't already know all this stuff?' And yet he constantly underrates himself. He doesn't take credit for anything. He points with his index finger toward the heavens, pulls on his earlobes with the same finger, and then, if he's standing up, he sits down, or if he's sitting down, he stands up. This is his peculiar way of expressing his modesty and his submission before God, and his friends and enemies alike are fond of this routine.

These three men provided me with glosses for the Persian poetry, which I wrote down to establish a standard and so that if I forgot what the poetry meant, then later I would have the glosses for reference and so wouldn't have to ask anyone. Especially Mukhtar Masood: after he got back from his official RCD* tour of Turkey where he watched with wonderment the astonishing dances of Rumi's whirling dervishes, ever since then he's been explaining Persian poetry as though it has something to do with Turkey. If I needed to, I guess I could have consulted with another of my oldest friends, Professor Qazi Abdul Quddus, MA, BT. But the thing about that is that with his infinite erudition, he ends up making even simple poetry impossible to understand.

* Translators' note: The RCD was the Regional Cooperation for Development, the multinational development organization established by Pakistan, Iran, and Turkey in 1964 and dissolved in 1979. It was followed in 1985 by the Economic Cooperation Organization.

You make what's simple hard.
Funny how if I don't pay you any heed
Even hard things turn out simple!

The truth is that today's readers can't survive an onslaught of Persian poetry. Especially when it drops in as if from outer space. Maulana Abul Kalam Azad gussies up his prose just so that he can work in his favourite lines of Persian poetry. You might say that with him it's not the poetry but the prose that's out of place: he weaves his wordy prose around the silken cocoon of his Persian poetry. But bear in mind that since ancient times there has only been one way to make silk: take a live silkworm and drop it into boiling water—up till its death, the silk is its own.

Mirza says that the hardest part of Ghalib's poetry is all the commentaries. That if it weren't for them, understanding Ghalib wouldn't be half so bad. That Ghalib is the only poet in the world whose poetry gives you twice as much pleasure when you don't understand it!

With these three men around, may God please have mercy on me! After I got sick, I started to worry about them—who knows where misfortune will strike next?

Once I commented to Manzur Ilahi that he had a lot of Persian poetry in his two books, and yet the new generation of readers is as ignorant of Persian as I am. I told him how, with my beginner's knowledge, I can try to guess at its meaning here and there, but in the end, this only kills it. I suggested that in any new edition he should explain this poetry in brackets so that everyone could understand him.

He paused. He closed his eyes, pursed his lips, and smiled in his pleasing way. Then he said, 'But then its whole point would be lost.'

Mirza chimed in on this subject: 'The same can be said about how many English words you've crammed into this book.' He went on: 'The British show great forethought and cunning in using words from other languages. For instance, food. Their food is insipid—just awful. But use French to describe it, and *ta-dah!* That's what the fancy restaurants do. Even today French is thought of as a language of politesse and sophistication. So whenever the British have something to say that either bears upon art or bares too much, they talk it up, or tame it down, in French. You must know that Samuel Pepys (1633–1703) wrote his world-famous diary—in which he wrote in great detail about his debauchery and "nightly exploits"—all in shorthand so that his butler couldn't read it. Whenever he got to a part where the British would usually rely upon their conventional understatement, say, "oh, so naughty!" and then move on, he wrote those parts in French. But when he got to parts that were so unmentionable that even French would seem too sultry (which were most parts), then without missing a beat he switched over to Spanish to narrate his nightly adventures. Almost like he chose a language to match the degree of debauchery in evidence! Now just take a look at some other disciplines. The British have taken their words for plants and most of their legal terms straight from Latin—as is. When they talk or try to act wise, they use Greek words in quotation marks so that no one will catch their drift. In opera, it's got to be Italian. And in philosophy, the hard words are always German. In doing so, they make incomprehensible language worse— they make it physically unbearable.' After this rambling primer, he added, 'We use English words only when we're sure that whatever we're hinting at could be expressed far better in Urdu.'

Despite this timely warning, you will have found English words here and there. The reasons for this are that either I didn't know their Urdu synonyms or that they appear in actual dialogue. Moreover not only have some English words become so common and ingrained in our experience, but also they are mispronounced in such a way that they should be considered nothing other than Urdu. An English speaker wouldn't recognize the words nor would they want them back in their new shape if they did.

My dear old friend Muhammad Abdul Jameel did me a huge favour by offering his useful advice during the revision of 'A Schoolteacher's Dream' and 'The First Memorable Poetry Festival of Dhiraj Ganj.' His suggestions were just as delicate and modest as he himself, and his marginal notes were so light that simply rubbing your finger across them erased them. He also suggested some corrections that I was not willing to make. For example, a Gujarati businessman was in a heated argument and happened to say, 'So I take the crippled fucking horse, and then what?' Jameel Sahib is from Lucknow, and his sense of decorum couldn't handle this. His gentle reproof didn't go so far as excising the entire sentence, but rather he just put a line through 'fucking' and wrote over it 'gosh darn.' At another point, he said, 'It might be just me, but what is this expression "hak dak"? Please write "hakka bakka." Here in Lucknow we don't say "hak dak."' I begged his indulgence, 'With "hakka bakka," all that comes to mind is wide-open eyes and a jaw dropped in astonishment, and yet with "hak dak," I aslo get how the heart just skipped a beat.' He answered, 'Then why don't you just go ahead and write "dhak dhak"? And, here, I was surprised to see you used the word "gay." It must have been a slip of the pen. You'll have to pardon my saying so, but, well, that word, isn't it too crude for you?'

'What should I write instead?' I asked. 'What's wrong with being gay?'

'Nothing.'

When I burst out laughing, he did a double take. He thought about the word's potential meanings, and then ended up laughing for quite a while as well. He wiped the tears from his eyes with his handkerchief and said, 'If you have to keep it, then write "queer." It's more decent.'

Hakka bakka! That's what happened to me while I thought back to how I'd used 'queer' in several instances to describe people when all I had meant was 'strange.' With this new euphemism in place, they would be able to sue me for slander and defamation!

After a little while, he turned up the starched sleeves of his muslin kurta, and as he riffled through the manuscript's pages, he said, 'You've used some words that aren't proper in Lucknow.' I replied that that was exactly why I had used them. This hit a nerve, and he exclaimed, 'At last you've said something worth listening to!' Then, as he lit one cigarette from the butt of another, he said, 'But, Mushtaq Sahib, what is this "bok"? I've never heard of it.'

'It's a young, horny goat that's used for breeding. Think horns, scraggly beard, and a bad smell. Its meat stinks too, and it's all stringy.'

'God! I've never heard of this word. Are there really goats like that? The word—its meaning—the idea of such meat—is just disgusting! It makes me want to retch. Can't you use some better-smelling animal in its place? Who's going to understand "bok" in Karachi?'

'Those who know what "retch" means,' I said. 'You've memorized all of Ghalib, right, first to last word? You must have noticed that he manages to slip in its polar opposite. In his letter to Alai, he wrote: "As I write this, you must be feasting on bok stew. With God as my witness, I don't envy you your stew and pulao. Yes, by God, I hope you never get your hands on a piece of rock candy from Bikaner. When I think how Mir Jan Sahib must be sucking away on a piece of that candy, that's when envy burns through me, and I start gnawing on my hand." But what did Ghalib mean by this rock candy? Just rock candy? If he really wanted some, he could get tons of its finest gems right where he was in Delhi. It's amazing that literary scholars haven't trained their beady little eyes on this delectable aporia, especially considering how in another letter Ghalib clearly mentions rock candy in connection with affairs of the heart.'

'Anyway, forget Ghalib,' Jameel Sahib said. 'But this word, "ruhar." Where's that from? It doesn't sit right on the tongue. It sounds quite uncouth. Is it Rajasthani?'

'I was wondering that myself,' I said. 'That's why I asked Majid Bhai...'

'Majid Bhai?'

'Mr Majid Ali, the former chief superintendent of Police, who moved to London. Everyone calls him Majid Bhai—his kids, his aunts and uncles, his colleagues. Majid Bhai. Except his wife, Zehra Nigah. She calls him Majid Uncle. Anyway, I went to check the word with him, and he confirmed that it means cotton taken out of an old quilt, carded by hand, and then stuffed into new quilts. That's what ruhar is. I consider Majid Bhai my guru, and I accept whatever he says as the unimpeachable truth. But just to doublecheck, I asked him, "Do people in Badaun use the same word?" "Look here," he said, throwing a fake look of anger onto his face and injecting an edgy stammer into his voice—a combination that during arguments has the same efficacy as Moses's staff. "We're friends and all, and a little intellectual banter is fine too. But only those from Badayun have the right to call "Badayun" "Badaun." I mean, imagine if one day you started calling me Majid Uncle instead of Majid Bhai. The police here in London would arrest me for polygamy! It wouldn't affect you. In any event, "ruhar" is the right word. In Badaun, the roving street-vendors used to go from house to house calling out for it. They bought it off people in exchange for sweet sesame crackers.' I thought this the opportune moment to put in check my great passion for intellectual enquiry, seeing as how he was soon to turn my mortar board into a washboard and beat me over the head with it. Even the best examples of humanity aren't able to put up with Majid Bhai's endless witticisms. Go ask the Oracle of Delphi. One time in front of Majid Bhai's boss's office, some people were standing a ways off and shouting slogans against his boss: 'Ayub Khan's ass-kisser! Ayub Khan's ass-kisser!' The minister asked Majid Bhai why the people outside were making such a racket, and Majid Bhai replied, 'Sir, I think they're talking about the childhood game Pin the Tail on the Donkey.'

Jameel Sahib relaxed a bit, hearing this drawn-out explanation cum authenticating narrative. He exhaled smoke through his nose and said, 'I guess if you're allergic to regular cotton, ruhar's good for you. But, you know, I see you're very taken with archaic words. I like them too, probably for the same reason that I like collecting antiques. But it's possible that readers won't. You should gloss them by putting their meanings in brackets.'

'Mirza often taunts me about this,' I replied. 'He says that I'm one of the very few who hasn't filed a claim for property abandoned back in India, and the reason for this is that before coming to Pakistan, I dug up all the local Rosetta Stones, stuffed them into my travel-all, and headed over here. He was just kidding, but, in fact, if I'm able to resurrect one word—yes, just one word—then I'll consider my life's work done.'

Jameel Sahib sighed, 'Yes, you keep saying that, don't you?'

* * *

Unfortunately, Jameel Sahib was able to help me with only two chapters before he passed away, and now I lack readers who are so perspicacious, perceptive, and punctilious, and whose suggestions are so spot-on, enriching, and assuring.

Finally, I must thank my better half, my wife Idris Fatima, who smiled indulgently whenever she found one of the many weaknesses in the text. Still you will probably be able to find mistakes that you might like to see corrected. After she read through the manuscript, I said, 'I can't get rid of my Rajasthani lilt, and my idioms. I keep washing my scarf but the stains remain!

Out, damned spot! Out, I say ...*

I'm surprised you didn't notice any errors this time.'

'As soon as I finished my schooling,' she began, 'I moved in with

---

* Shakespeare. Lady Macbeth dreams that she has blood on her hand and tries to get it off but can't manage to, whatever she tries.

you. From Aligarh, to this house, I mean, fort, or, really, *small* fort. It's been forty-three years. I can't remember anymore how I used to talk and how you used to talk. Now everything I hear just sounds right.'

Since we mixed up our cultural kit and caboodle long ago, and we sipped the cold, sweet waters of the Sindh and Ravi Rivers, this was bound to happen. But I have absolutely no complaints. Praise be to God, the Lord of all worlds!

LONDON

OCTOBER 6, 1989

Acknowledgments

We would like to thank Barbara Epler and Tynan Kogane at New Directions; Meru Gokhale, Fazal Rashid, and Archana Shankar at Random House India; Arshad and Zeba Yousufi for their generosity and time; and the PEN Foundation, whose grant helped us to complete this translation.

MATT REECK AND AFTAB AHMAD